# HERE BE
## DRAGONS

# HERE BE
# DRAGONS

*June Harris*

iUniverse, Inc.
New York   Bloomington

*iUniverse books may be ordered through booksellers or by contacting:*

*iUniverse*
*1663 Liberty Drive*
*Bloomington, IN 47403*
*www.iuniverse.com*
*1-800-Authors (1-800-288-4677)*

*Because of the dynamic nature of the Internet, any Web addresses or links contained in this book may have changed since publication and may no longer be valid. The views expressed in this work are solely those of the author and do not necessarily reflect the views of the publisher, and the publisher hereby disclaims any responsibility for them.*

*ISBN: 978-1-4401-5044-9 (sc)*
*ISBN: 978-1-4401-5045-6 (ebook)*

*Printed in the United States of America*

*iUniverse rev. date: 07/27/2009*

*In ancient times, mapmakers labeled unexplored regions, "Here be dragons." No region has been less explored than the human heart...*

# *Prologue*

THE DAY HER BROTHER Jamie was hanged, Jessalyn Kirke took the money he had stolen and fled England for the West Indies.

She'd had no plan to go to the West Indies; indeed she'd had no plan to leave England at all. But when the opportunity presented itself, she took the money, took passage on the first ship that was leaving, and set out to a place where, at least, she thought, I'll be anonymous. Where my name and history aren't known to every guttersnipe on the street.

She'd been a nine-days' wonder, a momentary subject of gossip, served up with the soup course in wealthy homes all over England, her name tossed about for a joke, a tantalizing anecdote. And then she was old news, no longer current enough to be discussed, but the memory of the name stayed. It was an odd name, strange enough to be remembered, and whenever it was mentioned, there was the inevitable pause, and then: "Jessalyn Kirke. Wasn't she the one who…"

They wouldn't forget the name. Not likely. She had managed to do what was never forgiven in those circles. She had made waves in an aristocratic pond.

*NEAR LONDON, 1856*

# Chapter One

MARCELLA MORRISEY WAS IN trouble of a classic sort. She'd been rising early, driven from her bed by seizures of nausea, losing her breakfast regularly, and, in general, displaying all the symptoms she had so feared when she had embarked on the affair with the duke. At first--at the *very* first--she'd been frightened of just this thing, and rather bothered by the moral concerns. But her conscience had been soothed into compliance soon enough. Stronger women than she had succumbed to the charms of the Duke of Bennington, and Marcella had never been a strong-minded woman.

She had come to the household as a governess for the duke's daughters--a lovely young thing. Too young and too lovely, the duchess had thought. She knew her husband, knew his weakness for a dimpled cheek, a cascade of blonde curls, and she suspected that it would only be a matter of time. She was prepared to turn a blind eye to his activities; she always did. She'd done her duty by him, and if she hadn't given him the son he'd wanted, well, neither had any of his paramours. Besides, she had no intentions of going through *that* again, son or no son. Let him take his pleasures where he would, she thought. It was not her concern.

What was her concern was a governess for her unruly daughters. She'd been through five in almost as many months, and she was becoming rather desperate. Her daughters were infamous, and apparently the word had spread along the grapevine that such people as governesses attended to, because no reputable, experienced women would even apply for the position of governing the young hellions. The

5

duchess had been reduced to hiring the most inexperienced, callow schoolgirls for the job, and Marcella had been the latest in the line.

Surprisingly, she proved rather more competent than the others. She was certainly bright enough. She spoke French like a native--she'd had a French mother, she said--and she was unusually well read. She had beautiful manners.

Perhaps because she was young and pretty and appealing, perhaps because she gave even dull lessons a spirit of fun, she had been effective in subduing the heretofore unmanageable threesome, and her tenure had lasted some six months now. The duchess had begun to hope she might be permanent.

The duke knew that the search for a new governess was about to resume.

"T-t-two months. About two months, I think." Marcella twisted her handkerchief in her lap and looked up at the duke, who was making little effort to disguise the contempt he was feeling for this whole procedure. Why did women always have to cry? The prettiest of them looked such a mess with their eyes red and their noses dripping. And the others--like his wife--well, they weren't even to be seen. None of them were improved by it. If she had managed a smile, flashed the dimple in that wicked way he was so fond of, he might have softened toward her a bit, and her fate might have been quite different. But crying women, he thought. God save me!

Now he sighed and considered the problem. He'd manage it, he was certain. He always did. But what a pity. They were such great sports going into these things, he thought with a certain disgust, but they never had any idea how to cope when it came to this.

"Now, now, my dear. Don't take on so. It isn't the end of the world, you know. It's happened to others." He used a fatherly tone with his mistresses, especially when he was about to discard them. He never used fatherly tones with his daughters. He preferred not to deal with his daughters at all.

"I suppose it isn't the end of the world for you, John," Marcella dabbed at her brimming eyes, "but it might very well be for me. I'll never be able to get a decent job again. I don't know what I'll do."

"Now, Marcie, you know I'll help you." He would, of course, particularly if it involved only money. The duke had never encountered a problem that couldn't be solved by liberal applications of money, and it was not as if this situation were new to him.

"Oh, I know you will, John. It's just that it's such a mess, and I feel so--dirty--about the whole thing." They always did, afterwards, he thought, when they'd been caught. In the beginning, it was always such luscious forbidden fun.

He was silent a moment, considering. Then he blurted out, "Look here, Marcie. Have you been seeing anyone else?"

"Seeing--you mean--are you asking me if it's *yours?*" Marcella was horrified. She had gone into the affair considering it to be an expression of "purest love, of soul meeting soul," as she confided to her diary. It was a measure of the duke's considerable charm that all the women he seduced thought that they were doing him a tremendous favor.

The duke, seeing her face crumble into fresh tears, hastened to reassure her. "No, no, my dear. Of course that's not what I'm asking." It was what he was asking. "Of course I know there's been no one else in that way." Curse the luck. "What I meant was, has any young man been calling on you, paying you certain attentions, that sort of thing?"

She shook her head and blew her nose loudly. "No. The only young man I've seen since I've been here has been that young curate from the church down the road, and he's engaged. And that tenant farmer of yours, Wilburn something or other."

The duke was not a cruel man. Cruelty took more effort than he was willing to expend. He was, simply, so totally self-concerned that it never occurred to him that there were lives besides his own, or affairs beyond those with which he was involved. When Marcella mentioned Wilburn Kirke, she put into his mind the solution to his problem, and beyond that, he had no further consideration. What he was doing to Marcella did not enter his mind, nor would it have interested him if it had. He was doing her a favor, and having done it, he would wash his hands of the whole affair.

Wilburn Kirke was in need of a wife. The duke was in need of Wilburn Kirke. Wilburn Kirke was the best farmer and most productive manager he had on his estates, but the man was considering leaving, going to America or Australia or somewhere. Since his first wife had died in childbirth, he'd been dissatisfied with his life here. He thought he could do better elsewhere, perhaps have his own farm.

Now the duke looked at Marcella and considered a plan. If Wilburn Kirke had a wife and baby to tie him to his place…

Jessalyn was born several weeks late, a fact that helped salve Wilburn Kirke's pride and probably made her life a bit easier than it would have been otherwise. He was a proud man, and taking on the duke's discarded mistress and bastard child was a task he found more distasteful than he would admit, sober. Drunk, he was sure he'd made a mistake.

He'd gone into it for a number of reasons, not the least of which was overawe for the wishes of his betters, as he thought of the duke. That the duke would come to *him,* a tenant farmer, and ask a favor, almost as a friend, well, Wilburn was too impressed by the gentry to consider saying no to him.

And to be married to a governess. Like most unlettered people, Wilburn, who could scratch his name and little more, held great respect for those who were educated. Marrying a governess was marrying above himself, no question about it. And he'd seen her. A pretty little thing. All those curls. They said she spoke French. She'd be something of a prize for a man like him.

Besides, the duke was prepared to make the offer even more appealing. More land, someone to help him work it, a smaller rental fee, and occasional unnamed favors hinted at. It was an offer to tempt a man, that was for sure. Wilburn Kirke agreed to it.

There were many who would have said he'd made a good bargain, and most days, Wilburn would have concurred. True, it took Marcella a while to learn her way around the farm kitchen--she who had never cooked a meal in her life--and the duties of a farmer's wife. Sometimes he thought she would be about as useful to him as one of those pampered lap dogs the duchess was so fond of carrying about with her. But if Marcella was weak in some ways, she was bright, and she was not ungrateful. Will Kirke was, she thought, a decent man, and he had done her a great favor. She was willing to work hard for him, to make a go of their lives together. She did all that she thought might please him, even to naming the child for his mother as well as her own. Jessie, his mother, and Carolyn, her mother, became Jessalyn.

Her chances for success in marriage would have been fair, had it not been for the girl.

Jessalyn was the living, breathing reminder of his wife's dalliance with another man, and Will Kirke could not look at her without thinking of the two of them together. It was fatal to the marriage that he had fallen in love with his wife. Indeed, it would have been better for them both had he been able to remain aloof from her, thinking of her as a kind of housekeeper. Then the jealousy that ate away at him might not have been, and he could have treated Jessalyn with the same careless kindness he showed the other children in the neighborhood.

But it was not to be. The more he loved his golden, frivolous wife, the more he resented the child she had borne of another man, and the resentment was to destroy what could have been a loving marriage.

It did not help that Jessalyn looked more like the duke than any of his legitimate children. She had his cleft chin, his dark blonde hair, his wide-set blue eyes. The mouth that on the duke appeared almost weak, was in her face, merely soft and feminine.

The duke, on the rare occasions when he saw the child, would shake his head over the strange ways of nature. What a pity the child's a bastard, he would think to himself. I could make a good marriage for that one. His own daughters resembled their mother, an heiress of great fortune and no beauty. They would make fine marriages--they stood to inherit enough money to insure it--but that one, he would think, that one would make a brilliant match. Then he would promptly forget her until the next time he happened upon her.

Will Kirke tried to forget her, tried to put her out of his mind, but there was no way for him to do so. Marcella, having seen how it was going to be, placed herself between the child and the man she was married to, keeping Jessalyn out of his way as much as she was able, and making as little of her as she could in front of Will.

It cost her to do it. Jessalyn was a good child, a sweet and loving little girl, a child that a mother like Marcella would have doted on if she could have. Instead, she kept the child at arm's length emotionally, resisting the urge to cuddle her, to hold her, to make much of her, except when Will could not see.

When Jamie was born, Marcella was free to indulge herself in all the affection and mother love she had resisted with Jessalyn. Will never quibbled about the care Jamie received, never resented that his own child became the center of Marcella's life. And Jessalyn, deprived so long of a place to center her own affections, turned to Jamie as a place to lavish her own love.

She was four when he was born, and she was bright and beautiful. Marcella had taught her to read, stealing time when Will was out of the house, filling the child's mind in compensation for the love she could not display. Jessalyn was quick and eager to learn, wanting to please her mother, and she came to associate learning with the only praise and attention she could get. She read everything she could find as she grew, and wrote on every scrap of paper she could collect. She learned French, chattering away in that language with her mother in Will's absence, not using it at all in his presence by unspoken understanding.

Jamie, a round little boy with a mop of bronze curls, was Jessalyn's darling. If he was spoiled and self-centered, she didn't know there was anything wrong with that. She thought he was her own special treasure, and from the time he could make his wishes know, she was his willing slave.

He was charming and sweet-tempered, loving when it suited him to be, peremptory and demanding when it did not. Will made quite clear from the start that this was *his* son, that he would be treated in an entirely different fashion from the way Jessalyn had been raised, and that whatever Jamie wanted, he should have.

Perhaps Will would have had more sense about raising children if Jessalyn had not been there; perhaps he could have learned if Marcella had produced a house full of noisy infants so that he was not forced by a misplaced sense of pride to emphasize the difference between his child and "that other one." But all the might-have-beens were not, of course. It was one of those ironic quirks of nature that the course Will pursued produced a son who was enough like the duke to have been his natural child, and a stepdaughter who was as proud and as fiercely independent as Will himself.

Jessalyn was ten when she learned the truth about her parentage. She and Jamie were outside after supper, eating strawberries in the corner formed by the large kitchen chimney, waiting to be called in to bed from the long summer twilight. The corner was deep and hidden by rose bushes that climbed to the window above. Jessalyn and Jamie found it to be their favorite place to take their treats. It was sheltered from the wind in fall and winter. The grownups didn't know about it, so they were safely out of sight and might escape a chore. And there was the "hidey-hole."

The "hidey-hole" was Jessalyn's name for a small crevice the two had made in the base of the chimney by removing a loose brick and digging away at the mortar around it. They had discovered the brick was loose a couple of years earlier, and had, idly at first, poked and prodded it until it came out. After some time, they managed to gouge out a hole beneath it where they kept small treasures--a colored stone, a bit of taffy, an apple, a bright feather. It was their secret and special place.

Tonight as they finished up the strawberries, Jessalyn reached for the brick, pulled it out, and put her hand inside the hole to draw out a small, cloth-wrapped parcel.

"What you got, Jess?" Jamie leaned over the little bundle.

"Tarts. I saved them from tea. There's two each."

"Oh, good." Jamie's eyes lit up as he reached for his two, and narrowed a bit as he debated a way to get one of Jessalyn's. He loved sweets, and greedy little boy that he was, searched for ways to supplement his share. Now he looked up at Jessalyn, his face innocent, and said, "I'd surely like a cup of milk to go with them."

"As would I," she said, nibbling around the edges of the tart. "I'd think Mum would say no, though. She's cleaned up from supper already."

"I'd go ask her."

"Is Father home yet?"

"Lemme look."

Jamie scampered around the corner of the chimney and out under the bushes so that he could see into the window of the room where his parents sat in the evenings. Will's habit was to spend his evenings in the local pub, from which he returned in conditions ranging from mildly intoxicated to roaring drunk. As time passed, he tended more toward the latter than the former, a situation that Marcella viewed with increasing alarm. Beyond a certain point, he was incapable of governing his tongue, and she had found that Jessalyn's presence was likely to send him into fits of rage that he would take out on the child or on Marcella herself. Best, Marcella had found, to keep the girl out of his sight.

Now Jamie crawled back into the corner and reported that his father was indeed at home.

"Well, then, "Jessalyn said, "you might go ask for a cup of milk. Make sure you do it in front of Father. And just ask for one for yourself. We'll share."

She knew Jamie would not be denied the milk, but best not to risk asking for one for herself.

Jamie looked at her, his mind calculating rapidly. "You go ask, Jess. I went to see if Father was there."

She shook her head. "No use my going, you know that. We'd never get the milk if I asked."

"Not fair that I have to do all the running. I'm smaller than you anyway."

Jessalyn sighed. They both knew how it was with the two of them. They just didn't know why. Because he's a boy, she thought. People always like boys better.

"I know you're smaller. That's why they'll give it to you."

"I'll do it if you'll give me one of your tarts."

Jessalyn looked at her brother, his eyes wide in the gloom, his face innocent. "Oh, all right. I will. But you'd best not stop and drink half the milk before you get back. It's to share, you know."

" 'Course I won't. Let me have the tart." He held out a grimy palm, and she gave him the tart. He crawled under the bushes and was gone around the corner.

She leaned against the chimney to wait. In a moment, a light shown through the window overhead, throwing a dim light onto the rose bushes. She smiled. That would be Mum, pouring out the milk for Jamie.

"...and that's all you get, young man," her mother was saying. "You've had enough to eat today."

"Yes, Mum, thank you, Mum." Jessalyn could see in her mind's eye the innocent, winning smile Jamie would be giving her mother, could see the indulgent look on her mother's face as she ruffled Jamie's auburn curls. She heard his footsteps as he left, heard the door close behind him.

"Leave off, Marcella." It was her father's voice. "He's a growing boy. No need to starve the lad."

"No need to allow him to become greedy and piggish, either."

"Humph. Begrudge *my* son a cup of milk, but nothing's too good for the duke's by-blow."

Jessalyn frowned. What was he talking about?"

"Hush, Will, you know that's not true. Why do you have to keep on about it?"

Her mother's voice sounded weary, as though she'd been over this before.

"Not true! Ha! The duke's daughter must learn to read, and the duke's daughter must speak French, and the duke's daughter must learn to be a lady. Humph! She'll wind up married to a tenant farmer like her mother did, and what good will all her fancy ways do her then?"

Jessalyn sat up straight, her face pale in the shadows.

Her mother's voice, usually so patient and resigned, was harsh as it came through the window. "I fervently hope not," she said, the anger obvious in her voice. "I'd certainly hope she would have more sense than her mother and not wind up married to a drunken lout of a tenant farmer."

Jessalyn heard the curse and the sound of the blow, and her mother's muffled sob, but they seemed to come to her through a fog. They were talking about her. She was the duke's daughter. Wilburn Kirke was not her father. That was why he'd always favored Jamie, not just because he was a boy.

She ran back through her memories, trying to recall the encounters she'd had with the duke. Was it her fancy, or did she remember a special look in his eye when it had fallen on her? Had he treated her in any particular way? She was still caught up in her thoughts when Jamie came crawling slowly back through the bushes, pushing the cup of milk before him.

"I had to drink some of it, Jess, " he was saying to explain the half-empty cup. "It was slopping over, all over, and I..." He looked up at her, straining to make out her expression in the near-darkness of the corner. She took the cup absently, forgetting in her absorption to scold him for drinking more than his share.

"Jess, what's wrong with you? You look like you've seen a ghost or something."

She dragged her mind back to the present and gave him a vacant smile. "Nothing like that. I was just thinking, that's all."

"About what?"

"About whatever. I don't have to tell you everything, you know."

Jamie's eyes narrowed. "You'd better tell, Jess. If you don't, I'll tell Father that you--"

"All right, all right," she sighed. Jamie was always threatening to tell father something, even if he had to make it up. Best to humor him, she thought, with something he wasn't even faintly interested in.

"I was thinking about the dress Mum's going to make me for Christmas. She said it's going to be blue, with lace on the sleeves, and…"

She went on about the imaginary dress until Jamie said, finally, "Oh, stop. I don't care about your silly dress. I thought there was something interesting. Like a ghost story. Tell me a ghost story."

She opened her mouth to start to make up a story for him and was interrupted by their mother, calling them to bed. They crawled out of the corner and headed around the house. Jessalyn glanced at her mother, at the spot on her cheek that would be a bruise by morning, and felt a sympathy for her that she'd never experienced before. She looked at Will Kirke as she passed the chair where he was slumped, a scowl on his face, his eyes bleary and unfocused.

The reading she had done had left her with an active imagination and a sense of romance that had stood her in good stead for the years in her life when she had little to comfort her, and now she began to weave a story about herself and her mother and the duke that combined all the elements of fantasy that her young mind could conjure up.

Her poor mother, she thought. Beloved of the duke, who was married and could do no more than yearn for her. They had had their fleeting moment of love, and then years of separation. So close, but so distant. She pictured the duke as a noble figure, married to one woman, but yearning for another. He must have watched me from afar, she thought. I'll bet he's sorry I'm not his real daughter. I'm prettier than his real daughters. This was not a thought prompted by vanity, merely a recognition of the truth. The duke's legitimate daughters tended to be a horse-faced lot, but it was of little consequence. They were heiresses and titled, and beauty would play no part in their destinies.

She could not know that with the passage of time, her mother had come to see the duke for the libertine that he was, and to greatly regret her affair with him. She could not know that the duke, far from longing after her mother and herself, seldom thought of them at all, and when he did, it was to congratulate himself on a situation well managed.

Hers was an uncomfortable world, and to make the best of it, she cushioned herself with the creation of a fantasy constructed around what she knew of her birth. That creation became more real to her than the world she lived it. Her fiction was to be abruptly shattered and her life altered entirely by that shattering at a later time, but throughout the rest of her childhood and adolescence, she was to be sustained by a vision of the duke as a tragic, romantic hero.

\*     \*     \*     \*     \*

Marcella's death shortly after Jessalyn's fourteenth birthday saved the girl from an early and unwanted marriage. It had been Will Kirke's intent to marry her off as soon as was practical--at fifteen, probably, and surely no later than sixteen--but when Marcella died of pneumonia during a long, unusually cold winter, he altered his plan.

If he married Jessalyn off, he'd be forced to marry himself or hire a housekeeper to look after Jamie and run the house. Neither of those options appealed to him. With Jessalyn at home, he could do with the one hired girl who had helped Marcella, and Jessalyn could do the rest and look after Jamie.

It was a huge task for a fourteen-year-old girl, running the house for a large farm, but Jessalyn was as well equipped to do it as any young woman her age could have been; Marcella had taught her all the things Marcella herself had been late learning, and the girl was very capable. Besides, given a choice, it was what Jessalyn would have taken. She could have married any time after her fifteenth birthday; there was no shortage of young farmers and an occasional old farmer to court her. But she felt no attraction for any of them.

Her life with Will had left her with misgivings about the whole question of marriage. When the other girls her age came to think of nothing else, she viewed the institution with distrust and foreboding. She had seen no good of marriage, no happiness to be gained from it. She was as well educated as her life with a capable governess could make her--considerably better educated than the duke's daughters-- and she was certain that there was more to life than scrubbing it away on a tenant farm.

Furthermore, she harbored notions that her father, the duke, would help her out of her situation. She was a bit vague on what she expected him to do. Sometimes she fantasized about a good marriage that he would arrange for her with someone in the world beyond farming; sometimes she thought she would go to him and ask him for references so that she could be a governess herself and get out of Will Kirke's kitchen.

Her favorite daydream was one in which she went to the duke, told him that she knew who she was, and he arranged for her to become his secretary or his traveling companion, or (in the version in which he was quite ill) his nurse, who cared for him constantly.

In this fashion, six years passed, six years during which Will Kirke settled into a kind of resigned acceptance of her position, in which he paid as little heed to her as possible, and in which they would pass days without exchanging five words. Jamie was the sole bond between them. As such, he provided the link for such communications as they had.

From time to time, Will would decide to marry Jessalyn off, and would say as much to Jamie. Jamie would convey the message to Jessalyn, who would express her displeasure at the prospect. Jamie would then tell Will that the proposed marriage was not for her, although he would express that as if it were his own idea. Will would drop it for a while until the notion occurred to him again.

Jessalyn turned twenty with no prospects for marriage. There were those who had called, those who had let it be known that they were interested in her, but having received no encouragement, they turned elsewhere. By the time she was twenty, speculation about her had almost ceased. Those who knew her considered that she had decided to devote her life to taking care of her father and her younger brother. They thought it admirable of her, if a trifle odd. Will was not at an age to need her care; he was still able to do the work of two men on the farm. And it was no secret among the neighbors that he treated Jessalyn in such a fashion as was hardly designed to inspire devotion.

Still, they could think of no other reason that she should choose not to marry.

Jessalyn could.

She chose life with Will as the lesser of evils. To say that she held herself above those who would have married her was less true than that she simply found nothing about them to interest her. She carried in her head the fantasy that was more satisfying that what life had to offer, and she felt that to desert her dreams would be to give up the possibilities of a future. And so she stayed home, caring for Jamie, doing for Will.

By the age of sixteen, Jamie had a reputation locally as a hellion and a scapegrace. He was handsome, true enough, and certainly charming; more than one feminine heart had fluttered when he favored its owner with a glance or a smile. But local fathers were not so easily enchanted as their daughters. He was not considered fit company for any of the daughters of the so-called "decent" families.

Jamie was troubled by this not a whit. If the "decent" girls were not available to him, there were plenty of "indecent" ones who were, and he took his pleasures where he found them.

Jessalyn knew her brother's reputation and was bothered by it. She was concerned that he did little or nothing to earn his keep, that he spent his time riding around the country with an assortment of unsavory companions, that he was frequently involved in pursuits which skirted the edges of the law. Once or twice she tried to approach Will to express her worries, but it was no use. Jessalyn knew that Will would never take any criticism of Jamie, real or implied, from her, no matter how gently she broached the subject, how subtly she tried to bring it to his attention. When she mentioned the subject, she was rebuffed harshly. Wild oats, Will said. All young men sow wild oats. Better to get them out now. He'd settle down when the time came.

Jessalyn thought not, but her efforts to deal with Jamie were just as ineffective as her efforts to deal with Will.

"Ah, Jess," he would say, "I'm just having fun. Don't be sour, Jess. I'm not doing any harm. You know what Father says. I have to sow my wild oats." And he'd give her a smile, his charming, lop-sided smile, and a hug or kiss on the cheek, and she'd not have the heart to scold any more.

Still, she worried. The wild oats bid fair to spoil the crop, she thought. But she was helpless to do more than fret.

# Chapter Two

J ESSALYN HAD BEEN SLEEPING soundly, or she probably would have awakened at the sound of Jamie's horse approaching the house. She was tired. The year was getting on into fall, and she had been working with the apples all day. She'd put up a batch of apple jelly today; that was Jamie's favorite. She still had to do the apple butter for Will.

Fall was her favorite time. The weather had been good for the apple picking--the days were golden with a touch of frost in the air, and the apple harvest had been better than usual. They'd have apples in the cellar all winter, and Jamie could have his fill of applesauce. There would be plenty of fruit to market and plenty to keep.

In fact, Jamie had been in London all day negotiating a sale with one of their regular customers who always ordered several dozen bushels from them in the fall. At least, Jamie had been in London for the purpose of selling the apples and setting the delivery date; what he had been doing after that bit of business was open to surmise.

Jessalyn usually heard him race his horse around the house on his way to the stables in back. Mother-like, she would sleep only lightly until she knew he was safe at home, but tonight, worn from her work during the day, she was first awakened by a noise downstairs.

She sat up in bed, listening, and heard a sound like a body falling against something, then a muffled sound of a voice, probably Jamie cursing the darkness and too drunk to light a candle. She sighed and reached for the light by her bed. She'd have to go down and help him up the steps before he wakened Will. She guessed that it was in the early morning hours, and once awake at this time, Will wouldn't go back to sleep. He'd get up and stay up and be angry and disgruntled for the rest of the day.

She fumbled with the candle and wrapped a shawl about her shoulders. By this time, she'd heard Jamie fall against something again, and she hurried down the stairs.

She crossed the entryway into the parlor from which the sounds had come, and held up her candle to make out Jamie's form, slumped on a chair near the door. She could smell the fumes of the liquor before she reached him, and she shook her head. He was holding his left arm with his right hand, and there were wine stains all over the front of his shirt. She sighed at his shabby condition.

"Jamie, for heaven's sake. Coming home at this hour, and drunk as a lord. I hope you haven't wakened Father."

He raised his head as she stood over him with the candle lifted, and in the pale light, his face looked like death.

"I'm …not…drunk, Jess," he said in a hoarse whisper, his eyes struggling to focus on her face.

She snorted. "Huh, not much you're not. Drunk and wine spilled all over you, and sick, too, by the look of you. Well, come on, give me your arm and let me help you up to your room before…" She stopped, her voice trailing off as she realized that the "wine stains" were slowly spreading down the sleeve of his shirt and seeping through the fingers of the hand he was using to clutch his arm.

"Oh, lord, Jamie," she gasped, setting the candle on the table at his side and reaching for her shawl to wrap his arm. "What happened to you? How'd you come by this?"

"Later…Jess. Help me…please."

She managed to get the shawl wrapped firmly around the injured arm and slipped her shoulders beneath the good one. He was a tall as a full-grown man, and looked older than his sixteen years, but he was slim, and she was tall, so she managed to support his weight as she helped him into the kitchen.

He half-led, half-dragged him to the chair before the fireplace. She hurried to poke up the fire and put the kettle on to boil, then she poured water and gathered washcloths and clean linen for bandages. Jamie slumped in the chair, his eyes closed, so still that she thought he'd lost consciousness.

She'd had experience in dressing wounds before--someone on the farm was always coming up with an injury of some sort--and she had her supply of bandages and medicines at hand. She set them down beside his chair and reached for his arm.

He almost screamed with pain when she moved it, and she stopped and used her scissors to cut away the shirtsleeve.

"How did you get this, Jamie? Tell me." Her voice was firm, and she ignored the shake of his head. "Tell me, Jamie. I need to know. What happened to you?"

He continued to shake his head and she stood back and put the scissors on the floor. "Well, then, treat your own arm. I'm going back to bed."

He turned to her quickly. "No, Jess...no, I need...you. I'll...tell you. Don't...tell Father."

"I never tell Father anything. You know that. What made this?"

"Pistol...pistol shot."

"A pistol shot!" Who on earth shot you? And why? Jamie, what were you doing?"

"It was...a mistake. All a...mistake. It was...Bennington."

"Bennington! The duke! Why on earth--what were you doing, Jamie?"

He told her the story, briefly, hesitantly, revived enough by the cup of tea she poured for him to sketch the details for her.

He had been on his way back from London, he said, when he had come upon the duke's carriage stopped by highwaymen. He had tried to go to the rescue, had tried to stop the robbery, but in the confusion when he rode up, the duke took him for one of the thieves, managed to pull a pistol, and shot him. The would-be robbers had fled, but not before killing one of the duke's party. Bennington's men had given chase, but he had hid in the bushes and escaped them.

"Jamie, how terrible! But when it's light, we'll have to ride over to the duke and explain what happened. I'm sure he'll understand. You only wanted to help, after all,

and--"

Jamie was shaking his head. "No, Jess, I've got to get away from here. He thinks I was one of the robbers. He'll never understand that I meant to help. I heard him, Jess. He yelled, 'I know you! You're Kirke's boy! I'll see you hang for this!' He won't ever believe me, Jess."

"Of course he will. He was angry. When he's cooled down and had time to think about it, he'll know you couldn't have been part of that gang, Jamie." She was wrapping a bandage around his arm after smearing it with salve. It was a flesh wound, the bullet having missed the bone, but he had lost a good deal of blood and he was weak.

"Jess, he won't listen. I know he won't. You didn't hear him. He'll have me hanged for it, and I won't wait around for them to come drag me away."

"You can't leave here now. Don't be a fool, Jamie. It can't be all that bad. You didn't do anything." Jessalyn stood up. "Father will take care of it. Come now. Let me put you to bed. You need the rest, and things will be better in the morning. She reached out a hand to smooth his hair. He was a boy, she thought. Little more than a child. It couldn't be so serious. A bit wilder than most of his pranks, obviously, but it couldn't be so bad.

"Please, Jess. Help me. Give me some food. Let me go. I've got to go before they get here. Please, Jess!"

His voice was desperate and his manner so unlike himself that she was almost caught up by his urgency. Had he been more able to ride, she might have given him what he asked for and sent him on his way. But somehow it was difficult for her to comprehend that Jamie, *her* Jamie, could be involved in a crime. Sitting here in the kitchen, the candle on the table throwing their shadows against the familiar walls, the fire warming them, she thought that highwaymen and pistol shots and the troubles he'd described seemed so far away that she couldn't believe that there was any real danger. The duke would never hang Jamie, she thought. Not the duke, her father. He wouldn't let that happen to her brother.

Jamie just needed a good night's sleep, she thought. He's tired out and he's lost a great deal of blood. She nodded at him, seeming to give in to his entreaties. "I'll fix you something to take," she said, "but you have to have something for that wound. You've lost a lot of blood. You'll never make it if I don't give you something for it."

"What is it?" he asked, turning toward her supply of ointments and syrups. "Something foul tasting, probably."

"I'd say it tastes quite foul, but it'll make your wound close up so you don't bleed to death on the way to wherever you're off to." Well, she thought, it isn't quite a lie. It will make him sleep, and the wound will be better in the morning.

"Well, stir it up, and be quick about it," he said, straining to lift himself from the chair. "I've got to change horses and be off in a hurry. I'm surprised they haven't been her already."

"You'll need help saddling your horse. You drink this." She handed him another cup of tea laced with the opiate she kept on hand. "I'll go see to the horses."

He sat back down and took the cup and drained it. She stepped out the door, but instead of racing through the chill night air to the stables to saddle a fresh horse for him, she went around the corner of the house and leaned against the warm chimney to look through the window to where he sat by the fire. She kept herself in the shadows, hugging herself in her flannel nightgown against the chill, and waited until she saw him start to nod. It didn't take long. Weakened by the loss of blood and tired has he was, he was susceptible to the effects of the narcotic, and in a few minutes she scurried back into the kitchen just in time to catch him as he fell forward out of the chair.

She dragged him up to his bed and covered him against the chill.

They came from him when the sun was just coming up over the hills.

# Chapter Three

`THE STORY THE DUKE told differed substantially from Jamie's version. According to the duke, he and his agent were leaving London with a large sum of money in gold that was to be used in payment for some breeding stock he was buying from German brokers. Ordinarily, cash wasn't necessary in such transactions, but on this occasion, the brokers had demanded, and were to receive, gold. Apparently they had had dealings with the duke before.

Bennington and his agent, a Mr. Weatherby, were traveling in the duke's coach, and they were attended by the outriders normal for such an excursion. Despite their precautions, they had been ambushed by a party of armed men and forced to surrender the gold and some of their personal effects--watches, rings, and the like.

The members of the group wore masks, but as one of them leaned over to take the agent's purse, the duke swung at his head with his walking stick and knocked his hat off, revealing the auburn curls of Jamie Kirke.

The duke had immediately recognized that hair, and had begun to shout, "I know who you are, Jamie Kirke! You can hide your face, but you can't hide that head of hair!"

That had been the signal for a general melee. The highwaymen, startled, turned to flee. One of them shot and killed Weatherby. The outriders pursued them, and in the confusion, Bennington grabbed a pistol from somewhere and fired at Jamie. He had seen the boy sway in the saddle from the shock of the bullet, but he had not fallen, nor had he dropped the gold he carried.

Jamie was taken back to London and thrown into prison to await trial. The duke's testimony and the wound in his arm seemed evidence enough to convict him, and Will was frantic. He hired counsel, he paid money to Jamie's prison guards to improve his living conditions, and to insure that he got sufficient food of good quality, and he went to visit the duke, hat in hand, to beg him to reconsider and let Jamie off.

He returned from that visit looking ten years older, his face gray and lined. He entered the kitchen where Jessalyn was making him a cup of tea and slumped into a chair in front of the fireplace.

"What did he--did he say--" she began. Will just shook his head.

"Nothing. He won't do nothing. He says he's sorry, but Jamie is guilty and has to be made an example." He stared at the fire. "An example, he says. My only son. Hang him for an example."

Jessalyn clenched her fists, digging her nails into her palms in an effort to fight back the tears. "Surely not. Surely he won't let him hang. Maybe he's just trying to scare Jamie. He's only a boy. They wouldn't."

"They've hanged younger. He's old enough to know better, that's what counts. No," his body sagged lower in the chair, seeming to shrink under the weight of his resignation, "the duke won't do anything. I thought he might. I did him a favor once, a big favor, too, and I thought--well, it's of no account now. They have short memories, do the gentry."

"Maybe if *I* went to talk to him. Maybe I could make him see the truth, that Jamie wasn't part of the gang, that he only meant to help. Maybe if I told him--"

Will looked up at her sharply. "Told him what? Why'd you think he'd listen to you and not to me, who's known him these thirty years"

She bit her tongue to keep from saying, "Because I'm his daughter." Instead, she shrugged and said, "Sometimes a woman can get a man to do things when another man can't." Will looked at her, thinking that she was going to offer the duke the same sort of favors her mother had given him, and his hatred and contempt for her twisted his face.

"Might've known you'd think of *that*, you being your mother's daughter," he said, and spat into the fire.

Jessalyn spun to face him, furious, her jaw jutting out at him. "How dare you say such things about my mother! She was much too good for the likes of you, that's certain. You didn't do her any favors by marrying her, you know. More likely the other way."

Will sprang from his chair and made for her to strike her, but she was too fast for him. Before he rounded the table, she was out the door, grabbing her cloak from a peg as she left, slamming the door behind her.

It was a mile through the lane to the duke's mansion. Ordinarily she'd have loved the walk through the tree-lined road. The day was clear and crisp, and the leaves along the lane were deep and golden. This was a place she usually treasured. But not today. Today was too important, too vital. She didn't even notice the countryside, so busy was she framing her request to the duke. But the time she reached the long gravel drive to the estate, she was out of breath and her cheeks were flushed from the autumn air.

She was too preoccupied to be intimidated by the imposing entry to the house or to think what she must look like, her hair hanging down her back in a thick braid, her work clothes on under her cloak. She scampered up the steep flight of steps that led to an ornately carved door. It was designed to be impressive, and usually she'd have been properly impressed. Today she didn't even notice, so intent was she on the purpose of her visit. She lifted the heavy brass knocker and banged it furiously. The door was opened by a butler who took one look at her disordered hair, her flushed face, her housedress, and said, "The servants' entrance is around back."

He tried to shut the door, but Jessalyn was in no mood to be shunted off so quickly.

"No!" she shouted, and shoved the door so hard and so quickly, that she caught the man off guard and almost knocked him down. "I am not a servant. I have come to see his grace, and you will please inform him that Jessalyn Kirke is here."

The butler, startled by the demand and the force with which it was delivered, was momentarily flustered. "But you can't--I mean, you can't just walk in here and demand to see the duke. Do you have an appointment? No, wait! What are you doing?"

Jessalyn had pushed her way past him and was standing in the center of the entryway. "If you do not go and announce me to the duke at this moment, I shall search every room in this house until I locate him, and I will shout at the top of my lungs while I do it."

By this time, the man, an old retainer of the duke's household, and a man not ordinarily thrown off course my any sort of contretemps, had recovered his dignity and presence of mind sufficiently to say to her, "My dear young woman, if you insist on pursuing this course of behavior, I shall have to have you bodily removed from this household."

Jessalyn planted her feet and crossed her arms and stared into his pompous face and said, "You may call out the entire staff of this place for all I care, but I'll be back every time you throw me out. I came to see his grace, and I mean to see him, and I shall see him, and if you were the devil himself, you should not stop me!"

Having delivered this fierce speech, she paused for breath. What the outcome of the battle of wills might have been is open to speculation, because at that moment, the duke himself, his attention captured by the noise, descended the stairs asking, "What seems to be the problem, Whitley?"

Whitley, relieved to have the problem taken from his hands, turned to the duke and said in his best officious manner, "It's this--person, sir. She says she wants to see you, but she has no appointment and apparently no card, and I can't seem to convince her that one doesn't simply come barging in like this and--"

"Never mind, Whitley, never mind. I'll see her." His attention had been arrested by the sight of a pretty face, and the duke was prepared to be his most gracious self to the "person" standing at the foot of the stairs. He didn't recognize her immediately.

"Who are you, young woman?"

"I am Jessalyn Kirke, sir. My --father is Wilburn Kirke."

The duke's eyebrows went up sharply. It had been several years since he had seen her, and time had improved her. It had not done the same for him. He had put on considerable weight, and even the most skillfully tailored waistcoat could not disguise the paunchy midsection. Twenty years of dissolute living showed in his face, in the bags beneath his eyes, in the sagging jowls. His nose was red and swollen and his hair had thinned.

Jessalyn didn't see any of that. She had come prepared to view him through the veil of her fantasy, and all she saw was her father, the duke, wonderful and tragic.

"I see. Miss Kirke, come into my library. Whitley, see that Miss Kirke and I are not disturbed."

The butler bowed, turned on his heel and left, his manner clearly indicating that he had washed his hands of the whole affair.

Jessalyn followed the duke into the library, sitting down in the chair he indicated to her, and watching him as he settled his bulk into the loveseat opposite her.

"Now, my dear, I must assume that you are here on your brother's account." Jessalyn nodded, and he spread his hands in a gesture of helplessness. "I thought I had made myself clear to your--to Wilburn Kirke earlier. There is nothing I can do. It is now in the hands of the law, as you know. Your brother committed a crime for which he must pay, and it is beyond my power to alter that situation."

Jessalyn looked at him, her gaze steady. "We both know that is not exactly true, your grace. You are a man of position. You have influence. And Jamie is entirely innocent. He was coming to help you, coming to your aid. He was not part of the gang that robbed you."

"Indeed," the duke sighed wearily. "If he were so eager to come to my rescue, why then did he flee, taking with him a great deal of money, none of which had been seen again? No, I'm very sorry, my dear. I was there. You were not. Besides, your brother's reputation is well known in this locale. He's hardly the sort to come to the assistance of those in need."

Jessalyn curbed her anger at the duke's seeming boredom with the whole interview, and remembering that he was her father, said to him imploringly, "Please, your grace, consider that the boy is only sixteen. He isn't bad, your grace, truly he isn't. Even if you could bring yourself to--suggest--that perhaps he could be shipped to Australia or somewhere, even if you still believe him to be guilty--he's so young, sir. I beg of you, for--for my sake, please."

"For your sake?" The duke's eyebrows lifted. "And why for your sake, may I ask?" He leaned forward a bit, eager to know what she knew.

"For--because--of my mother, your grace. You--knew my mother, I believe."

"Ah." He slumped back into his seat, regarding her with a faint smile. "You know about that, then, do you?"

She lowered her head, then looked up at him. "Yes, sir."

"I see. Well, my dear, it was unfortunate, but hardly to be helped under the circumstances. I did the best I could for Marcella, but this is a different thing entirely. Shame about her son, but he is what he is. Thieves are a danger to society, you know, and your brother has been a hellion all his life. It's just as well to have him out of the way of doing more damage."

He looked up at Jessalyn, and he thought for a moment she was going to faint. Her face had gone pale, and her eyes looked huge in her face. But she did not swoon, did not cry, did not scream, did not do any of the things he had come to expect from females. She merely said, through lips stiff enough to be frozen, "I see. I understand."

He would, in the future, wake from dreams of those eyes staring at him, through him, as if they could see every sin he had ever committed. He would wake, shaking, as if he had been accused by an avenging angel. He had little conscience. He had little concern for sins of omission or commission. Right was what was convenient and beneficial for him, wrong was the opposite.

But for that moment, and in the moments he was to come to dread in the night, he was pinned firmly to the truth by a pair of eyes that scorned and seared him. It was as if they were his own eyes, looking into his soul and despising what they saw there. Because he was so shaken by them, he hastened to cover his unease by saying quickly, "Of course, if he should give the money back, that would show some repentance, and it might alter the case, you know. I've no wish to seem harsh, my dear, it's just that--"

"He cannot give the money back, your grace." Her voice seemed to come from some place else, back past those eyes. He couldn't know that he had just shattered a dream, a fantasy she had held for half her life, and that in doing so he had left her looking at the man who was her father as he really was: An aging lecher, a fat old man with no more concern for her than if she had been a bothersome fly. The death of that fantasy left her face to face with the hopelessness of Jamie's position. She had played her trump card and had found that the game had been stacked against her before the cards were dealt.

"He doesn't have the money. I met him when he came in the house that night. He had nothing. There is no money."

"Then if he would name his companions, they must have it."

He would not look at her. His concern for the money rather than for the taking of a life was real enough to make him blurt out the conditions of his help for Jamie, but his guilt made him turn from her eyes.

"Then they must. But he doesn't know them, so he can't very well name them, you see." She rose from the chair. "I am sorry to have bothered you, sir. I'll find my way out."

Her dignity and composure had shamed and embarrassed him, and he found himself now trying to find a way to regain some stature in her sight, to find a way to make her look at him as she had at first. The look she gave him as she rose from her chair was the sort of stare she might have given to some repugnant creature crawling in the dirt. He was not accustomed to such treatment, and particularly not from women. Even now the title and the wealth proved little less seductive than his charm and appearance of earlier years.

He rose and held open the door for her. "My dear, I am truly sorry for this." She merely looked at him. "Perhaps there is something I can do for you, to help make it up, so to speak. I mean you are my--" He stopped short of acknowledging her and said, "I mean, I did know your mother. Perhaps you would like to leave here, to go somewhere else. A letter from me could help a great deal, you know, if you wanted to, say, take a position as a companion or--you do read, don't you?--a governess, or even…"

His voice trailed off as he glanced at the face, utterly expressionless, that looked back at him.

"No, thank you, your grace. I think not. Good day."

He watched her leave, closing the front door behind her softly, experiencing a feeling as close to regret has any he'd ever had. If only his own daughters had such poise, he thought. If only any woman he'd ever met had had it.

# Chapter Four

J AMIE'S TRIAL WAS QUICK, and the verdict was a forgone conclusion. It was, in effect, the word of his grace, the Duke of Bennington, against the word of Jamie Kirke, son of one of the duke's tenant farmers. There had never been any doubt as to the outcome of the trial--it was merely a formality that had to be preserved to lend legality to his hanging.

The trial was not uneventful, however, and the incident that decided Jessalyn's future occurred near the end.

Jessalyn had been called as a witness for her brother. His counsel believed that her testimony might lend enough doubt to the case that Jamie would be considered for deportation rather than hanging, and so she was called to tell about what had happened on the evening he returned to the farm.

The testimony was predictable enough at first. She swore that Jamie had come directly into the house, that he'd had nothing with him, that he had told her the story he still clung to, that he'd gone to the aid of the duke and his men.

But when the prosecutor rose to question her, he looked her over insolently, something like a sneer on his face. He was a small man with a nose like a hawk's beak, a man who was bored with his job, who sent dozens of men to their deaths regularly with no trace of conscience or concern. Standing before Jessalyn, slouched almost casually, his small black eyes peering out malevolently from beneath his wig, he saw a chance to relieve the boredom of his day and have a bit of fun with this young woman.

Seldom did a stir of the tub of human refuse with which he dealt turn up a specimen like her. She could have been highborn, he thought, standing there so straight, so proud. What had she to be proud of, this farm girl? Pretty, yes, but then so were dozens who walked the streets--at least, when they first started walking them.

"You say, Miss Kirke," he began, "that your brother had nothing with him when he came into the house that night. Is that true?"

"Yes. That's true."

"Why couldn't he have hidden the money before he came in?"

"Because he was hardly in any condition to do so. He was barely able to walk when he came in. Besides, he'd not had time to hide anything."

"Could it be, Miss Kirke," he continued, his voice deceptively smooth, "that you came to his aid, so to speak? That you hid the money for him?"

"That I--you think--do you mean that *I* might know where the money is?" Jessalyn's eyes were wide, shocked.

"I'm merely asking, Miss Kirke. It was quite a lot of money, you know. One could understand the temptation."

Jessalyn stood up a bit straighter, her teeth clenched, her anger obvious, but controlled. "There *was* no money. I saw no money. Not at any time."

"You are quite sure of that, Miss Kirke?" the unctuous voice went on. "Never? Not even a bit of it?"

"Sir, if I had any knowledge of that money or its whereabouts, I'd have returned it--all of it--after I talked to the duke about my brother."

The prosecutor raised his eyebrows. "You talked with the duke?"

"Yes. I went to see him, to tell him the truth about Jamie, that he wasn't part of the robbery. He said if Jamie returned the money, or if he named his companions, he might consider requesting leniency for my brother."

"I see." The prosecutor smiled at her, a knowing smile, a smirk, and said, "You went to the duke to beg for mercy for your brother, am I right?"

"Yes."

"To ask for--clemency, you say."

"Yes."

"Perhaps to offer--something--in exchange for his grace's mercy?"

The faces of the spectators in the courtroom all seemed to assume the same smirk as they began to understand what the prosecutor was driving toward.

Jessalyn, however, still did not understand.

"No--no, I just wanted to ask him, please, to give my brother a chance, he's so young, only sixteen, and--"

"We are all aware of your bother's age, Miss Kirke. What we are interested in right now is what you had in mind to offer to his grace in return for his consideration of your pleas, what--favors--you might have been willing to bestow by way of a bribe."

As the meaning of his words came clear to her, Jessalyn's face colored, and she said coldly, "Such a thing never occurred to me, sir. I had always considered that the duke was a fair-minded man, and that he might be willing to consider my request."

"Oh, I've no doubt that the duke is a fair-minded man. And indeed you are a fair young lady." The spectators snickered, and Jessalyn bit her lip, trying to keep her anger in check. "Nevertheless," the oily voice continued, "it hardly seems a fair trade. The duke has lost a great sum of money, and now you want him to let the thief--and accomplice to murder--off with a slap on the wrist? Fair-minded or not, does that seem quite fair to you?"

"It would seem fair-minded to me that the duke consider granting my request, yes sir, it *would* seem so."

"And why so, may I ask, Miss Kirke? Merely because you are of passing fair appearance? A man died that night. We've no doubt your brother is a thief. He may be a murderer, too."

"No, no! He isn't!" Jessalyn was becoming frantic. "He isn't either of those things!"

"At the very least, he's an accomplice to murder, Miss Kirke. A thief, an accomplice, possibly a murderer, and you wanted the duke to let him off?" The prosecutor pretended to be appalled, outraged.

"No! He's not those things! I went to ask the duke to listen to him, to show some mercy toward him!"

"Or, " his voice dropped, and an insinuating tone crept into his voice, "did you hope to get him off and keep the money, too?"

"NO!" she shouted, her control giving way to her anger, goaded into unthinking fury and fear by the unjust charges and the cynical, sneering manner of the man. "No, none of those things! I hoped he'd do it for me, for my sake!"

"For your sake? For *your* sake? And why on earth should he do it for *your* sake?"

"Because he's my father! I thought he'd do it for me!"

The prosecutor's mouth dropped open; he was shocked out of his ennui, for once. Jamie, watching her from the prisoner's box, stared, his mouth an O. Will Kirke's face contorted into a mask of hatred, and the duke flushed red. The courtroom was silent for a moment, the spectators looking back and forth from Jessalyn to the duke. Once mentioned, the resemblance was obvious, and the looks of shock were quickly replaced by knowing grins.

The duke, flustered by the charge, banged his cane on the floor and shouted, "Lies! The fool girl is lying! Not a bit of truth to it!"

Will Kirke rose and stormed from the courtroom.

Order was restored rapidly enough, and the trial proceeded to its inevitable conclusion, but Jessalyn's story had spread all over London by nightfall. That the duke had fathered numerous illegitimate children was no secret; it was no secret that numerous members of the aristocracy kept mistresses, frequented brothels, had bastards scattered throughout the countryside. But no one mentioned it, at least not in public. No one stood up and said, "He is my father," about some dissolute lord. There were unwritten rules about such things, and Jessalyn had just broken one of them.

Of course, the duke denied the statement vociferously. None of his, he said. Damned girl, anyway, trying to make him look bad because of her thieving brother.

But just as no one had believed a word of Jamie's denial of the theft, no one believed a word of the duke's denial of Jessalyn's paternity. It was much too juicy a tidbit of gossip not to be repeated, and it was believed because it's purveyors wanted to believe it.

"...stood right up, you know, and said it right out. 'The duke is my father.' And him sitting there, not fifteen feet away."

"...looks the image of him, they say, leastwise when he was younger. Gone to fat, now, you know."

"...Kirke, Jessalyn Kirke. She said it right in the courtroom with her father--the Kirke man, that is--sitting right there. And he didn't even deny it, just got up and walked out."

"...said the duchess left town to go to the country right away and at the height of the season, too. She wasn't seeing anyone."

Jessalyn's purpose in blurting out the truth about her parentage had not been to embarrass the duke, or to make him look bad, or any of several possible motives. Indeed, she had had no purpose when she said it other than to make that snide little man stop his evil insinuations. But it did have the effect of making the duke look malicious and lecherous.

Not quite sporting, the gossip ran, not to do something for the girl. Quite pretty, you know. And he'd not even say a word in favor of her brother. His own daughter. Very poor. Bad form.

The immediate effect on Jessalyn was to subject her to knowing looks and smiles from Jamie's jailers and to the fury of Will Kirke.

She made the trip to visit Jamie every day until the day he was to hang, and the jailers, heretofore indifferent to her, now looked at her with the smiles, the manners that said that they knew her for what she was.

She thought that they did not.

Will Kirke had left the courtroom to go out and get roaring drunk and came home shouting his fury and frustration to her locked door.

"If he hangs, missy," he shouted, his words slurred by the ale he'd consumed, "if he 'angs, you might as well hang with him, for yer dead for all of me." He paused, breathing heavily. "Your fault, all your fault. Hadn't been for you, he'd not be in this trouble. All your fault. Want you out of my house. Yer none of mine. Out, d'ye hear? If he hangs, never wanna see you again, hear?"

Inside the room, Jessalyn lay on her bed and silently concurred with his opinion that it was all her fault. Will's reason for accusing her was obscure, reasoning born of a liquor-soaked brain and a sense that perhaps his own indulgence had led Jamie to this place. But Jessalyn was eaten away by guilt at believing that she could have prevented this and had not.

Why didn't I listen to him, why didn't I help him get away? I practically turned him in myself. Why didn't I just send him running? If he'd been caught, it would have been no worse than it is now. She was hardly sleeping these days, her mind turning over all the ways she might prevent the hanging.

Will, on the other hand, slept much of the time. He spent most of his waking hours in the pubs, and he came home late to sleep off the drunk until he could return the next day.

On the eve of the date set for his hanging, Jessalyn made her usual visit to Jamie's cell. The guards, paid for their troubles, led her through the corridors, through the gates and doors to the small cell where she could see Jamie's red curls glowing in the dim light.

She had become accustomed to the smells of the place, smells of unwashed bodies, of vomit, of rancid grease, of human waste and decay. She had almost become accustomed to the slimy floors, the sweating stones, the smoke from the lamps. But she never became accustomed to the sight of Jamie, rising from the lice-infested straw on the floor of the cell, stepping over the other bodies to come to face her at the bars. She could never reconcile this gray, listless face, these dull eyes, with the Jamie she knew; memories of his laughing child's face tore at her insides and fed the worm of guilt that ate at her constantly.

On the last day of his life, she stood before him, reaching out to touch his hand. Warned to move back by the guard at her elbow, she stepped back, wrapping her cloak more closely about her.

"I've brought your food," she said, indicating the basket she carried. "It's still warm. It'll take the chill off."

"I'm not hungry, Jess. But hand it on in, anyway. My mates in here will be glad of it." The other three occupants of the cell had stirred when she arrived with the food, and now sat still in the background, their pinched faces yearning toward the basket she held.

The guards had already checked the basket, and one of them opened the small window for her, and she shoved the basket through. Jamie took it and passed it negligently to the scarecrow nearest him, who seized it and dragged it back toward the corner where the threesome fell on it.

"How's Father?" Jamie asked after a pause.

"All right, I suppose. He's drunk every night and sleeps all day. Has he been by to see you?"

"No. You're all the visitor I get. All my friends," he laughed, a humorless, dry sound, "all my good friends just disappeared, you know."

"Jamie, Jamie, I'm so sorry, I'm so sorry. I was wrong. I should have sent you out. This is so wrong, so terrible."

"Ah, Jess." His voice was comforting and he made an effort to smile at her. "It wouldn't have mattered what you did, they'd have got me anyway. Don't blame yourself, Jess."

"But I do, Jamie. It was my fault. I should have listened to you. I could have helped. It was my fault." Her voice broke at the end, and she grasped the bars, her hands clenched tightly around them, now that the guard had become careless of her and had wandered off somewhere else.

"Jess, it didn't matter. I was so near gone, I'd have fallen off the horse a mile from the house. Besides," he said, suddenly older than his sixteen years, "it wouldn't have saved me. I was bound to end up this way anyhow. I'd been headed for it all along."

"Oh, no, Jamie. No, you weren't. You were a little wild, maybe, but you didn't do this, you didn't, you'd change now, you know you would."

Jamie shook his head and patted her hand. "It's no good, Jess. It was bound to happen." He looked behind him at the three scavengers clustered over the basket, and turned his head to try to peer down the hall. "Where's the guard?" he asked, his voice almost a whisper.

Jessalyn glanced down the dim corridor to where the guard was leaning carelessly against a doorway and said, "He's down at the end of the hallway. Why?"

He pulled her closer, his manner conspiratorial. "Jess, when they've hanged me, I want you to take the money and leave. Take a ship, go away, get away from here. Promise me you will."

"Take what money?" She frowned at him, uncomprehending, and then the truth of what he was saying dawned on her. "Jamie, are you telling me you *have* the money?"

"Of course I have it, Jess. I've always had it. But now it'll be yours. Promise you'll take it."

"Oh, Jamie." She sagged against the door, closing her eyes, hanging onto the bars. "If only I'd known, if only you'd told me. Bennington said he'd speak for you if he'd got the money back. Oh, Jamie, maybe it's not too late, maybe if I went and got it and took it to him, maybe--"

"No." He shook his head vigorously and gripped her wrists. "No!

You are not to do that. I'll have paid in full for that money, and it's yours, do you hear? He'd not have spoken for me, not if you'd given it back, not if you'd begged him. Don't you understand, Jess?"

She shook her head, slowly, not convinced. "No, Jamie, surely not, surely if he got it back--"

"And do you think he'd speak for me now, Jess? Now that you've shown him up for the lecher and scoundrel he is? Ha! It was almost worth hanging, just to see his face that day in court."

Jessalyn opened her tightly closed eyes to see her brother's face twisted into a malicious grin. "But Jamie, I can't take the money. Where would I go? I wouldn't dare spend a cent of it. They'd have me. I can't--"

"Hush! I've been thinking in here for days now, and I waited till today to tell you for fear you'd try some fool thing like giving it back. Well, you're not going to. Where will you go and what will you do if you don't take it? You don't think you can stay with Father, do you? And what else can you do?"

"But I can't--"

"But you can!" he hissed, clutching her wrists more tightly. "There are ships leaving every day for Australia, the West Indies, America. Buy passage on one of them and get out of her. Go out and get married and forget me and Father and this whole thing. Promise me!"

"Jamie, I--"

"It's damned little enough the duke is doing for you at that. He *owes* you, Jess. Promise!"

"I--promise," she said finally, giving in to him from force of habit, and to sooth his last night. He released her hands then, and managed a smile reminiscent of his old, cocky self.

"I'll watch out for you, Jess. You go on, and I'll take care of you. You make something better for yourself. I won't let anything happen to you."

She looked up, her face pale in the feeble light. "Jamie, that's blasphemous. You won't be--"

"Oh, come on, Jess. I won't be off to Heaven, that's sure, and I've no inclination for Hell. I'll stick around and keep an eye out for you."

"Oh, Jamie," she sighed, her eyes filling with tears.

"Ah, now, Jess. No tears. You've not cried yet. Don't do it now, girl."

She wiped her eyes quickly with the back of her hand, trying to look composed. "Yes. Well. I'll be back in the morning before--time. Will they let me see you?"

"For a minute, but not alone. That's why I had to tell you tonight. Remember, you promised."

She nodded. "I know." Then she raised her head and said, "But, Jamie, where is it? Where did you put it?"

"Where?" He managed a lopsided smile. "Why, in the hidey-hole, of course. Where else?"

*   *   *   *   *

He was hanged in the early morning, one of several to die that day, with nothing special to mark his turn except the flame of his hair and his youth. Jessalyn had been allowed to see him for a moment, to hug him quickly, to tell him that she loved him, before he was dragged away with the others, down the corridor to the courtyard.

She stood in the back of the yard full of people, their raucous laughter and ribald jokes seeming to make a mockery of her grief. As long as Jamie could see her, she had kept back the tears, but now as he stepped up to the scaffold, she bit the knuckles of her hand until she tasted the blood, and the tears almost blurred the sight of the blindfolded youth, standing straight, his hands tied behind him, as the minister read from the prayer book.

The crowd paid little heed to him; he didn't have a brave gallows's joke, a last line to toss out to them before the trap was sprung. He was just a frightened boy, the bravado of last night gone, his face white, his lips bloodless.

The chill November wind scattered a few leaves across the cobblestones. The minister's voice, if not his words, came to her, and she forced herself to watch as the trap was sprung and his slim body dropped with a sickening thud through the opening. She moaned, a harsh, animal sound. His neck was broken at once, his lifeless form twisted a bit at the end of the rope.

Then she turned, and pulling her cloak about her and drawing her hood down close over her face, She fled the courtyard, running sobbing and stumbling from the awful place.

# Chapter Five

S HE RETURNED TO THE farm long enough to pack a bag with a few belongings and to locate the cache in the hidey-hole. It was all there, right enough, a bag of gold with a few pieces of jewelry, and after examining the contents quickly, she stuffed it into the bag with the rest of her belongings and headed for the coast.

She'd made no plans; she'd hardly had time to think about where she might go, and now when she reached the dock, she had no idea of a place to where she might book passage. As it happened, the choice was made almost by default. There was only one ship leaving immediately that took passengers. It was an old schooner, a former slaver that had been refitted for merchant and passenger service when slaveholding ended in the British territories. It was a small ship, old and disreputable, hardly, to the naked eye, even seaworthy; but it had been making the run back and forth to the West Indies with deceptive regularity. Jessalyn made inquiries and learned that it would be leaving in two days, and she signed up as a passenger and paid her passage in gold.

When she pushed the coins toward him, Captain William Scarsdale took the money and looked up at her. She was quite different, he thought, from the usual run of his passengers. The ones that paid their own ways usually looked as if they had starved themselves or their children to do it, and the balance were indentured.

Since slavery had been outlawed, he did most of his business with the indentured servants, the ones who sold their sold their services to the plantation owners to work in the cane for five, six, seven years to pay for their passage. They'd sign the papers here, and he would deliver them to the islands and collect on them. Servants out, sugar back.

Ones like her, ones who could pay their passage in gold, usually took the frigates, the big ships for passengers with money who were headed out to Australia or New Zealand or some other place to visit or for travel or for the government. He seldom saw the likes of her on his grimy little ship.

He counted the coins into his purse and looked up at her, his small eyes squinting over a bushy, unkempt black beard. "Don't get too many passengers as pay in gold, Miss--ah, what did you say your name was?"

Jessalyn dug her fingernails into her palms. The gold might have been a mistake, she thought. He'd remember that if someone asked. Perhaps she should have exchanged it, but it was too late now.

"Ah--Cook," she said, picking a name at random, quickly discarding her own as likely to be remembered, recognized. "Janet Cook."

He scratched her name onto his list of passengers. "Miss Cook, is it? And where are ye going, Miss Cook?"

"Where are you bound, Captain?"

He looked up at her, surprised. Ones like this usually had family, finances, jobs, something waiting for them. She must not be one of those. "Bound for Trinidad, Miss. Port of Spain. Was that where ye were wantin' to go?"

"It will do, Captain." Her voice was curiously flat, dead, and his interest was piqued. He scratched at the beard with fingernails that hadn't been clean in living memory, and narrowed his eyes at her.

"Going out in search of adventure, like, are ye?"

She realized that what she had said would make her sound strange. Everyone who went on these trips did so for a purpose; a woman alone didn't just board the first ship out of the harbor and take off to see the world.

She thought fast and said, "No, not really. You see, I'm an orphan, alone in the world, you know. I have no family and my health isn't what it should be. I--I've been considering going to a warmer climate for some time and the West Indies, well, that's a warm climate, wouldn't you say?"

He nodded, not believing a word of her story, and said, "Warm, sunny, fine place to be. Trinidad, now--that's a place. You'll like it there, Miss. Sure to be good for your health, Trinidad is."

She smiled and turned to leave. He watched her retreating back and muttered to himself, "For your health, indeed, Missy. More likely to keep that pretty little neck of yours out of a noose. Where would such a one come by that much gold honestly? And more of it in her purse, if I'm not mistaken. We'll see about your health, once we're well underway."

They sailed from England in the early morning. Jessalyn stood at the rail and watched the shore retreat from her view and pale in the distance.

Just as well, she thought. I've no wish to see any more of this country, anyway. Maybe someday I can come back. Maybe someday I'll want to see it again. But not now. Not anymore.

Her cabin was small and dirty, dim and nasty smelling, but she didn't complain of it after she saw the way the indentured passengers were shoved about in the hold. They were packed in, so many of them that they hardly had room to lie down to sleep. And the *Emmaline* was an old ship, leaky and badly kept. If they had been able to lie down, there was hardly a dry spot for them to do so. Water ran at their feet, mixed with vomit from those who were seasick, and the inevitable human wastes. The smell was vile, and that as many of them survived as did was more testimony to the strength of the human spirit than to any attention they received.

By contrast, Jessalyn's quarters seemed almost palatial, and by contrast to their meager diet of salt port and hard tack, her own meals seemed extravagant. Actually, her own were poor enough, and she regretted, after a few days of rancid, greasy stew, that she had not thought to bring along any of the apples that were so plentiful on the farm.

The apples were all she missed of the farm. Even in the face of poor food and the seasickness she was prone to, she didn't miss the farm, didn't miss Wilburn Kirke, didn't miss her occasional glimpses of the duke or his daughters riding past. To look back was to think of Jamie, and she couldn't think of him without being almost overwhelmed with grief and guilt and anger, so she put thoughts of her past behind her with a thorough firmness and concentrated on the moment.

For the first part of the trip, that constituted no problem, because she spent much of her time in her cabin fighting nausea and a chill and fever she had picked up from the damp autumn air before she had left. But when the days turned sunny and the weather was clear and the sailing smooth, the seasickness eased and the fever went away. She found, since she was spending less time in her cabin sleeping, that the days were long and there was little to occupy her time. She took to walking around the deck of the little ship frequently and staring out to sea.

She walked daily, hourly, around and around the ship, until the crew began to joke that she was going to wear a groove in the deck. She watched the sails overhead, she listened to, but did not join in, the talk among the men. They began to think of her as strange. She never exchanged more than "Good morning," with any of them, but she learned to know all of them by sight and many of them by name.

And as she walked, she was watched, not only by the men.

Captain William Scarsdale watched her. And watching, grew more and more curious. At some point, the curiosity was overcome by the lust that had been nagging at him almost from the moment he had first seen her.

He was an ugly man, dirty and crude. His matted beard and hair harbored a variety of lower life forms, and he couldn't remember when he'd had all his teeth. He was fat, seldom totally sober, and generally fortified with the contents of the flask of brandy he kept tucked beneath the folds of his food-stained clothing. He'd no illusions as to his own desirability. But then, on this ship, he didn't need to be desirable. He was the captain. His word was law here, and what he chose to do, he did. There was no one to argue the point with him. He maintained discipline among the members of his crew with impartial brutality, using flogging and keelhauling whenever he deemed such punishments appropriate.

Flogging was a standard punishment on any ship, and scarcely any of the experienced sailors had escaped it. Scarsdale employed it regularly for offenses as minor as cursing a fellow sailor or being slow to respond to orders.

But keelhauling was something else. It was a serious punishment, as likely as not to end in death. The man who was being keelhauled had a rope tied to his hands and another tied to his feet; then the rope attached to his feet was passed under the keel of the ship and fastened to a tackle on one of the yardarms. The offender was tossed overboard and dragged under the keel of the ship.

Death from keelhauling could come in a number of ways. A man might drown; that was not unusual, particularly if the rope snagged on its way beneath the ship. If he survived the sea, he might bleed to death from being scraped against the barnacles on the hull, or against rusty nails or spikes or whatever he was pulled across. If he should be alive when he was pulled from the sea, he was generally washed off with water or rum and left to recuperate or not, depending on the extent of his wounds. Infections often carried off survivors of the treatment.

Keelhauling was not a punishment to be contemplated lightly, and Scarsdale had reputation for using it more frequently than any other captain of the fleet. He would make bets on whether the victim would survive. His crew hated and feared him, and had no doubt as to his willingness to use the worst at his disposal if he were crossed. Not one of them, as a result, would stand in his way if he chose to press himself, however unwanted his attentions might be, upon the mysterious and apparently defenseless Miss Cook.

Jessalyn, meanwhile, was unaware that she was being watched. She was aware of little besides her own thoughts, and she paid so little heed to the captain that she would have been surprised to know how often he thought of her, how much she occupied his mind these days. In fact, when he invited her into his cabin some time into the voyage, she thought of it as only a kind of consideration on his part that might break up the monotony for the trip for her. It was, she thought, a relief from the tedium of the days, and she followed the young sailor who served as her escort to the captain's quarters with something akin to pleasure.

"Ah, Miss Cook." The captain smiled at her, his few teeth showing in a fashion that made them look a bit like fangs. "Come in, come in. Have a chair right here," he said, indicating a chair beside the table. She sat down on the once-red cushion, murmuring a greeting to him.

"How have you been weathering the voyage so far?" he asked. "Have you been seasick?"

"Some," she answered, making an effort to smile at him. "I've had some sickness. I'm afraid I'm not much of a sailor."

"Well, well, some aren't, ye know. I've had passengers sick from England to Port of Spain. Don't know how they kept alive on what they could keep down. You've done much better than some. But here now, I've asked you down for dinner and I've not even offered you a glass of wine. I've some fine sherry here, traded it off a Spaniard when I was last in Trinidad. Try a glass of that, now."

He poured her a glass of the amber wine, and poured a glass for himself. It was not his first glass of the evening; he'd sampled the sherry earlier and that on top of the brandy he'd nipped at during the day. Captain Scarsdale was well into the evening's drinking.

Jessalyn, on the other hand, wasn't much of a drinker at all. An occasional glass of cider in the fall at the harvest celebrations generally constituted the total of her drinking experience. She lived in a house with a man who drank a great deal too much, and she was leery of the effects of alcohol. Now she sipped at the sherry and resisted the captain's efforts to persuade her to take more.

As she took the sherry, she surveyed the captain's cabin. It was much like her own--small, dim, airless, and even dirtier. It looked as if it had not been given a good scrubbing in years. This was not the sort of ship she had grown up hearing about, she thought. "Ship-shape" applied to this vessel almost not at all. The condition of the deck and the care that was exercised with its rigging and the sails could perhaps use the term; apparently anything not obvious or necessary for the running of the ship was ignored.

The same young sailor who had brought her to the captain's cabin returned with a tray carrying the evening meal. It differed little from the meals she'd had since she boarded the ship, but there was a pitcher of stout and a rather heavy looking pastry for dessert.

While they ate, the captain plied her with questions about her background and her purpose in traveling to Trinidad, all of which Jessalyn evaded with a skill she seemed born to. She was not accustomed to lying. She'd always been used to telling the truth, even when it was sure to bring Will Kirke's wrath down upon her. Now she found that she was quite skillful at fabrication.

"You said you're an orphan, Miss Cook. How long have your parents been dead?"

"My mother died when I was fourteen," she said, bending her head to her plate. "My father died just a while back."

"Ah, that's too bad, now. Took ill, did he?"

She nodded, sipping the stout. "Pneumonia. The doctor said he got a chill out in the rain, and it took him quickly. Nothing to be done, the doctor said. He went right away."

"Happens like that sometimes," the captain nodded sagely. "Had a first mate died like that once. Think it were the cold in England. He hadn't been used to it for a while. One day he was fit, the next he was sick, the next he was dead. Didn't last a week from beginning to end." He glanced up at her, his small eyes taking in the amount of stout she was consuming, reaching to refill the glass she set down.

"And you'd no one else in your family?" he asked solicitously.

She shook her head. She appeared calm outwardly, but the lying was making her nervous and she was drinking more than she ever had. It seemed to make the stories come easier. "No one. My brother died recently, not long before my father, and I'd no other living relatives." At least none that would own me, she thought.

The captain sent the dinner dishes away with the young sailor, who noted the flush in Jessalyn's cheeks and reckoned that she'd not be returning to her own cabin that night. The captain set out glasses and poured brandy for the two of them. Jessalyn took a sip of hers and returned the glass to the table, sloshing the liquor over the rim of the glass as she set it down too hard.

"I think I'd best be going back to my cabin," she said, attempting to rise from her chair. "It's been a fine evening, Captain, but I think I'd best be--"

"Oh, now, Miss Cook. You'd not be leaving yet. You've not even finished your brandy." He laid a heavy hand on her shoulder and pushed her back into the chair.

Jessalyn's head was beginning to swim, and she was not feeling well. The liquor, combined with the greasy food and the motion of the ship, was making her feel queasy, and she tried once more to rise from her chair.

"You've really been most kind, Captain," she said, "but I have to go." Her stomach threatened to rebel at any moment, and she thought that if she didn't get some fresh air soon, she was likely to be sick right here at the captain's table.

The captain misinterpreted her attempts to leave. He was certain that she was trying to evade him, that she had seen his purpose, and now she was going to try to flee his advances.

For her age and background, Jessalyn was remarkably innocent. This was partly a product of her rearing at Marcella's hands--not wanting her daughter to make the same mistake she had, she'd instilled a great deal of sexual squeamishness in her--and partly a result of her treatment by Will Kirke. She had trouble understanding that men could like her, could want to be near her. She felt that like Will, all men must find her inadequate, unattractive, and she seldom interpreted their approaches properly. She did not understand the overtures of courtship, of seduction, of interest in her.

As a result, and because she was concerned primarily with the condition of her stomach, she did not understand the captain's motives until his hands were upon her. A more sophisticated woman would have known how things were early in the evening, or indeed, at the issuance of the invitation; Jessalyn's upbringing prevented her guessing.

When he reached for her, though, she was not in doubt. He grabbed her shoulders and pushed her up against the door of the cabin.

"Not so fast, *Miss Cook*, or whatever your name is. You're not going anywhere this night."

She pulled her arms up in front of her, attempting to shove him away, turning her head from his fetid breath as he tried to kiss her. "Captain, no, don't, please, stop. Don't, oh, please, Captain. I have to get out of here! Please let me go!"

"Not likely, Miss Cook. And don't play virtuous with me, missy. I know the only way you're likely to have come by that much gold, and it weren't no honest way, neither. Not your sort. Most likely took it off one of your customers and then run for it. Orphan, indeed."

He pulled at her dress, yanking at her sleeve until it tore, trying to force his knee between her legs. She screamed and shoved him, raking his cheek with her fingernails. Furious, he slapped her hitting her head against the door and splitting her lip so that the blood ran down the side of her mouth.

She turned her face toward him, stunned, and then suddenly, as he lunged for her again, nausea overcame her and she vomited, bending forward as the cramps took her, spewing the vomit all over the front of the captain.

He cursed her and shoved her from him, pushing her so that she slumped against the door and slipped to a sitting position.

"Damn you, you slut, look at this mess! You no-good wretch!" He turned to grab a rag to clean himself, gulped a slug of the brandy, and then turned back, intent on finishing what he had started.

As he turned to face her, however, he suddenly went pale, gasped, dropped the decanter of brandy, and began to shake all over.

"My god!" he choked, his eyes starting from his head.

Standing over the half-conscious girl was the figure of a youth, tall, slim, with reddish curls. He had a noose around his neck, and his face was purple, and his eyes were bulging from his head. He was staring at Scarsdale, those horrible eyes fixed on the captain's, and he was standing in front of the girl, legs spread apart, hands on his hips, his whole attitude leaving no doubt that he was going to protect her.

But the most frightening thing to the captain, the thing that sent him stumbling backwards over the shards of the broken decanter, was that he could see right through the body--the door and the girl behind the youth were visible, but the hideous apparition was equally visible.

The captain was no less superstitious than most of his profession. His face, pasty white, was sweating profusely, and he began to scream for someone, anyone. But by the time the young sailor opened the door, the vision had faded. When the boy entered, all he saw was the young woman, slumped down so that she almost fell out the door when he opened it, and the captain, white as the sails of his ship, leaning against the table opposite her.

The sailor surveyed the scene, confused. The captain, rubbing his eyes, thought that he must have overdone the brandy, and his fear rapidly turned to fury. He'd been done out of his bit of fun with this puking witch, and he'd been made to look a fool in front of his crewman. He swore loudly and kicked at the fragments of the bottle on the floor.

"That impudent wench tried to kill me!" he said to the astonished sailor. "Swung at me with the brandy bottle, she did. Would have smashed my head if she'd connected. Ever know a woman who could hold her liquor?" The sailor shook his head, glancing surreptitiously at the girl who was now trying to lift herself from the floor.

"Get her out of here!" the captain snarled. The sailor started to help Jessalyn to her feet, eyeing the bruised face and the split lip. Too bad she'd missed the old sot, he thought. The better for us if she'd hit him with that bottle.

"Shall I take her back to her cabin, sir?" he asked, helping her to stand as she swayed, moaning, against him.

"Yes, take her--no. No. Not to her cabin." I'll fix her, he thought. She-devil. Fight me, will she? We'll see how much fight she has left when she gets to Trinidad. "No. I can't be letting her run around loose. Throw her in the cargo hold. And chain her up. Put her in leg irons."

The sailor looked at the captain, surprised. Seldom was even the most belligerent sailor put in irons. Flogged, maybe. Tossed in the hold for a day or so. But not put in irons.

"Leg irons, sir?"

"Leg irons. You heard me. Now get it done." The captain tossed off another finger of brandy and glared at the young man, who was leading Jessalyn out the door. "If she gives you any trouble, fetch her a clout alongside the head. That'll slow her down a bit."

Jessalyn was still dazed as she was put into the hold, and she couldn't understand why she hadn't been returned to her cabin. She was lowered into the hold, chained, and left. When the sailor closed the hatch behind him, she was left alone in a pitch-black pit.

# *Chapter Six*

D OMINICK REYNOLDS FLUNG THE packet of papers from him, and the sheets hit the wall of his office, scattering like so much confetti.

"Damn! Damn him!" he shouted, and turned to the window, pounding his fist into his palm.

Across the room, Simon Alderly looked up, startled. His employer's eyes had taken on the look and color of polished steel, and the scar across his cheekbone had gone white, a sure sign of his rage.

"There's only one person capable of inspiring that sort of anger in you," he said. "What has our friend the Earl of Trenton come up with now?"

Reynolds sighed heavily and continued to stare out the window, his hands on his hips. He was a large man, broad shouldered, taller than the average by a full head. His plantation manager watched him in silence, thinking that Reynolds had little skill in dealing with frustration. Somehow it seemed to sit more awkwardly on him than on others. Finally the man turned and looked at Simon, running a hand through his heavy dark hair.

"That was a letter from Smythe in London. It seems that my former father-in-law has been plotting my life for me. Again."

"Ah, and what does he have in store for you now?"

"A new wife. Or perhaps I should say, a replacement for my first."

Alderly raised his eyebrows. "Indeed. And just who did he have in mind for the position?"

"Who else? My late wife's twin sister."

"Alida? He's sending out Alida Fitzhugh? Just like that?"

Dominick sank heavily into the chair behind the desk. "I thought I had anticipated him," he said. "I thought I had caught on to the way he thought. But I hadn't considered this possibility. Not at all. It never occurred to me that he would send her--*her*."

He slammed his palm on the desk and rose and began pacing back and forth on the carpet in front of Simon's chair. "I don't want to be married again. Not to anyone. Especially not to another one of Hartwell Trenton's witch daughters."

Alderly steepled his fingers, considering. "Is Smythe certain of this? How did he come by the information?"

"Straight from the old man himself, evidently. Trenton was making arrangements for some shipping, and he told Smythe that since Adelaide has been dead for almost a year now, and old Fitzhugh has been dead for nearly two, that he thought it only right that he send Alida out to me. Since, as he put it, I'm surely in need of a wife, and since there's undoubtedly no one suitable in the West Indies, he thought it was the least he could do. Humph," he snorted. "There's no one suitable under his roof either, but how do I go about telling him that?"

"It *is* a problem, all right." Simon paused. "Of course, you could always just tell him, 'No, thanks.'"

"Yes." Dominick sighed and sat back down at the desk. "Yes, I could. But he'd be thoroughly insulted, and I'd lose any hope of ever getting Bellefleur back."

"Um. There is that." The two were silent for a time, and then Alderly said, "It isn't as if you needed the place. You're certainly quite capable of buying any number of bigger, more impressive estates."

The cold gray eyes turned on him. "That isn't the point."

"I know. So, how distasteful *is* the idea of being married to Alida Trenton Fitzhugh?"

"Very. Very, very distasteful. I would do anything--well, not anything, but shall we say, many things? to avoid it.

"Um." Simon leaned his chin upon his fist, considering. He was devoted to Dominick Reynolds' best interests, because that man was not only his employer, but for some years now, his best friend. The two could hardly have been more dissimilar: Reynolds, tall, dark haired, bronzed, impetuous, given to quick bursts of temper; Alderly, slim, fair, practical, deliberate. Simon was a connoisseur of fine art, cuisine, literature. He was the sort of man who was always socially correct, impeccably dressed. He was a hostess' delight, a man who was absolutely correct, marvelous to invite to any party or to escort a visiting sister or aunt. He could be counted on to be very charming, listening to every word, however inane, brightening the conversation with anecdotes collected during a lifetime of travel.

Dominick, by contrast, had no patience with stupidity, whatever the source. He seldom noticed what he wore unless the occasion required formal attire. Clever chit-chat bored him to the point that he had been known to wander away in the middle of what some lovely young thing thought was her most successful flirtation, unaware that she was still babbling on. Women might fall in love with him, but they were seldom comfortable under that most masculine, no-nonsense scrutiny.

"Well, my friend, it seems to me that you didn't get any prizes when you beat the earl at cards. As to your current predicament, I'm not sure what to tell you. You have several options, you know. You could always send her packing."

"And lose any chance of getting my home back."

"True. Or you could marry her, and have some prospect of getting it, finally."

"But even that wouldn't be sure. And besides, the life I lived with Adelaide would probably seem like a glorious party compared to life with Alida. I'm not sure I can go through that again."

"Or, you could let her stay on here, but tell her that you couldn't possibly consider remarrying with the memory of her dear, dead sister fresh in your heart."

"Not only would she know that to be a lie--I'm sure Adelaide never wrote anything flattering about me--but she'd probably just stay here, applying pressure and manipulating until I caved in."

"Too bad you're not already married. That would certainly solve your problems."

"Maybe. Unless it created new ones. But it would be one way out of this."

Simon took out a long slim cigar and lighted it, watching the smoke rise, and pondering. "You didn't have any word about this from the earl himself, am I right?"

"No. Smythe sent the information on ahead on the first ship he could get to bring it. He said I probably wouldn't hear from Trenton for some two, three weeks. Evidently this marvelous little scheme just came to him when Alida's chance to marry someone more eligible didn't materialize, and he decided to cover his interests by marrying me into the family again."

"How much time does that give you, then?"

"Before she gets here? A month at the least, depending on whether she's already left or not. Six--eight weeks at the outside, depending. Why?" Reynolds scrutinized his friend. "What did you have in mind?"

"Well, I was just thinking. People have been married in less time."

"Married? You mean to someone else? That's out of the frying pan, Simon. Marriage is what I want to avoid."

"Um, yes, I know. But suppose it should be simply an arranged marriage. A marriage of convenience."

"A sort of legalized pretense, is that what you're getting at?"

Alderly spread his hands. "If it would work…"

Reynolds shrugged. "Oh, it would solve some problems, all right. It would provide a graceful way out of the dilemma with Trenton. After all, he would hardly fault me for refusing to be a bigamist. The worst complaint he could have would be that I'd not waited a full year to marry after Adelaide's death. But it's impossible, Simon. First of all, there's no one to marry on this little island. Second, what sort of woman would be willing to take on such a masquerade? What sort of woman would have a family that would allow it?"

"You underestimate your attractions, my friend. I know a hundred women who would jump at the chance to be Mrs. Dominick Reynolds. Even in name only." He smiled. "Some would even prefer 'name only.'"

"Huh. I'd probably be better off married to Alida. At least I'd know what I was getting into. No woman would be flattered by a proposition like that, and sooner or later I'd be the victim of my own cleverness."

"Still, it is a thought."

"It is. But impractical, my friend. Impractical. And I'm usually the one who comes up with those ideas. No, I'm afraid I'll have to deal with the problem in some other way."

"Well, then, as I see it, you have been effectively caught between Scylla and Charybdis, as the Greeks would say."

"Maybe. I have to think about it for a time."

He gathered the papers that littered the floor, flung them on his desk, and strode out of the room. He climbed two flights of stairs in the center of the house, coming out at the top of a small cupola from which he could survey his property for some distance. Ahead of him, over the tops of the trees, he could see the ocean, deep blue in the early twilight, fringed with coconut palms. The setting sun cast the lawns and gardens in shadow. The cane fields picked up the late afternoon sun, seeming to ripple under it. Tobago, he thought. Paradise. Why is it that Paradise is so miserable? He leaned forward, his elbows on the white rail encircling him. If anyone had told him when he was fifteen years old that he could have all this and not be happy, he'd have thought the idea foolish, or worse. But there it was. All that he could see--and much more--was his. "Rich as a Tobago planter," they used to say, and though the saying had lost much of its meaning since Tobago had fallen on hard times, he was indeed rich. Very. The richest of the Tobago planters. And the nagging, unhappy, dissatisfaction was there still, was as real, as constant as the prevailing breeze.

He couldn't put his finger on the exact time when it had begun to go wrong; it was tied up with Adelaide and her father, those two schemers, who, unable to achieve happiness themselves, set about seeing to it that no one else associated with them managed to have much, either. But he wasn't sure just how it had all come down to this. When he'd bought the original plantation from a near-bankrupt lord, it had been the culmination of a long-held ambition. His own place, his own land. He'd added to it, buying up pieces of property that came on the market as they were sold by over-extended planters who were hurt badly when slavery was abolished in the British Empire.

But a large part of it he'd won in what he'd come to think of as an ill-fated card game. He'd come by it in payment of a gambling debt incurred by the Earl of Trenton. And in dealing with the earl, he had met the earl's daughter. And had married the earl's daughter. And had taken on management of the earl's other plantation here. And was not, now, any closer to achieving his goal of reclaiming Bellefleur than he'd been when he went into the game at the first, hoping to bargain for that property.

Bellefleur...sometimes the image of it in his mind's eye was so sharp that it might have been yesterday when he saw it last. Sometimes it was blurry, faded through the twenty years since he'd last been there, since he'd last ridden up the graveled path to see it suddenly through the clearing in the trees. The rose brick walls, the steep gabled roof, the tall slender chimneys--he closed his mind on that thought now and straightened, his hands on his hips, and looked about him. Beneath him, a slender, graceful figure emerged from the house and started down the path toward the servants' quarters. Aurore, he thought. The beautiful Aurore. She carried her turbaned head high, her chin lifted, as if she were a princess. And indeed, she was desirable, he thought. In fact, he had considered--but no. No women, he thought. Perhaps on an occasional trip to Trinidad, but not close enough for entanglements on a permanent basis. No more women. I've had a wife, and I don't want to get involved with another. I don't need that. I'd not be in the predicament I'm in today if it were not for their scheming, conniving--He smashed his fist against the pillar of the cupola. What in the hell am I going to do about Alida?

# Chapter Seven

THE EFFECTS OF THE alcohol got Jessalyn through most of the first night in the hold. She slept, fitfully, uneasily, but enough to get through the long hours until dawn. With the first light that filtered through the cracks around the hatch cover, she awakened and fully realized her situation.

She was in a hold with no comforts and no facilities. There was no bed here, nothing but the bulky shapes of the cargo looming about her in the dim recesses of the ship. Her ankles were chained together. She could stand, but she couldn't move about, if indeed there had been any place to go. At the moment she was so thirsty she could hardly bear it, she was nauseated, her head ached, and her lip could scarcely stand the touch of her tongue. She tried to call for help, but her voice sounded weak, even to her own ears, and she sank back down into the pool of bilge water in which she had spent the night.

The water sloshed back and forth, tormenting her thirst, aggravating her nausea. She leaned back, her head throbbing, and waited for someone to come and take her out of this place. I won't cry, she thought. I won't. I won't cry. I cried for Jamie, but I won't cry over what that pig of a captain has done to me. When we reach port, I'll go to the authorities, I'll--I'll do something, anything, but I won't cry over it.

It was close to noon and the heat in the hold was fierce when one of the sailors came down to bring her some food and water. She gulped the water greedily, wretched tasting stuff that it was, but shook her head over the mess of hardtack and salt pork offered her.

"Best take it, miss," the sailor said. "It's all you're to get today, and you'll likely be right hungry after a while."

"I can't--I'm not--" She put a hand on her rebellious stomach and shook her head.

"I know how it is next morning after you've had a tot too much, miss, but you'll be wanting it later on." He put the food in her lap. "Let me just leave it here for you. You can have it later." He said the last quietly, glancing up at the opening overhead to see that he was not heard.

Jessalyn thanked him, and following his eyes, asked as quietly, "When do you think he'll let me out of here?"

The sailor shook his head. "No way to tell, miss. When he decides, I guess. Cap'n Scarsdale's a hard man to guess about sometimes. No way anyone can figure out when that might be."

She looked at him, her eyes wide. "You mean he might keep me here--not let me go back to my cabin--for the rest of the trip?"

The sailor was sure of it. He'd been close by when the captain ransacked her cabin earlier, searching for something, and apparently finding it, because he came out of the cabin smiling and muttering about the girl; he made no mention of letting her out.

But looking at Jessalyn's stricken face, he could not tell her that. "Oh, I wouldn't think so, miss, but I wouldn't count on getting out right away, if I'uz you. You must have scared the captain right proper when you swung that bottle at him, and he's not likely to get past that in a minute or two."

Jessalyn looked at him, her face first blank, then puzzled. "Bottle? What bottle are you talking about?"

"The one you swung at the captain, miss. Must'a come near hitting him with it, too, because he was sure in a foul temper over it. Don't you recollect that?"

"No--no, I don't," she said, putting a hand to her throbbing head, trying to remember. "Was that what he told you?"

"Sure did, miss. Said you went for 'im with murder in yer eye." He glanced up at the opening again, and lowered his voice once more. "Not a man on this ship but what was sorry you missed, too, if you know what I mean. Cap'n Billy Scar's a bad 'un to ship with."

"But I was sure--" She stared into space, recalling the events of the previous evening, and turned to the sailor suddenly, saying, "I didn't swing at him. I didn't do anything. He broke that bottle himself when he dropped it on the floor. All I did was--I mean, he tried to--I fought him and I was sick, but I didn't try to hit him with a bottle. I couldn't. He knocked me down, and I was too sick to get back up."

The sailor narrowed his eyes and stood up. "Well, it'd be a poor way to treat you, miss, if that's true." And all the more reason to keep her shut up down here, he thought. Poor girl. Not likely to see much more daylight this trip, if I know that scum Billy Scar.

"Oh, it's the truth, all right. I was sick, but I wasn't past seeing." The sailor had no doubt that she was right. He shook his head and climbed out of the hold, closing the hatch as he did so, shutting out the daylight. He was the last person she would talk to for the rest of the trip.

Had the journey been longer or had Jessalyn been weaker, she might very well not have survived the ordeal. There were times when she thought she was keeping herself alive and sane by sheer hatred.

Physically, the situation was miserable enough; she got very little food, and most of it was of such poor quality she'd have thrown it out of her own kitchen. Wilburn Kirke's dogs ate better. She got no sunlight, no exercise. The hold was dark and damp and rat infested. She itched from the fleabites, but the rats terrified her. They would scamper across her outstretched feet searching for crumbs, and she could see their little eyes glowing in the faint light of the hold. The first time one of them became bold enough to scamper upon her lap, she screamed so loudly that one of the sailors opened the hold to see what was wrong. After that, he slipped the ship's cat into her compartment, and the cat kept the rats at bay and kept Jessalyn company. She was almost pathetically grateful to that faceless sailor.

She was sick and feverish for more days than she could keep track of. She couldn't keep down the food she could eat, and that was little enough. The leg irons wore on her flesh until they rubbed sores, and the sores wouldn't heal. They festered and hurt. She tried to move as little as possible, but there was no way to prevent scraping the scabs off the sores and opening up the wounds. She tore strips from her petticoats to wrap them, finally, but the ankles would swell and she'd have to take off the bandages when they got too tight.

Beyond the physical, the mere fact of the confinement was disturbing her mind in frightening ways. Sometimes she thought she was going insane. She didn't know what day it was, couldn't tell, sometimes, whether it was day or night, didn't know, after a time, how long she'd been down there. Her mind began playing tricks on her, and sometimes she thought she was hallucinating. Probably she was. She kept down so little food that she was suffering the effects of starvation. But the loneliness, the crushing boredom, the sense of total deprivation was beginning to tell on her.

Sometimes she thought she saw other people in the hold with her, but they would vanish when she looked at them straight on. Sometimes she would sleep, and when she awakened, she would think that it was dawn, that she had slept all night, but she had not.

She tried to concentrate, to focus her thoughts, to keep her mind steady. She concentrated on hating Captain Scarsdale, thinking of everything she would have done to him, had she the power. To a large degree, that hate kept her from going mad.

That, and the presence of the cat, finally provided the threads that kept her fragile hold on reality intact. The cat came and went as she pleased, allowing herself to be stroked and scratched from time to time, sleeping for an hour at a stretch on Jessalyn's lap. The very presence of a living thing, a warm body in the midst of this misery, was immensely comforting to the young woman. She was sure that had the captain known what comfort she took from the presence of that small, self-sufficient yellow beast, he'd have thrown the animal overboard rather than let it stay with her.

The time dragged past so slowly that sometimes she was convinced she had died and was in hell. As the ship reached the tropic regions and the heat increased, she was sure of it. By the time the ship reached Trinidad, she had been in the hold more than a month that she could account for, and she felt as if she had spent most of her life there.

The wretched looking creature the sailors dragged out of the hold in Port of Spain bore little resemblance to the comely young woman who had boarded in England. The ragged, filthy dress hung on the skeletal frame of her body. Her hair, ordinarily honey colored, was dull brown, lank and matted. She'd not even been able to wash her face for a month, and she was filthy, and felt alive with fleas and lice. Only her eyes, blue and direct under the straight dark brows would have been identifiable to those who had known her, and they had become as hard and set as if they'd been chipped from china.

She came out of the hold blinking and shielding her eyes against the bright sunlight. She could hardly stand after a month with no exercise, and she stumbled as she was led down the gangplank. The sailor with her had to put his arm around her to support her.

Slowly her eyes adjusted to the light, and she sat down on a crate beside the edge of the wharf, savoring the sunlight and the absence of movement, the stillness of being off the ship. The activity around her was frenetic. The indentured servants were unloading from the ship and were standing in bunches, while groups of men, apparently English, negotiated with the captain for their services. Like a slave auction, Jessalyn thought. Glad I'm not one of those. I wonder when I can get my things off the ship and find a place to stay. I need to wash. A bed would be heaven.

She watched lethargically as the unloading of the cargo from the ship continued. The waterfront was busier and more colorful than any place she'd ever seen. Africans and East Indians bustled back and forth off and on the ship, pumping against turbaned Sikhs and Chinese in bright robes. She saw skin tones in all shades from ebony to alabaster. The occasional European looked almost pallid and out of place among this collection of exotic faces. She stood up and tried her legs, excited by the prospect of being in such a place.

The sailor who had brought her off the ship stood by her, not moving from her side. She turned to him now and said, "When will they be unloading my things? Or can I go back to my cabin to get them? I'm feeling better now. I think I could manage. Or perhaps you could help me a bit, if--"

"I'm afraid I can't help you, miss. I'm just staying here to keep you from running off, like the captain said. I don't know about any of your gear."

" 'Keep me from running off?' What does that mean? I paid my passage; I can go anywhere I choose. What does he think I'm going to do, leave without my money and clothes?"

The sailor, avoiding her eyes, shook his head. "I can't say, miss. I'm just doing what I'm told. The captain said to keep you here, and I'm going to until--oh, he wants you over there, now, miss. Better come with me. Here, let me help you."

He took Jessalyn's arm, and she, too weak to struggle and too startled to protest, walked with him across the way to a desk that had been made by stretching planks across two barrels. Captain Scarsdale stood beside the desk, and behind it stood a thin-faced man writing figures on a sheet of paper.

"This one's the one you got the paper on there," the captain was saying to the man. "Don't think she'll be worth much in the cane, but you may have some call for a kitchen wench, or some such thing. She should be able to handle that."

Jessalyn stood before the two, blinking at the proceedings, looking from one to the other in an effort to comprehend what she was hearing.

"I'm not sure she'd even be good for that, Scarsdale," the thin man was saying. "Looks sick to me. Pale as a sheet. Don't you feed those wretches on that miserable tub of yours?"

" 'Course I feed 'em. Feed 'em as good as any other captain. Man's got to make a profit, though, else what good is being in this business? Besides, this one was a troublemaker. Had to lock 'er in the hold better'n half the trip. Tried to kill me, she did. That's why she's so peaked. Few days in the sun'll take care of her."

The man looked Jessalyn over carefully. "Huh. You're right about the cane. She's too puny to do any good there. Couldn't do half a task a day. Let me see. Janet Cook. Is that her name?"

The captain nodded. Jessalyn watched the exchange without saying a word. "The papers are all in order," Scarsdale said. "That's her mark, there."

The man nodded and picked up a paper and was about to turn away, when a low, well-modulated female voice said in English that would have done credit to a lady of some rank, "Why should I make an illiterate mark? I'm quite capable of writing my own name."

His head jerked toward her, his mouth open in surprise, and Captain Scarsdale turned toward her, his face flushed. "What did you say, miss?" the man asked.

"She's just making that up," Scarsdale said, shoving her back from the desk. "She can no more write 'er name than she can fly. Crafty, that bitch is."

"I'll handle this, Scarsdale," the man said, giving the captain a look that stopped him short. "What did you say, miss?" he repeated.

"I said, why should I make a mark? I can write my name. I can also read. And if that paper says I'm indentured, it's a lie. I paid my passage."

"No more did she!" Scarsdale shouted. "Where would the likes of her get the money to pay 'er way out here? Tell me that, Miss High and Mighty!"

"Keep quiet, Scarsdale. Miss, I have a paper here that says that you are indentured for five years to pay for your passage, and the name under the mark is Janet Cook. Is that you?"

"It is, but it's not my mark."

The man looked at the captain and back at Jessalyn. He wouldn't put it past Billy Scar to come up with some scheme like this, but the scrawny, dirty figure standing before him hardly looked as if she could have obtained two coins to rub together, to say nothing of having saved the price of passage to the West Indies.

"If she's going to tell such lies, Oliver, make her say how she got the money for her passage. Tell us that, then, miss." Scarsdale looked at Jessalyn, a sneer curling his lip back over his yellow teeth. "Where'd you get the money, eh, girl?"

Jessalyn paused a moment, her mind racing over possible ways she could have obtained the money, knowing that she couldn't admit the truth, and certain now that the captain had taken the balance from her cabin.

"I'd been left it by my father," she said. "My father, who died a while back."

The captain smiled contemptuously. "And who'd yer father steal it off, eh?"

"I said I'd handle this, Scarsdale." Mr. Oliver gave the captain a hard look and turned back to Jessalyn. "You inherited it, you say, Miss Cook?" She nodded. "And you say you can read and write?"

"I can read and write English and French, and I had the money for my passage from my father." It wasn't quite a lie, after all.

The voice was low, but it carried well, and it reached the ears of Simon Alderly, who was examining some cargo across from the proceedings. He glanced up to see the young woman who was explaining her situation in such firm tones, and for a moment, he was puzzled. Somehow he had difficulty putting together that voice and the stated accomplishments with the wretched person he saw standing in front of the makeshift desk. English and French? She looked little more than a scrubwoman, and an ill-used one at that. He moved closer to the group.

Mr. Oliver was torn with doubts. He didn't trust Scarsdale as far as he could throw his horse, but these were serious charges. If the girl could read and write, it would certainly lend weight to her story. But no doubt Scarsdale would call up witnesses from that motley assortment of misfits that he called a crew who would swear to *his* story. Still, the girl seemed firm in what she had to say.

He had opened his mouth to say that he would call the magistrate to settle it, when he felt a tap on his shoulder.

"Ah, yes, Mr. Alderly." His expression smoothed itself into respectful lines as he turned to face the tall slim gentleman who stood beside him, looking past him at the girl. "What can I do to help you, sir?"

"Sorry to interrupt here, Oliver." The newcomer smiled at Jessalyn and nodded to the captain. "Captain Scarsdale. How are you?" His voice was correct, but aloof. Evidently, thought Jessalyn, he was no friend of the captain. "I couldn't help overhearing the young lady here, and I wondered if I might ask her a question or two."

"Oh, certainly, sir, certainly." Mr. Oliver was all deference. "Right, Captain?"

The captain nodded, surly, but with a certain respect. Jessalyn looked from one to the other of them, and back to the mysterious Mr. Alderly. Whoever he was, he must be someone to contend with, because the other two men were practically standing at attention.

"Miss--ah--Cook, is it?" Alderly glanced at the paper on the boards in front of him. Jessalyn nodded. "If I understood you correctly, I believe you said you read and write. Is that true?"

"Yes. I do." Jessalyn had her head up. She might be treated like a servant, but she refused to act like one. She didn't know who this man was, but since she could hardly make her position worse, she could a least maintain some pride.

"English and French, I believe you said."

"Yes."

"Do you cipher, also?"

"Yes. Some." She had kept the records at the farm for several years now.

"It's a lie," Scarsdale interrupted, spitting on the ground. "Where would the likes of her--" He stopped at a glance from Mr. Alderly. The look was not hostile, but it was authoritative, and the captain paused in mid-word.

"How did you come by such--ah--scholarly achievements, Miss Cook?"

"My mother was a governess," she answered with a sidelong glance of triumph at the captain, "and *her* mother was French. She taught me."

Alderly raised his eyebrows. "Et vous parlez bien francais?"

"Je parle francais assez bien," she said, "por une anglaise."

"Je suis d'accord," he murmured, and he smiled at her. The captain fidgeted, and Mr. Oliver shot him a furious look. Alderly turned to the two men.

"I think we can settle this problem without the necessity of calling in the local authorities, gentlemen," he said. The captain relaxed visibly, and Mr. Oliver nodded, relieved.

"Whatever you say, Mr. Alderly."

"My employer is always in need of people with Miss Cook's talents to help with record keeping on the plantation. Most of the people who come out here are usually not so gifted, you know."

"Of course, you're right," Mr. Oliver was smiling and nodding. "How fortunate for both of you, then."

Jessalyn looked from one to the other of the men, uncertain what they were talking about. Simon Alderly looked to her as if he represented some sort of rescue, but she was not ready to trust him. Her experience at the hands of men in the last months had been so bad, so wrenching, that she simply stood there, fatigue weakening her knees, waiting for the next decision, good or bad.

"Aye," Scarsdale was saying, "didn't know she was a smart 'un. Never let on, did ye now, miss?" Jessalyn said nothing. She merely looked at him. He dropped his eyes.

"We'll take care of the expenses, Captain. Simply draw up the papers, and I will sign them and have the money sent down to you. I trust that will be satisfactory?"

"Oh, yes, certainly, sir." The captain was delighted. He'd got the gold she'd had with her, he'd collected twice for her passage, and the woman was off his hands. "She'll be a fine one, sir." He glanced at the miserable looking creature before him a bit doubtfully, his look belying his words. It's bad luck, she is, he thought, and they'll have no good from her. The image of that ghastly--thing--standing over her body was still with him, and he would not have gone near her for twice what'd he'd made off her.

Jessalyn turned to Mr. Alderly. "And am I to be indentured to--your employer?"

"I think, Miss Cook, we may be able to work out something that will be satisfactory to both of us. My employer is a reasonable man. We will discuss the problem with him."

Jessalyn nodded. The encounter had sapped the last of her strength, and at this moment, she hardly cared. She wanted some decent food and a few creature comforts, and she would consider her way paid.

*     *     *     *     *

Simon Alderly studied the scrawny girl sitting across from him in the carriage as carefully and as covertly as he could. He'd been serious when he told the two men that the plantation could always use someone with her talents. Tobago was too small to offer much to people who could do the work they needed done and too small to provide the people to do it. Correspondence was voluminous; he and Dominick Reynolds both worked on it and were always behind. There was a great deal of bookkeeping, and they both worked on that, too, often into the night. Reynolds had hired young men to do the work so that he and his manager could be freed for more pressing duties, but they didn't last long. It was difficult to attract them to the tiny island that offered so little in the way of social life or advancement. They could do better in places like America or Australia. So they came and went, and the work piled up. If this young woman could do the work, there would be a place for her in any event.

But Alderly had in mind another possibility, too, one that might appeal to his employer, and one that the girl across from him could hardly choose to refuse. He'd not given up on the plan he'd suggested to Reynolds earlier. In fact, the idea of a convenient marriage to shelter his friend from the possibility of a more detestable fate seemed daily more feasible. It was only the lack of the appropriate woman to play the part of the dutiful wife that stood in the way of his idea. And this one--dirty and unappealing as she was--offered some potentiality. She was obviously intelligent and as well educated as any young woman was expected to be. She had a good voice, and though frail, carried herself well. Even the unattractiveness had its advantages. There would be no danger of involvement for Dominick Reynolds. He had had his emotional entanglements, and they had proved destructive and unpleasant. He would not be interested in another. Best of all, she was apparently without roots or attachments. No family to consider, most likely. He intended to find out what he could about her, but if he should be right, she might do well. Quite nicely, in fact.

Jessalyn leaned forward in the carriage seat, looking at everything she could take in. She had been deprived for so long of any sights and sounds outside the hold of the ship that she thought she could not absorb enough of all that the carriage was passing. The streets of Port of Spain were as crowded with interesting faces and styles of dress as the waterfront had been. The air was fragrant with scents she had never smelled before, and the carriage rolled along beneath the shade of blossoming trees that were as strange to her as if she were in another world. She knew that when she had rested and recovered for a bit, she would have a thousand questions, but for now, she was silent, hungry for the sights and sounds around her, lost in seeing and smelling and hearing all that was there.

She started suddenly to realize that Simon Alderly was addressing her, and that she had not responded to his "Miss Cook?" although it was apparent from his tone that he must have said it several times.

"I--I'm very sorry, Mr. Alderly. I was looking at everything. It's so strange, you know. I've never seen anything to compare with this place."

"Nor have I, Miss Cook, and I'd venture to guess that I've traveled rather more extensively than you have. Trinidad is unlike any other place I've ever seen. I just wanted to tell you to enjoy the sights, because we leave tomorrow for the plantation, but that was unnecessary advice, I see."

"Quite unnecessary, Mr. Alderly. I can hardly look at everything, there's so much to see."

"We're going to a boarding house not far from the waterfront, and I'll see to it that you are provided with facilities for bathing and with some suitable clothing. Mrs. Brundage should be able to help you with that. She seems a sympathetic person."

"I should be very grateful, I assure you. It's--I'm--frankly, I shouldn't be surprised or offended if you didn't want to be seen riding in the carriage with me. I must look quite frightful, I know, and you are being very kind to me. I want you to know that I am grateful, and that I shall not disappoint you or behave so as to reflect badly on your judgment."

Simon Alderly was touched by the speech and a bit startled. He had assessed her as intelligent, but she was also more articulate than he had anticipated. She regarded him seriously, her gaze direct and steady from eyes that were so blue and deep that he wondered briefly whether there might not be more to her appearance under all that grime than was apparent. But he dismissed the thought. Direct eyes, no matter their color or intensity, do not make beauty, he told himself.

Simon was something of an expert on beauty. He was forty-eight years old, his hair the sandy sort that grays late, if at all, his eyes hazel. He was taller than the average, but not as tall as his employer and much thinner than Reynolds' broad-shouldered frame. He was a life-long bachelor, an observer of women, an admirer of women, but he'd never met the one he would want to spend a lifetime with. In a way, the fact of his confirmed bachelorhood contributed much to his social success. He would not be considered a good match for the daughter of an earl or the sister of a marquis or even the niece of a wealthy, thought untitled, landowner. He was, after all, an estate manager, and though his social credentials were impeccable and his connections excellent, he was not thought eligible. But how convenient, how fortunate to have someone like dear Simon, someone to make a fourth at whist, to even out the dinner party. If Dominick Reynolds was rich enough to overcome his lack of social prominence, at least in this part of the world, Simon was not; but he did have his uses, according to the local custom.

Simon found the situation privately amusing. He was not a believer in the popular cliches regarding breeding, or in the notion that patrician birth was recognizable by any quality more remarkable than the possession of money. He had known serving girls with more natural grace and charm than duchesses of his acquaintance; he had known a princess or two with less of either of those qualities than fishwives he'd met. He liked women, found them fascinating and pleasant, and was not fooled by them any more than he was by their equally pretentious husbands, fathers, and brothers. He'd been raised by an unusual mother, a woman who was direct and plain spoken, who had no use for artifice and affectation, and she'd spoiled him for other women. He'd spent much of his life as a young man looking for another such woman. He had decided that she did not exist.

Simplicity and directness were not popular qualities of the day; indeed they were anathema to most young women, and were shunned like the proverbial plague. That the young woman across from him had spoken to him so simply and directly was surprising to him. He was not accustomed to such a lack of pretense, such a lack of coyness, from women, even those who were as wretched as this one. A flicker of something crossed his mind momentarily, disturbing him briefly, but it was no more than a breeze that ruffles an otherwise smooth lake. He pushed it down. He had a bargain in this young woman, he was certain. Even if Dominick didn't choose to agree to his plan, she was worth a good deal to them for the work she could do. And she'd cause no problems. She was properly grateful and would make no trouble. He was satisfied with her.

The carriage pulled up in front of what Jessalyn first took to be a spacious residence, but which was, in fact, a boarding house. Agnes Brundage took great care to see that it did not resemble a typical boarding house, however; she went to considerable pains to see that her place offered the appearance and the comforts of an elegant home. By doing so, she attracted a first-class clientele--plantation owners who were looking for homes; wealthy guests of islanders who had to have places to stay until their hosts could transport them to their houses. Drivers of the local rented conveyances sized up potential customers and brought the best to Agnes. They were well rewarded for their efforts, and so was she. There was no hotel on the island, no inn at which guests received the pampering, the care, the indulgence with which they were treated at Mrs. Brundage's.

Simon extended his hand to Jessalyn, helping her from the carriage, and sent the young man who approached to find Agnes herself. That good woman gasped when she first saw Jessalyn, but years of dealing with people had taught her to mask her feelings. When she approached the pair, her demeanor was as cordial as if she'd been greeting relatives.

"Mrs. Brundage," Simon began, "this is Miss Cook. She's had an unfortunate voyage and needs your help. Can you give her a room and arrange for what she needs? She's going to be employed by Mr. Reynolds."

Agnes Brundage inclined her head. She was a short, round woman, although she gave the impression of greater height because she carried herself with great poise. That fact, combined with the iron gray hair that she wore pulled tightly into a bun on the back of her neck gave her the appearance of being a stiff, cold, rigid woman. It was not so. She was a soft-hearted, kind, motherly woman, a woman who used her nurturing on her guests to make up for the lack of children of her own. She was appalled at Jessalyn's condition, but her first instincts were to do something for the poor child.

"Certainly, Mr. Alderly. I'll put you in my best corner room, Miss Cook. That way you'll get the breeze. Have you any luggage?"

"I--no, Mrs. Brundage. It was all stolen on the trip."

"Everything was lost, Mrs. Brundage," Alderly said. "Perhaps you can help her locate some clothing to do until we can arrange otherwise."

"Oh, of course. Poor dear. Are you hungry?"

"Well, yes, rather. I've not eaten recently."

"Come with me, dear, and I'll show you to the room."

Odd, Agnes Brundage thought, as she talked with the girl while they climbed the stairs to the room. I'd have taken her for one of those starving beggars off the streets of London. Before she opened her mouth, that is. Agnes had been exposed to what she thought of as "the quality" long enough to recognize one of them when she heard one, and unless she was sadly mistaken, this one was something besides what she appeared to be. Filthy or not, she'd known better times, Agnes decided, and she was curious as to how such a girl came to be in this condition. Not curious enough to ask, though; Agnes was nothing if not discreet.

She opened the door to the room and let Jessalyn precede her into the chamber. The room wasn't large, but it was immaculate and cool. The furniture was heavy and dark, and almost filled the room. A large bed with a white spread stood against one wall; a bulky dressing table with a large mirror stood opposite. A chest and a wardrobe covered another wall, and in the corner between the windows was a table with a pitcher and bowl and a folding screen to hide them.

"Now then, dear," Agnes said, "I'm going to have the girls bring in a bath for you, and we'll start getting you a bit more comfortable. You must have had an awful trip." She shook her head at the girl. "I've seen some come off those boats looking poorly, but my stars, child. You look like you've been dragged through the hedgerow backwards."

Jessalyn glanced at herself in the mirror, closed her eyes, and turned away. "Yes," she said, "I certainly do that."

"Poor child," The widowed Agnes clucked over young people as if they were her own children. It was not the least secret of her considerable success. "You do look ill. Were you sick on the trip?"

"Yes. Quite a lot."

Agnes nodded and smoothed her quite smooth hair. "I thought so. I know how to deal with that. Now. The first thing is to get you out of those clothes and into some fresh ones. You can change behind that screen over there and hand those things to me." She paused, glancing up and down the length of the girl. "If you ask me dear, that dress is only good for burning, unless you object."

"No. You can burn everything I'm wearing. I'd as soon not ever have to see these garments again."

"Fine. Then you hand me those things, and I'll send the girls with the hot water."

Jessalyn stepped behind the screen and began to remove the filthy garments, hanging them across the top. Mrs. Brundage handed her a sheet to wrap around herself. "I know there are those who don't believe in bathing all over, but I say, this isn't England. No danger of catching a chill here, you know. And if you'll forgive me for saying so, my dear, you do need a good scrubbing."

Jessalyn, behind the screen, smiled for the first time at this, and the motherly tone. "I'll forgive you saying so, Mrs. Brundage, if you'll forgive my wretched appearance. I usually look neater, truly I do."

"I'm sure of it. But we'll have you put to rights shortly."

The maids came in with the tub and the hot water, and Jessalyn climbed into it, sinking into the water with gratitude and a bit of pain. The sores from bites and scratches, the raw places where the irons had rubbed, stung when the warm water hit them. She ignored the pain. She'd suffered worse, and her desire to be clean was stronger than her discomfort.

More acute than her physical misery, though, was the pain she felt when she caught a glimpse of her body in the mirror. Every rib showed, her breasts were shrunken, her skin blotched and discolored. She turned her head away quickly. She was not inordinately vain, but the sudden loss of the beauty to which she was accustomed, which she took entirely for granted, struck her hard. She wanted to shrivel inside herself, to hide from people, to cover up as fast as possible.

She scrubbed her body and her hair, using a foul-smelling solution Mrs. Brundage sent to destroy her unwanted parasites. She was weak and the bath took a long time, but when she dried herself and slipped into the stockings and petticoats and the prim black dress that the maids left, she looked and felt like a different person.

She set to work combing and brushing the tangles from the waist-length hair, and was still at it when Mrs. Brundage entered the room carrying a tray for her.

"My heavens, child, I'd never have known you." She set the tray on a table beside the bed. "Here. Let me help you with that hair. My, you do have a lot of it. Lucky you didn't start to lose it on the trip." She took the brush from Jessalyn and began to smooth the masses of damp gold hair back from her face.

"No, that trip didn't hurt your hair any, and that's a blessing. I've seen it start to fall out. I brought some pins with me, and I'll pin it up off your neck. It's hot enough here without that heavy hair hanging down your back. Here. I'll braid it, and you hand me the pins."

Jessalyn sat still under Mrs. Brundage's capable hands, not moving as her hair was braided and pinned up high on her head. It was the first time her hair had been brushed for her since she was a child, since long before her mother died, and though all of the brutality at the captain's hands had not wrung a tear from her, this simple act of kindness threatened to bring on floods.

"There, now, that should feel better, having your hair clean and pinned up out of--my goodness, child, whatever is wrong? Did I hurt your head? You look about to cry."

Jessalyn shook her head and bit a knuckle to keep from crying, but the tears spilled over anyway, and Mrs. Brundage gathered the girl into her arms and wiped her face with the edge of her apron.

"There, there, dear, I know from the looks of you that you must have had a bad time of it. Don't cry now. You're going to the biggest plantation in the Indies, and you ought to do well for yourself. Now, then, come on; wipe your eyes a bit. There's a good girl. I've brought you something to eat and a pot of tea, and you'll feel better when you've had something."

Jessalyn's sobs subsided into sniffles and she took the handkerchief Mrs. Brundage offered and wiped her nose and dabbed at her eyes. "I'm--I--I'm sorry--t-t-to cry all over you like this, Mrs. Brundage, but it's just--that--that--you've been so kind, and I'm so g-g-glad to be here."

"Of course you are. Now here. Drink this tea. Not much a good cup of tea can't make right." She handed Jessalyn a cup of the tea, strong and steaming and sweet, and the girl sipped it greedily. It seemed years since she'd had any, and she'd thought sometimes, in the hold, that she could tolerate almost anything if they'd only give her a cup of tea once in a while.

"Not so fast there. You stomach's not used to much, and you don't want it coming back up. Now, here. She uncovered the other dishes on the tray. She had brought up a dish of chicken broth and bread, thinly sliced and spread with butter. She watched as Jessalyn consumed the food, hungrily, and wondered how long it had been since the girl had eaten. She cautioned her to slow down, to take a bit at a time.

"Ummm." Jessalyn leaned back and wiped her buttery fingers on the napkin Mrs. Brundage handed her. "That was so good. You don't know how heavenly hot food tastes."

"Oh, yes, I do, my girl. I've not forgotten my trip out here, you know. Ships' food can keep you alive, and that's all the good that can be said of it. Now, you'll need some rest. Mr. Alderly will be back later and wants to see you after dinner. He said you are to rest until then. I'll leave you now, and you try to get some sleep."

Jessalyn didn't have to try. She thought that she had no sooner stretched out on the bed than she was asleep, and she was still sleeping soundly when Mrs. Brundage tapped on the door. Simon Alderly was waiting to see her in the parlor.

She stood and smoothed her hair back into place, then followed Mrs. Brundage's ample back down the stairs. Mr. Alderly was waiting in the small parlor just off the entry to the boarding house. The room was one that Mrs. Brundage kept especially for private meetings requested by her guests. It contrasted with the large parlor, farther back, which served as a general gathering place where residents could socialize. The small parlor was, like the other rooms, filled with heavy, dark furniture. A burgundy velvet loveseat faced a larger, dark pink sofa, and large chairs and small tables filled the room. Lace curtains stirred in the evening breeze. Simon Alderly stood when Jessalyn entered the room, struggling, with some degree of success, to mask his surprise at her improved appearance.

"Miss Cook. You are looking much better, if I may say so."

Jessalyn sat down on the loveseat across from him. "Thank you, Mr. Alderly. I am feeling much better, thanks to Mrs. Brundage."

"She appears to have taken good care of you." He glanced at Mrs. Brundage and nodded his approval.

"She's been very kind, and I am most grateful to her."

Mrs. Brundage, a bit flustered at the praise, said, "Now, then, child, I was only doing what Mr. Alderly said to do."

"You were very good, Mrs. Brundage. I will not forget it."

Simon saw the direct gaze settle on Mrs. Brundage as if the young woman made a commitment to the person to whom she spoke, and somehow, he believed her when she said she'd not forget. Odd. It's the sort of thing people *say*, but…

"I'm having a drink, Miss Cook, one of Mrs. Brundage's special rum swizzles. Would you care for one? Or a glass of sherry?"

Jessalyn shook her head, remembering her last encounter with spirits. "Thank you no, Mr. Alderly, none for me."

"Perhaps some tea, then?" Mrs. Brundage offered, and Jessalyn agreed.

"Oh, yes, some tea would be lovely."

When Mrs. Brundage was gone, Simon Alderly looked across at Jessalyn and said, "Now, then, Miss Cook suppose you tell me how you came to be in the hands of such a rotter as Captain Scarsdale. I've checked the papers he said you signed, and I've no doubt they're forged."

"They are. I paid my passage."

"Scarsdale is a fool. He underestimated you. He assumed that because most young women in a position to take passage from England can't read and write, that you'd not be able to, either. But what would cause him to do such a thing?"

Jessalyn looked at her hands and then up at Simon Alderly. She opened her mouth to speak, then closed it, struggling to find some way to tell him what had happened. He leaned forward and said to her, "Now, look here, Miss Cook. I don't care what you did, or why you're here. If you were in some sort of trouble in England, well, half the people in these islands were, before they came here, if the truth were known. I'm not going to turn you in to the magistrate or send you back to England or any of those things. Do you understand?"

The girl nodded, looking at him straight on.

"Still," he continued, I would like to assure my employer--and now yours, also--that we do not have an axe murderess in the household. Do you see my point?"

She smiled at him, the first time he'd seen her smile, a sudden smile of such swift amusement that the flicker of doubt he'd had about her returned. Perhaps--but surely not, he thought. Those hollows under her eyes, that emaciated frame, the sores about her mouth, that pallid skin stretched over her skull--surely there can be no beauty hiding in there, he thought. But the smile--the smile does something for her. It does light her up remarkably well.

"Of course I do, Mr. Alderly. And I can reassure you on that point. I am indeed no axe murderess. In fact, I am not in any trouble with the authorities in England, to the best of my knowledge. My difficulties were of a more--personal nature." She paused, considered, then said, "To begin with, my name is not Janet Cook. It is Jessalyn Kirke." She hesitated again, waiting to see if this name had any effect on him, but he did not respond, except to nod.

"I had thought you were traveling--ah--incognito. Miss Kirke, it is then. Why did you feel it necessary to hide your identity, Miss Kirke?"

"Because I left England after I stole some money from my father, and I didn't want him to be able to locate me." It is true, after a fashion, she thought. I did steal it and he *is* my father.

"I see." Simon Alderly raised his eyebrows and rested his chin on his fingertips. "Then your father is not dead as you said."

"Not when I left, although I can't speak for him now. He was drinking heavily, and he might very well be dead by now. You see, my brother was--my brother died recently, and my father blamed me for his death. My brother was his favorite, you know, and Father was rather badly hit by it. He told me to get out of his house, that he'd not shelter me any longer." She looked at him straight on, that direct blue gaze. "And so I took the money and came here."

"I see," he murmured again. He took a sip of the rum and looked at her. He believed the story, and it was less awful than he'd imagined. Merely a runaway daughter, no ghastly stories here. "But if you were going to start a new life for yourself, Miss Kirke, and since you'd made up your mind to take the money anyway, why didn't you take enough to sustain yourself for a while once you got here? Why did you take only enough for your passage?"

"Oh, there was more. I had sufficient to live for some time."

"What happened--wait. Don't tell me. I can guess. Captain Scarsdale."

She sighed. "Indeed. Captain Scarsdale."

"What did you do to run afoul of that one?"

"Not very much, but I suppose it was enough. He invited me to his cabin for dinner one night, and I had too much to drink. I don't drink, you know, and that and the seasickness--at any rate, he tried to--I mean, he--I didn't understand--"

"I do. You refused him, and he threw you into the hold and took your money and tried to pass you off as indentured. Is that it?"

"Yes." She closed her eyes, remembering the shame of that night.

"Sounds very typical of our captain. Well, you survived it, which is more than some have, and you're here now. I suppose you'd like to hear a bit more about your new position."

At this point the maid bustled in with tea and an assortment of pastries for Jessalyn, and a fresh rum swizzle for Mr. Alderly, set it on a table between them, and bustled back out again. Jessalyn poured herself a cup of tea and settled back in her chair. Now that she was comfortable enough to listen to him, she was very curious about what she had taken on in her new employment.

"I have a great many questions, Mr. Alderly, and I'm sure I'll think of more. Is the plantation far from here?"

"Some distance. It's not located on the island of Trinidad, actually. It's on Tobago."

"Tobago? You mean as in, 'rich as a Tobago planter'?"

Alderly smiled. "As in that very expression, though I'll have to tell you that it is relatively inaccurate these days. Tobago planters--indeed, all the planters in the West Indies--have come on hard times since the abolition of slavery. Many of the old island families have had to virtually abandon their holdings. Or, they've lost them to the merchant consignees who advanced them money. Tobago planters aren't what they used to be. Many of them are just managing to hang on these days." He paused and sipped his drink. "Fortunately for both of us, though, Dominick Reynolds is not among that group."

"I see. His plantation is still flourishing, then."

"Not exactly. Oh, I don't mean to mislead you. He has an enormous plantation, and most of his land--though not all, by any means--is planted in sugar. But each year a smaller and smaller portion of his income is derived from the actual sale of the sugar. He has increasingly diversified interests. And that's where your job comes in."

"Oh?"

"Yes. You see, Mr. Reynolds has considered his situation and decided that it's foolhardy for his income, or anyone else's for that matter, to be entirely dependent on one source. Or, in this case, one crop. If anything should happen to that one source--" He spread his hands--"bankruptcy. So he has many interests in many places, and he needs a person who can maintain correspondence with those interests. Am I making myself clear?"

"Oh, yes, quite clear, Mr. Alderly."

"You would correspond with his agents in various places and keep records for him, that sort of thing. That you speak French is a major asset, since he has holdings in France and Switzerland. Does this sound like a position that you could manage?"

"Yes…yes, I'm sure I can do it. I should warn you, though, that I know very little about business."

"That isn't a problem. I'll be working with you, as will Mr. Reynolds. I'm sure you can handle it."

She murmured assent, and he studied her over the rim of his glass. Indeed, after what she'd been through, he suspected that she could handle quite a number of things. Nonetheless, he thought it best not to mention any more of his plan to her at the moment. First he'd have to talk to Dominick Reynolds; then there would be time to see whether Miss Kirke could handle a bit more of a surprise.

# Chapter Eight

D OMINICK REYNOLDS WAS PACING his plantation docks by the time the ship arrived bearing Simon Alderly and Jessalyn Kirke. He didn't know about Jessalyn's arrival, of course, but he had come to the docks himself to meet Simon and to get his hands on any further word from England as soon as possible.

Reynolds was a solitary man, confiding little even in Simon, and almost nothing in anyone else. The relationship between the two was an unusual one; they'd both have described themselves as "friends," but the word "friendship" didn't quite describe it, since Dominick Reynolds could scarcely be said to have any friends in the customary sense of that word. Still, they were much closer than a mere business association, and Alderly was as near to being a friend to his employer as anyone had ever been. The two of them were always careful to preserve the sort of formality that made true closeness impossible. For years, they remained "Alderly" and "Mr. Reynolds" to each other. Only recently had they become just "Simon" and "Dominick." Unless he happened to be cornered in a situation such as he faced now with the impending disaster of an unwanted bride, Dominick seldom discussed personal affairs or feelings with his manager. Nonetheless, the extent to which Simon was familiar with the intimate details of his employer's life would have greatly surprised the taciturn Reynolds.

Simon had known when Reynolds quarreled with his late wife, and what the quarrels were about. He had known why Dominick left Adelaide's bed and when he returned. He knew what other women there had been, and when. Simon had his sources of information, and if little of his knowledge came from his employer, none of it left the manager, either. He was, in his own way, as secretive as Reynolds.

Now Reynolds stood at the end of the dock and watched his manager escort a starved-looking young woman down the gangplank, and her appearance momentarily diverted him from contemplation of his own problems. Where on earth had Simon found *her* and what did he plan to do with her? Lord, she looked awful!

"Dominick," Simon extended his hand. "Good of you to meet us. Miss Kirke, may I present my employer--and now yours, as well--Dominick Reynolds. This is Miss Jessalyn Kirke, I have engaged her as the secretary we so badly need to handle our correspondence."

Dominick kept his face carefully neutral as he bowed to the young woman. "Miss Kirke. Welcome to Tobago and to Dragonsong Plantation." He turned to Simon. "How did you happen to meet Miss Kirke?"

"She arrived on Captain Scarsdale's ship from England yesterday. She'd had a bit of difficulty; I can give you the particulars later. But I believe she can handle the job, and I consider that we're fortunate to have her."

Jessalyn was surveying her new employer, thinking that whatever she had expected, Dominick Reynolds certainly was not it. She had pictured him older, perhaps overweight as many of the wealthy men she had known had been, a result of their lives of ease. Further, all the wealthy men she had known had dressed the part, wearing expensive, if not always fashionable, clothes, and watches and rings and such things.

Dominick Reynolds didn't fit any of her preconceptions. He didn't appear to be a day over thirty-five. He was muscular and bronzed like a man who did hard labor for a living. He was large--well over six feet and very broad through the shoulders. He was dressed as casually as one of his field workers, in rough trousers and boots, a shirt open at the neck with the sleeves rolled up to the elbows, and a battered straw hat shielding his face from the tropical sun.

Now he looked at her, the cool gray eyes showing nothing. "I'm sure Mr. Alderly has told you how much we need help here, Miss Kirke." And we do, he thought. Why is it that I think there's more here than he's telling me?

"Yes."

"Good. I came down to pick up the mail. I'll have a chance to talk to you later, after you've had time to get settled." He took the packet Alderly extended to him and said to her, "The men will load your luggage and you two will follow in the carriage momentarily." He turned and began to walk toward the horse a servant was holding for him.

"I have no luggage, Mr. Reynolds."

He turned and frowned at her. "No luggage? You brought nothing with you?"

"Of course I did. It was all stolen from me, and I've nothing but what you see--and that was given to me."

He glanced at Simon and back at the girl. "I see. Well, we can take care of that. We'll discuss it later." He turned and strode away from them, mounting his horse and racing away as they watched. Simon led Jessalyn to the waiting carriage.

Jessalyn watched the departing figure over her shoulder as Simon helped her into the carriage, and as he disappeared, she looked up to see her escort regarding her with a faint smile.

"What do you think of your new employer?"

"He is certainly not at all what I'd expected. When you told me about him, I thought perhaps he was--well, older, for one thing, and more--I don't know exactly. Different, you know. Like the rich men I'd seen in England, I suppose."

"Actually, most of the planters here are rather like their counterparts in England. But Dominick Reynolds is a bit of a puzzle, even for this part of the world. He acquired this plantation--or at least the start of it--when he was twenty-three. Local legend has it that he won it gambling."

"Gambling?" Her eyebrows went up.

"Umm. Like most legends, it's only partly true. He bought the first portion from a bankrupt nobleman who was glad to be rid of it. He did win a part of it from the Earl of Trenton, but that was a relatively small portion. In fact, Trenton himself had won it from someone else, so he didn't consider it a great loss. He still has his major holdings here; Dominick manages the earl's plantation as well as his own."

"I see," she murmured.

"Some say he won the hand of the earl's daughter in that same card game, but I tend to doubt that. The late Mrs. Reynolds was not one to consent to be wagered like a horse or a piece of property."

"Mr. Reynolds is a widower, then."

"Yes. At any rate, however he got the first bit of land, he's hacked much of the rest of it out of the jungle, practically with his bare hands at first. He is a driven man, is our Mr. Reynolds. An unusual man."

The carriage was loaded quickly, and they began the trip up the gentle slope from the docks to the main house. The house was not visible from the beach, and the road, once it left the waterfront, wound through groves of palms and greenery more lush and beautiful than Jessalyn had known existed. Trees and vines dropped over the roadway, and she caught sight of brilliantly colored birds among the foliage.

One spectacularly lovely one, a large crimson bird, swept over the carriage and she gasped. "How beautiful! What was that?"

"It's called a scarlet ibis, or a flamant, as the French say. If you like birds, you'll love Tobago. I've never seen any place that had as many and as colorful ones as here. When we have the time, we can take a ride back through the jungle, and I'll show you the flamingos."

"Oh, yes," she breathed. "I'd love that. And the flowers here. So many of them. Were they planted, or do they grow wild?" She was looking about her, trying to take in the trees and flowering shrubs on either side of the drive. She thought, rather extravagantly, that this was the way Paradise was supposed to look.

"Both, actually. These grow wild, although Mr. Reynolds has the gardeners take special pains to keep this drive lovely. If you miss the sort of flowers you had at home, there's a garden behind the house with the flowers Mrs. Reynolds had imported. Roses, daisies, that sort of thing. The ones you'd recognize. Mrs. Reynolds was quite homesick, and the English garden comforted her."

The were passing under a tree whose pick blossoms, stirred by an ocean breeze, dropped in a shower in Jessalyn's lap.

"How lovely," she said, scooping the petals into her hands. "What sort of tree is that?"

"It's called a poui. Most of them here have pink blossoms, but there are also yellow ones. This is the first time they've bloomed since the rainy season."

By the time the carriage came in sight of Dragonsong, Jessalyn was quite in love with her surroundings. The air was warm, but made pleasant by a gentle ocean breeze, the vegetation was lush and exotic, and the flowers were enchantingly fragrant. She felt as if she had somehow stumbled into a fairy tale place, a dreamland, and that she would suddenly discover that it was not real. She turned to Simon Alderly and said, "I think this place must look like the Garden of Eden."

He smiled wryly. "Don't forget that Eden had its serpent, and you will probably find that Tobago does, too. You may find several, in fact. The island is lovely, but it isn't perfect, and it isn't always safe, even. You'll have to be careful about wandering off alone until you've had time to learn about it." He pointed past her shoulder as the carriage rounded a curve on the gravel drive and said, "There, now, you can see the house from here."

She turned to look at the enormous white house that was set like a diamond against a green velvet background. It seemed, at first glance, that the house was all windows and verandas, and it stretched over a vast area. It did not resemble any of the estates or large homes she had seen in England in any way except size; it was as large as any she'd seen.

The house was on a slight rise, facing the direction of the ocean, and it had deep shaded galleries on both levels. All of the rooms that she could see appeared to have French doors opening onto the shaded balconies. Many of the doors were open, and she could see filmy draperies floating in the breeze. On one corner of the house a flowering vine climbed to shelter the veranda from the sun; it ran all the way to the second story.

Jessalyn thought the house looked to be perfect for this place. It was different, but somehow it satisfied her sense of rightness, of the proper house for the place. She thought she'd have been disappointed to have found a square Georgian mansion in this jungle; it would simply have looked out of place, and she said so to Simon.

"You will find them, though, and Swiss chalets and Scottish baronial manors, and any other sort of house that is built in Europe. People build what they knew at home, however inappropriate. Mr. Reynolds designed this place himself. He wanted a house that would stay cool, catch the ocean breezes, and Dragonsong does it very well. You'll see the difference if you have occasion to visit some of the other plantations."

She examined the house carefully as the carriage drew closer, and then she asked, "Why did he call it *Dragonsong*?"

"Ah, I should have thought to mention that as we left Trinidad. Do you recall my pointing out to you the strait we came through, the place where I showed you how close we were to South America, to the Venezuelan coast?"

She did. She had seen the jungles, green against the horizon, as they sailed through the narrows.

"That strait is called the Mouth of the Dragon. The one at the south end of Trinidad is called the Serpent's Mouth. It was Mr. Reynolds' fancy that this island was the song that came out of the dragon's mouth. Thus, Dragonsong."

She smiled. "Interesting. It sounds like poetry."

"Ah, you'll find Mr. Reynolds a man of many parts."

The carriage stopped and her helped her down. The door to the mansion was held open for them by a tall, thin black man with white hair, who smiled at them as they climbed the steps.

"Mr. Alderly, how fine to see you back, sir," he said, bowing and taking the manager's hat.

"Thank you, Douglas," Alderly said. "It's fine to be back. Miss Kirke," he said, turning to Jessalyn, "this is George Douglas, Mr. Reynolds' butler, who has been with him for many years. Douglas, this is Miss Kirke, who has come to be a secretary for Mr. Reynolds."

"Miss Kirke," Douglas bowed to her, making an obvious effort not to stare. "Mr. Reynolds said you were coming. This is Mrs. Simms, the housekeeper," he said, gesturing toward a tall woman in black who moved so silently out of the background that Jessalyn had not been aware of her presence until that moment Mrs. Simms nodded. She had mouse-colored hair slicked back in a tight knot at the back of her neck and hooded eyes of an indeterminate color. The look she gave Jessalyn merely acknowledged her presence; there was neither friendship nor animosity there. It seemed to say, "Well, you're here. We'll wait and see about you."

"Mr. Alderly," Douglas continued, "you are to meet with Mr.

Reynolds in his office. Miss Kirke, I will have someone take you up to your room. Mr. Reynolds felt that you would want to rest this evening, and he said he would see you early tomorrow."

His speech was carefully correct, but a bit oddly inflected, the speech of a person who has learned English as a second language. Jessalyn was curious about him, but she filed her questions away for later, and looked up at the young woman coming toward her across the entryway.

"Miss Kirke, this is Celestine, my daughter. Celestine, this is Miss Kirke, the new secretary." Douglas turned to Jessalyn. "Celestine will take you upstairs to your room. I welcome you to Dragonsong, Miss Kirke, and I hope you are to be happy here."

"Thank you very much," Jessalyn said. "I'm sure I shall be."

She turned to Celestine who was eyeing her with frank curiosity. That young woman appeared to be in her late twenties or early thirties. She was quite dark, but her features were almost sharp, and she didn't resemble Douglas. Jessalyn wondered if she looked like her mother. She was reed slim, with long narrow hands and tapering fingers, and her eyes were large and dark and tilted. She wore a long, bright red garment that flowed about her as she walked, and her head was wrapped with a bright yellow scarf. She gave Jessalyn a welcoming smile that flashed even, white teeth, and said to her, "You come with me, miss. I will show you to your room."

Jessalyn followed her upstairs. Celestine moved with a kind of smooth glide, her feet in their soft slippers soundless on the polished floors. As she followed her guide, Jessalyn looked about the house. It was a light, airy, open house, with clean lines and a lack of clutter she'd never seen in houses in England. It was clearly built for this climate. The floors, made of light wood, were uncarpeted and buffed to a high gloss. Through open doors along the corridor, she caught glimpses of brightly colored rugs. The windows all seemed to be covered with the filmy draperies she'd seen earlier, and some of them had screens made of thin strips of bamboo.

It seemed to Jessalyn that they had walked for half a city block before Celestine opened a door and allowed her to enter a large room. It was much like the other rooms she'd seen. French doors opened onto the gallery, and the draperies floated in the breeze. Above the door a split bamboo shade was rolled up. The furnishings were simple but beautiful and obviously costly--a polished brass bedstead, a large white armoire, white tables beside the bed with crystal lamps on them, a beautiful dressing table with a gilt framed mirror hanging over it. The room was predominantly white, but it was saved from tedium by a rug that exploded with bright red flowers. A full-length mirror stood opposite her, and Jessalyn turned quickly from her reflection.

"I--I'm not accustomed to seeing myself looking like this. I've never been so--so thin before." She sank down on the bed. "Or so ugly," she whispered to the bemused Celestine. She looked down at her hands and thought that they were little more than claws.

"Ah, Miss Kirke," Celestine's voice was warm and soothing. "The trip does that to some people, I think," Jessalyn raised her eyes to the dark face. "Not to worry, Miss. You will be fat and fine very soon. My mama, Marguerite, she will make you all special food, you get fattened up again in no time. You will see."

Jessalyn smiled. "You are very kind," she said. "I won't need anything special, though. Just food will do."

"Ah, Miss Kirke, you do not know my mama. She is one fine cook, and she has one big heart. She take one look at you, looking like a starved bird, and she will pull you into the kitchen and make you eat. You will see. Now," she turned to the window, "you been in a house like this one before? You know how everything works?"

"No. Never. I only came off the ship on Tuesday. I don't know how anything works."

Celestine smiled at her, flashing white teeth. "I will show you. Anything you want to know, I will show you. This is the way to keep out the sun," she said as she raised and lowered the bamboo blind. "This is how to keep out the mosquitoes at night." She showed her how to drape the mosquito netting around the bed. "This is the wardrobe," she opened the door to the armoire and closed it. "I will hang up your clothes when they come."

"No," Jessalyn said. "I have nothing. It was all stolen."

"Stolen! Ahh! Bad luck to whoever did that, I say. Well, you speak to Mr. Reynolds about that. That Mrs. Reynolds, she had thousands of clothes. Some should fit you, no problem. You ask him. Now, I will bring you warm water to wash." She took the pitcher out of the bowl on the dressing table. "You like to lie down, now is a good time. Mama will send something to eat. Dinner is a time yet. You rest now, how about that?"

She left the room, closed the door gently, and Jessalyn lay back on the bed and closed her eyes, glad of the chance to lie down. She was more fatigued that she had thought, and she was asleep before Celestine returned.

She didn't know how long she had slept, but the late afternoon sun had thrown the gallery into deep shadow before she heard Celestine's voice calling to her. She roused herself to see that young woman standing over her, calling her name.

"Umm." She shook her head, trying to clear the sleep from it. "I didn't know I was so tired. Have I been asleep a long time?"

"Oh, yes, miss, a long time. I have brought you something to eat and a nightgown. Mr. Reynolds says you are to have whatever you need until we get somebody up her to make clothes for you. Now, you eat."

The tray contained a thick, rich soup, bread with butter, sliced fruit, and a pot of tea. "Mama said you must eat it all. She said it is special for somebody who was sick, and you must eat every bit. I am to see to it."

"But there's so much! I'm not sure I can."

"You must try. You need it. Besides, you don't eat, Mama fuss at me. I'm not crazy about that, I tell you."

Jessalyn laughed. "I'll try to keep you out of trouble, then."

She did manage to finish most of it. She'd had nothing to eat since breakfast at Mrs. Brundage's, and the food was so good, she ate more than she thought she could. By the time Celestine returned for the tray, the sudden tropical darkness had fallen, and it was time for the lamps to be lighted.

Celestine had put a nightgown, a dressing gown, and slippers in the armoire, and now she came back into the room, carrying armloads of clothes that she dumped on the bed. "Mr. Reynolds says you are to have any of these clothes you need. Whatever you want, we go through, pick out some things for you. I can take the rest back."

Jessalyn stared at the pile of clothing. She picked up one dress, a pale pink with ruffles cascading down the back of the skirt, and held it up to her. "These are lovely things, Celestine. They belonged to Mrs. Reynolds?"

"Oh, yes. Those and lots more. They be a little bit short on you, I think. She was not so tall."

"Um. Yes, I can see."

"Probably rounder, too. At least, until you get well, put on some weight. But no problem. You tell me what you want done, we take care of it."

Jessalyn sorted through the garments. There were lovely dresses, hand embroidered lingerie, silk stockings. She could have bet that the cost of this lot alone would have been more than she'd spent on all the clothes she'd had in her life.

They chose some dresses, and Celestine helped her try them on and pinned them to fit and measured the hems. "We can have these done tomorrow, no problem." She folded the undergarments and put them away, then draped the dresses over her arm. "I will put these out for the girl to do tomorrow. You put on your nightgown, now, and I will be back to brush your hair."

"Brush my hair? Celestine, I--I'm very grateful, but I think I should tell you that I--well, it's that--I'm not really used to having anyone do these things for me, you now. I mean, I've not had that sort of upbringing."

"I know. You are used to do for yourself."

"Well, yes. Can you tell?"

"Sure." She shrugged. "You are not used to give orders. Anybody can see that. But Mr. Reynolds, he said I am to help you. So--" Another shrug. "I will help you. Besides," she said, "you are tired, you are not feeling very well. I am glad to do it."

When she had gone, Jessalyn went to the wardrobe and took out the nightgown. It was white batiste, sheer and embroidered with sprays of tiny blue flowers. There was a matching dressing gown. Mrs. Reynolds certainly had good taste in clothes, she thought. She put on the gown and the robe, which didn't reach her ankles, and she thought that Mrs. Reynolds must have been shorter than she by a good three inches.

Celestine tapped on the door. "You sit down here," she said, indicating the chair in front of the dressing table, "and let me see your hair. She removed the pins deftly, and loosened the mass of dark blonde hair. "Ahh," she said, "you have the most beautiful hair. I can make it look gor-ge-ous."

She rolled the word out and Jessalyn laughed. Celestine caught sight of the laughing face in the mirror, and smiled to herself. Somebody, she thought, is going to get one big surprise when this one gets fattened up a bit. Never mind she looks like a plucked chicken now. Later on--she sighed a bit. Sometimes white people got no sense.

Celestine turned down the covers before she left, and Jessalyn slipped into bed, ready to sleep in spite of the long nap. So many things to ask, she thought. So many things I need to learn, Can I be happy here? What's going to happen to me? What sort of future...but then she dozed, dropping off into dreamless sleep.

In the corner of the veranda, shadowed from the moonlight by the vine that covered the end of the house, two figures had watched the light in Jessalyn's room go out. Now they stood in silence, still, as though waiting for something. At last, one of them said softly, "She brings trouble."

The other laughed, a quiet chuckle. "Trouble? She is too skinny to carry enough trouble to do harm."

"Never mind," the first voice replied. "She brings trouble. I have seen it. And she don't know that she does, poor thing. She don't know what trouble she carries."

# Chapter Nine

JESSALYN WAS AWAKENED ON her first morning at Dragonsong by what seemed to be hundreds of birds chirping and singing. She pushed aside the mosquito netting and padded across the floor on bare feet to raise the blind and look out. The sun was just up, and it filtered through the trees, casting long shadows over the veranda.

She washed and dressed quickly, pulling on the only dress that fit her. She brushed her hair, pinning it high on her head, and slipped quietly from the room.

She had not asked about breakfast, and no one had thought to mention it. She'd been too tired last night to remember, and now she was hungry. She found the dining room, but it was empty. On a sideboard, covered chafing dishes stood ready, warming their contents, and plates and silverware were laid out. She gathered that one served oneself breakfast whenever it was convenient, so she picked up a plate, and lifting the lid on one of the dishes, was preparing to help herself. The door opened behind her.

She turned to see a short, round black woman entering the dining room smiling at her.

"Miss Kirke, you must be."

Jessalyn said, "Yes, I am. Are we supposed to help ourselves to breakfast? Is that the custom?"

"For the others, yes. Mr. Reynolds and Mr. Alderly leave before sunrise every day, then come back and eat later. Others come down when they wake up. For you, no. I have special instructions from Mr. Reynolds for you. I am Marguerite."

"Oh, yes. You are the cook; am I right?"

"You are very right. I am the wife of Douglas, the butler, do you know? Mr. Reynolds says you have one very bad trip from England and I am to feed you special." She shook her head. "He very much right. You nothing but skin and bones. You come with me. I take care of you fine."

Jessalyn set down the plate she was holding and followed Marguerite from the dining room, down a short passageway to the kitchen. The cook held the door open for her and indicated that she was to sit down at the large kitchen table.

"First thing for you, a big cup of tea, right?"

"Oh, yes, I do need a cup."

"Sure. And you are to drink it, plenty of cream, lots of honey. That helps fatten you up. And start with this fruit while I fix your eggs."

She set a large mug before Jessalyn, poured the strong, dark tea, and laced it generously with cream and honey. She handed the young woman a knife and pushed toward her a big wooden bowl filled with fresh fruit. There were oranges, pineapples, avocados, mangoes, papayas, bananas--Jessalyn didn't know the names for all of them, and some, like the cashew fruit and the tiny fig bananas, she had never even heard of. She finally selected a mango and peeled the fruit while she sipped her tea and watched Marguerite.

"You get up this early every morning, you come down and talk to me. Mr. Reynolds, Mr. Alderly, they go out to the sugar as soon as daylight comes. They work till it gets hot, then come back. You get up early, you gonna be lonely around here, you know. Come down and talk to me and my girls."

"How many girls do you have, Marguerite?"

"Two. Celestine and Aurore. They my girls since they mama died. George and me, we never have children of our own, you know." She sighed, and the bright face shadowed briefly. "We took Celestine and Aurore to raise when they mama died, and they just like my own. I call them my girls, you know. You met Celestine yesterday."

Jessalyn nodded, sipping the tea.

"Here now, you start with this." She set a plate of eggs smothered with a rich sauce in front of Jessalyn, and stood by expectantly while she sampled them.

"This is delicious, Marguerite," she said, and the woman beamed. "What's in this sauce?"

Marguerite smiled and shook her head. "That is secret. Special secret sauce, help fatten you up." She turned back to the stove and speared two thick slices of bread which were sautéing in butter, and placed them on a saucer beside Jessalyn's plate. "Here is toasted bread. You put on honey, or maybe you like better this lime marmalade."

She set the pot of marmalade on the table.

"I'll try the marmalade," Jessalyn said. "I've never had lime marmalade before."

"You will like it. I made it myself."

By the time she had finished the toast and marmalade and the eggs and the mango and the tea, Jessalyn was stuffed, but as she began to rise from her place, Marguerite motioned for her to be seated, saying, "No, no, you have not enough yet. You have some more. Just a minute."

"More?" Jessalyn placed a hand over her bulging stomach. "Marguerite, I couldn't possibly eat another bite."

"Yes, yes, you sit down, you eat this."

She placed a dish of rice before the girl, rice served hot with honey and cream, like oatmeal. Jessalyn groaned.

"Listen, I'm sure Mr. Reynolds would be happy that I ate the breakfast you've already served me…"

"No. No. You must eat more." Marguerite stood over her, her round form planted firmly beside Jessalyn's chair, her mouth set in a line that announced firmly her intention to stay there until the bowl was clean. Jessalyn sighed and began to spoon up the rice, wondering as she did so where she was going to put it all.

Fortunately for her overloaded digestive system, the door to the kitchen opened at that moment, and she took advantage of Marguerite's distraction to spoon a large portion of the mixture into the capacious napkin on her lap.

Celestine came into the room, followed by a younger woman.

"Ah, Aurore," Marguerite said, turning to the new arrival, "you have not met Miss Kirke. She is new here. You come in and meet her."

Jessalyn looked up from the napkin, smiled at Celestine, and turned to see the loveliest creature, she thought, that she had ever beheld. Aurore was as small and delicate as a child, but with a body whose curves were far beyond childishness. Her skin was the color of Jessalyn's cream-laced tea, and her hair was deep coffee brown. It hung down her back in a thick braid that ended below her waist in a cluster of curls. Wisps of hair made ringlets around her small pointed face. But her eyes were her most arresting features. They were deep gold, long and slightly tilted at the corners. They were fixed on Jessalyn now in an expression that mingled open curiosity and disdain, and Jessalyn thought that she had never felt so ugly, so conscious of her lost beauty, as she did under the scrutiny of those unblinking eyes.

"How do you do, Miss Kirke?" she said in a soft voice. The gentle correctness of that phrase was belied by the expression in her eyes, an expression that said as plainly as if it had been voiced, "My, you are an ugly one. No competition here." But the soft voice continued, "Welcome to Dragonsong. We hope you will be happy here." The right words. All the right phrases. Jessalyn found herself shrinking from them, feeling, rather than knowing, the insincerity.

But she answered, equally polite, "Thank you very much. I'm sure I shall be."

It was easier to smile at Celestine, to answer her greetings.

"How did you sleep, Miss Kirke?"

"Very well, Celestine. Very well indeed, thank you."

"Mrs. Simms said to tell you that Mr. Reynolds has sent for the seamstress and she'll come this afternoon to measure you. He says you need all new clothes."

Aurore raised an eyebrow. "You didn't bring any clothes with you?"

"All stolen. Mr. Reynolds told Mrs. Simms everything she had--all gone."

"It's all right, really," Jessalyn said. "I could do with the things I have that were Mrs. Reynolds'. There are certainly enough of them."

"Huh. I guess so." Celestine shook her head. " 'Bout all that woman did was order new clothes and read books."

"And drink gin," Aurore added acidly.

"Aurore!" Marguerite frowned at her youngest. "Not good to speak bad about the dead."

"Don't know why it's wrong to tell the truth. Even about the dead.

Everybody knows it. Besides," she glanced at Jessalyn, "you want your own clothes anyway. Wouldn't catch *me* wearing some dead woman's clothes." She shuddered faintly.

"That's nonsense, Aurore," Celestine sneered. "Clothes don't know whether the owner alive or dead. You need some new ones, though, anyway," she said to Jessalyn. You not be comfortable in her things. Too short."

"Don't you two have something to do 'sides coming down here to gossip?" Marguerite regarded the two narrowly. "Didn't Mrs. Simms tell you something you had to do?"

The girls glanced at each other and Celestine said, "Umm. We're on our way, Mama, don't you fuss about it." They moved out the back door, and as Marguerite watched them go, Jessalyn loaded the rest of the rice into the napkin. She looked about for a place to dispose of it, but didn't see any such place, so she determined to smuggle the napkin outside with her.

She sat still, waiting for her chance to leave unnoticed.

"Ah," Marguerite said, picking up the empty bowl, "you see. You did finish. I told you."

Jessalyn just smiled, clutching the napkin in her lap, and cast about for a way to change the subject. "Celestine and Aurore don't look much alike, do they?"

"No, but you see, they had different papas. Celestine's mama, she came here from India. East Indian, we say. She marry with Celestine's papa, he African. Celestine both. We call her people *dougla.*

"Celestine's mama," Marguerite sighed and shook her head, "she never have no luck with the men she marry. Celestine's papa, he died before Celestine was born. Her mama, she mourn for him, long, long time. She didn't marry with nobody else.

"Then when Celestine, oh, about ten years old, her mama marry with Aurore's papa. He French, he sailed on ships. He stay with Aurore's mama, they have Aurore, they very happy. Aurore, she such a pretty little thing.

"Then," she sighed, "one day he go off on that ship, he never come back. Nobody ever hear of that ship again. Never. Aurore's mama, she wait and wait and wait. Finally, I think she just die of the waiting. George and me, we took those girls. We never have no children of our own, but those girls, they just like ours. But they different. Oh, my, yes. They nothing alike." She shook her head, smiling.

"That Celestine, she is one good girl. Whatever she say she do, she do it. Do it right, do it now. Aurore, well, she *mean* to do it, but something come up, she see a flower or a butterfly, it go right out of her head. She sorry later, but it is not done, all the same."

Jessalyn thought that perhaps Marguerite was seeing Aurore through the prejudiced eyes of a mother. From her glimpse of those strange gold eyes, that voice so in contrast to the expression, Jessalyn would have bet that what Aurore meant to do, she did, and those things which "went right out of her head" did so because Aurore did not choose to think of them.

Bur perhaps, she thought, I may be the prejudiced one. She only knew that until she had met the fragile and lovely Aurore, she had felt thin and ugly, but she knew it was only temporary. Under Aurore's unmistakably superior smile, though, she had felt old and disfigured. She had never been vain, but she had always been conscious of being--appreciated, of seeing faces brighten or clear at her approach. Now, confronted with the beauty that was Aurore, she had a vague feeling that the girl had sized her up, classified her as worthless, and dumped her into the group reserved for those who were insignificant. It was a decidedly uncomfortable feeling. Do I treat people like that? Lump them like that? She was uneasy thinking that she might have done so.

Marguerite turned back to something on the stove, and Jessalyn knew that she had held the soggy napkin on her lap as long as she dared. She slipped from the chair, hiding the thing in a fold of her skirt, and said, "I think I'll be going. I'd like to see the gardens a bit this morning."

She left hurriedly by the back door that led to the outside. She skirted the edge of the house quickly, ducking around the corner out of sight of the kitchen window. Once away from the kitchen and out of sight of Marguerite, she paused by a large hibiscus bush and dumped the rice under it, pushing it back where it could not be seen.

"What is it you're using as compost for the hibiscus?"

Startled, she jumped and whirled around to face Dominick Reynolds, who was regarding her with interest and faint amusement.

"Oh! Mr. Reynolds! I didn't know anyone else was here."

"My apologies for frightening you, Miss Kirke, but I must know what you were hiding so carefully in the bushes. Or is it a terrible secret?

Jessalyn laughed. "Only from Marguerite. Apparently she took quite seriously your order to feed me well. She fed me *so* well that I couldn't finish all my rice. Rather than displease her," she glanced at him and blushed, a bit like a school girl caught in some prank, "I hid it in my napkin and--ah--disposed of it here."

He smiled, and she thought that his face was transformed when he did so. He looks much younger, she thought, and if he isn't particularly handsome, he could pass for it when he smiles.

"I promise not to tell Marguerite," he said. "Of course, you may have compounded your problem, you know. If she thinks you ate all that food she made today, she may serve you twice as much tomorrow."

"Oh, no! I hadn't thought of that. I can't go on filling up the flower beds with rice."

"Well, who knows? They may thrive on it. I don't imagine it's been tried. But I will tell Marguerite to take it a bit easier for a while. I wanted you to be healthy, but not necessarily stuffed to bursting." He paused and the smile faded, and he looked down at his feet for a moment as if hesitating before plunging into something he was not looking forward to.

"I was looking for you because Mr. Alderly and I--because *I* have something to discuss with you. Can you come with me to the office now?"

"Certainly." She wiped her hands on the napkin and looked down at it, hesitating to take it with her. "I'll just take this back to the kitchen--"

"Leave it." He snatched the cloth from her hand and flung it into the bushes almost angrily, then strode off in the direction of the front of the house. She hurried after him, wondering if she'd done something wrong, unable to fathom what it might be.

She couldn't know, of course, that he was not angry--at least, not at her. He was feeling a mixture of emotions: embarrassment, irritation, nervousness, and not a small trace of shame. Not quite right, in his eyes. Unfair, perhaps. Yes, all of that. Making a mockery, a business arrangement of what ought to be something entirely different. But then, let's face it, Reynolds. Your first marriage turned out to be a sort of business deal, too, didn't it? Only much less straightforward. He bit his lip and pushed the thought out of his mind. He held the door open for her, and she preceded him into the foyer.

"To the right," he said, indicating the hallway that led to his office. She went into the large room, a room more like a library than an office. It faced the front of the house, looking out on the expanse of lawn. All of the wall space not occupied by windows held floor-to-ceiling shelves of books. She stopped for a moment, looking around her at all those books. Dominick went past her and sat down at a large desk. Across from the desk, Simon Alderly rose from his chair to greet her.

"Miss Kirke," he said. "Did you have a good rest?"

"Oh, yes, I do feel much better, thank you, Mr. Alderly."

"You're looking well," he said. "I think the rest and the food must be taking effect already."

Dominick scraped the chair and jerked it forward impatiently. "Shall we get on with this?" he asked.

"Certainly." Simon pulled up a chair for Jessalyn, and sat back down in his own.

"Miss Kirke, I'm going to get straight to the point about this. Mr. Alderly--that is, I--have a business proposition for you. I want you to consider it carefully, but please be assured that you are under no obligation to accept it, or to feel that you are under pressure to do so."

She regarded him steadily, a faint pucker between her eyes. He was not a handsome man, she thought again. Not really. He had cool gray eyes and very dark hair and there was that scar across his cheek. Further, the scowl he wore appeared to be almost habitual. No, she thought, not precisely handsome, but he definitely had something, some quality, which made him appear attractive. Presence, she thought, for lack of a better word. He has presence. He'd be noticed in a crowd if he were half as tall and blatantly ugly.

She nodded at him now in answer to his, "Do you understand?"

"Yes," she said. "I believe so. What--exactly--is this, um, proposition?"

He looked at Simon Alderly, who looked at his laced fingers, then turned his glower on Jessalyn.

"We--*I*--want you to marry me."

It was out then. He clenched his teeth and the muscle in his jaw jumped. Her eyes grew large and her mouth opened, then shut quickly. It was a moment before she said, almost in a whisper, "*Marry* you? Is that what you said?"

"Yes." The word was a single shot. "That's what I said."

"But…I don't understand…"

He sighed and looked at his desktop, then back at her. "It isn't a particularly easy situation to understand, Miss Kirke, and I'm not sure that you could appreciate my position, even if I explained. Suffice it to say that I am in need of a wife as soon as possible. It has to do with some property I stand to lose if I'm not married. That may not be very clear, but I'm not going to elucidate. My proposal to you is a business one, and in fact, there is some advantage to your being unaware of all the details, if you can make any sense of that."

She could not, but the explanation, such as it was, had at least given her time to compose herself. "I--see. But surely there is someone you know already, someone more suitable--"

"Actually, Miss Kirke," Simon Alderly raised his eyes to hers, "that is a bit of a problem, you know. Tobago is a small island, and while there are indeed eligible young women, there are--reasons--why this situation requires that Mr. Reynolds choose someone unfamiliar."

There was an uncomfortable pause, then Dominick said, "I told you it was a business proposition, Miss Kirke. This is the arrangement, if you choose to accept it. I am asking you to be my wife--in name only, I might stress--for the period of one year. During that time you will be able to lay claim to all the privileges that entails. You may have whatever clothes, servants, jewelry, within reason--" He waved a hand, dismissing the details--"to which my wife would be entitled. At the end of that time, you will seek an annulment, and I will settle an annual sum of five thousand pounds on you. I will see that you are satisfactorily settled anywhere in the wold you choose, as long as it is outside the West Indies."

"I see." She regarded him silently for a moment. "And suppose," there was an odd note in her voice, and both the men looked up at her. "Suppose at the end of the year, I don't wish to go. Suppose I should like being Mrs. Dominick Reynolds. What then?"

The men looked at each other. This was a possibility they had not considered. Could this homely little mouse cause problems they'd not thought of?

Dominick Reynolds shook his head. "That is not an option, Miss Kirke. Contracts will be drawn up. If we make the agreement, it will be as stated."

"I see."

"I'll give you some time to consider it, but you must know that I'll need to have your answer within twenty-four hours, since time is a factor that--"

"There's no need for that, Mr. Reynolds." She rose and went to stand at the window. On the brilliant lawn, a bird hopped about crazily, chasing some skittering insect. Flowering bushes framed the grass, and beyond that, palms bend in the breeze, shielding from her view the ocean she knew was out there.

"Your choice for this--unusual--arrangement was marvelously made in some respects, Mr. Alderly. I am, as you know quite well, rather short of options these days. I have no money. I have no place to go. I have no one to go to. There was a time when I could have perhaps bartered my appearance for something--someone--but I haven't that anymore, either." Behind her back the men exchanged guilty looks, and Dominick Reynolds snapped a pen holder between his fingers. "I accept your conditions, Mr. Reynolds. Your offer is extremely generous, in fact. When is the marriage to take place?"

"In three days."

"Three days? But don't the banns have to be read?"

"We can get a waiver. The time can be reduced from three weeks to three days."

"I see."

"I've sent for Mrs. Cummings, the seamstress. She'll be able to make you something suitable to wear for the--ah--ceremony."

"Thank you, Mr. Reynolds. I'm very grateful."

"Don't you think it would be a good idea--since we're to be married--for you to call me Dominick?"

"Yes. Certainly...Dominick."

"And your name is...Jocelyn?"

"Jessalyn."

"Of course. Jessalyn. It's rather a different name, isn't it?"

"My mother made it up. It was a combination of my two grandmothers' names--Jessie and Carolyn."

"I see."

There was an awkward silence, and then she said, "Would you mind if I went to my room now? I have rather a lot to think about."

"Of course. Certainly."

"Good day…Dominick. Mr. Alderly."

She turned and started toward the door. Halfway there, she turned back to the man she was to marry and said, "Do you mind if I borrow your books? I love reading, and you have so many."

"Of course not. Use them any time you like. Any time the office door is closed, I'm not to be disturbed. Otherwise, you may come in whenever you wish."

"Thank you."

She closed the door quietly behind her, and the two men looked at each other.

Finally, Simon Alderly spoke. "Done, then."

Dominick stood up quickly and shoved his chair back so abruptly that it overturned. "I suppose so. But dammit, sir!" He stopped in front of the window and spun to face his manager. "There should be another way."

Alderly shrugged. "You could marry Alida."

"I'd sooner be in hell."

"Besides, Miss Kirke is intelligent and agreeable. She may even be presentable, once she gains a bit of weight."

"Frankly, I'm ashamed of us both. I've a feeling she's worth a great deal more than this sham of a marriage."

"So much the better. She'll be less of a burden that way. Besides, you have no reason to feel guilty. She'll come out of this unscathed and a rich woman to boot. You've been the making of her fortune."

\*    \*    \*    \*    \*

Jessalyn spent the night before her wedding sitting up in her bed, her knees drawn up under her chin, watching the patch of moonlight on the floor move slowly across the rug, then disappear altogether. It isn't the way I always thought about it, she mused. I was always sure--

when I considered it at all--that I'd be in love with someone, that the night before my wedding would be a night I'd look forward to, waiting impatiently for the next day, for the next hour. Not a night I'd sit awake dreading the dawn as if I were going to the gallows. Not the gallows. She thought of Jamie, tried to think of something else, could not, and finally cried, wiping the tears on her nightgown.

Across from her, the pale ghost that was her wedding dress hung on the door of the wardrobe. The seamstress and her helpers had worked on it steadily for three days, and it was, she had to admit, a lovely dress, the loveliest she'd ever owned. A yoke of sheer ivory lace spread out to the shoulders and up to her neck, concealing the fact that she scarcely had a bosom any more. A voluminous satin skirt over enormous hoops draped beautifully to reveal a full lace underskirt. Simon Alderly, himself, had traveled to Trinidad to procure the white kid slippers.

But the dress couldn't fill the emptiness she felt about this marriage, the sinking feeling that she was getting into something beyond her capabilities, beyond her depth.

How did one behave as the wife of a wealthy planter, anyway? She knew how to pour out tea, thank to her mother, and she knew about the protocol of making social calls, and she had Mrs. Simms, that black draped shadow, to help her. But suppose she did something awful, some dreadful faux pas that brought shame on her and on her--on Dominick Reynolds. She could not think of him as her husband. Would he hate her? Would he send her away in disgrace? *What am I getting into? Why did I say I would do this?*

Because, Jessalyn Kirke, you had no other choice, that's why. Because if you can survive this year, you can go out into the world and make a life for yourself. Five thousand pounds a year. It's a considerable fortune. Nothing to Dominick Reynolds. Everything to me. I've made a bargain. Pray God I can keep it.

*     *     *     *     *

They met early the next morning to sign the contracts. The wedding was held that afternoon.

It was, she though, as tense and as restrained as a funeral. Indeed, the brevity of the ceremony and the expressionless faces of the witnesses made her think there was something of a mockery in wearing the beautiful dress. She could have worn anything, anything at all. No one would have noticed. She stood beside Dominick, her cold hand in his warm one, her other hand clutching a bouquet of white roses, listening to the minister drone the few words. Simon Alderly and Mrs. Simms stood as the witnesses; Celestine and Aurore and Marguerite and George and such of the servants as could get into the drawing room watched.

At the end of the ceremony, Dominick dropped a chaste kiss on her forehead. She thought that his lips trembled, but when she looked at his face, she saw no sign of that. How odd that she'd have thought it.

Everyone toasted them with a glass of champagne. It was a distinctly joyless occasion, a particularly spiritless toast. She had a glass of limeade, made for her especially by Marguerite, cooled by the ice imported from America by ship and kept in storage for such events.

She went to bed early and alone.

"I have had the servants move your things into the suite which adjoins mine," Dominick had said. "It's a more luxurious place and you'll be more comfortable there. And it's more...suitable."

"Of course," she murmured.

But for tonight she returned to her own room.

She felt no different, she thought. The only outward sign of her new state was a heavy, too-large gold band that she twisted about her finger.

I'm likely to lose it, she thought. I'd best tie it to my finger. Best not to lose it. I'll have to give it back when my term is up. How sad and funny. My term as his wife. But she couldn't laugh. She slept fitfully and lightly that night.

*   *   *   *   *

"Something wrong here, you know. Something very much wrong. You know that, don't you?"

"I don't know about wrong. Just ain't natural, that's all."

"Wrong, too. This will cause trouble, just you wait."

"What kind of trouble?"

"I don't know yet. Just trouble. I have seen it."

# Chapter Ten

S HE WAS UP EARLY the next morning, dressing quickly and washing, doing her hair hurriedly. She went down the hall and down the stairs rapidly, through the dining room to the kitchen. She looked forward to early mornings. The house was large and quite empty during the day, but in the early mornings, before they went back to their own homes to tend their gardens and take care of their own affairs, the Douglases and Celestine and Aurore were about and good for a bit of gossip and information. Now she pushed open the swinging door and went in to get her breakfast.

Marguerite spun about to look at her, and her eyebrows went up.

"Miss--Mrs. Reynolds! You should not be here!"

Jessalyn looked about, confused. "I should not? Is something wrong?"

"Nothing is wrong. But you are the *maitress*--the wife of Mr. Reynolds. It is not proper that you should eat in the kitchen with the servants."

"But I thought--"

"It is not done." Marguerite set her small feet firmly, her hands on her ample hips. "You go back to your room. Celestine is your maid now. She will bring you your breakfast, take care of you. You don't come eat with the help."

"But I'm not--"

"I fix your breakfast, see, right here. You go. I'll send it up with Celestine."

Jessalyn backed out of the kitchen, confused and disheartened.

There was no one else here to talk to. What was she to do with her days? She'd come to look forward to the morning talks and laughter in the kitchen. Now they had set a distance between themselves and her, and she was to observe it whether she chose to or not. She wandered back up the stairs and turned the opposite way at the top, strolling down the long corridor to the suite she was to occupy now. She had been in it once, but only briefly. It had been dim then, the shutters closed on it, dust covers on the furniture. Now she opened the door and looked about. The rooms had been dusted and aired now, prepared for her to move in.

She was in the sitting room of the suite, and her first impression was that there was more furniture in the room than any room its size really needed. Her second was that most families she'd know in England could have lived for a year or more on the price paid for any item here. In front of her was a chaise covered in red velvet, and in the center of the room stood a tufted, fringed ottoman of gray satin. A bombe secretary stood against one wall, an enormous highboy against another. Marble-topped tables with prism-hung lamps upon them stood against ornate chairs and velvet loveseats. An elaborate gaming table with a marble top, an onyx and marble chess board inlaid in its surface, stood in a corner between two heavy chairs.

The bedroom was dominated by a great canopied bed with peach silk draperies and a matching coverlet. A dark, carved chest stood at the end of the bed, and a huge wardrobe almost covered one wall. In both rooms, rococo whatnots hung on the walls; small figurines crowded them. She wandered through the bedroom into the dressing room. A large bathtub stood on gilded feet, enameled flowers spreading over its ivory colored backrest. A tall mirror stood in the corner; a small silver one on the dressing table cast her image back. She picked up a heavy silver hairbrush; the initial *A* was woven into a spray of flowers on its back. In the wall across from her were two doors, and she tried the first, which opened to reveal a well-filled linen closet. The second was locked.

Of course. It would be. It would be the door that joined this suite to Dominick's, and it would be locked.

She found that the two rooms depressed her. The furniture was all heavy and dark and ornate, and it was not the sort of décor that she found appealing. It looked, well, rich, she thought, but not cozy or comfortable or inviting.

She sighed. It was to be her home, at least for a year. Perhaps she could--As she stepped back into the sitting room, she looked up to see a pair of dark eyes looking back at her. A large portrait of a young woman hung on the wall at the end of the room, a picture she'd missed before because it hung on the wall through which she'd entered.

The woman in the picture was quite beautiful, Jessalyn thought. A delicate face, with arched brows, laughing eyes, and a full pink mouth. Long slim hands. Ivory skin. A mass of dark curls falling across one shoulder. How very lovely she was. Jessalyn stepped up to read the little bronze plate at the bottom of the portrait: "Adelaide Trenton," she murmured. "His wife." She felt an almost unreasonable twinge of-- what? Guilt? Jealousy? She felt suddenly an intruder in the place. Those laughing eyes smiled down at her, almost accusing her. But of what?

"I'm hardly trying to take her place, after all," Jessalyn muttered to no one at all. But somehow, here she was, wearing a dead woman's clothes, sleeping in a dead woman's bed, married to a dead woman's husband. She shuddered.

Celestine knocked gently at the door and she called, "Come in."

Celestine entered, smiling. "I brought your breakfast. Isn't this a fine place? You will like this room, I think."

Jessalyn managed a small smile. "Oh, yes," she said, trying to sound convincing. "I suppose I will."

"Where will you have this?" she asked.

"Oh, just set it on the gaming table," Jessalyn said.

Celestine set the tray on the table and pulled out a chair for her. Jessalyn sat down and began to uncover the dishes. No need to hide the rice in the bushes now. She could simply eat it or not, as she chose. Whatever. Actually, she thought, that sounds very dull.

If the servants thought the situation between Jessalyn and Dominick Reynolds odd, not by one glance, one raised eyebrow, one badly concealed snicker did they betray their thoughts. One would have thought that it was an everyday occurrence for the richest planter on Tobago to marry a woman he'd known four days, a woman who looked a perfect wretch. Jessalyn glanced at Celestine, who was busying herself with straightening the few things hanging in the wardrobe in the bedroom, attempting to improve on what was already perfect.

She finished as much of the breakfast as she could, in spite of the fact that she had little appetite, and stood up. Celestine was there immediately to take the tray.

"Celestine, I think I'd better talk to Mrs. Simms. Where can I find her?"

"You do not need to find her, Mrs. Reynolds." ("Mrs. Reynolds." Would that ever sound familiar to her?) "I will send her up to see you."

"But it really isn't necessary. I can go to see--"

"But she should come to see *you*. That is how it is done."

How it is done. If the servants could tell that she didn't know how it was done, whatever would other planters and their wives think of her?

She dreaded those confrontations.

The meeting with Mrs. Simms was less than satisfactory, too. Jessalyn did not know what she had expected, or even what she had wanted from a discussion with the housekeeper, but Alice Simms did not offer much help in her search for occupation.

They discussed the menus--Mrs. Simms always wrote them up--and the day-to-day running of the house--Mrs. Simms handled it all--and the servants--Mrs. Simms gave them their instructions when Mr. Reynolds did not--and in the end, Jessalyn sighed and folded her hands in her lap.

"There doesn't seem to be much for me to do around here, then, does there?"

"You needn't bother yourself, Mrs. Reynolds. I can handle it for you." She was not hostile or unkind; she was merely doing her job as competently as she was able.

"I know. Tell me, what did Mrs. Reynolds--Adelaide? Was that her name?--do to occupy her time?"

Mrs. Simms seemed momentarily at a loss and Jessalyn was puzzled. The silent Alice Simms appeared never to have any loss of composure, and this simple question almost disconcerted her.

"Well--ah--I--she--she had her hobbies, you know, she read a great deal, I believe, and she had her friends, and she paid her calls, and she wrote a great many letters, you know. Letters home. To England, that is."

Of course, Jessalyn thought. It isn't any of my business. She would resent my asking about her former mistress. But she merely said, "I see."

When Mrs. Simms had gone, she strolled down the stairs and out of the house to the gardens.

Dragonsong had three gardens. Simon Alderly had described for her the "English garden," as the residents called it. There was also a kitchen garden where vegetables were raised for the house. But there was another garden, one that Alderly had told her was unique in his experience. It was called the "jungle garden," and it was a lavish display of flora native to the islands. The jungle garden was planted and carefully tended to preserve an image of jungle growth, of wilderness, but it was a fantasy jungle. Flowering plants and bushes were planted everywhere, and grouped so as to be most pleasing to the eye. The result was that flowers were everywhere together in a wild, exuberant display. Bougainvillea, jacaranda, frangipani, anthurium, flamboyand, cassia- -they all made a wonderful and extravagant tableau that threatened to overwhelm the senses. Jessalyn loved it, but she thought perhaps it indicated some sort of perverseness in her nature. She had been repelled by the ostentatious display in the furnishings of her suite, but she was delighted by the grandiose flamboyance of the jungle garden. By comparison, the restraint of the English garden seemed pallid and dull.

The garden cheered her; it had before. Nevertheless, she thought, she could hardly make a life for herself pacing about in the gardens. As much as she loved reading, she wasn't prepared to spend all of her time doing that, either. She sat at a table in the garden for some time, watching the birds, listening to the hum of the bees in the flowers. Finally, she stood up and walked back to the house. She let herself in and walked down the hallway to Dominick Reynolds' office. The door was open, so she entered.

He looked up from his desk.

"Ah, Jessalyn, I'm glad you came down. I needed to talk to you. Sit down for a moment."

He did not look at her, avoiding her eyes as he spread papers in front of him and surveyed them. "The seamstress will be back this afternoon. I've engaged her to work out a complete wardrobe for you, and she'll bring fabric samples and such things. Order everything you need. If you are in doubt about anything, order it. Mrs. Simms may be able to advise you if you have any questions."

"I see. Thank you."

He glanced at her quickly, then back at the papers. "I am going to be gone for the next month or so on a business trip. Not far, actually, just to Trinidad, but I do have business to take care of that I must do myself. I'm sure you and Simon will manage well enough."

"Certainly."

He was off to Trinidad to try to intercept Alida Fitzhugh before she showed up at the plantation, damn her. If he could catch her before she got here and ship her back home quickly, he could avoid an awkward and uncomfortable scene. It would be ugly enough as it was, but no point in letting it disturb things here if it could be avoided.

"Is there anything I can do for you before I leave?"

"Yes, actually," she said, "there are two things that I wanted to ask you about."

"What are they?" He finally raised his eyes to hers, curious enough to forget his embarrassment in dealing with her.

"When Mr. Alderly brought me here, he said there was work for a secretary. Was that accurate?"

Interesting bit of phrasing, he thought. Not "true." "Accurate." No accusations. Just an interesting clarity.

"That is, in fact, very true. There's always more paper work than Simon and I can keep up with, but it is not precisely the sort of thing that the mistress of a plantation does, you know."

"I fully understand that. The servants have been quite clear in keeping me apprised of those things that the mistress does and those things that she does not do." Her mouth dropped at the corner in a tiny, wry smile. "Still, I'm not quite what you might call your typical plantation mistress, so I don't believe that if I break the rules a bit anyone would be terribly scandalized, do you?"

"What did you have in mind?"

"Doing what I was brought here to do, actually. I'm not going to be able to do the things the first Mrs. Reynolds did to amuse herself, you know. I do want to read, and you have a fine library, but that won't occupy all my time. Mrs. Simms said that writing letters home and paying calls are things that other women do to occupy themselves, but for obvious reasons, those avenues are closed to me for the moment. I've no experience in leisure, Mr...Dominick. I truly need some occupation."

"I see. Well, I think we can risk the servants being appalled at the thought of a mistress doing such things, if you're quite sure that you want to involve yourself in them."

"Oh, I'm quite certain. I'd much prefer it."

"Then I'll have Mr. Alderly see to it. We would be grateful for the assistance. Where would you like to work?"

"It doesn't matter, really. There's a fine writing desk in my sitting room." She hesitated. She'd rather not work under the portrait of Adelaide Reynolds, but she hesitated to say so. She'd not want to offend him.

"It would be more convenient if you could work here where the files are kept. I'll have a desk moved in and you can work in here if you wouldn't mind. I'll be gone for a while, and Simon uses this desk when I'm absent."

He paused. She rose from her chair.

"You said two things. What was the other?" he asked.

"Well..." She paused. "It's...Look, I don't want to offend you, so if this is asking a bit much, please just say so. It's about the suite...the new suite?"

"Are you not going to be comfortable there?"

"Oh, good heavens, no, that isn't the problem. It may be too comfortable, in fact. You see, there's quite a lot of--well, just *things* in those rooms. It's a bit crowded for my tastes, and I was wondering if I could have some of the servants move a few chairs and tables and such things out."

"Oh, of course, certainly." He shook his head. "Look, you don't have to ask about things like that. Anything short of knocking out a wall that you want to do, do it. Feel free. Hang a trapeze if you like. Make yourself comfortable."

She laughed. "I hadn't thought of a trapeze," she said. "Maybe later."

He smiled. The tension had lessened. She was, he thought, quite likeable. They might yet be friends. "I've asked Simon to show you about a bit while I'm gone, if you're interested. He said you seemed to appreciate the island scenery."

"Oh, yes." Her face was lighted by sudden interest. "It's lovely. At least, I've loved what I've seen."

"There's much more than you've seen here. Simon will drive you about, show you some interesting things. Do you ride?"

"Yes."

"Good. Have the seamstress include a riding habit. You'll have a mount at your disposal."

How money simplified things, she thought. "You'll have a mount at your disposal." On the farm, there had been horses, but most of them weren't for riding, and she'd had to wait until one was free before she could ride. Here, she had a mount "at her disposal." She'd need a bit of adjustment in her thinking. She smiled, murmured her thanks, and left the room.

The desk was moved into the office before he left in the afternoon. He had her oversee the placement of it, allowing her to select the spot where she'd prefer to work. She chose to have it in front of the window that overlooked the lawns and the driveway, and she was settled in front of it by the time she saw him leave that day for the short sail to Trinidad.

She was in the same place two weeks later when she saw the carriage go whipping off down the drive at a run. She looked up, puzzled. She'd been aware, vaguely, of some minor disturbance in the foyer; someone had run in and whispered something to Douglas, who went racing from the room. Then the carriage had hurtled past her window. Shortly, the carriage returned, and she looked up to see the driver helping someone from it--a young woman, apparently, and after her, an older woman was handed down from the steps.

"Mrs. Reynolds, ma'am?" She looked up to see Douglas standing in the doorway, shifting from foot to foot, quite obviously agitated.

"Yes, Douglas?"

"Uh, Mrs. Reynolds, ma'am, if you could come please, there's someone here, and perhaps you'd best see to it?"

She frowned, but she followed him back to the foyer.

Standing in the foyer, tapping her foot, her lovely face set in a petulant scowl, was Adelaide Reynolds.

Jessalyn experienced a moment of what felt like vertigo--the marble floor seemed to turn slightly beneath her feet.

But that's impossible, she thought. Adelaide Reynolds is dead. Pull yourself together.

"How do you do?" she said, extending her hand. "May I help you?"

The young woman ignored her hand and looked past her. The older woman, standing just at her elbow, eyed Jessalyn curiously. "I want to see Dominick," the younger woman said. "Where is he? Wasn't he expecting me?"

"I've no idea," Jessalyn said. "He didn't mention it."

"He must have been. Father notified him that I was coming. He should have been here to meet me."

"Perhaps Mr. Alderly will know something--"

The young woman turned her gaze on Jessalyn for the first time. "I certainly hope so. Who are you, if I may ask? The housekeeper?"

"No." Jessalyn almost flinched. "I'm Jessalyn Reynolds."

"Reynolds? Are you his sister?"

"No...his wife."

"His WIFE!" The woman's eyes flew open, and she almost spat the words. "That's impossible! You aren't his wife!"

"Yes...I am...I'm Jessalyn Reynolds..."

"You *cannot* be his wife. I'm here to marry him. I'm his fiancée."

# *Chapter Eleven*

T HE FURY, THE HUMILIATION, the embarrassment of the moment hung in the air briefly as the two women stared at each other, as Douglas moved from foot to foot uncomfortably, as the older woman in the background assumed an odd expression that Jessalyn thought looked strangely like amusement.

Before the situation could worsen, Simon Alderly arrived. He greeted the two women and gave immediate instructions to have them placed in comfortable suites. He sent the servants scurrying about with refreshments for them and with their luggage. He assigned maids to the two women, since their own personal maids had apparently been left in Trinidad. And when all of that was done, he turned to Jessalyn who had sunk onto a bench in the foyer, bewildered by the scene, and crushed by the entire confrontation.

"And now," he said, offering her his hand, "please come into the office with me, Miss--Mrs. Reynolds. I very much regret this. More, I'm terribly afraid we--Mr. Reynolds and I--have caused you unnecessary embarrassment, and you need an explanation."

He thought that the blue eyes she turned on him held an odd combination of despair and defiance.

"You owe me no explanations, Mr. Alderly. Of course I'm curious about this. Who would not be? But Mr. Reynolds and I have a business arrangement. Nowhere in the contract does it say that I am to receive explanations."

Touché, he thought. But aloud he said, "Nevertheless, I'd like to have you come into the office with me. I think you'll understand several things more clearly if I explain a bit of family background to you."

She followed him into the office and he closed the door behind them. "I hope you will not repeat what I'm going to tell you, Mrs. Reynolds. Dominick would tell you much of it himself if he were here, but there are parts of this that --well, he might be hesitant to mention."

"I don't gossip, Mr. Alderly." Of course she did, she thought, but that sounds best. "But as I said, you don't have to tell me these things."

"Umm. Perhaps not, but perhaps I do. You see, Mr. Reynolds went to Trinidad to try to forestall this visit. He was aware that Mrs. Fitzhugh--the younger woman that you more or less met--was on her way, but he thought that she would not be here for at least two more weeks. He had received her father's letter quite recently, and I don't know how he managed to miss her in Trinidad, but--" he shrugged-- "he did. We'll find out what happened when he arrives."

"Is she--was she--really his fiancée? She looked so much like the picture of his first wife that I almost fainted when I saw her."

"Indeed. They are twins. Identical twin sisters. So alike, in fact, that I got the same start when I saw her. I don't believe that I've ever seen two people who more closely resembled each other. And as to your question, I think the word *fiancée* is at best misleading. The fact is, her father sent her out here to marry Dominick Reynolds. Without consulting Dominick about it, I might add. The earl--Adelaide and Alida's father--apparently decided that it would be to his advantage to have his remaining daughter married to Mr. Reynolds, and so he sent her out."

"What on earth made him think that Dominick Reynolds would cooperate with such high-handed treatment? Dominick certainly doesn't seem the sort of man to be so casually pushed about."

"True. Perhaps it would be clearer to you if I started from the beginning. The Earl of Trenton--that was his sister Heloise with Alida, by the way--and the Reynolds family go back quite a way..."

Dominick Reynolds had been a boy of twelve when the Earl of Trenton took the family estate, Bellefleur, from the Reynolds family. Jason Reynolds, his father, had owed the earl money, and while it was not a sum he'd have found impossible to pay, it was a rather heavy debt. The earl wanted the money--all of it, all at one time. Jason Reynolds still might have managed to pay it. He was working to raise the money, and had good prospects of doing so, until the earl managed to lure him into a wager, a card game, a chance, he said, to clear the total of the debt. It was a fool's wager. Jason's wife begged him not to play. He was no gambler, she said, and the earl was. Worse, the earl had no reputation for honesty.

The game turned out as badly as she had feared. It was, in fact, dishonest. The earl cheated dreadfully at cards. By the time it was over, the earl had won Bellefleur, and the Reynolds family had been forced to leave.

"But if he cheated," Jessalyn interrupted, "why couldn't Jason Reynolds go to the courts? Why couldn't something be done?"

No one had been willing to stand against the earl, and there was only Jason Reynolds' word. And that only for a short time. After the loss of Bellefleur, in the process of moving from the home that had been in his family for a hundred and fifty years, Jason Reynolds collapsed and died, and after that there was nothing to be done at all. His wife died three years later.

Dominick Reynolds, meanwhile, grew up nursing a hatred for the earl and a driving need to get his own back. The earl had never lived in Bellefleur, had never even rented it out. He merely kept it, and Dominick wanted it.

"As a young man," Alderly went on, "he learned to gamble and became quite successful at it. I don't think he ever intended to make a life of it, and I don't think he was ever addicted to it as some are. I think he merely saw it as a means to an end. His father had lost Bellefleur in a game of chance; he would win it back the same way."

Things had not worked out precisely that way. He had eventually confronted the earl, after he had acquired a considerable fortune and could finance his way into the prosperous establishments that gentlemen frequented. His holdings had not been so large then, but they were large enough. Large enough to make him a very eligible suitor in the eyes of a man with two marriageable daughters and huge gambling debts.

"There is the story I mentioned to you earlier that Dominick won the hand of the earl's daughter in a card game, but that isn't quite the truth. He did win the portion of the plantation I told you about; that's no secret. How he got the earl's daughter for a bride is a bit different."

He had gone into the game to win Bellefleur back, but the earl was rather shrewd enough to hold out on that. He wagered a portion of his plantation on Tobago, and Dominick won it, but he would never put Bellefleur on the table, even though young Reynolds offered enticing odds. He was more devious than that. Having seen what the young man was after, that became the very thing that he was least likely to risk. The earl was after other things.

"Adelaide Trenton was a lovely girl. I don't have to tell you that. You've seen her picture, and you've seen her twin--you've seen her, for all practical purposes. But she was vicious, as vicious as any woman I've ever known, and she made her husband's life as close to hell as she was able. She used to taunt Dominick with the accusation that he had bought her from her father, but that wasn't the truth.

"Adelaide said--and indeed, perhaps believed--that he only married her for her name, that he was a nouveau riche social climber. But that isn't true, either, and wasn't then. Dominick did indeed pay a great deal for Adelaide's hand, but it was extortion by the Earl of Trenton that required it."

"Extortion? You mean, her father--"

"I mean, Mrs. Reynolds, that when he married Adelaide Trenton, Dominick Reynolds was entirely captivated by her. He was quite in love with her. He could have had several young ladies, some of whom had more--shall we say, social prominence?--than the Trentons, title and all, could lay claim to, and who would have come much cheaper. Don't ever misunderstand this, my dear. No matter what sort of posturing and snobbery the aristocracy may indulge in with regard to 'family name' and 'breeding' and 'social acceptability,' enough money can buy all sorts of social acceptance, and Dominick Reynolds, even then, had enough money to buy his way into Buckingham Palace, I'd wager.

"The earl saw how things were with Dominick and made the most of it. He mouthed things about the family name and Reynolds' lack of background and all of that, but he knew exactly how much in love that young man was, and he held out for quite a sum."

"That sounds so--calculating."

"Oh, quite." Simon Alderly smiled. "Quite calculating. Dominick paid all of the earl's gambling debts before he was allowed to have the dubious pleasure of marrying Adelaide. And it was worse than calculating, really. The earl has a mean streak. He made Adelaide believe that Dominick had forced the marriage by buying up his gambling debts, that the option was to be forced into bankruptcy. I suppose he invoked debtor's prison, or some such thing. He allowed the young upstart to have his bride, but he saw to it that he would never have any pleasure in the bargain."

"How utterly cruel."

"Yes, though in his own way, Dominick repaid him. He let it be known after the wedding that he'd have paid twice the price, and the greedy old buzzard almost had an apoplectic seizure. But the marriage--" He shrugged. "The marriage was doomed from the start. Adelaide held herself above him, ridiculed him, made his life miserable. He wanted children and she refused to have children. He had his plantation here, his home. She hated it and constantly threatened to return to England."

"Why didn't he simply let her?"

"He would have. Her father wouldn't. Dominick oversees the portion of the earl's plantation that he doesn't own, and makes it pay better than anyone else ever has. The earl kept her here so that his interests were protected. And that brings us to Alida."

"Her father wants her here for the same reason that he kept Adelaide here."

"You're a very shrewd woman, Mrs. Reynolds. Of course. It is to the earl's advantage to keep Dominick Reynolds closely tied to the family. Furthermore, as long as Dominick yearns to recoup Bellefleur, he too, has an interest in preventing the earl from becoming angered. It's an unhappy situation, Mrs. Reynolds. Both Dominick and I were hoping to keep you from becoming enmeshed in it."

"I see. But I am enmeshed, I'm afraid. So I take it then, that Dominick married me because that was the only way he could gracefully refuse to marry Alida--Fitzhugh? Is that right? Has she been married before?"

"Yes and yes. If he had a wife, of course, he could hardly put her aside for another. Alida was married to Roman Fitzhugh, who was thirty years older than she. Hartwell Trenton was outfoxed on that one. He thought he was marrying Alida to money, and it turned out that Fitzhugh was more in debt than *he* was. Debts took his whole estate when he died. Left Alida next to nothing, and she was back on her father's hands. I suppose that having used Dominick Reynolds thoroughly well once, he thought he'd use him that same way again. But Dominick is older now and considerably wiser, especially about the Trenton women. You were a fortunate find for him."

"Perhaps we were both fortunate."

"You may not think so after dealing with Alida for a while. I fear that this situation is not calculated to make her any easier to live with. You know about a woman scorned and all that."

"Mr. Alderly, I've been starved, kept in chains, robbed, thrown out of my house. I've lost my mother and my brother in death, and whatever looks I had are gone. What terrors can a spoiled, malicious woman hold for me?"

He looked at her, startled by the intensity and wisdom of those words. "You are a sensible woman, Jessalyn Kirke Reynolds. Dominick may be more fortunate than he knows."

She smiled at him, a warm, wonderful smile, and that curious pulse of doubt about her looks flashed through his mind again. It was an odd sensation, as if he were seeing someone else slip into her skin, someone lovely and warm and meltingly beautiful. He brushed the thought from his mind. Nonsense, he told himself. Impossible. She'd not a thread of beauty. But the thought nagged at him and he worried it about a bit, like probing a sore tooth. If she should turn out to be pretty, that might be worse for her than if she were plain.

"Nonetheless, I am making a point of putting myself at your disposal until Dominick returns from Trinidad. You may escape from the fearful clutches of the Trenton women as often as necessary by visiting me, and besides, you've seen nothing of the island. I shall take it upon myself to see that you are shown all the sights. And there are some lovely ones, I might add."

"That sounds wonderful, if you're sure you won't be too busy. I'd love to get out and about."

"Good. So we shall. No let us concoct some story about how you and Dominick met and married and let the Trenton ladies believe it.

No point in having Alida believe that he married you just to avoid having to marry her, even though it is true."

"Ah," she sighed, "I do so hate lying. And I'm not even very good at it, as you've already seen."

"Then we'll simply make it as nearly the truth as we're able. Let's see. You've been corresponding with Mr. Reynolds for some time. An affection developed between you. He wrote you asking for your hand, and you came out and married him. How does that sound?"

"Close enough. How did we begin corresponding?"

"Umm. Let's see. He bought something--what could he buy?-- from your father?"

"Apples?"

"Oh, yes, very good. Apples are a luxury here, definitely imported. He sent you a gift, you wrote a proper thanks, you began writing. How's that?"

"Sounds plausible. Are those things done?"

"Marriages like that? Oh, dear, yes. The Dutch on some of the other islands make what are called 'glove marriages.' They're a kind of proxy marriage to get good Dutch wives out here."

"But the servants must know that I was originally supposed to be a secretary of some sort."

"Merely a story we told the servants to prevent embarrassment to you in the event that Mr. Reynolds and you changed your minds after you met. But of course, you did not. In fact, you decided to be married at once since Dominick was going to have to be gone for a time, and you didn't wish to postpone the marriage."

"You're quite good at invention, you know."

"My dear, I've had years of practice at circumventing curious hostesses. I'm a master at instant romance."

She laughed, almost a giggle. He felt better at having amused her.

"Then," she said, "we'll use your version. Will you tell Dominick when he gets back?"

"Of course. Now I have to go attend to our guests. How early can you be ready to go on an excursion tomorrow?"

"As early as you like. I'm quite an early riser. Is six too early?"

"Make it seven. Have you a riding habit?"

"Yes. The seamstress delivered it yesterday."

"Good. Then I'll see you early then. And Mrs. Reynolds?"

"Do call me Jessalyn, Mr. Alderly."

"Then do call me Simon, Mrs. Reynolds."

She smiled.

"Whatever you have to do to stay away from Alida Fitzhugh for the balance of the evening--feign illness, hide, lock yourself in your room, whatever--do so. Avoid her at all costs. She will strike out rather viciously at the first person to cross her, but if she runs true to form, she'll be more easily handled after she's been allowed to vent her spleen. Do not see her tonight."

Jessalyn frowned, but she nodded. She had no desire to have any contact with Mrs. Fitzhugh at all, but the longer she could put it off, the better she'd feel about it. Perhaps in twenty-four hours she could develop some strategy to cope with the situation.

It wasn't difficult to avoid Alida Fitzhugh for the rest of the afternoon. The seamstress was scheduled to be there again, and the selection of fabrics and styles took up the balance of the day. By dinner time, Alida's maid, Miriam, knocked at Jessalyn's door to say that Mrs. Fitzhugh would like to talk to her.

Jessalyn shook her head. "Tell Mrs. Fitzhugh that I'm still feeling the effects of my voyage, and I'm retiring early, but that I'll be delighted to have tea with her tomorrow." There, she thought. I'm starting to get this "maitress" thing down.

Miriam nodded and started out the door. "Miriam," Jessalyn called before she could leave. The girl turned toward her. "How...*is* Mrs. Fitzhugh, would you say?"

The girl rolled her eyes and leaned against the door. "I say she real *mean*, Miz Reynolds. Real mad and real mean. She scream at her aunt, you know, Lady Heloise" That lady come with her? She scream at her loud, long time. She say she been made a fool, somebody gonna pay for making her look like a fool. She scream about Mr. Reynolds, she scream about her father, she scream about--beggin' your pardon ma'am--about you. She scream about her sister." The girl glanced about her, uneasy. "That real bad, Miz Reynolds, say bad about the dead. That real bad luck."

"Um. I suppose you're right, Miriam. It might be worse luck to talk about the living, especially if they find out."

Miriam smiled hugely. "Mos' specially if it Mr. Reynolds. He don't put up with that bad talk. He didn't with the other Mrs. Reynolds, he won't with her sister neither." She slipped out the door and Jessalyn stared after her.

She's probably right, she thought. He doesn't strike me as the sort to take a great deal of abuse.

*     *     *     *     *

She was up at first light, and she dressed quickly, pulling on her riding boots, delighted with their fit, and buttoning up the snug jacket of the dark blue riding habit. She noted that it was already fitting more tightly than it had when it had been made for her. She'd asked the seamstress to make all the clothes so that they could be let out, knowing that she'd regain at least some of the weight that she had lost. The seamstress had given her a knowing smile, but she'd ignored it. She didn't bother to explain that she hadn't the usual reason for requiring large seams in the new things. Let her think what she would.

She massed her hair in a chignon on the back of her neck and pulled the hat that matched the outfit to a jaunty angle low on her forehead. I'm getting better, she thought. It's been almost three weeks, and I'm starting to look better. I don't have all my weight back yet, but most of the sores are healing, thanks to Marguerite's medicines, and the circles under my eyes are going away.

She made her way down the stairs quietly. Simon wasn't there yet, but then, she was early. The house was quiet and seemingly empty. For a place that employed as many servants as this one did--and Dominick Reynolds kept fewer servants than most--the place could seem amazingly deserted. She glanced at the tray on the table inside the front door. It had a number of calling cards from island women, wives of planters, according to Mrs. Simms, who had come to pay their respects when they learned of the marriage. Tobago was such a small island that news traveled very fast. She looked over the names. Mrs. Harrington, Mrs. Despain, Mrs. Anderson, Mrs. Basil, Mrs. Delaney, Mrs. Newell--the names meant nothing to her, of course. She'd not been "at home" to any of her callers yet, offering as an excuse that she had not yet recovered from the effects of her trip. She smiled a bit at the irony of the deception. She, who had so seldom been sick in her entire life that it was remarked upon in the family if she mentioned a headache.

She heard Simon Alderly's footstep on the veranda, and she opened the door quickly before he could knock.

"So," he said, smiling down at her, "you're already here. I was prepared to wait."

"I'm afraid, Simon, that I'm unfashionably punctual. I was looking over some of the calling cards that have been left. You know these women, of course?"

He thumbed through the cards. "Oh, yes, indeed. You'll need to start paying your calls as soon as it is feasible for you to do so. In fact, I'd suggest that as soon as your two 'guests' are up to it, you might take them along with you. That will give you a diversion and keep them busy enough to give them something to do besides look for ways to make your life miserable."

"Perhaps you could tell me a bit about these women before I begin my calls. Let me know what to expect."

"Oh, I suppose they're the standard lot of planters' wives, with a few exceptions. Margaret Harrington is the nearest. We'll ride past the Harrington place, Solitude, on our way this morning. Margaret does little besides eat bonbons and collect hideous furniture. Her husband keeps a mistress on Trinidad and comes home as little as possible. You won't find much to interest you there, but you'll want to make the call." They were strolling down the graveled pathway to the stables, and Jessalyn laughed.

"Do all the island wives have such colorful characteristics?"

"No, not all. Lila Despain, for instance, is a kind, lovely lady, older than you by twenty years, perhaps, but a gentle and gracious person. You'll like her. Kitty Anderson and Bethany Basil are best friends, a bit gossipy, but harmless enough. Susan Newell is the oldest of the lot, probably sixty, opinionated and outspoken, but if she likes you, you're accepted on the island socially, without question."

"The local *grande dame*?"

"As close to one as we have. It's just that Mrs. Newell has a sharp tongue and no reason not to use it."

"And Mrs. Delaney?"

"Ah, the lovely Lacey Delaney. She's another story entirely, I suppose."

He opened the door to the stable and let her in, the preceded her down the long corridor to lead out her mare.

"I told the stable crew I'd saddle the mounts myself. This is Josephine, the mare Dominick said you were to have."

"Did she belong to the late Mrs. Reynolds?"

He looked at her a bit strangely. "No, actually, Mrs. Reynolds didn't ride. She hated horses. The result of a fall from a horse as a child, I believe. Mr. Reynolds has always kept a stable of fine horses, a bit of a hobby with him. Josephine has always been a favorite of his. She has a wonderful disposition."

Jessalyn stepped forward and stroked the mare's muzzle and scratched behind her ears. "She does seem pleasant enough. Not put off at all by strangers, is she?"

"Not a bit."

Jessalyn ran a hand over the smooth chestnut coat. "How lovely. Probably the loveliest horse I've ever ridden."

"She's yours now, you know. Mr. Reynolds left word that if you two got on, she belonged to you. If you want her, that is."

"Oh," Jessalyn breathed, "I want her. I do indeed."

Simon helped her mount, and they started off down the drive.

"You were going to tell me about Mrs. Delaney, I believe."

"Oh, yes, I was. Lacey Delaney. Mrs. Delaney was an actress, a performer on the stage in London. Woodrow Delaney met her there on one of his trips to England after his first wife died and was absolutely besotted by her, I understand. I can also understand why, and so will you when you see her. She's quite attractive."

"I see. An actress. Were any of the island women--umm--reluctant to associate with her because of that?"

"Oh, they might have been. There was some talk of actresses being socially unacceptable, and all that, but it didn't last long. For one thing, Susan Newell was the first to call on her, and whatever Susan says, usually goes. For another, Dominick made Adelaide call on her too, and that sealed it. From then on, Lacey Delaney's place on the island was assured. There was never any talk of treating her other than as one of the planters' wives."

"How did he do that? Make his wife call on Mrs. Delaney, I mean. It seems to me that she had the reputation of doing nothing she didn't want to do."

"He has his ways. I know why he made her go, even if I'm not certain of the leverage used. Woodrow Delaney was one of the first planters on the island to help Dominick out, help him get started, learn the ropes of raising and selling sugar. Dominick wouldn't have let his wife snub Woodrow Delaney's wife had the woman been a gutter snipe."

"Is that why--I mean, all those women have already called on me without knowing--I mean, is Dominick Reynolds' wife automatically accepted as well?"

He smiled at her. "Of course. Were you worried?"

"I hadn't even thought about it until now. But it would be better for him, wouldn't it, if I were acceptable?"

"Quite frankly, Jessalyn, I don't think Dominick cares a jot. But it will make your life more pleasant in many ways. By the way," He glanced at her, "I haven't said so, but allow me to comment on how well you're looking these days. That riding habit is uncommonly becoming to you."

She thanked him and smiled, and he frowned a bit. She was more than looking well; she was looking lovelier each day. Not a beauty yet, but getting there. That might prove to be a problem. It certainly wouldn't make her any more popular with Alida.

The road they took wound along the edge of the island, between the ocean and the jungle. Between the road and the sea, a stretch of dark gold beach curved smoothly northward, butting up against a stretch of rocky cliffs. The other side of the road was fringed with coconut palms that crowded together like sentinels, keeping back a jungle growth that pressed against them. The tangle of vines and thick growth was sparked here and there with bursts of color, flowering plants that sprang up where sunlight reached through the lush growth. And birds--the ever present birds--flashed through the trees or chattered in bushes beside the roadway.

"Ah," Jessalyn said, "how lovely. I must be quite primitive at heart. I find the jungle very beautiful."

"So do I," her companion answered, "but you can see how difficult the problem of planting on this island becomes when you realize that the area cleared for cane fields was once just like this. I'm afraid you and I may be among the few who appreciate jungles."

"I can understand that, but it's so lovely here, so pleasant, so beautiful. How lucky the people are who live here. They must feel very fortunate."

Simon Alderly laughed out loud. "Mrs. Reynolds, you have much to learn about conditions on the islands. Most of the English residents hate it here. They hate it so much, in fact, that for the most part they pretend they are not here at all, that they are still in England. And they behave in such a way as to make this whole experience as English as possible."

"I see. Perhaps I feel as I do because I don't have fond memories of England, then."

"Perhaps. Or perhaps you're a realist."

"In what way?"

He hesitated. "I want to show you something. I'm taking you around the island to a marshland, a kind of swampy area where we can see some flamingoes. Have you ever seen flamingoes?"

She shook her head.

"This is a lovely place. I've noticed you appear to be interested in birds, and I want you to see this place. But we have time to stop and see something else before we get there, and this may help you to understand the islanders a bit before you meet them."

They rode along the coast for another half mile before the road they were on turned inward and cut through the jungle growth, giving Jessalyn a feeling of riding through a green tunnel. Another half mile along, a graveled drive turned off the main road, and Simon Alderly took the turnoff. She followed him.

The road appeared not to have been used in some time; vines crawled across it, and in some places the gravel was almost gone. Alderly pulled a machete from a scabbard on his saddle and swung at the vines that dropped over the path. A bit further along, they went through what appeared to have been a gate; the halves of it now hung open, and one side dangled from a single hinge. The brick pillars from which the gates had hung were almost indistinguishable from the rest of the trees and bushes.

They rounded a curve in the path, and she sat up in her saddle and said, "Oh!" Ahead of them was the ruin of what appeared to have once been a magnificent house. It was brick--or had been, and large wings attached at oblique angles to a gracefully shaped central section seemed to reach out toward her in the green stillness. The house had had white shutters, and apparently, large expanses of lawn, and beautiful hedges and shrubs. But she could only make out those things by guesswork now. Jungle growth crawled through the windows, tore at the shutters, climbed the brick walls. The shrubs had grown wild; rose bushes that looked as large as trees hung heavily across a crumbling garden wall. The hedges loomed over the drive they were supposed to edge.

"This is--was--Serendipity," Simon murmured. He dismounted and gave her his hand to help her from her horse. "It belonged to a family named Quincy. He was one of the wealthier planters on the island, or was thought to be."

"But how could he--I mean, what could cause a family to simply go away and leave a place like this? Couldn't he sell it? It must have been so beautiful."

"It was. Let me show you."

They walked up the steps to the front entry, and he pushed open the door. It shrieked on hinges long rusted, and she stepped inside the foyer. The floor was pale pink marble--or had been. It was cracked and moldy now, discolored where rain had seeped under the door. She lifted her skirts against the debris on the floor and wandered down the hallway. She stopped in front of a door that opened into a long, narrow room, evidently a ballroom. Mirrors in gilt frames, some of them cracked, threw her image back to her.

There were light spots on the walls where pictures had hung, and the wallpaper was peeling away in strips.

Simon's image appeared behind hers in the mirror. "What happened?" she asked.

"Jeremiah Quincy went bankrupt. Lost everything he had. He managed to sell most of the cultivated land, but there was no buyer for a house like this. He had to leave it. He and his family took what they could, but what they couldn't take--" He shrugged. "Some of the islanders took the rest, they gave some of it away, they sold what they could."

"How sad for them. How terrible to lose so much."

"Sadder than you know. Jeremiah Quincy shot himself soon after the family returned to England. Couldn't face the disgrace. His wife and children are living on the charity of relatives. But the worst of it is, I could take you to half a dozen places just like this, right here on this island, and another half dozen on Trinidad. Or more, perhaps. Trinidad is larger. This is one reason the English are uneasy here. They know the jungle is just sitting here, waiting to take back what they've stolen from it."

"But. Simon, how could this happen? How can people get the money to build all this--" she gestured about her--"and then lose it all?"

"It's a bit complicated, actually, but then I suppose financial dealings are always a bit complex. Some of the planters were badly hurt when slavery was outlawed in the '30s. Of course, some managed to recover from that through careful planning and good management, simply because they were given enough notice to arrange for the transfer. Most shifted to indentured servants, for instance. But there were other things.

"Quincy, for instance, got caught in overspeculation. He borrowed against his sugar crop, the price dropped, he lost everything. He wasn't the only one. Several West Indian banks failed. It was devastating for some planters. There were other things, too. In 1854, the West Indian Encumbered Estates Act was passed, and what that did was give the merchant consignees, who had advanced money to the planters, first lien on their property. Some of the old West Indian families lost their estates to the merchants. That frightened investors away from the islands.

"Fortunately, Trinidad and Tobago hadn't ever been members of the group controlled by the Corporation of British West Indian Merchants. That group picked the consignees, the people with whom the planters were forced to ship. The consignees set the terms for shipping the sugar, and the planters had no place else to go. They had to take the consignees' prices, their terms, and they had to grow the only produce that the consignees would buy, which meant sugar. Only sugar."

"But you told me Dominick had some of his land planted in other crops."

"He does. He's experimenting with cocoa, for instance, and that is promising to be a profitable venture. He's looking into raising some of the more exotic spices, too. As I said, planters on Tobago didn't get caught in the trap that got some of the other islanders. Part of that was Dominick's doing, too."

"How so?"

"He promised the planters that if they didn't sign on to the West Indian Encumbered Estates Act--it looked good to some of them who were on the verge at the time--that he'd see to it that their crops were shipped. It meant he had to invest in a shipping line of his own, but it's been a profitable venture, both for him and for the others. The other islanders owe him a great deal. Do you understand now why there's very little chance of your being snubbed by the other planters' wives?"

"I'm beginning to."

She started toward the door, the jumped back with a shriek. A "vine" that she'd almost stepped on had curled suddenly and shot across the floor--a small green snake.

"I'm terribly sorry," Simon was instantly at her elbow. "I should have checked for snakes. Are you all right?"

"Yes. Oh! It simply gave me a start. I'm very--I'm frightened of snakes, really, I'm sorry if I--I didn't mean to be quite silly."

"I don't find that silly at all. I'm not overly fond of the crawly things myself. Fortunately, most of the ones on Tobago are small and non-poisonous, helpful for keeping down the rat population, and not at all dangerous. Scary, though, nonetheless."

"Yes. Yes, very, for me."

"On some of the islands," Simon continued, helping her back up on her mare, "the planters introduced the fer-de-lance or *mapepire* as it's known around here. Luckily, that was not done on Tobago. All the ones I've seen here have been quite thoroughly in captivity."

"Are those poisonous?"

"Very. Although, for my money, I'd face one of them any day before I'd choose another set-to with a bushmaster."

"Bushmaster? Are those more deadly than the fer-de-lance?"

"That would be hard to say. They're different, and that's the problem. You see, most snakes, the fer-de-lance included, are nonagressive. They prefer to run rather than attack. Generally, when someone is bitten by a snake, it's because he stepped on the snake, or otherwise cornered it. The bushmaster, though, is aggressive. He will pursue. One of my most persistent nightmares revolves around the time I stumbled into one in Venezuela. Had I not been with a man who swung a quick machete, I might not be here to tell about it."

Time and distance seemed not to have dulled the memory for him; he shuddered visibly at the recollection.

"I cannot conceive of anything more frightening," Jessalyn said, "and yet, in spite of that, I've been aware that you have very carefully preceded me into any places where there might be snakes hanging from trees. I thank you for that."

He looked at her quickly. A most unusual woman, he thought, not for the first time or even the second time. That she expressed appreciation for what all the other women he knew merely took for granted seemed quite remarkable.

"It's a fear I've had to face long since, working on a plantation in the jungle, Jessalyn. But let's talk about something more pleasant, shall we? I think you're going to enjoy our short tour of the island today."

They went back to the main road and followed it for some distance. At length, he turned off the road and took a narrow trail that led for a time through the jungle. Finally he turned his horse aside and held back a veil of vines so that she could go through the space ahead of him. As she peered through the space he had cleared for her, she breathed an involuntary, "Ahhh."

Ahead of her lay a dark pool of water surrounded by mangrove trees on three sides. On the fourth, the water stretched away into the jungle. The whole of the small pool seemed filled with the bright pink bodies of flamingoes.

"How beautiful," she murmured. "And how strange. I've seen drawings of them, but I'd never realized how exotic they are. What thin legs and what large bodies."

"Indeed. They are not a shapely bird, I find, but I forgive them their awkward shapes for the lovely color they have. Notice the black tips on their wings as they fly. See, there's one landing over there."

"Can we get closer?"

"No, not really. They frighten rather easily."

"Is this a swamp?"

"Not a true swamp, actually. It's more like an estuary. The water here is salt, and the flamingoes feed on brine shrimp and such small sea creatures. There is a true swamp farther in, complete with alligators, or caymans, as the natives call them, and monkeys, parrots, too, I hear, but it's a much more difficult trip, I'm afraid."

"I'm glad we came," Jessalyn said. "I'd not have missed it. Flamingoes are not like anything I've ever seen before." She watched the birds dipping their beaks into the water and lifting them on necks that seemed too small to carry the heads. A bird stood on one thin leg, and then the other, and she watched, fascinated, for a time. She was so engrossed that she did not observe her companion slide off his horse and slip away.

"Here," he said a moment later. She turned, surprised, to see him extend to her a pair of peach-pink feathers. "I managed to get these for you without their taking flight. I've no idea what they're good for, if anything, but I thought you might like to have them."

"Oh," she said, reaching down to take them, "how lovely. And how very kind of you to get them for me. They would make nice bookmarks, don't you think?"

"I should think so," he said, swinging back into his saddle. "Sounds the perfect use for flamingo feathers."

She stroked them with one finger, admiring the unusual shade. "A lovely color. It would make an attractive gown, wouldn't it?"

"I do. Perhaps you should have it made for the Delaneys' carnival masque."

"What is a carnival masque?"

"A splendid masquerade party. Lacey Delaney has a great gala every year, and everyone on the island goes. It's Tobago's version of the great carnival celebration on Trinidad."

"What is the carnival? I really must sound awfully ignorant to you, but I don't know about carnival."

"Ah. Of course not. If you were Catholic, of course, or if you'd lived in one of the Catholic countries, you'd know. Leave it to the English to preserve Lent, but to take all the fun out of it. Catholics celebrate carnival during the week before they begin doing their penance for Lent. It's one last great fling before the deprivations begin. At least, here on the islands it is. In the United States, in New Orleans, they call it 'Mardi Gras' and celebrate it in much the same fashion. Used to be that all the planters went to Trinidad for carnival and a round of parties, but now the thing to do has come to be staying here and going to Lacey's party. Not that it approaches the spirit of Trinidad; there's nothing like carnival on Trinidad."

"What's it like? Parties? Costumes? That sort of thing?"

"More Everything on Trinidad stops for carnival. Everyone wears costumes for three days or more, everyone parades. It is unrestrained gaiety. You cannot imagine the exotic costumes, the dancing, the calypso singers. No, even Lacey's best pales before Trinidad at carnival. But you needn't tell her I said that."

Jessalyn laughed. "I shall not. But what are calypso singers?"

"My, you haven't been here long, have you?" He shook his head, pretending to be appalled at her ignorance. "Calypso singers are--how shall I describe them?--singers of catchy little tunes designed to deflate the most pompous of the powers that be, usually. They are sung in a kind of French patois, and are based most often on the latest gossip, the most obvious vanity, or the most recent faux pas of the gentry. Oh, sometimes one is created to extol the virtues of some admirable sort, but usually they are either wickedly pointed or lewd or both."

"Don't the people being sung about take offense?"

He laughed. "They don't understand. Most of the white people on these islands--a very small minority, by the way--haven't the faintest understanding of calypso melodies. They think they are just quaint native tunes. And the quaint natives do nothing to disabuse them of that belief."

"But how do you know? Do you understand them?"

"Hm. Yes, as a matter of fact, I do. You see, Jessalyn, I have an insatiable curiosity, and when none of my servants would translate for me, or, when pressed, came up with versions that were obviously not even close to accurate, well, I took it upon myself to learn. I found a--friend--who taught me."

"I see. But aren't they careful what they sing about in front of you now?"

He smiled, lifting one eyebrow. "I don't tell them. It's my private joke, after a fashion. They have their secrets. I have mine. And," he added as an afterthought, "I hope I can trust you to keep my secret?"

"Certainly, but only on the condition that you'll translate some of them for me if I have the chance to hear any."

"If they are not too indelicate for your feminine ears, my dear. Now I suppose we'd better start back. You probably will have to face the fierce Alida over tea this afternoon."

"Yes." She closed her eyes momentarily. "I'm quite dreading it, you know."

"I'm certain. But there are two things you must know. I'll be there to help get you through the initial unpleasantries. Follow my lead, and I'll do all I can to blunt her rapier tongue."

"And the other thing?"

"It should be obvious, Jessalyn. You are the mistress of Dragonsong now. Adelaide Trenton Reynolds is dead, no matter how she may seem to be reincarnated in the person of her sister. And whatever the conditions of your marriage, you are in charge of the house, just as if you had been brought here on purpose to be so. Don't let her abuse you or intimidate you. Dominick would have no part of it, were he here, and you must not either."

# Chapter Twelve

S HE THOUGHT LATER THAT what he'd said sounded wonderful, but those brave words were less easily put into practice. Facing Alida Fitzhugh over tea was, she thought, an ordeal.

Give Marguerite credit, the tea was magnificent. Jessalyn had it served in a small bower on the side of the house, a gazebo-like porch that lent itself well to the occasion. The silver tea service had been polished until it gleamed in the green light of the vine-covered enclosure, and the assortment of tarts and other delicacies was beautiful and tempting. Jessalyn suspected that Alice Simms, the silent, capable Mrs. Simms, was largely responsible for the service. She must, she thought, remember to thank her. The staff could easily have made me look as if I managed poorly, she thought. Instead, they all seemed in league to make me look accomplished at this.

If the two visitors had anticipated anything less than perfection here in the wilds, they didn't show it. Lady Heloise attacked the tarts with a vengeance; Alida nibbled at one, leaving the bulk of it on her plate. Simon Alderly stretched his long legs in front of him, seemingly as relaxed as if he'd been in his own parlor, and led the conversation into topics of general interest, eliciting from the ladies the latest in London gossip and news.

The ploy worked for a while, but there was no keeping the two women from the matter they wanted most to discuss: Jessalyn.

Eventually Alida Fitzhugh leaned forward and set her teacup down and said, "Do tell us a bit about yourself, Mrs. Reynolds. Dear me, that sounds so formal. What is your first name again? I can never remember those--odd names."

"Jessalyn," she murmured. "I suppose it is different."

"I should say. And what was your maiden name?"

"Cooke," Simon spoke up quickly. "Spelled with an E. Am I right, Jessalyn?"

She smiled at him, grateful. "Yes, that's right."

"Jessalyn Cooke. With an E. I'm sure I've never heard it before, have I, Aunt? Still, there's something vaguely familiar about the sound of it."

Jessalyn felt her face grow tight, but she merely poured another cup of tea and said, "Oh, I suppose it's a common enough sounding name, when you come right down to it. More tea, Lady Heloise?"

"Oh, yes, I think so." She extended her cup. "No, I think you couldn't have heard it before, Alida. Where do you come from, then?"

"Outside of London. We lived on a farm, not far from Enfield."

"Strange that we haven't met," Alida said with a glance at her aunt, "don't you think?"

"Not at all," Jessalyn looked at her straight on, fixing her firmly with a direct, unflinching gaze. "You couldn't possibly have heard of me, Mrs. Fitzhugh. I have absolutely no social connections. My mother was a governess and my father was a farmer, and there would be no reason on earth for you to have been aware of my existence."

She caught a glimpse of Simon's smile out of the corner of her eye, and he winked at her.

"Ahh," Lady Heloise said, "how did you and Dominick meet, then?"

She told them the story she and Simon had rehearsed.

"I see." Alida Fitzhugh smiled and shrugged, dismissing the young woman with that gesture. "It must be an interesting situation for dear Dominick, you know. From the daughter of an earl to the daughter of a farmer. Really, my dear, you'd have to have no sense of humor to miss the irony of it all."

It was Jessalyn's turn to shrug. "So far, he's not complained. Besides," she added, looking up at the pair in front of her from beneath seemingly lowered lashes, "I dare say he's found me much less expensive."

Simon Alderly managed to turn a snort of laughter into a hearty cough, Lady Heloise stopped her attack on a tart in mid-bite and stared at the girl, and Mrs. Fitzhugh froze, then picked up her cup, rattled it, and set it down hard.

"Well, I suppose," she said in iced tones, "one gets what one pays for."

"Oh," said Jessalyn lightly, "not always. I'm sure Mr. Alderly can attest to that."

"Indeed." Simon appeared eager to jump into the conversation. "As a matter of fact, Mrs. Reynolds paid quite well for her voyage over, only to be robbed in the course of the trip. And on top of that, she was quite ill most of the way."

"Pity," Mrs. Fitzhugh snapped.

"Wasn't it? Although she seems to be recovering quite well, aren't you, Jessalyn? In fact, I believe you mentioned that you were feeling up to making some calls this week."

"Yes," Jessalyn picked up on the cue. "I've had calls from several of the ladies on the island, though I've not been up to receiving them. Perhaps the two of you would like to accompany me on a few calls this week."

"Oh, I suppose," Alida said carelessly. "Obviously there's very little else to do on this god-forsaken island. Adelaide's letters always deplored the total ennui of the plantation life. And perhaps we could play whist in the evenings. You do play, don't you?"

"No, I never learned."

"Ah, but you must," Simon leaned toward them. "A splendid idea, Mrs. Fitzhugh. There are four of us, and we can teach Mrs. Reynolds. She'll learn quickly."

"I suppose. At least it will do until Dominick gets back."

"You'll be disappointed even then, I'm afraid." He shook his head. Dominick won't learn. Adelaide was always after him, but he would never learn to play."

"How disappointing. After all I've heard about Dominick's skill at the gaming tables, too."

"Umm. True enough. Still, he wouldn't play whist. Considered it just a social pastime, not a real card game. A waste of time, he said."

"When is he coming back, anyway?"

"Probably another two weeks. He has been informed of your

arrival--I sent him notice yesterday--but he has a great deal of business that can only be handled in Trinidad, and I don't expect him for another two weeks. I'm sure he'll be back in time for the Delaneys' masque."

Jessalyn lifted her cup to her lips to cover a smile. The talk of the masque would keep them occupied long enough to allow her to escape gracefully from the tea. She'd have done her duty and she could plead other demands on her time.

She slipped into the house as soon as she was able and went in search of Alice Simms. She found her in the kitchen going over menus with Marguerite.

"Ah," she said, "I'm glad to find both of you. I wanted to thank you for the lovely tea."

"No need, ma'am," said Mrs. Simms. "It was a simple enough tea."

"Ho!" Marguerite's eyes sparkled with mischief. "Worked hours on them tarts, I did. We had to make it *special*."

"It was indeed special, and I thank you both."

"We're glad you liked it, ma'am."

"Right we are," Marguerite nodded. "Couldn't let you be shamed in front of--*them*." She almost spat the last word.

"I see." Jessalyn smiled at the pair, and they exchanged brief glances. "I gather that you both already know that we'll probably have our hands full with the two of them."

"We know," Marguerite said. Mrs. Simms merely nodded. "if that one turn out to be something like her sister--" Alice Simms shot her a quick look and Marguerite stopped. Jessalyn looked from one to the other of them.

"Is there something I should know about Mrs. Fitzhugh, perhaps?"

"No point in spreading malicious gossip, ma'am, now is there?" Simms answered, and Marguerite, who'd had her mouth open to answer, closed it and looked down.

"Don't matter what we say anyway," she said. "If we say, if we don't say, all the same. Things be what they be."

"Was there something else, then, ma'am?" Simms was beautifully efficient at dismissing her, she thought.

"No, not really. I plan to take Mrs. Fitzhugh and Lady Heloise with me when I return some calls this week, and I'd like your advice, Simms, on what to wear."

"Certainly, ma'am. I'll be glad to help. Mrs. Reynolds, a lady in your position is certainly entitled to have a lady's maid. Would you like me to see to arranging one for you?"

"No, thank you, Simms. I'm much more comfortable doing for myself. If I need help, I'm sure Celestine will be able to give it."

"That Mrs. Fitzhugh, she got two maids."

Jessalyn said, "We were raised differently, Marguerite. I'm sure she thinks she can't do without them."

"Lots of things she thinks she can't do 'thout," Marguerite muttered.

*     *     *     *     *

Until they began making social calls together, Jessalyn had not realized the animosity that lay between Alida Fitzhugh and her Aunt Heloise. Perhaps there was animosity between Alida and everyone, but to this point she and her aunt had managed to keep a united front in Jessalyn's presence. Perhaps they thought they had a common enemy. But on the long carriage ride to the other planters' homes, the façade broke down, and the behavior that was apparently customary between them came to the surface.

The first skirmish began over a remark Lady Heloise made about Jessalyn's health.

"Your appearance does seem to have improved a bit since we've been here, my dear," she said. "You aren't looking quite so thin."

"Yes, I do believe I'm regaining the weight I lost on the trip over."

"Hmm. You must have had a wretched voyage," Alida said. "Of course, even under the best of conditions, and heaven knows, we had the best accommodations money could buy, I found it dreadfully tiring."

"I dare say," Lady Heloise said, glancing at her. "You're still showing the effects of it, my dear."

Alida's eyes narrowed. "At least, *dear* Aunt, I'm of an age at which time and rest *do* make improvements in one's appearance. Thank heaven for that."

Lady Heloise colored. "Dear, dear, let's not be sharp with each other in front of Jessalyn. She'll not think well of us."

Alida rolled her eyes, clearly indicating that she didn't give a flip for what Jessalyn thought. Then she looked across at Jessalyn and smiled a tight little smile. "You see, Jessalyn, my aunt is one of those unfortunate ladies, who, having never married, is really not at home anywhere. She and my mother loathe each other, and so she spends as little time at her ancestral home as Mother can manage. Sometimes she visits others of her brothers and sisters, or, as on this occasion, chaperones a young woman on her travels. She was quite looking forward to my marriage to Dominick so that she could manage a year or so in the tropics at my expense."

Lady Heloise's lips were pursed, her face flushed, her eyes averted from her niece's. She twisted her hands upon each other, as if, Jessalyn thought, she were twisting Alida Fitzhugh's slim neck, but when she spoke, her tones were calculated to sooth, as if she were speaking to an annoying child.

"Now, now, Alida," she said. "I know you must have your little joke, dear, but let's not give Jessalyn the wrong impression."

"Oh, I'm certain that I'm not, Aunt Heloise. I'm quite sure I'm giving her the impression I intended to give."

Lady Heloise smoothed her face with some effort and glanced sideways at her niece. She sighed softly, and then said, "You must know, of course, Jessalyn, that Alida is right about me in some ways. Not that even maiden aunts don't have their uses, of course. I suppose it must be much worse to be a penniless widow."

The emphasis on the last two words was delicate but distinct, and Alida Fitzhugh snapped her head around and glared at the older woman.

"Just what do you mean by that?" she snarled.

"I only meant, Alida dear, that having never married, I obviously haven't known what I might have had. That's all."

Alida's face was furious, and she seemed about to attack her aunt viciously, but at that moment the driver announced that they were at the Harrington place. By the time they'd descended from the carriage, Alida's face had undergone an astonishing change. The normally petulant mouth had curved into a smile, the brow had smoothed itself magically, the eyes were widened, the chin lifted. When the door was opened and their hostess appeared, her face was as serene, her manner as calm and assured as if she had never spoken a harsh word or had a troubling thought. Jessalyn thought she'd have made a superb actress; her technique was flawless.

Margaret Harrington was, Jessalyn decided, the roundest woman she'd ever seen. Her bright pink dress practically burst its seams displaying her round arms and her round body. She had enormous round breasts, a round face, and a round O of a mouth. In fact, she looked like a series of O's arranged to represent a woman.

She welcomed her visitors delightedly. How nice to have guests! How lovely to meet the new Mrs. Reynolds! How wonderful to see someone just over from England! "Do tell me all the latest gossip!" she said, and she giggled. Jessalyn understood why her husband had a mistress on Trinidad; that piercing, incessant giggle would be enough to account for it.

After her curiosity about Jessalyn had been satisfied, Margaret turned to the other two ladies. She found them and their recent news of people she knew much more entertaining. Jessalyn sipped weak tea and surveyed her surroundings. The Harrington home didn't look anything like Dragonsong, she thought. It was a large brick Georgian mansion, much like houses in England. The interior could have been imported directly from that country, also. The furniture was upholstered in silk, the draperies were heavy damask, the carpets were thick and plush, and the colors were all shades of dark red or burgundy. The effect was dark enough and gloomy enough to make Jessalyn grateful for the air and sunlight of Dragonsong. And for the space.

The parlor was the most crowded room she thought she'd ever been in. Bric-a-brac covered every available surface, with china cupids vying for room with ceramic shepherd girls, crystal birds nudging hand painted plates. The room was so filled with furniture (and Simon was right; it was hideous) that the ladies had a bit of difficulty moving among it in their hoops. There were loveseats, sofas, large tables, small tables, whatnot shelves, curio cabinets, etageres, bookshelves--all crowded together in a clutter Jessalyn found fascinating and repulsive. After Dragonsong, this room was suffocating and oppressive.

Margaret Harrington sat down beside a box of chocolates--"I have them shipped in from England, special"--offered some to her guests, and then proceeded to demolish the contents. By the time they left, Jessalyn observed that the box was quite empty.

Back in the carriage, Alida murmured pleasantries to her aunt about Mrs. Harrington: "Lovely woman. Quite a nice home," and so on. Her aunt said nothing, but after a few moments, she turned to Jessalyn and asked, "What did you think of Mrs. Harrington, my dear?"

Jessalyn blinked. "I thought she looked like a talking bonbon."

Had she been thinking, she'd probably not have said it, but caught a bit off guard, she simply blurted out the first thing that popped into her head. Alida gasped. "How absurd!" she said. "Margaret Harrington is from one of the best families in England
and--"

But Lady Heloise let out a whoop of laughter. "Didn't she just! I've never seen anyone put away so many chocolates so fast!"

Their next call, on Kitty Anderson, was much like the first, but the visit with Susan Newell, Jessalyn quite enjoyed.

Mrs. Newell was precisely as Simon had described her. She looked all of her sixty-odd years; her hair was quite white, and she wore it piled on top of her head. She was unfashionably brown, as if she worked out of doors; Jessalyn was to learn that indeed, that was exactly what she did. She did gardening as a hobby--"Seems the thing to do. Grow anything here, you know"--and her flowers were wonderful. She made the three of them, with their wide-brimmed hats and their carefully opened parasols seem pale and washed out.

"Ah, my dear," she said to Jessalyn when they were seated, "I hear you had a most dreadful trip over."

"Yes, quite awful. I was sick the entire way."

"You needn't tell me. Oh, dear, I do remember. Had the same problem, you know, but complicated by Geoffrey."

"Geoffrey?"

"My oldest, you know."

"Was he ill, too?"

"Not a bit of it. Wasn't born yet. I suffered enough for both of us. Thought it might harm him, but no such thing. Turned into a great strapping lout of a man."

Jessalyn laughed. Alida smiled politely. Lady Heloise coughed a bit.

"I'm so glad to see you at last. Can't tell you how happy I was to hear that Dominick had married. Thought his first marriage might have spoiled him for good and all."

Alida stiffened. "Thank you, Mrs. Newell..." Jessalyn murmured.

"So glad he married a different sort of woman this time."

"May I remind you, Mrs. Newell," Alida said coldly, "we are discussing my late sister?"

"Oh, of course, of course, and not to speak ill of the dead, but I've said it to her face often enough. Real harridan, your sister Adelaide. More spoiled, selfish woman I've never seen. You must know that yourself. Heard she took Dominick away from you."

Alida's face went red, and she glared at the older woman. "You heard incorrectly, then. And as for her marriage, I'm sure Adelaide did the best she could."

"Oh, no. Did the worst she could, actually. But that's an old story. Now my dear Mrs. Reynolds--may I call you Jessalyn? What a pretty name. Where have you called so far?"

"Well, we just came from visiting Mrs. Anderson, and before that, we called on Margaret Harrington."

"Oh, poor dear Margaret. What did you think of her?"

"Jessalyn said she looked like a talking bonbon," Lady Heloise said.

Mrs. Newell laughed loudly. "Oh, indeed, indeed." She wiped her eyes. "Ah, well, I suppose everyone has to have something. Charles has his mistress on Trinidad, and Margaret has her chocolates."

Alida and Lady Heloise stared. "Mistress?" they said in unison.

"Dear me, you two are new here aren't you? Rather common knowledge. Dare say Dominick told you about it, Jessalyn."

"I had heard something, yes."

"Lovely woman. Mulatto, I think. Has several children by her."

"How disgusting," Alida snapped.

Mrs. Newell looked at her, surprise. "Hardly disgusting. How'd you like being married to Margaret Harrington?"

"That's hardly the point. She comes from a lovely family in England. I'd think they'd do something, put pressure on him, something."

"Oh, my dear, how silly." Susan Newell waved the suggestion away. "That lovely family stays lovely on Charles Harrington's money. How are *they* going to pressure *him*? They're very lucky Margaret managed to snag old Charles. Going under fast, they were. He pulled them out. Most of them think the family's lucky in two regards--they got Charles' money, and they got rid of Margaret."

Alida was silent, her mouth a tight line, but Lady Heloise was enjoying this thoroughly.

"I quite agree, Mrs. Newell. Have you ever heard a more irritating giggle?"

"Hardly. I'm sure Charles thought he was getting a prize. Quite an armful, she was, when he married her. Long since outgrown Charles' arm, though. Or anybody else's. Now," she turned to Jessalyn, "when you leave here, you must go call on Lacey Delaney. You'll love Lacey. Quite a character."

"Oh, yes, we're planning to go there next. Isn't she the one who used to be an actress?"

"Oh, dear, yes. Good one, too, I understand. Such fun, she is."

"An *actress?*" Alida spoke as if the word were something disgraceful.

"Quite." Mrs. Newell spoke with such an air of finality and fixed Alida with such a pointed look that she precluded any further comment, but as they were leaving, she called Jessalyn back for a moment.

"My dear," she whispered, "however did you get that snob of a Fitzhugh woman foisted off on you?"

"She didn't know Dominick was married to me. She came out here to marry him herself."

"Dreadful. Simply dreadful. But how *terribly* lucky for Dominick. Do get rid of her as soon as you can."

Lacey Delaney's home was the most imposing of the mansions they had visited. It was a huge white Greek revival structure with marble columns across the front and green shutters on the windows. Acres of velvet-green lawns spread around it, and beds of flowers set like jewels in the formal gardens gleamed in the sun.

The inside of the house was not like the others, either. It was not like Dragonsong; this house did not have the same open air of cool tranquility. This was a very formal atmosphere with a feeling of luxury and sophistication, quite lovely and quite composed. A fragile staircase seemed to float, spiraling, from the floor of the entryway to the second level. There the stairwell was circled by a curved railing and a skylight shed soft light on the entry and the stairs. There were few paintings on the walls, but they were impressive. The large room to which they were shown was uncluttered and elegant. The upholstery, the carpets, the draperies, were all shades of yellow, ranging from pastel to gold, and the effect was that of captured sunlight. The walls and furniture were white and cream. Vases of flowers provided most of the ornamentation, although there were several crystal and silver bibelots placed carefully about the room.

Jessalyn thought the room delightful, but Alida was unimpressed.

"She certainly keep this place *bare*," she said. "Heaven knows they must be able to afford more."

"At least it's not like that dreadful mess at Harrington's," Lady Heloise said.

"But ye gods. *Yellow*? At least Margaret used subdued colors."

Jessalyn decided that she had never truly understood the meaning of the phrase "swept into the room" until she saw Lacey Delaney enter. There was no other way to describe the way that lady simply seemed to take possession of the room. She was not tall, but she appeared to be. She wore her silver-gilt hair piled high on her head, and she held herself as if she were quite an imposing figure. Which, Jessalyn though, she was.

Now she extended a small hand to Jessalyn and to the others and seated herself opposite them, spreading pale gray silk about her with a bit of a flourish.

"How delightful to meet you, Mrs. Reynolds," she said. "You must be quite improved to be up to making calls."

"Oh, yes, I'm feeling much better. And of course, Mrs. Fitzhugh and Lady Heloise wanted to meet some of the ladies on the island, too."

"Are you recently arrived from England, then?" she asked the pair sitting opposite her. Her voice was warm and throaty, and she seemed to purr, rather than speak. She must have been an impressive actress, Jessalyn thought.

"Yes," Alida said. "Last week."

"How lovely. Perhaps you could bring me up to date on some gossip, then. I've simply been dying to know, and letters are so unsatisfactory."

"Oh, if we can," said Lady Heloise. "What was it you wanted to know?"

"Well, I got this letter from a friend, and she said--you know that annoying way they have of doing this--'I guess you heard about that old devil, the Duke of Bennington.' And that was all. Not another word. I've been asking everyone, but no one knows what she meant."

Jessalyn felt her breath almost stop, and her hands curled into fists on her lap.

"Oh, dear, yes, of course. It was a scandal. I'm surprised you didn't hear." Alida smiled maliciously. "Let me see if I can remember how it goes. It seems that some highwayman robbed him--wasn't that it, Aunt?--and they caught the thief and brought him to trial. Then during the trial, the thief's sister stood up in the dock and testified ('Under oath, mind you,' Lady Heloise inserted) that she was the duke's daughter."

"His daughter!"

"One of his many by-blows, I suppose," Lady Heloise said, "but I heard from someone who was in the court when it happened that there was no doubt the girl was telling the truth. He said you had only to look at her and the duke and you could tell they were blood kin. At any rate, she'd gone to him to beg mercy for her brother, and he'd do nothing."

"That sounds like him. Did they hang the brother?"

Alida shrugged. "Oh, yes. Bennington had his pound of flesh. But the duchess left London for their country place at the height of the season. She was that upset."

"Bennington was always a petty old sot."

Alida raised her eyebrows as if to condemn such talk coming from a mere actress about her betters, but she said nothing. Lady Heloise said, "Bennington hasn't a decent bone in his entire bloated body."

"What happened to the girl?"

"No one knows," Alida said. "She disappeared. I mean, that sort always does, I suppose."

"I suppose. Ah, here is the tea. How do you take your tea, Mrs. Reynolds?"

No answer.

"Mrs. Reynolds?" They all looked at Jessalyn who appeared about to faint. "Mrs. Reynolds, are you quite all right?"

Jessalyn took a deep breath. "Yes, y-y-yes, I think so. It's the first time I've been out, and the heat and all--I must not be as well as I thought."

Lacey rang for a servant and had her bring a damp cloth to bathe Jessalyn's wrists and forehead.

"Better now?"

"Yes, thank you, much."

"It does take some time to adapt to the tropics. In fact, some never do manage to be comfortable here, although I find that I really prefer this climate to the cold dampness of England."

"Not I," Alida said firmly. "I believe that should I live here fifty years, I'd still prefer England."

"Ah, but you've hardly been here long enough to give our little island a chance, now, have you? Perhaps you'll come to like it better later." The tones were warm, but the blue eyes had a hint of mockery. Alida didn't seem to notice.

"I'm sure it seems lovely to me," Lady Heloise said. "As I get older, I withstand the cold less well."

"Well, perhaps your niece will be more interested in our island when she comes to know some of the families here. You'll meet almost everyone at our gala. You are coming, aren't you?"

"I'm sure we shall, " Jessalyn murmured. "In fact, we have to have the seamstress out soon to start on our costumes before she is overwhelmed by your other guests' outfits."

"Does everyone come in costume?" Lady Heloise asked.

"Almost. Oh, a few simply refuse, and nothing will move them. Your Dominick, for instance, will wear a mask with his evening clothes, and that's his only concession. Of course, *I* can't criticize. I've never been able to get Woodrow into costume, either. Dear Simon makes up for it, though. He always wears a wonderful costume."

They left a few minutes later, and the drive home was largely silent. When they drove past the entry to Susan Newell's home, Alida muttered, "Awful woman. I shan't call on *her* again."

Jessalyn said nothing. She was certain that *she* would call there often.

She lay in bed that night, recounting to herself the events of the day. She'd liked Susan Newell, hadn't liked Margaret Harrington, had no opinion yet of Kitty Anderson, and Lacey Delaney--Lacy Delaney. What about Lacey Delaney? She'd been charming, certainly. And beautiful. She was certainly gracious. Why then, was Jessalyn slightly uneasy in her company? Because she had raised the story about the duke? Because in her house the tragedy that had so scarred Jessalyn's life had been tossed about as so much casual gossip?

No...no, she thought, not that. That had been unfortunate, but it wasn't just that. She looked up at the mosquito netting draped about her bed and silvered by the moonlight. I think it was...her hands, she thought drowsily. Everything about her was calm, serene, except her hands. They moved, looking, with their long fingers and small bones, like pale spiders, hovering, pouncing, grasping. She has grasping hands. She wants something, anything, everything. If I had something she wanted, Jessalyn thought, I should be very anxious about it.

And then the thought faded and she slept.

# Chapter Thirteen

T HE NEXT FEW DAYS were peaceful and pleasant ones for Jessalyn, in spite of the Trenton women. Alida Fitzhugh, Jessalyn learned, began drinking in the late afternoons, and consequently slept very late in the mornings.

"Nothing else to do on this god-forsaken island," she muttered the first time Jessalyn encountered her in an advanced state of intoxication. "Wonder how my sister stood it as long as she did." She had discovered the rum swizzle, a drink mixed in a tall glass with rum, lime, and the ice which Dominick imported. Douglas made them for her, swizzling them to a froth with a long stick, and Alida declared the concoction the only civilized contribution the islands had made to English culture. Jessalyn abstained, even from the sherry and bitters popular with many of the islanders and the special favorite of Lady Heloise. She stayed with the iced limeades that Marguerite made for her.

Jessalyn was accustomed to rising early, and since her guests slept late, early morning became her favorite time of day. She'd be up at dawn, bathe, dress, and slip out of the quiet house into the cool morning air to explore the gardens and the areas around the house. Early morning was, she found, the best time to observe the birds on the island, and as Simon Alderly had promised, their variety and color were splendid. She caught an occasional flash of color as she startled a scarlet ibis from its perch; once she thought she saw a parrot. Sometimes she would see one of the larger birds, an egret or a heron, fly over, but there were always smaller birds, and she was learning to recognize the blue tanager, the yellow and black bananaquits, the cornbird.

She loved the beaches and would wander down through the thick groves of coconut palms to watch gulls and terns wheeling overhead. She would stroll along the golden sand, sometimes taking off her shoes to play in the surf, and watch small fishing boats work their way back and forth along the coast.

She would wander back to the house for breakfast when the sun began to warm the sand, and have one of Marguerite's "special" breakfasts.

She confronted Marguerite about having breakfast in the kitchen after the arrival of her "guests."

"It is not done," Marguerite insisted.

"Nonetheless, I plan to have my breakfast down here. I am the *maitress,* am I not?"

"Well, yes, certainly, Miss, and that is why--"

"Then, if I am the *maitress,* I can decide how things are to be done, right?"

"Yes, of course, Miss, but--"

"Then I have decided that I need to have breakfast down here where I can discuss running the household with you and Simms. It serves my purposes to do so, and it allows me to stay aware of what's going on. I'm sure Mr. Reynolds would expect that."

Marguerite smiled widely. Given a reason she could accept, she was all too happy to capitulate.

" 'Sides, " she said with a wink, "you need to spend *some* time with people what *likes* you, not allatime pick-pick-pick at you."

"I certainly do," Jessalyn sighed. And so it was settled.

Marguerite had informally adopted Jessalyn, and while she gave the occasional nod to her position as *maitress,* she largely treated the young woman as if she were one of her own girls. Marguerite was incapable of ignoring a stray, be it human or animal, and as a result, her kitchen was frequented by adoptees of both species. The kitchen, Jessalyn decided, was the heart of the plantation. Children and grownups dropped into Marguerite's kitchen for care and feeding, for gossip and laughter. It was a rare day when there wasn't a child bringing in a cat or dog or a bird with a broken wing or even an orphaned lamb to be treated by the tender Marguerite.

Jessalyn was more at home in the kitchen than anywhere else on the plantation. She fed the animals, helped with the cooking on occasion, and chatted with Marguerite. Those few days were the most peaceful time she had ever known, and the calm and care suited her. Her guests were demanding and Dominick's correspondence was heavy, but it was still less strenuous work than she had been accustomed to. She laughed with the warm and loving Marguerite, made friends with Celestine, and even managed a kind of uneasy acquaintance with Aurore. She had a treasure in Dominick Reynolds' library; it was filled with all sorts of books, and more arrived weekly.

It seemed a good life. It was not to last.

Later, when she looked back, she thought that the tranquility of that period had ended on the day she first saw Marmles. She had gone into the kitchen early and found Marguerite and Celestine arguing about something, and it didn't take her long to find out what the problem was.

"Celestine, we can't just leave them there. Aurore said she won't set foot out the house as long as they're there. You know how she is."

"HO!" Celestine rolled her eyes heavenward. "I know better than anybody else in the world how she is. But I don't see know reason to put those poor bitty mites out just to please Princess Aurore. They don't bother her no way. She can just walk around them, that's all." She smiled at Jessalyn. "Good morning, Miz Jess."

"Celestine, you so hardheaded. Miz Jess, you talk to her. She just won't see reason, no way."

"ME hardheaded!" Celestine was indignant. "I not the one sitting in that house refusing to come out on account of some poor baby kittens. You say hardheaded, nobody so hardheaded as that Aurore."

Jessalyn looked from one to the other, puzzled. "What's the trouble?" she asked, peeling a banana and leaning against the pantry door. "What's the matter with Aurore?"

Jessalyn was somewhat uncomfortable about Aurore. She didn't know whether the girl avoided her deliberately or whether their paths simply never crossed, but she saw a great deal less of her than she did of the others, and their relationship had remained cool, and distant. Jessalyn felt, always, the same cool disdain she'd felt the first time that she had seen the girl.

Celestine looked up at her. "You know that big old mama cat been wandering around here, that one Mama said have her kittens any day now?"

Jessalyn nodded.

"Well, she have them, all right. Right under the steps to our house. Now Aurore won't come out of the house. She do hate cats. And she not set foot out of that door till them cats be gone. I say, Aurore just have to get over it, that's all. I don't see no reason to make those bitty little kittens move just to cater to Aurore."

Marguerite shook her head. "You just don't understand, Celestine. Aurore got scratched by a cat when was a little tiny child, and she scared of them a lot."

"Scared, hoo!" Celestine hooted. "Aurore not scared of the very devil, she just looking for an excuse, that's all. She not want to do her work."

"Celestine, she really scared! Really. Now you go move them kittens, move the cat, move it all, please!"

Celestine looked at her mama and sighed. "Oh, all right. I guess I have to if I don't want to end up doing her work."

Marguerite reached into the depths of a large cupboard and pulled out a big basket and lined it with a frayed towel. "Here. You put them in this and bring them up. We find a place to put them."

Celestine took the basket, and Jessalyn said, "Could I come with you? I love cats."

"Sure, come on. I could probably use the help with that big old mama cat anyway. She won't be one little bit happy when I start messin' with her babies."

The two of them followed a graveled path out the back way, across the lawns past the hedges that marked the boundaries of the gardens and out to the compound where the plantation workers lived. Each family had its own wooden cabin, built up high on stilts, and its own garden plot. The cane workers left for the fields as soon as the day was light enough to see, and came home when the sun was high. That way they had time to work their own small kitchen gardens and raise their own vegetables. Of fruit there was no limit; it could be picked from trees that grew wild in and around the compound, and there were groves of citrus trees maintained by common labor.

Jessalyn followed Celestine back to the house she and Aurore shared with George and Marguerite.

Celestine set the basket she carried on the ground at the foot of the steps that went up to the porch above their heads. "Now then. There they are, just under there. Can you see?"

Jessalyn followed her pointed finger to the mass of wiggling bodies under the steps. "Oh, yes! I see!" She squatted down to peer under the steps. "Aren't they sweet?" she asked, smiling over her shoulder to Celestine. "Look, Celestine, how little they are."

"Little or not," said a voice over her head, "they cats, nonetheless. Fair make my skin crawl."

She looked up to see Aurore leaning on the rail around the porch, looking down on them, her face contorted with loathing.

"Never you mind, Aurore," Celestine said," you got your way-- again. Mama said move them up to the house. Then you can do your work," she added significantly.

"You don't have to see them again, Aurore, unless you chose," Jessalyn said.

"I never choose to see no cat, never, no way."

Jessalyn had reached under the steps and was handing the kittens back to Celestine, one at a time. When the sixth and last was tucked into the basket, she reached for the mother, who was by this time pacing nervously back and forth, howling at them.

"Can't you do something with that yowling car, Celestine?" Aurore snapped. She leaned over the railing. "She making me nervous." And she shuddered.

"Just one moment," Jessalyn picked up the cat and turned to settle her in with the litter. "There." She stood up and brushed off her skirts, and looked up at Aurore with a smile. Aurore was wearing a white, loose-fitting garment that set off her creamy skin to perfection. Wisps of her hair escaped from the braid coiled on top of her head and curled around her face. She was so lovely, Jessalyn thought, that the effect was only spoiled by the sullen expression on her face. As the girl looked down at Jessalyn, the scowl deepened.

"You certainly starting to look different, Miz Jess," she said finally. "Not so scrawny like you was."

"Oh, I hope so," Jessalyn said happily. "Marguerite has certainly been feeding me well enough."

Celestine grinned at her. "I told you Mama fix you up. Didn't I tell you? You lookin' real pretty."

Jessalyn laughed, and the pair started back down the path, but Aurore studied the retreating Mrs. Reynolds with a speculative frown. Huh, she thought. She *is* starting to look pretty. She starting to look *good*. Too bad about that. Wonder if Miz Fitzhugh notice that yet. Wonder what happen if somebody happen to bring it to her attention. She smiled to herself, and hurried down the steps and along the path to the kitchen.

Celestine and Jessalyn were busy settling the kittens and their mother in a new spot when Miriam rang for the ladies' morning trays. Celestine turned to Jessalyn and said, "I got to go take up the trays. Can you stay here and see to them for a minute or two? Maybe if that mama cat happy here, she not move them back."

Jessalyn sat alone by the basket for a moment or two, stroking the mother cat, running a finger over the kittens. Her heart had been taken by one of them in particular, a small fluffy ball of orange fur that reminded her of the ship's cat in miniature.

"I think, " she said to the meowing mite, "that if no one objects, I will have you for my own. I don't see how anyone could take exception to my keeping a cat."

"Miz Reynolds would--the *old* Miz Reynolds, I mean, if she was here. She hated cats as bad as Aurore. Wonder if Miz Alida the same way?"

Jessalyn turned to Celestine, surprised. "My, that was quick. What did you do, run up the stairs?"

"No. Aurore was there. She offer to take Miz Alida's tray, so I only had Lady Heloise." She smiled a wicked little smile. "Might as well let Aurore do some work when she in the mood. Lord knows, the mood don't strike her very often."

Jessalyn laughed and picked up the little cat. "This one is my favorite," she said. "Think Marguerite would mind if I took him when he's a bit bigger?"

" 'Sakes, no. Mama got all she can do getting rid of them cats. But they's better looking cats in the litter than that one. He looks kinda like he been dipped in a pot of orange marmalade."

Jessalyn tucked the kitten back in the basket by his mother. "No, that one is my favorite. He reminds me of a cat that I was--fond of, once. And you're right about his color. Maybe I'll call him Marmalade."

"Huh," Celestine snorted. "That too much name for that runty cat. How about just Marmie?"

"Umm. That sounds like a mother cat. How about Marmles?"

Celestine laughed. "That one silly name. But that one silly looking cat. Marmles he be."

Upstairs, Aurore brushed past Miriam to take the breakfast tray to Alida's bedside and set it on her table.

"Good morning, Mrs. Fitzhugh. Fine morning, ain'it?"

Alida straightened up in bed, brushed her hair back from her face, and fixed the girl with slightly bloodshot eyes. "Not yet it isn't. And who are you?"

"I'm Aurore, ma'am. I brought you your breakfast."

"I see. Thank you. You may--"

"Marguerite, the cook, she my mama. She make you special breakfast. Not so special like she do for Miz Jess, but special for you."

"I do think you'd be better advised to refer to your employer's wife as 'Mrs. Reynolds.' 'Miz Jess' strikes me as entirely too familiar, young woman."

"Yes'm. I guess you right. Course, Miz J--Mrs. Reynolds, I mean, she probably don't know no better, seeing as how she not quite like you. Not used to being a *maitress*, you know."

Alida leaned forward, signaling the girl to fluff the pillows behind her. "Oh, I know. That's obvious even to the servants, isn't it?"

"Well, yes'm, I guess so. See when she came here, first few days, Mr. Reynolds, Mr. Alderly, they say she gonna be a secretary here, something like that. Then, who woulda thought it? Mr. Reynolds up and marries her. That before he find out you coming, of course. He sure mad when he find out you coming. He real sorry he didn't wait, I bet."

She had settled the breakfast tray across Alida's lap and poured her tea, and Alida, stirring it, stopped and looked at her.

"What makes you think that?"

"Heard him say so. Course, you gotta know, you mustn't tell no one I said that. I was--um--listening, kind of. I wasn't s'pose to be there, you know?"

"Eavesdropping, you mean."

"Well, not really. It was sort of an accident. Only, when I heard them talking--Mr. Reynolds and Mr. Alderly--I just sort of didn't move."

"What did they say, exactly?"

"Well, Mr. Reynolds say he wish he'd known you coming, and now it was too late, or something like that, but what's done is done, and that how it is."

"How--interesting." Alida smiled into her cup.

"Yes'm. Then he take off for Trinidad right after the wedding, and he not been back since."

"Right after the wedding?"

"Oh, yes, ma'am, real soon after. They have this little ol' wedding, nobody here but us and the preacher, and Mr. Alderly, you know, then he took off. He didn't even take the time to--well," she giggled, "you know."

Alida looked up at her, frowning. "You mean--are you trying to tell me--wait a minute. When did he find out I was coming?"

"Umm, that be right after the wedding. Just *right* after. Then he left."

"Then as far as you know, the wedding has never been consummated?"

"What?"

"They've never shared a bed."

"Oh, I know that for certain-sure."

"How can you be so certain-sure?"

Aurore shrugged. "I know the maid does they rooms. She say. She know. She lowered her voice. "They *ways* to tell."

"Umm." Alida leaned back against her pillows, a little smile playing about her mouth. "How very interesting."

"Yes'm, but I guess that be taken care of pretty soon when he get back."

"Why do you say that?"

"Well, you should have seen her when she first got here. My

goodness, she one scrawny, ugly thing. Looked like a plucked chicken. Mama been working on fattening her up. Mr. Dominick say for her to do it. Guess he know she be real pretty once she get a little meat on them bones, so I guess he been waiting for that."

"Um. She is thin. I thought when I first saw her, how on earth could Dominick have married such a woman?"

"Hey, Miz Fitzhugh, I think she over that bad spell. You looked at her lately? She looking real fine these days. *Real* fine. My mama fatten her up just like Mr. Reynolds say, and she looking real pretty. Bet he be surprised when he come home."

Alida's eyes narrowed. "Yes, I'll bet he will. I'll just bet he will." She looked over at Aurore and the tray. "Take this back to the kitchen. I'm getting up. I think I have some other things to do."

Aurore scooped up the tray and started for the door. Miriam opened it for her and gave her a hard scowl. Aurore only smiled at her and when she was out of her sight and hearing, laughed out loud. To herself she muttered, "White women such fools. Act the lackey and you can make them believe anything."

\*       \*       \*       \*       \*

Jessalyn was tired. The seamstress who was working on their costumes for Lacey's masque had been and gone, and she found the fittings tiring. She'd prefer a day of walking and climbing stairs to an hour of standing still and being poked and prodded, she decided. And the fifteenth century costume she'd chosen to wear as Lucrezia Borgia hadn't helped, either. Next year, something simple, she thought. Then she reminded herself that she'd not be here next year. This was her only Delaney masque.

She'd consulted with Susan Newell about her choice of costume, and when she'd decided on the infamous Italian lady, Susan had smiled. "A bit of a contrast, is it? Go to it, then. I've never seen anyone do Lucrezia. Lots of Cleopatras, Marie Antoinettes. Those well known ones. One year, Margaret Harrington came as Elizabeth, complete with ruff and farthingale. The shortest, fattest Elizabeth in English history."

She related her findings about the ball over tea to Alida and Lady Heloise who were busy debating their own costumes.

"She said Cleopatras and Marie Antoinettes abound," Jessalyn said. "Have you thought of Anne Boleyn?"

"Too ordinary," Alida grumbled. "Besides, she got beheaded. I'd rather go as someone more--I don't know--reminiscent of pleasant things."

"How about further back? Eleanor of Aquitaine?

"Um I like the period, but she sounds too old."

"Maybe I could go as Eleanor," Lady Heloise said.

"You're too dumpy, Aunt," Alida said.

"What about Berengaria?"

Who?"

"Berengaria. She was a princess from Navarre, you know, in Spain, who married Richard the Lion Hearted. Eleanor's daughter-in-law, actually."

"Hmm. Alida tapped a tooth with a fingernail and considered. "Was she pretty?"

"Who knows? She was a princess and then queen of England. Even if she were not, who'd say so? Besides you have the right coloring for a Spanish princess."

"What sort of thing did she wear?"

"I think there are some books in the library with drawings. Let me get them and show you,"

Jessalyn brought in the books and spread them open to show Alida the twelfth century costumes. She considered them, frowning.

"Not awful, really. Those headdresses cover all your hair, though."

"Oh, yes, well, they do, but you could wear them. It takes a lovely face to carry off having all the hair covered."

She'd said the right thing. Alida's vanity was touched, and she determined that Berengaria was her choice.

As for Lady Heloise--"I'll need a lady-in-waiting if I'm to be a queen, aunt," Alida said, "you may be my attendant."

Lady Heloise sighed. She'd hoped for something more glamorous, but she settled for lady-in -waiting.

Now Jessalyn stretched out on her bed hoping to have a short nap before dinner. It was warm this afternoon, and tired as she was, she dropped off to sleep quickly.

When she woke, it was pitch black and the house was silent.

Someone had drawn the mosquito netting around her, and she was still fully clothed. She lit a candle and walked out on the balcony, but there was no moon and the impenetrable tropical darkness was complete.

I must have slept for hours, she thought. I've missed dinner, and I'm ravenous. She walked back in and sat down on the bed. Well, nothing to be done for it now. She undressed, put on her nightgown, and crawled into bed, then snuffed out the candle.

But she lay there and stared into the darkness for the better part of an hour and decided, finally, that she'd never get to sleep until she got something to eat. Besides, she thought, sitting up and scratching her arms, the mosquitoes must have had a feast on me before Celestine or whoever put the mosquito netting down.

She relit the candle and slipped from the room barefoot, closing her door softly so that she wouldn't awaken anyone. Downstairs in Marguerite's kitchen, she sliced a piece of bread and spread it with butter and honey, and washed it down with a glass of tepid milk. She wiped up the utensils she had used and put them away, dusting up the crumbs to prevent their attracting ants, then peeked into the pantry to check on the kittens. The mother cat eyed her suspiciously, but he neither moved nor meowed; Jessalyn stroked her until she purred, arching her head under the young woman's hand. She allowed Jessalyn to stroke each of the kittens in turn, then Jessalyn rose, stepped out, and closed the door softly.

Still wide awake, she started for the stairway, then stopped. I won't get to sleep for a while, she thought. I think I'll stop in the library and get something to read.

She padded down the hallway, let herself into the office, and searched among the books for a title she'd seen earlier. She spotted it and another one that seemed intriguing. She set the candle on the floor and sat down beside it, putting one book in her lap and holding the other in her hand.

Outside in the darkness, Dominick Reynolds saw the faint light from his office window and he frowned. Who would be in the office at this hour? He'd just come from Simon Alderly's home where the two men had spent the entire time since his arrival late in the day. They'd been involved in business discussions for much of the time, but a great deal of talk was given over to the problem of Alida Fitzhugh. What was to be done about her? She caused an uncomfortable situation. He could hardly, under the circumstances, order her to leave. Certainly she had a right to visit her late sister's home. But how long did she plan to stay? Days? Months? A year? She hadn't said. Visits of longer than a year were not uncommon, given the time the trip took, and six months was probably a minimum. One could not expect a pleasant experience in any event, and Simon didn't hold out much hope for the situation improving. She'd been drinking, he said. Heavily. True, she tried to hide it for the most part--a couple of drinks in the evening before dinner, perhaps one after, but when she retired to her room she'd consume a great deal more.

"How do you know?" Dominick asked.

His manager shrugged. "I have my sources. Servants talk, you know."

Dominick was silent. It wasn't wise to ask more. Simon wouldn't tell him, and there was no point in pushing him to evasion. Dominick always wondered how much Simon knew about his marriage to Adelaide. Probably most of it. Probably *all* of it. He'd never asked. Simon had never mentioned it.

But tonight Simon said one interesting thing.

"Our Miss Kirke--Mrs. Reynolds--has turned out to be a most interesting person," he said, "in more ways than one. I think you will find her an unusual surprise."

"Oh? How so?"

"I shall leave that for you to discover. However, she is--shall we say--rather more than we thought we were getting."

That was all he would say. Dominick dropped it. Let Simon have his little mysteries, he thought. I'll learn soon enough.

Now he entered the house, approached the door of the office, glanced inside, and stopped.

Jessalyn was sitting cross-legged on the floor, a book open on her lap. Her head, bent over the book, was tilted to one side. Her left hand was raised to her hair, holding one side of it out of her face, and the other side fell loose in the light of the candle, a gleaming gold curtain. Gone were the scabrous sores she'd had when she arrived. Gone were the hollows under her eyes, the transparent, pasty skin stretched skull-like over her face. Gone was the stick of a body, the paper-thin wrists. My god, he thought. No wonder Simon warned me.

She hadn't seen him enter, her attention entirely captured by the book she was reading. At his soft "Jessalyn?" she started, gasped, and jumped to her feet, and the book hit the floor with a noise that seemed to reverberate through the still house. He knelt to pick it up for her, and as he handed it to her, she giggled. The sound was odd coming from her; he thought it might have been the first time he'd heard her laugh.

"I was trying to be so quiet," she said, "and now I've made a noise to wake the dead."

He looked at her, a sudden constriction in his throat, and the smile faded from her face. She mistook his silence for displeasure, and she said, "I hope I'm not wrong to be here? You said I might borrow the books if I wished, and I've been very careful to replace them where I got them."

"Oh, no, no, Jessalyn, " he said quickly. "I'm sorry, my mind was elsewhere. Of course it's all right. Quite all right. I was merely-- surprised, that's all. Your appearance is very--improved."

Oh, much improved, he thought. Even in her nightgown, barefoot, with her hair about her shoulders, she's a beauty. How could she have- -who'd have thought--how could that wretched creature have become- -he bent and picked up the other book to cover his confusion, and handed it to her.

"Thank you," she said. "Marguerite has been following your orders conscientiously. She feeds me very well."

She stooped to retrieve the candle, and he suddenly didn't want her to go, hated to have her leave, as if by leaving she took the light, not just of the candle, but of herself.

He said, for lack of better conversation, "Has she made you callaloo soup?"

She smiled, her mouth curving and pushing a dimple into one cheek. "Oh, yes, that's my favorite. What does she put into it, anyway? I've asked, but she only says, 'Oh, a bit of this, a bit of that.' "

He laughed. "That's all you'll get from her, too. Marguerite learned to make callaloo soup on Trinidad. It's a specialty there, but each cook has her own version. Marguerite will never give away her secrets."

She looked down at the books in her hand and a lock of her hair fell across her cheek. He found the urge to smooth that lock back into place so nearly irresistible that he had to clench his fists to keep from touching her. She looked up and said, "I'll take this one. I can read the other next."

"Take them both," he said. "In fact, if you like, I'll have more bookshelves moved into your room so you can keep more books there."

"Thank you," she said, and flashed the quick smile once more. "I'd like that." She started toward the door, and he called after her.

"Wait."

She turned. "Let me walk with you," he said. "I'm likely to break my neck stumbling about in the dark down here."

He took the candle from her, holding it up to throw a path of light ahead of them. "Have you seen any of the plantation yet?"

"Only a bit. Mr. Alderly took me to see the flamingoes, but he's been so busy since you've been gone that he hasn't had much time to show me around."

"Have you been riding?"

"Oh, yes!" She looked up at him and her face glowed from more than just the candlelight. "Thank you for Josephine. She's just lovely."

"Why don't you comewith me on my rounds tomorrow morning? I'll show you some more of the place?"

"Oh, I'd like that."

"I'm up quite early. Shall I knock on your door?"

"No need. I'm an early riser." She took the candle from him. "Good night, then, Mr.--Dominick."

"Good night, Jessalyn."

He watched her go into her room, then sighed and entered his own. Damn, why did I do that? Why is she *like* that? I never thought I'd feel--I've worked *not* to feel that--that sudden lurch of the heart, that longing--for another woman. I never want to love another one of those wretched creatures--why did she have to look so--so young, so lovely. So touching and tender and innocent. He sighed and leaned his head against his hand on the doorjamb. I should stay away from her, he thought. I shouldn't spend time with her. But surely it can't hurt, this once, to go riding with her. Surely I can withstand--besides, he told himself, she *is* my wife. It ought to look natural, at least.

From the darkness, eyes which had seen the conversation watched until the lights beneath each door went out. A door opened. A door closed. And the house slept.

*　　*　　*　　*　　*

Marguerite Douglas sat up in her bed, staring ahead of her, he hands clutching a sheet to her bosom.

Beside her, her husband stirred. "Marguerite? What's the matter?"

"It starting now."

He was awake now, frightened. "What? What starting now?"

"The trouble."

"What is this trouble, Marguerite?"

"I don't know. I know it is bad. I don't know what it is. I can't see."

In thirty-odd years of marriage, he had seen this happen several times, and it never failed to frighten him, never failed to leave his knees weak and his heart pounding. They'd been newlyweds the first time, and he didn't pay much attention. He'd tried to shrug it off the second time, too, but no more. Never again. He hated these moments, dreaded them. The only faint consolation was that Marguerite hated them dreaded them, more than he did.

"Is it about Miz Jess?"

"It some about her. She sort of like a match to black powder, I guess. Not the match's fault the powder blow up. Somebody else have to set it all up. Match just *there*. All the same, it bad. Poor girl. It gonna be bad."

George Douglas sighed. "No way to stop it, huh?"

"No. It gonna be." She rocked back and forth. "It gonna be."

# Chapter Fourteen

J ESSALYN WAS DRESSED IN her riding habit and waiting at the foot of the stairs when Dominick came down.

"Ah, Jessalyn, you *are* an early riser. Have you been waiting long?"

"No. I just got here."

They walked in silence to the stables, where Dominick was greeted with some enthusiasm by the stable hands.

"That Spaniard hoss gonna be too glad to see you, maitre," one of them said. "He don't want nothing to do with us."

"Gave you trouble, did he?"

"Give everbody trouble 'cept you, maitre."

Jessalyn understood their concerns as soon as she saw the horse. Spaniard was a large animal, black with a blaze of white on his forehead. He was a magnificent beast, but obviously a temperamental one; the stable workers all seemed terrified of him. She could hear him stamping about in his stall, nervous, edgy. But the minute he heard Dominick's voice, he thrust his head forward, craned his neck to see his master, and whinnied. He was, she observed, obviously a one-man horse.

"Ho, there, boy." Dominick Reynolds put an arm about the great head, leaning close to him, patting his neck, stroking him. "Calm down a bit. We've got a visitor. Best manners, now, you understand?"

Indeed, the animal seemed to calm a bit. He nuzzled Dominick, and took the sugar cubes his owner proffered on a flat palm, then settled down. He tossed his head a bit, but he submitted to being saddled with little protest.

"He loves you, "Jessalyn said. "You must be very good to him."

161

"We're friends of a sort, I suppose. I raised him from a colt."

The truth was that Dominick Reynolds loved the horse as, perhaps, he loved no other living being, having turned from a bad marriage to the animal as a place to center his affection. But he didn't talk about either of those things--the marriage or the horse.

When Jessalyn's mare was brought around, they mounted and rode off down and road back of the house at a fairly rapid gallop. Spaniard needed to work off some energy, and Josephine kept pace with him well for a time. When she began to fall behind, Dominick reined in, and they slowed for a bit.

"We're going to ride past some of the cane fields, then I'm going to take you to one of the sheds where the sugar is made."

"How many sheds are there?"

"Two, now. The big one, close to the house, is the new one. It's my showpiece. It has the first steam engine on the island for grinding cane. Some of the others are getting them now, but I had the first. The one we're going to is an old mill. We still use oxen to turn the grinding wheel."

They rode past cane fields in all stages of growth, from just planted to harvest.

"How long does it take to harvest?"

"Fifteen months, from planting to harvest."

As they passed a field where workers with machetes were cutting the cane, she stopped and watched while they loaded it onto donkeys for the trip to the sugar mill.

"Wouldn't it be better to use wagons or something to transport the cane?" she asked. "Those little donkeys don't look as if they can carry much."

"Well, a couple of things about that. First, the donkeys can carry a great deal more than they seem to be able to. And second, I thought the same thing when I started. In fact, I got some wagons, some mules, and tried them out. The problem is that wagons mire too badly. As soon as the wagons are loaded, they sink into that damp soil so deeply that nothing can get them out. So," he said, "we went back to donkeys. It's more efficient than it looks, actually."

At the mill, she watched the sugar processing with interest. Two workers fed the cane between rollers which were turned by oxen trudging in a circle, harnessed to long sweeps. The juice from the cane drained into a tray that fed to an underground pipe leading to a collecting cistern in the boiling-house. A pair of young women removed the rushed cane. "We dry it and use it for fuel for the fires under the boilers," Dominick said.

The juice was piped from the cistern into the first of a series of "coppers" to be boiled clear.

There were five coppers. In the first two, the syrup was boiled, and the scum removed. After it had boiled for enough time in each kettle, it was ladled into the next. The scum from the remaining coppers was piped down into what Dominick called the "still-house." "We use it in making rum," he said.

The boiling-house was sweltering. Jessalyn could feel sweat run between her shoulder blades, and Dominick wiped his face until his handkerchief was soaked. While they were there, the workers doing the ladling were relieved by others, and Jessalyn asked, "How often do they change? It must be hard on them."

"Most places every two hours. Mine change every hour. When the planters used slaves for this, they changed every four hours, and that was considered generous."

"I think I'd melt in four hours.'

" I *know* I would."

Gradually the juice thickened, and by the fifth copper, when the "temper" was added--"temper is made of water and ashes," she was told--it was ready for crystallization.

"How do they know when it's ready?" she asked.

"Well, it's like--ever make Christmas candy?"

"Oh, yes," she smiled. "In fact, this place smells just like my mother's kitchen at Christmas."

"Well, how do you know when it's ready to pour?"

"You just know. The way it looks. Test it, add a bit to some water, things like that."

"Well, my sugar boiler 'just knows.' He's done this so long, he knows exactly when to take it out and put it in the cooling tank."

"And then it's done."

"Not exactly. Come with me."

He took her into the filling room, where a lukewarm mixture of crystal and molasses was being poured into wooden pots, roughly sixteen inches across the top, twenty-six to twenty-eight inches deep. "It stays here for two days, then it goes to the curing house."

"Why is that boy beating on those pots?" She pointed to a young man who was knocking on each of the pots and listening to the sound that each gave back.

"He's rapping it. Good sugar has a different sound from bad sugar. The good ones have a sort of, oh, ring to them. The bad ones sound dead."

In the curing house, the pots stood in long rows close together, draining molasses into hollowed wooden gutters. The gutters drained the molasses into large collecting tanks, one at each corner.

There were no windows in the two-story building, and it was quite close. "It's one of the ironies of sugar production that the cane needs a moist tropical climate to grow, but the same moist air is the enemy of the curing process. During the rainy season, we have to keep pans of coals in here to help the sugar dry out."

"How long does the sugar stay here?"

"A month. The pots are taken down to the knocking room, turned upside down, and dropped on the floor. The sugar comes out in a thirty-pound pyramid. We knock off the top and the bottom of the pyramid and make what we call *penneles* sugar with it. That's a slightly inferior grade, but doing that step leaves the rest better quality. At least, most of the planters do that. Some don't bother."

"What's next? Is it sugar then?"

He glanced at her, pleased with her interest. "Yes and no. It's a sugar of a sort. At this point we pack up most of it and ship it to Europe for refining. It isn't the sort of sugar you're used to--not the fine-grained white. It's a sort of bright yellow-brown. Some of it we take through another step to make it white. That's a long process, though. It involves covering the pot with a mixture of clay and water, and it takes about four months."

"An what do you do with the syrup that drains out of the pots in the curing house?

"Add it to the scum from the coppers and make rum out of it."

"You don't waste much, do you?"

"We try not to."

"How do you make rum?"

He looked down at her. "Are you sure you aren't bored with all this?" They were standing outside, and she had turned her face to the breeze. "It's my work, and I find it interesting, but most people find it quite dull."

"No," she looked at him, her face open. "I'm not easily bored. I like learning new things."

He looked at her for a long minute. "You'd have to. Come on then. Down to the still house."

After they left the distillery, they rode along a bit further to see some of the other crops.

"Simon told me you were diversifying. He said you were raising cocoa, for instance."

"I'm experimenting with several things. Some spices. Some cacao. I'm thinking about harvesting bananas."

"Bananas? But what would you do with them? Beyond eating them on the plantation, I mean."

"Nothing yet, but if steam travel becomes widely used and cuts the shipping time, we can get them to England or America before they ripen. They can be cut green and ripening time is slow enough to make that possible some time in the future. Of course," he smiled wryly, "most of the other planters think I'm crazy."

"I don't."

"I just don't believe in having my money tied up in one place. One crop failure--" He shook his head. "Of course, most of the others don't feel that way. Sugar production is quite expensive, and they think they can't afford to invest in other ventures. I think they can't afford not to. So far, though, only Woodrow Delaney has gone along with my ideas."

"Ah. Has he really? We've called on his wife."

"Lacey? Did you meet Woodrow, then?"

"No. He wasn't there. She's quite lovely, isn't she?"

"I suppose. Not my sort, but Woodrow thinks she's wonderful." He paused, reined in his horse, and looked out into the distance. "My first wife hated her."

It seemed a surprising revelation. He'd said almost nothing personal to her all morning, certainly nothing at all about his late wife.

"Did she really? Why?"

"Most likely because I made her call on Lacey when she first arrived. Lacey was an actress, you know, and Adelaide considered her to be a social inferior. More likely because people like Lacey. She gives fine parties and dinners. She's popular."

"And Adelaide wasn't?"

"No. Of course, it's difficult to be popular with people for whom you have only contempt."

She was silent for a moment. And then, risking a bit, she asked, "Did that include you?"

He gave her a long look, and she thought for a moment that he was going to tell her to mind her own business, but at last one corner of his mouth rose and he said, "Me, most of all."

"Why wouldn't she like you?" Jessalyn thought she knew the answer, thought she understood the story from Simon, but she was curious to know what he'd say, and she decided to let discretion go by the way. "You're very wealthy, you're well read and intelligent. Mr. Alderly said that many women in England wanted to marry you. I'd think she'd consider herself quite fortunate."

"You and Simon must have had quite a conversation about me."

She looked down, her face pink. "We did, a bit. It isn't entirely necessary, of course, but it is interesting to know something of the man one is married to."

He laughed out loud and was surprised how good that felt.

"She resented being married to me for the same reasons she disliked Lacey Delaney, I suppose. My father died when I was young, and my mother a few years later. I left my relatives' home--I couldn't stand being treated as a charity case--to try and make a life of my own. I went to sea, for a time. That's when I got this." He touched the scar on his cheek.

"'An accident?"

"A fight. With my captain. After the fight, I had to flee the ship to avoid being keelhauled or hanged. Lucky we were in port. I'd probably be dead by now if we'd been at sea."

"What did you fight about?"

"He was beating the cabin boy. I thought it was too much, so I hit him. He laid a blow across my face with the stick he was using on the boy, and I almost killed him. They had to drag me off."

He stopped, looking out across the fields at nothing in particular. She said nothing. "Do you find that sort of behavior appalling, Jessalyn?"

She turned faintly astonished eyes on him. "No. On the contrary. I was thinking that I wished you had been on my ship."

He raised an eyebrow. "You are very honest, anyway. Are you always so direct?"

"No. At least, I try not to be. Most people don't like too much honesty."

"Ah. So they don't. At any rate, we were discussing my late wife's opinion of me. She had a great distaste for the sort of past I've just related to you. Considered it distinctly unsavory, if not criminal. She'd have been much happier if I'd just inherited my money."

"But good heavens! Her own father prevented that!"

"Simon told you that part too, did he?"

"He had to. There was little he could do to avoid it once Mrs. Fitzhugh showed up."

"True. However, Adelaide didn't see it that way. I suppose she couldn't be expected to."

They had come in sight of the house now, and he turned to her. "Simon tells me you've managed to handle my sister-in-law quite well."

"If avoiding her is handling her, I suppose I have."

"Avoiding her may be the only way to handle her."

"We have made calls together, and we have tea and dinner on occasion. Other than that, we don't see each other."

"I've no idea how long she plans to stay. I'm hoping not very long."

"I wouldn't count on it," she sighed. "She complains constantly about being here, but I'm sure she doesn't relish going back England and facing the humiliation there."

After they turned their horses over to the grooms, they strolled back toward the house, and she said. "I'm ravenous. As soon as I bathe, I'm going to be able to eat everything Marguerite feeds me, for once."

"Oh, you can bathe after. Come and join me. I hate eating alone. That's why Simon usually comes and shares breakfast."

"Will he be there today?"

"No. He had and early errand. Come with me and we'll have--"

He had opened the door for her, and as they entered the foyer, she heard, "Dominick!"

They both turned toward the stairs, where Alida Fitzhugh virtually floated down, every silken curl in place, every carefully ironed ruffle crisp. Jessalyn thought she had never seen her look lovelier; indeed, she'd never seen her at this time of day at all. Dominick stared at her. "Alida," he said finally, and as she reached him, she twined both slim white arms around his neck and pulled his head down to hers and kissed him on the mouth.

Jessalyn watched them, an unfamiliar and uncomfortable feeling growing in the pit of her stomach.

When at last Alida released him, she hot a glance at the young woman and said, "I do hope you don't mind, Jessalyn, dear. It's been such a long time since I saw dear Nick."

"Of course not," Jessalyn murmured, but Alida wasn't listening.

"Nick, you are looking wonderful. Better than I'd remembered. I was just coming down to breakfast. How lovely to have you here."

Jessalyn blinked. Alida hadn't come down to breakfast since she'd been here. She had tea and toast in her bedroom, usually, and sometimes that came back untouched.

"Thank you, Alida. Jessalyn and I were just going in to eat. We've been out to see the sugar production."

"How fascinating," she said, smiling up at him. "You must take me quite soon."

"I'm not sure you'd enjoy it. It requires getting up quite early."

"Oh, dear, that's no problem. I only sleep late when there's nothing else to do. Now that you're here, I'm sure there will be lots of things we can do."

"I'm sure."

Jessalyn wasn't sure whether his tone was ironic.

"Shall we go it?" Alida smoothed her skirt. She looked Jessalyn up and down. "I'm sure Jessalyn will want to get out of that dusty riding habit before she joins us."

"Yes," Jessalyn said, starting for the stairs, "I certainly do."

"But I thought--"Dominick looked after her, then stopped. Damn women anyway. Now he was stuck with this bitch Alida, when what he wanted--What had he wanted? Better for her to go. I don't want to get attached to her. When she leaves--he didn't finish the thought. He followed Alida to the breakfast table.

*    *    *    *    *

Jessalyn went to her room and rang for breakfast to be sent up. She had her bath and rested, then took a book and went out to the gallery to sit and read for a time. She stared at the pages, unable to concentrate, her thoughts running over and over the time she had spent with Dominick Reynolds this morning. An unusual man, she thought. A difficult man to know, somehow. Most of the men in her life had been fairly simple to comprehend, at least after she got to know them. Dominick Reynolds became more complex the more she knew of him. Still, she thought, no point in getting caught up with him. All the troubles in my life came from trusting men. Jamie and my father were certainly not men to inspire trust, she thought. Nor was the duke. And as for Captain Scarsdale--but it had occurred to her that her rescue from the hands of the vile captain had been brought about by men. Simon Alderly was certainly to be trusted, and she had given him her confidence. Surely Dominick Reynolds was--or maybe it was *she* who could not be trusted. Perhaps listening to her heart instead of her head caused the trouble. If that were the case, then, it made sense to ignore that most untrustworthy organ. Surely it was *feeling* that had caused such confusion in her mind when she'd watched Alida Fitzhugh embrace him. Rational *thought* told her that there was nothing there to do with her. It was his choice to kiss or not to kiss Alida. She had made a bargain, a contract, a business arrangement. It was nothing to do with feelings. I'll keep the contract, she thought, the bargain, the business arrangement, and put down fiercely any feelings that arise for Dominick Reynolds. Those were no part of the deal. At the end of the year, ten months or a bit more now, I'll be gone. I'll have money to live, to travel, to enjoy myself. And without any encumbrances. She tried to revel in this thought. Why, she asked herself, do I find no comfort in it?

She was still in her room when Simms knocked to tell her that Simon Alderly wanted to talk to her.

"Certainly," she said. "Is he in the office?"

"No, ma'am, he said to meet him at the gazebo in the jungle garden."

"The jungle garden? But why on earth--"

"I've no idea, ma'am. I did get the idea the he wanted to meet you quietly, if you understand."

"I'm sure I don't, but I thank you, Simms. I'll go right away."

Simon Alderly stood as she entered the gazebo. "Jessalyn, how nice of you to come so promptly."

"Curiosity, Simon. I couldn't imagine what would cause such secretiveness."

"Nothing as major as all that, actually. I wanted to ask whether you were aware of Mr. Reynolds' birthday next week."

"Heavens no," she said. "He'd certainly not have mentioned it, if I've assessed him correctly, and no one else has."

"Oh, I'm sure you've assessed him correctly. He'd have let it pass without a word. Still, it might appear strange if his new bride--that it, if you, let it go by."

"Indeed. New brides would make a fuss, wouldn't they?"

"Exactly. That's why I thought I might warn you. What might we do, do you think?"

"Well, considering that I'm new here, perhaps a small dinner party--nothing elaborate. Say, the Delaneys, the Newells, perhaps the Harringtons, if we must--maybe one or two other couples? Do you think that would suit?"

"I think that would suit wonderfully well. Speak to Simms and Marguerite about it, and I'll get someone to deliver the invitations."

"Good. I'm glad you told me. It would have looked odd to have skipped it."

"By the way, might I mention how well you're looking these days? You've made quite a metamorphosis."

"Have I really? I know I'm looking better--I could hardly have looked worse--but I am pleased to be improved."

"Oh, indeed. You've no idea. You're quite the talk of the plantation."

"Oh, hardly that, Simon, I'm sure. Unless they're quite desperate for conversation topics."

"Umm. You'd be surprised what makes for interesting news around here." They both laughed.

Eventually she and Simms made the guest list to include the Delaneys, the Harringtons, the Newells, the Andersons, the Basils, and the Despains. "And with the two of us, Mrs. Fitzhugh and Lady Heloise, and Mr. Alderly, that will be seventeen. Sounds a manageable number, don't you think?"

Simms agreed. "Odd number, though, ma'am."

"I'm not sure that's awful," she said, "and besides, I don't know who to invite to even it up."

It turned out to be odder than she'd planned. The Harringtons sent regrets; Charles Harrington was on Trinidad--"As usual," Simms said--and Margaret didn't go out alone. Then Philo Anderson took a fall from his horse and broke his leg. "That leaves thirteen for dinner," Jessalyn said, frowning over Kitty Anderson's note. "How superstitious are you, Simms?"

Simms didn't look too happy, but she said, "I don't suppose it really matters, ma'am. It's too late to invite someone else now."

So it was. It was the day before the dinner when Jessalyn received the note and too late to ask someone else to fill in. "Too late to cancel out the dinner, too," she said. "We'll just have to make do."

Later, after the dinner was over, she wondered if the number had been somehow a premonition. Certainly the entire party seemed to suffer under some sort of bad spell.

She should have been warned, she thought later, when Alice Simms and Marguerite shook their heads over her proposed dinner menu.

She had asked Marguerite for Dominick's favorite dishes, and those were the ones she'd included. The roast beef and Yorkshire pudding were traditional enough, but the rest of the list included a number of native dishes: turtle soup, for instance, and yams, sautéed plantains, avocados--hardly the typical English meal. Simms shook her head over it.

"Surely you may serve anything you wish, ma'am," she said, "but it is at best unusual."

And Marguerite said, "It look fine to me, Miz Jess, but it don't look much like what I fix for dinner parties before."

Jessalyn ignored them. "It's Dominick's birthday," she said, "and we'll have his favorites."

On the evening of the gathering, Jessalyn fussed over the preparations so long that she was almost late getting dressed, and her guests had begun to arrive by the time she came down the stairs. She'd chosen a light blue gown with a wide neckline that bared her shoulders. Celestine had done her hair high on her head with curls cascading down her back. As she came down the stairs, Dominick was standing in the foyer talking to his manager, and when he glanced up and saw her, he stopped in mid-sentence, his mouth open, watching her descend. Simon Alderly followed his gaze to the young woman, then looked back at his employer. For a second the look on Dominick Reynolds' face was so strange that Simon was puzzled. What was it? Displeasure? Surprise? Shock? None those, he decided. It was there and gone so quickly that he couldn't precisely analyze it, but he'd have sworn it was naked longing, yearning. How interesting, he thought. Imagine falling in love with one's wife. Unique.

Douglas was circulating with a tray of rum punch, and when he saw Jessalyn enter, he set the tray down and exited to return with a tray of limeades. All the servants had become aware that Jessalyn didn't drink, and on occasions when others did, Marguerite made tall iced glasses of limeade for her.

The Newells had arrived, and almost at the same time, the Delaneys.

"Rum punch? It does look tasty, Jessalyn, but what's that you're having?" Susan Newell peered at Jessalyn's glass, turning away from the silver punch cups.

"Limeade," Jessalyn said, "I'm afraid I'm not terribly fond of spirits."

"Oh, I do like the occasional tot, you know," Susan said, "but I find that if I start before dinner, I tend to fall asleep over the soup course. I think I'll join you in the limeade."

The Despains had arrived earlier, and Lila Despain and Lacey Delaney were deep in conversation about some new dress pattern that Lila's dressmaker had acquired. It was a conventional enough gathering, a quiet group chatting about this and that. The Basils arrived, and Bethany Basil joined Jessalyn and Susan. Lady Heloise came into the room, was greeted, and took a rum punch.

And then, last of the group, Alida Fitzhugh swept into the room. She was wearing bright red silk, a vivid shade that not only set off her dark hair and fair skin to perfection, but which had the immediate effect Jessalyn thought, of making all the other ladies' pastel gowns pale in comparison.

She ignored everyone else in the room as she floated up to Dominick Reynolds, her lovely face raised to his, smiling. "Dominick! How dashing you look in eveningwear. Heavens, I haven't seen you dressed like this since--I believe it was the Duke of Somerset's ball. You danced twice with that horrid Elizabeth Sherbourne, and I was insanely jealous."

Douglas offered her a rum punch and she took the cup and drank it down. "My, this does seem terribly tame after your luscious swizzles, Douglas. Why don't you make me one of those, instead?"

Douglas inclined his head and left the room.

"Is this all you're serving before dinner, Jessalyn?" she said, looking down at her punch cup. "Most places offer more variety. Unless there's champagne, of course. Though I suppose a place as remote as this wouldn't have champagne."

"Oh, you'd be surprised," Susan Newell glanced at her. "We do have some of the amenities, you know. Got the wheel last year. Plan to get a printing press one of these days."

The others laughed, and Alida flushed angrily. "I only meant that it is rather out of the way here, and--"

"Oh, we understand, dear," Lila Despain said. "Susan was just having her little joke. I think probably the rum punch is in honor of Dominick's birthday. I happen to know this is his favorite."

Jessalyn smiled at her, and Alida turned back to Dominick. "Of course! I almost forgot. Happy birthday, dear Nick."

She moved quite close to him and stood on tiptoe to kiss him, another of those long embraces. At least, it started to be, but he disentangled her arms from his neck and moved back from her before the moment could become embarrassing. As it was, Lila Despain looked at her cup, and Bethany Basil regarded a painting opposite her with intense interest. Only Susan Newell raised an eyebrow, and Lacey Delaney looked at Jessalyn and rolled her eyes.

When Douglas brought the swizzle, Alida drank that almost as rapidly as she had downed the punch, and Dominick said mildly, "Better watch those swizzles, Alida. They're deadly the way Douglas makes them."

"Darling, I'm quite accustomed to the occasional drink," Alida said testily, "and I'm certainly old enough to make my own decisions about how much to have."

"I'd say so," Lacey Delaney muttered. Bethany Basil giggled, and Alida glared at the pair.

"Besides, Mrs. Fitzhugh, we're playing whist later, and it's always best to have your wits about you."

"Oh, never fear, Simon," she said, "I play rather better when I'm relaxed."

"A popular misconception, actually," Simon murmured. "Almost everyone thinks he plays better after a few drinks, but almost no one does."

Alida glared at him, but at that moment, Douglas announced dinner. Dominick turned as if to seek out Jessalyn, but before he could locate her, Alida had grasped his arm firmly and said, "I'm sure you'll be seating me for dinner, Dominick, as your guest."

He looked at her for a second, as if he intended to withdraw his arm, but then he smiled at her and said, "Of course, you're correct as always, Alida. And my other arm is for our other guest, Lady Heloise."

Alida's smile faded as he gave his left arm to her aunt, but Lady Heloise merely giggled and took it. Simon escorted Jessalyn to her place.

When the turtle soup was served, Alida looked at it disdainfully and said, "What on earth is *this*?"

Jessalyn looked up, startled. "It's turtle soup," she said.

"*Turtle soup*? Is that some sort of *native* dish?"

"An island delicacy," Dominick said. "My favorite. I presume that's why it was chosen."

Jessalyn smiled at him the length of the table. "Of course," she said.

"How clever of you, Jessalyn," Susan Newell said. "How nice to do something different for a change. Do get tired of the same old things, don't we ladies?"

They murmured assent. If they'd been prepared to try and avoid the turtle soup before, they were all determined to eat it now, following Susan's example.

As the other courses were served and the guests realized the purpose of the dinner, they dug in with some enthusiasm, intent on making Jessalyn's first dinner party a success, supporting her against the torrent of criticism from Alida.

Having failed to gain support for her attack on native food--"I am too envious that you thought of this first, Jessalyn," Lacey Delaney declared. "What a deliciously novel idea"--Alida turned to other complaints. The beef was undercooked, the wines were wrong, the dessert was too heavy.

No one answered her. She drank all the wine and was by now becoming increasingly careless in her speech.

The guests were becoming more and more uncomfortable, and less and less able to carry on small talk among themselves, over and around Alida. As soon as the dessert plates were removed, the Basils excused themselves. Bethany complained of a headache.

"Probably this awful food," Alida sneered.

"Oh, dear, no," she said, quick to avoid giving offense. "I've had it two days now."

The ladies adjourned to the drawing room, but the men didn't linger over their port and cigars. The gentlemen soon joined them, and the Despains took their leave, too.

The others tried to be discreet, but it was clear that no one had the heart for continuing the party. As she left, Susan Newell turned to Jessalyn and said, "Sorry about this dear, but there's one good thing."

"What's that," Jessalyn asked.

"The contrast between the two of you. Alida and her sister could have been the same person. Adelaide used to do this. Get drunk, scream at Dominick. Get rid of her, young lady. Get her out of your house. She's poison. Just like her sister. Pure poison."

As the last of the company filtered out of the house, Jessalyn started up the stairs to her room Halfway up the flight, Alida called her name, and when she stopped, the woman came up the stairs to where she stood.

"Quite an interesting party, don't you think?" she said. Her words were beginning to slur. Jessalyn wondered how much she'd had to drink before she came down and whether she'd had more since dinner.

"Y-yes," Jessalyn said, "I suppose you could call it interesting, all right."

"Amazing how provincial people become when they've been away from England for a while. I could scarcely imagine anyone in England eating *native* food."

She moved a step up ahead of Jessalyn, blocking the young woman's way. "Of course, I don't suppose *you* know any better, but *they* certainly should."

"I suppose. Good night, Mrs. Fitzhugh."

Alida backed up one step so that she stood over the girl, but she didn't move out of her way.

"Actually, I can't see how my sister could stand it those years she was here, except--" She smiled a sly smile, "for Dominick, of course. Dear Nick is a bit of a rough diamond, but he does have his virtues. Not that Adelaide would have appreciated the most obvious of them."

Jessalyn moved as if to pass her, but she blocked the way.

"Oh, Adelaide and I were much alike, just as we appeared, except in one or two ways. Adelaide was rather--shall we say--cold? She didn't take any pleasure in the joys of the marriage bed, for instance."

"Mrs. Fitzhugh, I--"

"I, on the other hand, have had some knowledge of that side of marriage. Not that I got it from old Roman Fitzhugh, heaven knows. He certainly wouldn't be the one to inspire raptures in any woman. But when you're married, there are always avenues open to a woman who is interested in--adventure."

"I think I'd better go"

"Ahh. Ahh, yes. I forget. You don't know of such things, do you?"

Jessalyn's head snapped up.

"Still the virgin bride, I understand. And with that luscious man available to you--you must be worse than Adelaide. You must have a body as cold as the--"

"Mrs. Fitzhugh."

They both turned, startled. Alida's face seemed to pale. It was Simms. She stood at the top of the stairs, a tall slim figure in black, her face as expressionless as ever.

"I think that's quite enough, Mrs. Fitzhugh. It's time for your bed, I think.Alida wavered a moment. "I was just telling this--young bride--Simms--"

"It's time, Mrs. Fitzhugh."

Alida turned without another word and mounted the stairs to her room. Jessalyn stood there a moment longer, her mouth open, trying to assess the scene. What on earth? Simms--the silent, imperturbable Simms--had ordered Alida Fitzhugh to her room, and the woman had simply turned and--gone. Without a word. How--strange. How very strange. Jessalyn climbed the stairs to her room slowly. The evening, she thought, had been a disaster from start to finish. She changed to her nightgown and blew out the lamp. But once in bed, she couldn't seem to fall asleep. The moonlight was bright on the lawns, but the shadows were black. She wandered down to the end of the balcony to a place where a vine climbed over the railing and reached for one of the blossoms spilling its fragrance into the night air.

As she turned, she heard the sound of a voice below her, and still standing in the shadows, she leaned over the rail to see a slim figure emerge into the moonlight. Aurore, she thought. What is she doing here at this time of the night? The girl seemed to glide over the grass, and as she did she spoke to someone standing in the shadows. Her voice was soft, and Jessalyn could hear the sound but not the words. She heard a man's voice reply, and as she watched, Dominick stepped from the shadows to meet her. They stood there for a moment, Aurore's face pale in the moonlight, and the sound of her soft laughter rose to the balcony where Jessalyn stood. And then, as she watched, Aurore reached out and touched Dominick's cheek. It was a touch, Jessalyn thought, that spoke volumes about an intimacy between them, and intimacy that must be, by its very nature, clandestine. And then Aurore moved away, slipping into the shadows, and Dominick disappeared beneath the balcony.

Jessalyn returned to her room, feelings of anger and disappointment and sadness twisting inside her. How bitter, she thought, to find that Dominick Reynolds was simply like all rich, powerful men. How deceptive her first impression of him. Did all employers take advantage of those within their power, she wondered, hating the knowledge of what she had just seen. Were they all like the duke? And what of herself? Had he, seeing that she was not as wretched as she'd first appeared, sought her out for the same thing?

It doesn't matter, it doesn't matter, she said to herself. It's nothing to me, it means nothing, it has nothing to do with me.

But she was confused and angry and close to despair. She didn't sleep for a long time.

# Chapter Fifteen

Lacey Delaney's gala was well underway before the Reynolds' carriage arrived to drop them at the front door. The guests filled the ballroom and spilled over onto the lawns where torches had been set up to light the area and to discourage insects.

Alida Fitzhugh's medieval costume as the queen, Berengaria, was admired extravagantly. Indeed, it was quite becoming. The gown was gold brocade, with long sleeves fitted almost to the wrist, then widening to drape to the floor. The sleeves were lined with scarlet silk, and her headdress had a veil held with a gold circlet to mark her rank.

Jessalyn's costume was a deep burgundy, and consisted of a close-fitting outer garment with wide sleeves that covered a long, flowing, rose-colored undergarment. The sleeves of the undergarment were snug to the wrists, and the sleeves of the overdress were trimmed with borders of the rose fabric. She wore a small hat that tied beneath her chin, and her hair, wrapped with ribbons, hung down her back in a long thick braid.

Jessalyn thought that she had never seen a more glittering sight than the huge ballroom with its vast crystal chandeliers lighting the dancers below. Costumes from fairy tales and from history sparkled as their owners moved to the music. A matron of ancient Greece waltzed by in the arms of a chubby pharaoh; a dour Charlemagne whirled a laughing Juliet; a stalwart Viking smiled down at a diminutive shepherdess.

Jessalyn stood at the top of the steps and watched the merry assembly for a moment, but only for a moment. Dominick took her hand just as it appeared he was about to be claimed by Alida for a dance, and swept her off into the waltz.

"You dance very well," he murmured, his chin against her hair.

"As do you," she said. "There seems to be no end to your accomplishments."

He drew back to look at her face to see whether she was being sarcastic, decided she was not, and pulled her to him again. "There's an end," he said. "I've yet to accomplish those things that are important to me."

"Such as?"

"Reclaiming my estate. Achieving some--happiness in my life."

"But I noticed that first came the estate."

"It means a great deal to me."

"You might have bargained for it with Alida Fitzhugh."

"That wouldn't have been a bargain."

She smiled. "And what would constitute happiness in your life, do you think? Can you have it without the estate?"

"I don't know. Perhaps I can't have it at any price. Still, there may be possibilities. For instance, I've wanted to ask you--"

At this moment, a dashing cavalier swept off his plumed hat, made a deep bow to her and asked, "May I cut in?"

She laughed. "Of course, Sim--" but he put his finger to his lips.

"We are all in disguise until the unmasking at midnight, dear lady. It wouldn't do to guess at our identities."

"Of course not, sir. How clumsy of me to have forgotten."

Dominick bowed and left the floor. At the edge of the dance floor, he turned and glanced over his shoulder at the couple he'd just left, then moved away to where a group of men were laughing and talking.

Several pairs of eyes observed the exchange and the subsequent glance.

Lacey Delaney, ready to step in and rescue Dominick from Alida, had her mouth open to deliver some witticism she'd been framing for him, when she saw his gaze shift and follow his wife and manager about the floor. Ah, how interesting, she thought. Who'd have guessed that little Jessalyn would turn out to be such a beauty? Something odd about that whole marriage, though it seems obvious to me that he's smitten with her. *She* seems much more at ease with Simon Alderly, of all the odd things. Ah, well. If this one is no more successful than his last, perhaps I'll finally have the chance to--console him. It would be delightful to find him receptive to my ever-so-subtle offers at last.

Alida Fitzhugh saw her former brother-in-law leave the dance floor and regretted that she'd taken a dance with her host. Damn, she thought. If I'd known, I'd have been there waiting. It's a good excuse to be in your arms, dear Dominick, and you can hardly avoid touching me when we dance.

Lady Heloise saw the couples change, and saw her niece bite her lip in vexation. She smiled to herself a bit, rather satisfied. There, Alida, she thought. How does it feel to be rejected by him--twice? She watched Alida's eyes narrow a bit and shuddered. Truth be told, she was a little frightened by her niece. At one time, she'd been terrified of the two of them. When they were young, when they were together, there was nothing they wouldn't do, nothing they wouldn't try, no matter who was hurt, no matter what the consequences. Not that there ever were any consequences for those two, thought. Their specialty was seeing to it that someone else took the blame for them. She wondered that Adelaide had ever died. Seemed as if she could have got someone else to do it for her.

When the dance was ended, Lacey's husband Woodrow, Alida on his arm, joined Dominick and Lacey at the end of the ballroom, and Simon led Jessalyn to the group. Margaret and Charles Harrington (Margaret, in a Red Riding Hood costume looking remarkably like an apple, Jessalyn thought), drifted over to join them.

"Lovely costume, Ali--Ooops!" Margaret giggled. "Ah, your highness. Who are you, by the way?"

Alida lifted her head slightly. "I am Berengaria, queen to Richard the Lion-Heart."

Woodrow Delaney nodded. "Yes, yes, very original, my dear. Not too many people even know about Berengaria. Interesting woman, very interesting."

"*You* would know about her, of course, dear Woodrow," Lacey murmured. "Woodrow reads history by the hour. Indeed, he reads little else."

"Don't find anything else as interesting, my dear," her husband said. "Still, that Berengaria. She was a sort of enigma. Tragic, really, I'd say."

"Oh?" Alida was curious. "How so?"

"Well, she was a Spanish princess. Navarre, she was from, and Richard married her, then promptly went off crusading and fighting wars and who knows what all. Neglected her rather badly, you now."

Alida's mouth tightened under her mask. "No," she said, her voice a bit hard, "I didn't know."

Woodrow Delaney went on, caught up in his subject and oblivious to the tone in her voice. "Yes, yes, he did. Of course, he wanted an heir, you know, kings always do, and when she didn't give him one, well, I suppose he lost interest. She never had any children. Rather sad, Berengaria. Course, 'twasn't her fault, most likely. Most believe Richard wasn't interested in women anyway, that he was--"

"Woodrow," Lacey patted his arm. "Not a topic for public conversation, dear, really."

"Oh. Oh, yes, you're right, m'love. Can't discuss those things in public."

Alida's mouth had become a thin white line, and she turned now to Jessalyn, her eyes furious behind the mask, and said, "I'm not feeling quite well, Jessalyn, could you come with me please?"

Jessalyn murmured, "Of course," and turned to follow Alida who was hurrying from the room.

In a small study off the ballroom, an enraged Alida slammed the door, ripped off her mask, and screamed, "How dare you do this to me!"

For a moment, Jessalyn was too astonished to speak, and then in as calm a tone as she could manage, she asked, "Do what, Mrs. Fitzhugh? I've no idea what you mean."

"Do what, indeed! You do know! You planned it! You're jealous and you wanted to make me look the fool! I know you did!"

"Mrs. Fitzhugh, I haven't the faintest idea what you're talking about."

"Do you think I'm entirely stupid? You tricked me into coming here as a-a-a barren, cast-off queen, that's what you did! You wanted me to look ridiculous in front of all these people! You're nothing yourself, and you wanted me to look like nothing, too! You--you vicious little wretch!"

Alida had had several drinks and she was screaming, not even aware of what she was saying, just furious and vengeful.

Jessalyn shook her head. "You're imagining things, Mrs. Fitzhugh. First of all, I didn't even know those things about Berengaria, and no one else did either, except Woodrow Delaney. I only knew who she was, that's all. Most people don't even know *that*, as you saw for yourself. Besides, why should it matter to you? Simon Alderly told me someone always shows up as Anne Boleyn, and her husband murdered her, for heaven's sake."

But by now, Alida had worked herself into such a fury that she was shaking and far beyond reason. "You lie! You did it on purpose! You sneaky little baggage! You wanted me to look the fool! I could kill you! Don't you know who I am, you stupid little ninny? I'm the daughter of an earl, you ignorant hussy!"

Stung past caution by the injustice and idiocy of the attack, Jessalyn finally snapped. "So what, Mrs. Fitzhugh? I'm the daughter of a duke, for all that I was born on the wrong side of the blanket, and what good has the fact of our birth done either of us?"

Alida, angry and incoherent, screamed and spun around, looking for something, anything. Outside, someone was pounding on the door. Alida's eye fell on an object on one of the small tables, a heavy brass unicorn, and she grabbed it and raised it over her head to hurl it at the young woman. Jessalyn had moved over to open the door, and as Alida released the unicorn, two things happened. Just as the unicorn left her hand, Alida screamed, this time not in anger but in fright. Her face went pale, her hands went to her cheeks, and she dropped to the floor in a dead faint. The other thing was that the unicorn, on a path to Jessalyn's head, was blocked by the door she flung open, and it smashed against that door, leaving splinters and a dent in the center panel.

Jessalyn rushed to Alida's side, cradled her head in her lap, and alternately slapped her cheeks and chafed her wrists. By this time, Dominick was in the room, and several of the others crowded in behind him. Lacey Delaney rummaged in the desk for smelling salts, and Alida began to come around, muttering, "It was awful, horrible, his--he was--face was purple--red hair--face all twisted--could see right through him, could see right through--"

Dominick looked at Jessalyn, puzzled, but she shook her head in answer to his unspoken question. "There was no one else in here, only the two of us. There was no one in a costume or a mask like that."

"Then she must be, um, delirious," he said. Some of the others glanced at each other. "Lacey, where can we put her to bed?"

"This way," she said. "Come with me."

Dominick scooped up the dazed Alida and followed Lacey. Jessalyn slipped out, and skirting the edges of the ballroom, found her way out onto the terrace and then into the garden. She moved away from the torch-lit area into the darkness, and when she came upon a table with chairs under some trees, she sat down and leaned her head on her hand.

What had happened in there, she asked herself. What had caused Alida to scream and faint? And what good fortune had kept her from being hit by that unicorn? At the distance, she could hardly have missed being struck, and considering the damage the object did to the door, she'd have been damaged rather severely herself. The unicorn had been heavy, with sharp edges and points, and she shuddered when she thought of it.

She was still sitting in the chair when a figure moved out of the shadows toward her.

"Jessalyn?"

"I'm over here, Dominick."

Dominick seated himself in the chair opposite her and said, "What happened in there, anyway?"

She sighed. "To be honest, I'm not sure I know. She was furious at me, screaming that I'd tricked her into dressing as a barren, cast-off queen, that everyone was laughing at her. It was absolutely untrue, but I couldn't begin to reason with her. She was almost hysterical."

"I'm familiar with the state. Her sister was quite the same."

"At any rate, she was quite wrong. I didn't know any of those things Woodrow said about Berengaria. Not any of them."

"Good lord, who does? Woodrow has a fascination with the backwaters of history. He delights in collecting odd bits of trivial information. No one knew those things. And what difference would it have made if they did?"

"I've no idea. As I said, she seemed quite irrational to me."

"Hmm." She could not see his face in the darkness. She could see only a faint glow of the white of his shirt. He was silent for a moment, then asked, "What's this about a redheaded man? She keeps mumbling about someone. Do you know anything about that?"

"Nothing. Absolutely nothing. There was no one else there at all. Only the two of us, and then she threw the unicorn and screamed and... Oh! Oh, my! Oh, no, it isn't possible! Those things don't happen!"

Had he been able to see her face, he'd have seen all the color drain from it, would have seen her eyes widen as a sudden thought occurred to her, as she heard a voice in her head saying, "...I'll stick around and keep an eye out for you..."

"What is it? What's the matter?"

"No  Nothing. Nothing at all. I have to go now. I have to get back inside, back to the light--"

She stood, and he sensed, if he couldn't see, her agitation.

She turned to go, but he grabbed her and spun her about to face him, barely able to make out her face in the gloom. "Tell me what's the matter. You're acting as touched as Alida."

She closed her eyes and he could feel her body shaking under his hands. "No, no! I can't! It's just a bad, bad memory, that's all! It really has nothing to do with any of this. I can't tell you!"

"Whatever it is, it's gone now. You don't have to be frightened. It's over. I'm sending Alida back, and that will be the end of most of this."

Impulsively, he pulled her to him, his arms about her, holding her body to his in an effort to sooth her, to stop the trembling.

They stood there a moment, and then his hand moved up to smooth her hair, to touch her cheek. Almost without thinking of what he was doing, he tilted her face to his and bent to kiss her, feeling the warmth of her, the sweetness of her. He lingered over her lips, kissed her eyes, her face; he murmured her name against her skin and held her as if afraid to let her go.

For a moment she clung to him, feeling her body glow in response to his touch, feeling momentary release from the cold loneliness in which she'd lived for so long. But images flooded her mind, killed the joy she wanted to take in this moment: images of her mother, of the duke, of Aurore--images of betrayal and loss--and she twisted from his arms and fled into the darkness.

He didn't follow her. He watched her go, bitterness filling him, until, unable to bear the feeling of despair that rushed into the void she'd left, he cursed and smashed his fist into a tree, tearing the flesh of his knuckles. He felt the pain almost with pleasure; at least it turned his mind from the sense of terrible loss that threatened to suffocate him.

Other eyes watched her go, also. Lacey Delaney, on her way to find Dominick to tell him that Alida had dropped off to sleep--with the help of a dram of brandy--saw Jessalyn run toward the house, heard the muffled curse and the sound of the blow, and smiled to herself. Ahh, she thought. Trouble in paradise, Dominick? Whatever has come between you and your young bride? With any luck, she thought, this marriage will be no more successful than your last. First, we'll have to see to getting rid of that sot of a sister-in-law of yours, then we'll see what can be done about the young wife. Dear Dominick. How silly of you to have scruples about such things as your wife or my husband. I've absolutely none, actually. And I do intend to have you. With your wife--or without her, it really doesn't matter. I *shall* have you. And no wide-eyed child of a bride will stand in my way, either.

\*       \*       \*       \*       \*

George Douglas sat at the table in the large kitchen and stirred his coffee thoughtfully. From time to time he glanced at his wife. She had her back to him, and occasionally she muttered something to herself. She looked worn, Marguerite did, and there were dark circles under her eyes.

"You still having bad dreams?" he asked.

She nodded. "Uh huh. Now and then."

"Huh. Looks like mostly *now*."

"Last night was bad."

"I guess so. I looked up once, saw you standing out on the front. You talkin' about it?"

"No need. Same thing."

"Tell me anyway."

She sighed deeply. "Nothing I can tell about, really. Just something very bad, George. People crying, people screaming, bad things happening. Something terrible is coming, and I don't know how to try to stop it."

"If you knew, could you stop it?"

"One time I did. I told a woman I dreamed her house on fire, her in it. She believe me, she leave the house, and sure enough, it burn, but she didn't."

Her husband shook his head. "Nothing you can do, Marguerite. Nothing you can do till it happens, or till you see more."

"Bad for all of us. Just bad. That's all I know."

"You think Mr. Reynolds been expecting something bad, too? He sure been acting strange lately."

"How?"

"Well, near as I can put it, right after carnival, he start acting like he running away from something. Miss Jess and him don't act like they hardly know each other. Mr. Reynolds been working like the devil after him."

"I don't know. That carnival party of Delaneys', that when Miz Fitzhugh have that falling-down fit."

"Yeah. That is one mean woman. I heard from Louis, that butler of Delaneys', she tried to kill Miz Jess. Louis said she threw something at her, nearly hit her with it."

Marguerite shuddered. "I feel just a whole lot better soon as that Fitzhugh woman leave this place. She never bring nothing good with her. Neither one of them sisters bring nothing good to this place."

"I know. Aurore call them the Ugly Twins."

At the mention of her foster daughter's name, Marguerite stared off into space, frowning. "They ugly on the inside, that for sure." She said. "They not ugly enough on the outside, that one thing upset Aurore."

"Why do you say so?"

"Aurore fancies being the only beauty around here. That why she started to hate Miz Jess so much."

George looked surprised. "She hate Miz Jess? How come? She got nothing to be jealous about that skinny little girl."

Marguerite's mouth twisted into a wry smile. "You taken a good look at that 'skinny little girl' lately? She turn into one beautiful lady."

"I guess. She still a tad skinny for my taste."

"Good thing she not too skinny for Mr. Dominick, that one thing that upset Aurore."

"What for? Aurore got nothing to do with Mr. Dominick."

His wife sighed. "George, sometimes I think you half blind. Aurore been following Mr. Dominick around looking like a sick calf since she been old enough to know he a man, she a woman."

"Huh," George snorted. "I put a stop to *that*. What good that gonna do her? I won't have no daughter of mine be a--a--"

"Watch your language, George."

"All the same," he said, angry now, "Mr. Reynolds is a rich man. Rich men pay attention to servant girls for just one thing. Then she not be fit for marrying anybody else."

"True, but she don't think that way. She know his wife dead a long time, she know he not sleeping with Miz Jess--"

"He's not? How do you know? Why not?"

"Who know? But the maid who keeps their rooms swears it, and I got no reason to doubt it. Anyway, Aurore figure one day, he look around, see she turned into a woman, and think maybe he *need* a woman. She gonna be ready if he ever look at her."

"That is stupid!" George spat. "I don't want her to be a--a toy for some white man. Even for Mr. Reynolds. I want her to get married, have babies, do something we don't have to be ashamed for her."

"Don't mean much what *you* want, George. Don't mean much what *I* want. Aurore only interested in what *she* want. She been that way, always, even when she one tiny baby. You know that."

George slumped a bit and set his coffee cup down. Then he looked up and said, "I know that. Think it do any good to get her married? Two or three been asking. She past old enough."

"No. I think she either refuse to do it, or do it, then run away. Either way, we still have a problem." She turned toward the door that Jessalyn had just entered. "Morning, Miz Jess. You have a good walk this morning?"

Jessalyn managed a faint smile. "Oh, yes. A good walk. I saw a parrot this morning."

"Ah." George smiled at her. "Hardly see those any more so close to the house. They mostly moved back in the jungle now."

Mr. Dominick wasn't the only one who had been acting strangely since the party, Marguerite thought. Miz Jess acted like she'd lost her spirit, somehow. She was looking prettier than ever; she had filled out more, the sun had given her skin an apricot blush and her hair golden tones. But she had been spending most of her time alone. She didn't go riding with Mr. Reynolds any more. She had dinner in her room, mostly, and she spent hours reading.

Alida Fitzhugh took to her own room and mostly to her bed. Dominick had tried locking the liquor cabinet, but had given it up as useless. It hadn't even slowed down her drinking, Marguerite knew. Rum was too readily available on this plantation, and rum seemed to make up most of her diet. The trays sent to her room came back nearly untouched. Lady Heloise, intent on doing what she saw as her duty to her niece, knocked on the closed door each day. Some days the maid turned her away. Some days she was admitted, but she usually left in a huff, the sounds of Alida's screams or derisive laughter following her down the hall.

This morning Jessalyn was picking at her breakfast and talking with George when Miriam, Alida's maid, brought her tray back. It appeared untouched.

"What is the matter this time?" Marguerite asked.

Miriam shrugged. "The tea too cold, the fruit too ripe, the toast not buttered right, what could be wrong? Anything, everything. Who knows what that woman think?"

Marguerite shook her head. "No way to please that woman."

Aurore had entered the kitchen in time to hear the last exchange. "She just like her sister. No way to please her either. She so miserable all the time, she better off dead. This one the same."

"Aurore! You watch what you say!"

"Well," Aurore muttered. "it's true, just the same. She glanced over at Jessalyn. "Miz Jess know. That woman try to kill her."

"Oh, I wouldn't say--"Jessalyn began.

"You hush up, Aurore," her mother said. She was genuinely angry now, and Aurore dropped her eyes. Marguerite was seldom this angry with her.

"Everybody say so," the girl mumbled.

"Let me take the tray up to her, Marguerite," Jessalyn said. "She needs to eat something. She can't just stay in her room drinking all the time."

"Don't know if you can do anything, Miz Jess," Miriam said. "You know how she is."

"Besides," Marguerite said," it's not fit, you carrying trays up, Miz Jess. You the *maitress*. That's a maid's job."

"Then Miriam can carry it, if that will please you. I'm going to see to the breakfast, anyway."

Jessalyn prepared the tea, making sure it was quite strong and very hot. She trimmed and buttered the toast herself. She chose the fruit--a fresh mango--and peeled and sliced it precisely. Then she and Miriam left with the tray.

Alida looked up from the bed as they entered. She looked terrible. She had dark circles under her eyes, she was thin, and her hair hung limply about her face.

"What are you doing here?" she snapped. "And why are you bringing this tray? I sent this mess back to the kitchen once."

"This, Mrs. Fitzhugh, is an entirely new and fresh mess," Jessalyn said lightly, spreading the napkin for her. "I made the tea myself, I buttered the toast, I sliced the fruit. It's as nearly perfect as I could make it, and you must eat some of it or the chances are excellent that you will reduce yourself to such as state that you'll be prey to the fever."

"The fever?"

"Tropical fever." She wasn't sure precisely what she was talking about, but she knew for a fact that Alida didn't either, so she went on. "It's quite devastating. I've heard it can turn one's hair white in a week."

Alida touched her hair unconsciously, as if checking to see whether it was turning gray. "Women are especially susceptible to it, isn't that right, Miriam?"

Miriam nodded gravely. "Awful for women," she murmured, going along with Jessalyn.

"In fact," Jessalyn continued, "it can age a woman ten years, I've heard." Alida sat up, more attentive. Jessalyn had touched her vanity, and she was responsive now.

"Why should you care whether I get it or not?"

"For the best of selfish reasons, Mrs. Fitzhugh. You are scheduled to leave for England in two weeks. I would hate for anything to interfere with your departure. You might not miss with whatever was at hand next time."

"Hah!" Alida snorted. "I'll say this for you; you are honest."

"Besides, it's in your best interests," Jessalyn continued. "You came here for my husband, and you'll certainly not charm him looking like that."

Alida snatched the mirror from her bedside and surveyed herself. She frowned at the reflection. "Why do you care? You certainly don't want me taking him, do you?"

"Of course not," Jessalyn said. "But you can hardly even put up a fight like that. We might at least make it competitive--in the time you have left."

Alida's eyes narrowed. "With any luck, I might even arrange for an extension of my visit," she said, "and see whether I can offer your husband what you--so far--have not."

Jessalyn lowered her eyes, then raised them and smiled at her adversary. "You might be surprised what has gone on during your--illness, Mrs. Fitzhugh."

Alida looked at her sharply, but Jessalyn rose and went to the door. "Do finish your breakfast, Mrs. Fitzhugh," she said sweetly. "Dominick hates bony women. At least, that did get *our* marriage off to a slow start."

She opened the door and started out, and Alida called to her, "Just a minute. I'd been meaning to ask you something."

Jessalyn paused.

"You said something to me--I didn't remember it until later--the night of our little, umm, contretemps, about your father having been a duke. Do you want to explain that?"

Jessalyn shrugged. Miriam looked at her, wide-eyed. "I'm sorry I said it. It wasn't important."

"It was quite interesting, though. Who was he?"

"I'd rather not say."

"Let's see--not Somerset, not Marlborough, not--wait. Bennington! No wonder that name sounded so familiar! Only it wasn't Cooke. That wasn't right." She frowned and shook her head. "I remember. You're that girl! Only it wasn't Cooke. That's not quite it. It was--it was--"

"Kirke," Jessalyn said.

Alida relaxed, and smiled a sly, insinuating smile "Ah, yes. Quite. Jessalyn Kirke. The talk of England last season. How very interesting to find you here. How did you get here? And how did you manage to acquire Dominick Reynolds?"

Jessalyn drew herself up and managed to look down her nose at Alida quite as if she'd been doing it all her life. "Mrs. Fitzhugh, I've no intention of telling you any of that." And with that, she left the room,

Back in the kitchen, Marguerite asked, "What happen up there?"

"We had a talk. I think she's going to eat something now."

"We'll see. You better look in on that cat of yours. He been underfoot something terrible these days."

"Has he, now? When will he be big enough to leave his mama, Marguerite?"

"He plenty big now. You want to take him up to your room? I get somebody to fix it."

"Do you think I might?" Her face lit up, and Marguerite smiled.

" 'Course you can. Who gonna say no?"

And so she moved Marmles up to her bedroom. Marguerite sent someone to fix a bed for him in a basket, and the cat became her companion and confidant.

During the first night, she was reading in bed after dinner, and Marmles climbed the covers, meowing and crying. She stroked him and offered him bits of bread she'd saved from her dinner, but he wasn't interested. When he tried nibbling at her fingers, she understood what he wanted.

"Milk, of course. I didn't bring any up for you." Milk wasn't readily available on the islands. It soured too quickly in the heat and humidity, and besides, Simon had told her, there was evidence that it carried disease unless you were certain of its origin. Dominick Reynolds kept two cows for milking, though, and Marguerite kept the milk cool with ice to prevent its spoiling.

She got out of bed now and shoved her feet into her slippers and pulled on her dressing gown. "Come on, then," she said to the kitten. "Let's go downstairs and take care of you."

She picked him up and made her way down the stairs, poured his dish of milk, and waited while he drank it. When he was finished, she picked him up and snuggled him to her. He purred loudly and closed his eyes. "Silly kitten," she murmured, and planted a kiss on the top of his head. As she passed the wing to the servants' quarters, she saw a light under Simms' door, and on impulse, she walked down the hall and knocked.

Simms opened the door, her knitting clutched in her hand, and said, "Why, Mrs. Reynolds. Is something wrong?"

"No, nothing. I just had a thought, and I wanted to ask you about it."

"I see. Do come in."

Simms stepped back and she entered the room. It was almost painfully neat and sparsely furnished. That must be by choice, Jessalyn thought. Dominick would give Simms anything she wanted for her room.

There was a rocking chair that was still moving, evidence that Simms had risen from it hurriedly. Jessalyn sat in a straight-backed chair opposite.

"Do take the rocker, Mrs. Reynolds. It's much the more comfortable."

"I couldn't think of it," Jessalyn said. She put the sluggish Marmles in her lap. He curled up, eyes closed. "I thought of something the other day, and I've been meaning to ask you about it ever since." Simms was still standing, her knitting grasped tightly in both hands. "Do sit down and go on with your knitting, Simms. I hate feeling I've interrupted you."

Simms sat down, almost reluctantly, and resumed her knitting, but she seemed ill at ease, almost as if she were sitting at attention. "If I can help you, ma'am..."

"Do you remember the night of Mr. Reynolds' birthday? After the party, when Mrs. Fitzhugh cornered me on the stairs?"

For a moment or two, Jessalyn thought she wasn't going to answer, but after a few seconds, she looked up warily at the young woman, began knitting very rapidly, and said finally, "Yes, I do believe I recall that incident, ma'am."

"Mrs. Fitzhugh was rather badgering me, and you came up behind us and called her name, and she looked almost frightened, then she stopped and went up to her room, just as you told her to do. Why would she do that?"

Simms looked at her once more over her knitting needles, the look impossible to read. "I'm not sure I can answer that, ma'am."

"Oh, I've no doubt you *can,* Simms."

Simms looked at her once more, and then smiled. Jessalyn almost jumped. It was the first smile she'd ever seen on that most immobile of faces.

"I mean, I'm not sure I want to, ma'am."

"I understood that, Simms."

Another long pause. "I've been in service to the Trenton family since I was fourteen years old. Did you know that, ma'am?"

"No. I didn't. I thought you worked for Mr. Reynolds."

"I came out with Mrs. Reynolds--the first Mrs. Reynolds--when she came here as a bride. I'd been with the Trentons since the girls were born."

"I see."

"They were--a different lot, ma'am."

"Were they always as unhappy as Mrs. Fitzhugh seems?"

"Unhappy, ma'am? Angry, more like. Angry from the day they were born. As if they were furious at having had to share the same womb, even. Jealous of each other. What one had, the other had to have the same or better. Never satisfied, either of them. They had the world, I thought, but it wasn't enough. Turned them mean, it did, ma'am. They used to have fights so fierce they'd bring blood, even as babies."

She paused, thinking. "I know you think I'm beating about the bush, ma'am, not answering your question, but I'm just trying to think how to tell it. There's part of it I can't tell. I'm sworn not to. But there's a part of it you can know. Doesn't matter.

"You see, both of the girls had a terrible urge for anything that someone else had that they didn't. They'd nag and coax and make a real fuss until they got it. When they were young--but not children, mind you--quite old enough to know better--they did a vicious thing to someone. A cousin, it was, and I'm the only one who knows they're responsible. It gave me the only power anyone ever had over them, ma'am. I don't push it, but Mrs. Fitzhugh, she knows that I know, and she's not like to fight me." She stopped knitting and looked directly at Jessalyn. "That's all there is, Miss. Not a great deal, but I'm sworn, you know."

"I see. But if they feared you so, why did Mrs. Reynolds bring you out her with her?"

"Smart thing to do, ma'am. Kept me away from those I might have told behind her, and kept me where she could keep an eye on me."

"Then, I suppose--well, I just thought they'd become--cruel as they got older, didn't have life turn out as they'd wanted it. I suppose not, then."

Simms looked over her knitting needles for a long moment, her face expressionless. Then she put the needles down and began to roll up her sleeve. She extended her forearm to Jessalyn, her face still expressionless. Across the inside of her arm was a long, ugly scar.

Jessalyn winced at the sight of the scar and raised a puzzled face to Simms.

"I used to do their hair when they were young girls. I wasn't too adept at it, then, but they were young and their mother thought I was good enough. Adelaide was just a girl, and she was wiggling about, and I made a slip with the curling iron and burned her neck a bit. She screamed at me and grabbed the iron out of my hand. I thought she wanted to do it herself, you know. She heated the iron in the lamp, then she grabbed my arm and pressed the iron to it, held it hard. I screamed. I remember it seemed an age I screamed."

"How *awful*! Did you tell anyone? What happened to her?"

Simms rolled her sleeve back down, buttoned it, and resumed her knitting. "No point, Miss. I needed the job."

"But Simms, how could you stay with her after that? Why would you come here with her?"

"She begged me to come. And Mr. Dominick pays me a salary I couldn't get anywhere else. My sister, her youngsters, depend on the money I send. That's why, ma'am." There was silence between them for a moment. "But I did get my revenge, ma'am, in a manner of speaking."

"How was that?"

"I watched her die the most painful, the worst death I ever hope to see anyone suffer through. She got hers back, in the end, and then some."

"Ahh," Jessalyn sighed. "She died in childbirth, didn't she?"

"Not exactly, ma'am. Indeed that is one of the reasons Mr. Reynolds is so bitter about the marriage, and I suppose, so anxious to be rid of her sister who reminds him of the pain of it."

"What do you mean? Simon Alderly said she miscarried, that she died of it."

"That was the story they put about, ma'am."

"But it wasn't true."

"Not exactly."

Jessalyn was suddenly not sure she wanted to hear, not sure she wanted to know the truth. She had a premonition, a cold chill of misgiving, that there was something almost evil about Adelaide's death.

"Mrs. Reynolds didn't want to have any children, ma'am. She especially didn't want to have Mr. Reynolds' children. She screamed horrid things at him when she learned she was with child. But he was happy about it. He would at last have someone to love, perhaps. She was set on not having it. She did everything the doctor told her not to do. She went to some old witch-woman who gave her a powder to lose it with. That didn't work. It just made her vomit for three days."

"But finally she found a way."

"Yes, ma'am."

"How--what--"

"One of my needles, ma'am."

Jessalyn's hand flew to her mouth. "My god--oh my--"

"She bungled the job, ma'am. She hurt herself, you know, and she bled and bled, and then she got infected, like, and she died a screaming death. It was very ugly, ma'am."

# Chapter Sixteen

THE END OF THE dry season was approaching. "Another month, perhaps two, depends on what sort of year we have," Simon told her, "and we'll be into the rainy season. I suspect it will be on us early this year."

"What makes you think so?" Jessalyn asked.

"I don't know," he said. "Just a suspicion. We've had more rain than usual during the dry season, for one thing. Makes me think we're in for a long rainy season."

Alida Fitzhugh hadn't left yet. In fact, she'd stirred herself out of bed early enough to go riding with Dominick, Jessalyn had noticed, and had managed to convince him to take her on a tour of the little island. Jessalyn had not been invited; she had not expected to be. Dominick had avoided her since the carnival party, treating her with scrupulous courtesy when they had met, but not seeking her out.

She didn't know how she felt about him. She tried not to think of him at all. She'd awakened during the night several times, stirred by a curious longing, an emptiness not accountable by anything she could name, but she tried not to think that had anything to do with him. It couldn't have. It couldn't have.

By the first of April, passage had been set for Alida and Lady Heloise. Jessalyn didn't know how she felt about that, either. Earlier, she'd have said she'd be glad to see the pair go--at least Alida--but now, she hardly cared. Let her stay, let her go. It seemed all one.

She busied herself with reading and with correspondence for Dominick. Most afternoons when there was no rain, she took a book with her into the jungle garden, hiding in the gazebo with table and chairs, reading until tea. That was where Dominick found her when at last he went searching.

The rain had just stopped, and Jessalyn, armed with a cloth to dry her chair, had gone into the jungle garden to her usual place. The birds had begun to chirp again. She could hear a keskeedee bird somewhere in the banana tree that dripped water onto the path. ("Keskeedee?" she'd said to Simon. "That sounds almost like--" "Like 'Qu'est-ce qu'il dit?' "he'd said. "Of course! 'What does he say?' Keskeedee, indeed.") A yellow-tailed cornbird flashed by as she sat down. She took out the flamingo feathers she'd used as book marks since the trip with Simon and put them on the table. She was well into the book when she heard her name spoken.

"Jessalyn?" It was Dominick. She looked up into his face and felt her heart begin to pound. She glanced down quickly, confused and unhappy with herself.

"Oh! Hello. I usually come out here to read during the afternoons. Were you looking for me? I mean, obviously you were." She felt as if she were babbling inanely. "Was there something…"

He sat down in the chair opposite her. "Yes. I did want to talk to you. I mean--you know--I wanted--"

He stopped. Silence hung there, filled only by the noise of the birds. She glanced up at him, caught him looking at her, blushed, and looked away. At last he sighed heavily.

"Jessalyn, " he said softly, "we have to talk."

She didn't look up. "What about?" she asked.

"Jessalyn," he said again, "look at me."

I dare not, she thought, but she raised her eyes to his calm gray ones and felt that curious leap inside her once more. "Jessalyn, this--arrangement we have. We have to talk about it. It simply isn't working out. At least, not for me."

"I see, " she murmured. "And you want me to leave before the year is finished, is that it?"

"No! God, no!" He leaned toward her frowning. "That isn't it at all. It's--I've spent the time since the carnival going over that moment--that pitifully short moment in the Delaneys' garden with you, and I've done everything I can to get it out of my mind, and nothing works.

Nothing, absolutely nothing, makes the slightest bit of difference. I thought, at first, to apologize to you, but I couldn't do that. I wasn't sorry then. I'm not sorry now." His gaze was intense. "What I'm trying to say--" he stopped, stood up, paced back and forth, and finally put his hands on the back of his chair and faced her. "Dammit, I don't know how to do this. How do you propose to a woman who is already your wife? What I'm saying to you is that I want you to *be* my wife-- not just in name. In fact, too."

She stared at him, her hand at her mouth, her eyes wide. She'd not expected this. Quite the opposite. Her first impulse was to throw herself into his arms and cling to him, but she resisted that, for several reasons. Her second was to turn and run, but she resisted that, too. Instead, she sat very still for a moment, frozen under his intense concentration.

Finally she said, "I don't know how to answer you, Dominick."

He sighed and flung himself into the chair, slouching down and glaring at her. "At least you didn't say no. That's something."

"But I might yet. You have to know this. I'm very frightened of you and of this situation."

The breeze ruffled the greenery about them and made a pattern of light and shadows about his face. "It's just that..." she spread her fingers and shook her head. "Dominick, when I was--let's be honest, when I was ugly--" she looked at him straight on, "you didn't even *see* me. You didn't even recognize me as a *person*. Now I look, well, pretty good. And now you profess to love me. But, Dominick, I'm the same *person*. I'm the same woman I was when I was ugly, and you didn't even see me then. How can I believe you love *me*, when you didn't even see the me that was there?"

"Jessalyn," he took her hand. "Jessalyn, you may be right. But how could I have seen the person that was there? I saw you for three days. Maybe the marriage was a hasty venture, but I didn't have time to know you. Would I have loved you before you regained your beauty? I think so. The *you* that I love is so much outside your lovely self that I do think I wouldn't have cared what you looked like. There are lovely women here that I could have married, but none that brought to me what you...what you are, what you bring."

"It's just that...I can't blame you for your failing to love me at first sight, really. I mean, when you stop to think of it, we know so little of each other. It isn't precisely a normal sort of thing, you know, two strangers marrying, and I keep thinking that if you knew me, knew *of* me, you might not like what you know, might not want to be married to someone like me."

"I know more of you than you think," he said. "I know, for instance, that Wilburn Kirke was not your father."

Her mouth dropped open. "You know about that?"

"About Bennington? Yes. I know."

"How?"

"I have agents in England. They made inquiries."

"I see."

"Jessalyn, you're right. This hasn't been a normal marriage. No courtship, no getting to know each other. None of the usual preliminaries. What if we start over? Couldn't we spend some time together? Go on picnics? Ride around the island, do those things for a time? I'm a patient man, Jessalyn, but I do want you. I wish you could try to--to get to know me--to--to--"

"To learn to love you."

"Yes," he sighed as if relieved, and ran his hand through his hair. "Exactly that."

After what seemed to him a very long moment, she murmured, "Perhaps we could try it."

He thought he'd never heard a phrase that lifted his spirits as much as those five short words.

They sat in the bower and talked for a time, and when they finally rose to go in for tea, he gave her his arm and took her book. In the exchange, one of the flamingo feathers was dropped, but neither of them noticed. Someone else did, though. Someone watched them leave, and slipped out, and picked up the flamingo feather, then slipped back into the tangle of green.

Other eyes watched them come out of the jungle garden and were not pleased by the sight. Alida Fitzhugh stamped her foot. One more card, she thought. I have played all my trumps but one, and if that one doesn't work, damn him anyway.

Alida dressed for bed that night with unusual care. She wore a filmy silk gown, cut low in the bodice to virtually bare a pair of smooth, rounded breasts; she had Miriam brush her long dark hair until it hung down her back in a gleaming fall. She slipped on a negligee over the gown and donned satin slippers. Then she dismissed her maid and waited. When the house was quiet and settled for the night, she left her room, looking in each direction, and padded down the hall to Dominick's room. She tapped at the door.

Dominick, stripped to the waist, pulled the door open. He'd been expecting George Douglas, who was commissioned to bring him a snifter of brandy, and he was confused when Alida glided into the room.

"Nick, love, I've got to talk with you."

"Alida, what on earth are you doing here at this time of night?"

"I've come with a sort of--business arrangement, Nick. A proposal of sorts."

"Well, at least let me get my shirt on so we can talk."

"Oh, dear, don't bother." She moved closer to him and ran her hands over his chest. "You look lovely, and besides, I'm hardly dressed for dinner, as you can see."

He saw. She slipped from the dressing gown, and the pale silk of her nightgown concealed almost nothing.

"Alida, I am really not in the mood for this sort of game. Put your dressing gown back on and go to your room. We'll talk in the morning."

"Oh, no." She smoothed her hands over his chest again and around his back, pulling him close to her. "We'll talk now. You know quite well, don't you love, that I don't want to go back to England."

He shrugged and removed her hands. "I really don't see what that has to do with anything, Alida. You're leaving in a week. Arrangements have been made."

"Arrangements--like beds--can be unmade. Suppose we tell your sweet little bride that I'm leaving, and I shall. But I'll only go as far as Trinidad, then I'll take a place and wait for you to come. I simply won't go back."

"What are you talking about?"

"I should think it would be obvious. I have to admit being a mistress is second best to being a wife, but it's better than returning to England. At least, at the moment. As long as you have qualms about putting aside your little wife--untouched though she may be--I suppose I'll have to settle for that."

He closed his eyes and shook his head. "Alida, I don't think you understand. What is between me and my wife is our affair, but keep this in mind: I love her. I love her very much. I will not have any part of an unsavory affair. Do you get that?"

Alida smiled. "Not even if it involves Bellefleur?"

He looked at her. "What did you say?"

"I said, my sweet, simple dear, not even if it involves Bellefleur?"

"How do you mean?"

"I mean just this. I am in a position to acquire Bellefleur for you, or to keep it from you forever. You choose."

It would have astonished a woman as greedy as Alida Fitzhugh to know that there wasn't a second's hesitation in Dominick's thoughts. He had already weighed the possibility of never regaining Bellefleur against the possible loss of Jessalyn, and had decided that nothing was worth losing her, not the house, not anything.

He said, "I've already chosen. Please leave, Alida."

He strode across the room and opened the door, behind which stood a startled Douglas carrying a tray with a snifter of brandy. He took in the scene, then backed up, stammered, and started to go.

"Come in and set the tray on the table, George," said Dominick. "Mrs. Fitzhugh was just leaving."

Alida laughed, a long silvery peal of laughter, and picked up her dressing gown and was gone.

In the room next door, Jessalyn had heard the voices. She couldn't make out what was being said, but she could distinguish Dominick's voice and a woman's tones. She'd seldom heard anyone in the room with Dominick, and she was surprised that the voices carried so clearly through the dressing room door. She stood in the dressing room, curious, and paused to listen. Then, ashamed of herself for eavesdropping, she started out. I've no right to snoop, she thought. It's probably just the maid. But at that moment, she heard the unmistakable sound of Alida Fitzhugh's laughter, and heard Dominick say, "...Mrs. Fitzhugh was just leaving." She closed her eyes and bit a knuckle until she tasted blood--blood and hot, bitter, scalding tears. She stuffed her fist into her mouth to stifle the sound of sobs and went into her bedroom, crawled into her bed, huddled into a corner of it beneath the mosquito netting and cried. She thought that it was the first time since she was ten that she had cried herself to sleep.

In spite of her restless night--or perhaps because of it--she slept later than usual the next morning. When she rose, she looked at her puffy face in the mirror and decided it would never do. She sent to the kitchen for some ice and a pot of tea, and told Simms she wasn't feeling well, and to please tell Mr. Reynolds not to expect her down. She patted the ice on her swollen eyelids, drank the tea, then crawled back into her bed. How do I deal with this, she wondered. What do I do, what do I say? Better nothing, she thought. I'm not committed to anything. Better to say nothing. Let it go by, tell him at the end of the year I've decided to leave, then go. Better that way.

When she thought back on that day--and she was to do so many, many times--it seemed to her somehow ordered and planned, as though everything that happened had been foreordained in some way. Everything seemed to have an inevitability, a purpose, as if the day were moving to a conclusion none of them would have been capable of preventing. Looking back, she would always see herself moving slowly, slowly, as if under water, though she knew that she had not done so, that she had gone about the day with perhaps a bit of lethargy, but no more than that.

She had gone down to tea that afternoon with Simon and Lady Heloise. Dominick had been out, then, and she had been glad of it. "He rode over to Delaneys', " Simon told her. "Something about a shipment Woodrow planned to send on the same ship the ladies are taking back to Trinidad."

Lady Heloise seemed distracted and irritable. She spilled her tea once and then upset the sugar bowl.

Jessalyn was too upset herself to notice much of that, but Simon asked her once if she were all right. "Oh, yes--I suppose. I'm just not myself. I never am when Alida is in one of her moods."

"Moods" was Lady Heloise's euphemism for Alida's screaming, tyrannical rages. Jessalyn looked up at her. "What seems to be the problem today?"

"Oh, dear, I don't know. Whatever is the problem with Alida? I know," she sighed, "that I'm getting old. I know I've never married and that I'm not much use to anyone. Only I do wish she'd leave off taunting me with it." Jessalyn felt sorry for her and reached over and patted her hand.

"You mustn't let it bother you. Everyone knows how she is, you know."

"I should say," Simon murmured.

"I know. And I know most of anyone. Only it doesn't help a great deal, sometimes. Sometimes--sometimes I'd just like to kill her."

"Oh, dear, Lady Heloise," Simon managed a small smile. "You'd have to take your place in quite a long line."

They all laughed, looking about a bit to make certain the wrath of Alida wasn't anywhere near to descend suddenly upon them.

Dominick sent word from Delaneys' that he was dining there and would look in on Jessalyn when he returned. Lady Heloise went to her room, saying that she had a fierce headache and planned to take some of her headache medicine and retire early. Simon went back to his own house. Alida had never come out of her room that day. Jessalyn read for a while, and when dinnertime came, had a light supper sent up, then dressed for bed. She went down to the kitchen once to get some food for Marmles. She'd taken the back stairs in her gown and slippers, and was surprised to find Celestine and Aurore still in the kitchen.

"Hello! What are you two doing still here?"

"We came over to help with the packing for Lady Heloise and--"

"And that ugly old witch up there," Aurore finished.

"You'd best be careful, Aurore," her sister said.

"Ha, careful. She best be careful. Somebody gonna cut her throat someday, everbody gonna cheer. They have a two-day party when the put her in the ground."

"Aurore!"

"What's she done now, Aurore?" Jessalyn asked.

"What she always do. Scream about nothing, about everything. Nobody make her happy, nobody do nothing right. She have a fit because I pack one of her precious dresses wrong, and she so drunk she can't see what I been doing anyway. Somebody gonna put the light on her."

"Aurore!" Celestine hissed. "You watch what you say!"

"Do what to her, Aurore?"

"She don't mean nothing, Miz Jess," Celestine said.

"Oh, I know. She's just angry. But what did she say? Put the light on her? What does that mean?"

The girls looked at each other, and Aurore, sullen, looked down. Celestine waved her hands and tried to laugh about it. "It just a superstition, Miz Jess. That stuff is *obeah* talk."

"Obeah?"

"Yeah, you know, like evil spirits, stuff like that. Papa--George--he said on Haiti they call it voodoo."

"Oh. With witch doctors and like that."

"Yeah, but you know, here, they usually obeah women. They say they give you the evil eye, put a spell on you, stuff like that." She shrugged, trying to pretend it was nonsense, but Jessalyn thought she was cautious about condemning the obeah women. "Anyway, one of the things they do, they got a fight going with you, they write down all the names of the people they want to hurt--kill--whatever, and they put it under the house with a candle on it, lit. The candle burn down, burn part of the paper, or all of the paper. Whoever name is on it, they hurt. Or die, even."

"Oh. And does it really happen?"

The girls looked at each other. "They this woman live up in Charlottesville," Aurore said. "Somebody put the light on her, and the next day a tree fall on her and she never did walk again."

Celestine made a face. "Ah, Aurore, you don't *know* that."

"*I* know it," Aurore said, giving her an angry look. "You know it, too."

"But if the names are burned off, how can you be sure they were on the list?" Jessalyn asked.

"Sometimes you can't. Just find little bits of paper, little candle, you *know*," Aurore said. "Sometimes you can read some of what's left and tell it was *your* name."

"I see." Jessalyn yawned. "Well, I think I'm going to bed. I've not been feeling well today, and besides--"

"Oh, Mrs. Reynolds." It was Simms. "There you are. I've been looking for you. Mrs. Fitzhugh would like to see you in her room."

Aurore rolled her eyes. "Now it be your turn to get yelled at. You tell me, I get obeah woman to take care of her."

Jessalyn laughed. "No need, Aurore. She'll be gone soon enough."

She followed Simms up the back stairs, carrying Marmles. When they reached the top, Simms said, "She's in a foul temper, ma'am. Let me take the cat. She hates cats. I'll put him in your room. And you be careful."

"I shall." She started down the hall, then called Simms back. "Oh, Simms, as long as Aurore and Celestine haven't left yet, would you have one of them make up a couple of limeades and bring them up for me and Mrs. Fitzhugh?"

"I will ma'am, but she'd not drink it. She's been on much stronger drink than limeade."

"Well, at least send one for me, will you?"

"Of course, ma'am."

She knocked on the door of Alida's room and entered when bidden. Alida was lounging on her bed, still dressed, but showing the effects of a daylong drinking bout.

"Siddown, Mrs. Reynolds," she said, waving her arm to indicate the chair beside the bed, slurring her words. Jessalyn thought she had never seen her quite so far gone. She sat down.

"Simms said you wanted to talk to me."

"Umm-hmm. I did. I wanted to tell you I've decided to go home, leave the field to you, dear Jessalyn. I'm not going to take Dominick from you after all."

Jessalyn thought that since her departure was quite eminent, this was hardly striking news, After last night, however, the second part, about Dominick, interested her. "Oh? What made you change your mind?"

Alida shrugged. "Poor performance, actually." Jessalyn stiffened. "I see."

"Instead, I'm going to get revenge on dear old Dominick. Revenge for insulting me. Revenge for killing my poor sister. Revenge for all the Trentons."

"How do you plan to do that?"

"I have my ways," she said with a wobbly smile. "I have my lit-tle ways." She wagged a finger at Jessalyn. At this moment there was a knock on the door, and Alida yelled, "Who's there!"

Jessalyn rose and opened the door and took the tray with the single limeade on it. "It's just Aurore with my limeade," she said. "I wanted a glass before bed."

"Jus' too wonderful, aren't you, dear Jessalyn? Jus' too perfect. Don't even touch spirits. Wonderful woman. Wonderful wife."

Jessalyn set the glass on a table beside the bed. As she did, Alida reached under her pillow and pulled out a silver flask. "Not too wonderful, though. Didn't order a limeade for me. Bad hostess. You're a terrible hostess."

"I suppose. But I didn't think you liked limeade."

"Don't," Alida said as she reached for Jessalyn's glass. "Weak stuff. Trouble is, this wretched rum is so awful, least this last batch Miriam got, needs something to mix it with. I've been using tea all day. This will work better though."

She pulled the glass to her, spilling some of it, then looked at the glass in one hand and the unopened flask in the other, as if puzzled over how to get the contents of the one into the first.

Finally Jessalyn said, "Here. Let me." She took the flask, twisted open the top, and poured a bit into the limeade.

"More," Alida said.

"It's empty, first, and second, you'll have to drink some of the limeade or it's going to spill over."

Alida gulped half the glass, then held it out. "More," she said.

"The flask is empty."

"Decanter's in the dressing room," Alida said. "Fill it up in there."

Jessalyn took the flask, refilled it from the decanter, then returned with the rum and poured part of it into the glass. Alida drank most of what was left.

"You were telling me you'd found a way to get revenge on Dominick," she said.

"Oh, yes. Oh, yes, yes, yes. Get to him, I will. Told him so, too."

"How?"

"Bellefleur."

"Oh?"

"You can't know him very well, Jessalyn, dear, if you don't know what an ob-ob-obsession he has with that place. Don't know why, lord knows, don't know why. But he does. I plan to see that he never gets it. Never. Nevernevernever."

"But why? How?"

Alida seemed to be sinking into a drowsy state, but she roused herself long enough to smile at Jessalyn. "Why? Because he wants it, that's why. I can't have what I want, he shan't have what he wants. And how? Dear Papa. I'll see that dear Papa never gives in. If I have to lie and invent a thousand stories to stir him up. Never give in." She sank back onto her pillow, her eyes closing. "See he never gives in." she mumbled. "Never. Nnn…"

And she was out.

Jessalyn sighed and rose from the chair. She looked around the room. She picked up the glass and started to take it back to the kitchen, but she couldn't find the heart to make that trip down and back once more. Miriam would be in soon and straighten up, anyway. She set it down with the other dishes on a tray, a tea pitcher and other things, and left.

She would remember those details later, and would recall exactly how Alida Fitzhugh had looked, her head lolling on the pillow, would remember where she had put the glass, would recall the details of her conversation at length.

She would have reason to; by morning Alida Fitzhugh was dead.

# Chapter Seventeen

A LIGHT DRIZZLE WAS FALLING during the services, but by the time the mourners gathered at graveside to see Alida Fitzhugh's casket lowered into the ground, the sun was out and birds were chirping. Inappropriate, Jessalyn thought. It should still be gray and gloomy for the funeral. Wrong, somehow, for the weather to clear and be lovely.

She glanced around at the faces of the people she recognized, all wearing proper funereal expressions assumed for the occasion, and she thought that the saddest thing about Alida's death was not the fact of it, but that she was utterly unmourned. Not a soul at the edge of the grave had suffered a real loss with Alida's passing; indeed, there were those who viewed her death with something akin to satisfaction.

Lady Heloise dabbed at totally dry eyes and held a lace handkerchief to her mouth to cover the tight little smile into which her lips had curved. One shouldn't smile at the funeral of one's niece, after all; at least, one shouldn't be *seen* smiling at the funeral of one's niece. Too unfortunate for Alida, but actually, a stroke of some luck for me, Lady Heloise thought. Certainly I can postpone the trip to England for a time. It's rather pleasant here. I'm nothing in England, less than nothing. The sister of a titled man, no husband, no family of my own, no social position to speak of, dependent on someone else for my very existence. At least here the smallest title counts for something, carries some weight. Dominick won't be in such a hurry to send *me* back, now that she's gone. He'll let me stay on for a while, if I just stay out of the way. Maybe I can linger on a bit. Life is certainly nicer here. At least, it will be, without *her.* And it isn't as if Alida didn't deserve what happened...

Margaret Harrington, standing a short distance from Lady Heloise, heard that lady sigh, and took it for a sigh of grief. Too bad for Lady Heloise, she thought. Her own niece, after all. She has undoubtedly taken it hard. It makes me think so much of Adelaide's funeral; it almost could have been...the same people, the same time of year--even Dominick Reynolds looks the same. He looks grim, carved from stone, almost. He wore that same set face at Adelaide's funeral. Adelaide... Alida...the same body, almost. She shuddered. She shifted her weight to her other foot. I do hope this is over soon. I want to get a bite of something to eat. She glanced up at her husband, in attendance today. I wonder if Charles will be so--unfeeling at my funeral. My funeral! The color drained from her face. I shan't die before him, can't possibly, and leave him with that--woman! She looked over at Dominick and Jessalyn Reynolds. Nothing on their faces, either of them. Are they upset? Are they glad? She felt her husband move and heard him clear his throat a bit. Charles would be glad if it were me. She allowed herself the thought for the first time, clearly, admitting to herself the truth about her marriage. He'd be glad, she thought. How did we come to this? He used to love me. He used to think I was so wonderful. How did I get this way? I used to be so pretty...

Lacey Delaney smoothed her black glove over the back of her hand and glanced at Mrs. Harrington. Poor Margaret, she thought. I wonder if Alida Fitzhugh was her friend. She certainly looks as though she's lost one. She really looks more upset than either of the Reynolds. Of course, one can hardly blame Jessalyn. The gossip was that Alida was here to take her husband, and that she did everything she could think of to get him. Hard to tell with Dominick. Does he feel anything? She tucked a wisp of her fair hair back into place. Black is not an unbecoming color for me, actually. I shall not regret having to wear it when Woodrow dies. I wonder how long that will take. He is thirty years older than I am; I should be widowed fairly early. She frowned. Too bad Dominick's bride appears to be so young and so--increasingly--healthy. But perhaps by the time Woodrow goes, he'll have tired of her, and we can work something out...

Susan Newell patted her husband Rufford's arm. A tiny pat,

counseling patience. Rufford hated funerals. He avoided all that were not absolutely necessary for him to attend, but one this close to the Reynolds, their good friends...Susan shook her head over the ironies of life--or, in this case, death. All that nonsense about the good dying young was certainly disproved this time. And in the death of Adelaide, too. A meaner, more selfish pair she'd never run across in her life, and she'd known a few. Hard to mourn when justice seemed to be so very well served. Surely the pious pastor would be quite shocked had she suggested that he stop all that drivel about "the passing of our dear friend and family member" and offer up a prayer of thanksgiving. She'd bet neither of the Reynolds was shedding tears over this; she'd heard stories that the vixen had quite deliberately tried to come between them, and from what she'd seen, she could quite believe it. Indeed, the look on Lacey Delaney's face suggested some satisfaction with the whole situation. Susan had known for some time that Lacey had a yen for Dominick, though so far she appeared to have done nothing about it. Just that look, that hungry, grasping, Lacey look...

The minister's interminable prayer finally drew to a close, and the collective sigh of relief was more felt than heard. Jessalyn moved away from the grave, holding Dominick's arm. She felt only relieved that the service was over; the last two days had seemed an age.

Alida's body had been discovered yesterday morning. Miriam had gone in early to see whether she was waking. She needed to be up earlier than usual to leave for Trinidad, to take the ship to England. The maid had entered the room, had moved about, picking up this and that, anticipating that Alida would stir as soon as she heard her movements. But she had not. That she was still dressed wasn't unusual. When Mrs. Reynolds came out last night, she'd said Alida was quite asleep, and that perhaps Miriam would like to put her into a nightgown. Miriam shook her head. "Unh-uh. Not me. If that other maid wants to, let her. She don't do nothing but curl her hair and fluff her pillow, anyway. I tried changing her once before. It like trying to dress and undress a dead body. She don't seem to care none how she dressed when she had that much to drink." Alida might yell at her in the morning, but she'd yell at her anyway.

Miriam pulled the draperies open, and the moment the sunlight fell across the bed, she knew something was wrong. In the light, Alida looked exactly like what she was--a corpse. Miriam screamed, backed away from the bed, and fled. Simms came rushing up the stairs at her screams and grabbed the hysterical young woman. "What is it?" She shook her shoulders, but Miriam just closed her eyes and continued screaming. "Tell me, you silly girl! Whatever is wrong?"

Finally Miriam gathered enough presence of mind to point to Alida's room, and Simms left her standing where she was and rushed in. Like Miriam, she didn't need a second look to tell her that the woman was dead--and probably had been dead for some time.

Pale and flustered, she hurried from the room. She stopped at the head of the stairs for a moment and stood, her hand on the railing, trying to think what to do. Mr. Reynolds, that was it. She must find Mr. Reynolds.

She went downstairs to his office, but he was gone. She went out to the kitchen where she found Marguerite and Celestine.

"Have you seen Mr. Reynolds?" she asked. They both shook their heads, eyeing her curiously. Simms was nervous, almost frantic, a condition as foreign to her as any that could be imagined. Simms was never upset; she seldom displayed any emotion whatsoever.

"Will you send someone for him, please?" She was almost wringing her hands now. "I--he--it's an emergency, please send for him at once."

Celestine left to send a messenger to the fields, and Marguerite bustled over to the distraught Simms. "Sit down here," she said. "You look like you about to faint. You sit right down. I get you some tea." She pulled Simms over to the chair. The woman looked about as if wondering whether she shouldn't be doing something else, but she sat down, her hands clutching each other tightly in her lap.

"What is the matter?" Marguerite poured the tea and set it beside her. "You look like you seen a ghost."

Simms looked at her quickly, opened her mouth, but nothing came out. Then she shook her head and picked up the cup of tea, holding it between her trembling hands.

By the time Dominick Reynolds arrived, she had regained control of herself, and she took him upstairs to Alida's room.

The doctor was sent for and taken to the bedroom. Shortly after, the constable arrived. The three of them held a conference in Dominick's office, and when they came out, Dominick Reynolds looked grim, the constable had taken over his office, and Alida's body was removed to the doctor's office for an autopsy. By midafternoon, the word had spread throughout the plantation: Alida Fitzhugh had been poisoned.

"Poisoned!" Jessalyn stared at her husband. "How? By whom? When?"

He shrugged. "That's what the constable wants to know. Last night, evidently, apparently by something she drank, but as to the other-- that's the question."

"But--" She sank into a chair. "She was fine when I was with her, and as far as I know, I was the last one to see her. At least, she seemed to have dropped off to sleep when I was there; I poured her some rum. In fact, I refilled her flask for her. I thought at the time that refilling it wasn't the best idea, but--" she waved her hands helplessly--"you know how she could be."

"Yes. I do, indeed."

"Now what?"

"Now the constable will talk to everyone on the place and see if he can come to any conclusions."

"Today?"

"Probably. At least, he'll start today. And he'll probably continue after the funeral tomorrow morning."

"The funeral will be that soon, then…"

"Island law. Burial must take place within twenty-four hours of the death, or as close to that as possible. I'll be sending notes around to all the island families that were acquainted with Alida, informing them of the time of the service."

"I'll help you with the notes, if you'd like."

"Would you? I'd appreciate it."

Writing the notes had taken some time, and when they'd finally finished, Jessalyn had gone out to the kitchen to supervise the preparation of the food. Guests would be coming here after the services tomorrow and refreshments had to be readied for them. It was late when she went to bed, but she'd had some difficulty going to sleep. Who would kill Alida? The thought went round and round in her head, and she considered all those she thought might have motives. Just as she was beginning to doze, the idea popped into her head, awakening her, that the best motive of all belonged to Dominick. If Alida died, she couldn't make good on her promise to keep her father from relinquishing Bellefleur. His was the most obvious motive of all. Though, of course, he wouldn't have. Not if they were having an affair. But were they? That's what Alida seemed to be telling her the night she died, that they were not. And she seemed angry about it. But no--that wasn't what she'd said. She'd said, "…poor performance, actually." Did she mean that in the cruder interpretation, or did she simply mean his behavior? Or was she simply being deliberately mean and misleading? Confusing, she thought. Too confusing. I'll have to wait until the constable sorts it out.

*    *    *    *    *

Walter Rhodes was not happy about having a murder on his small, generally pleasant island. Indeed, when Dr. Lambert had sent for him, he had inquired, rather hopefully, as to whether there had been some mistake. An accident, perhaps? Not likely, the doctor had said. "I suspected it right off," he'd said, "with her so young and no illness reported. But then, the autopsy confirmed it. No question. Poison."

"Umm. What about the glass, the cup, that sort of thing. What did she take it from?"

"That's a strange bit, really. There was nothing there. The servants had gone through, apparently, and cleaned up the dishes, tidied up. There was nothing with any poison in it."

"Drat. Bad luck. I'd like to know what she took it in."

The doctor shrugged. "If the gossip is to be trusted--and I've no reason to suspect that it can't be, in this case--probably in liquor. Evidently, she was quite a tippler."

"Ahh."

The constable sighed. Nasty, he thought. Not something one wants to have to deal with. He was hardly a squeamish man. He was not unused to violence. They didn't happen frequently, but fights among the cane workers did break out on occasion, and one of them would hack another to death with a cutlass, as they called the machetes they used on the sugar cane. But those were open and shut cases, usually, with witnesses and participants who tended to admit freely their parts in the brawls.

But this--nasty business, this. Difficult when it involved a man of Dominick Reynolds' stature. Have to be careful not to step on any toes. He lit his pipe and puffed on it between interviews. Mr. Reynolds himself had been unable to shed any light on the situation. Mrs. Reynolds was said to have been the last person to have seen her, with the exception of the servant who cleared the dishes away. He consulted his notes and frowned. Walter Rhodes was an honorable man, not one to beat about the bush, not one to hush up information just on the basis of a person's name or social position. But he was cautious, too. No point to blacken the reputation of a respected citizen without proof. No point in making unnecessary enemies of those with influence. Caution, he thought. That was the key word.

He had taken Dominick Reynolds' office to use during his interviews, and he was seated behind the desk, making notes. As Jessalyn Reynolds entered, he glanced up, began to make the obligatory half rise, looked again, and stood up, watching her as she came in. He'd not seen the new Mrs. Reynolds, and she was not at all what he'd expected. The former Mrs. Reynolds was small and dark haired. The new one was tall, fair, her golden hair coiled in a braid on the back of her neck, her blue eyes direct under dark brows. A lovely woman. Very lovely, he thought.

"I'm Jessalyn Reynolds," she said. "I believe you'd asked to see me."

"Yes--oh, yes, Mrs. Reynolds. Indeed. Right. If you'll just be seated, please."

She spread her skirts and sat down in a chair opposite.

"Now. Um, let me see. Your husband said that you were the last to see Mrs. Fitzhugh, is that right?" He looked at her over the rims of his glasses.

"As nearly as I know. I was in her room last night, and I left after she fell asleep. At least, I thought she had fallen asleep."

"Suppose you tell me the circumstances under which you last saw her."

Jessalyn related to him the events of the previous evening, avoiding as best she could references to Dominick. When she had finished, he nodded and looked over his notes. "You say she poured the rum out of a flask into the limeade?"

He looked up at her and she nodded.

"Mrs. Reynolds, I've heard it mentioned that Mrs. Fitzhugh--ahh, how shall we put it?--rather enjoyed spirits, shall we say."

Jessalyn looked at him. "She drank quite a lot, if that's what you mean."

"Where did she get the rum she was drinking?"

"As I said, from a flask."

"No, I mean, who filled her flask?"

"Usually, the maid did it, although I did it the last time."

"You?"

"Yes. You see, I'd sent for the limeade, as I told you, and she wanted to have it to mix with her rum. She said it was not very good rum, that she wanted to have something to drink it with. Only, she ran short, so I refilled it for her from a decanter in her dressing room."

"Umm. Where are the flask and the decanter now?"

"In the room, I suppose. I haven't seen them since night before last."

"No. They weren't there. I looked and I sent one of my men to look, but there was nothing there. No spirits of any sort in the room."

Jessalyn frowned. "That's strange," she said. "But you might check with Mrs. Simms. She'd be the one who'd know if anyone had put them away."

"Ah, I see. Yes, I'll do that. Mrs. Reynolds, by the way, did you taste the limeade at all?"

"No, I had no chance."

"Did Mrs. Fitzhugh remark on the strange taste, anything like that?"

"No, but then, she'd had quite a lot to drink, as I said, and if she tasted anything odd at all, she probably attributed it to the rum. She'd already said that was bad."

When she left the room, Rhodes puzzled over his notes. Strange about that flask. The girl Miriam had mentioned it too, but it hadn't been anywhere in the room when he'd searched. He and his man and the doctor had been very careful to search for anything into which poison could have been placed, anything that might have contained a liquid. Important to find that. Did the poison come from the flask? Or from the decanter of rum? Or was it in the limeade brought up from the kitchen? The flask was the most likely source, he thought. Or the decanter. Had it come in the limeade, he'd have to assume that it had been intended for Mrs. Reynolds. Still, there was no indication that she had any enemies waiting to do her in. Mrs. Fitzhugh, by contrast, had enough enemies that he might pick and choose among them.

Still, if it had been the flask, rather than the bottle, that would clearly point the finger at Mrs. Reynolds, who, by her own admission, had filled it last. Curious. Quite curious. He made a note to himself to ask Dominick Reynolds where the decanter of rum had come from.

The more he proceeded with the questioning, the more questions he raised. Simms acknowledged the dead woman's possession of a flask, but denied having seen it since her death. She produced the decanter that had been in the room, now washed thoroughly clean.

Lady Heloise refused to admit that dear Alida had ever tasted a drop of anything stronger than the occasional sherry, but the constable discounted that. In addition to Jessalyn, Simms and other members of the staff confirmed the victim's drinking habits.

Celestine, daughter of the cook, said that she had made the limeade and that her sister Aurore had taken it upstairs.

When Aurore entered the room, the constable thought that she was quite as lovely in her own way as Mrs. Reynolds--if one appreciated that native sort, of course. The girl sat down opposite him, her hands in her lap, quite composed.

Yes, she had taken the limeade to Mrs. Fitzhugh's room. No, she was not aware of any flask. No, she hadn't let the limeade out of her sight from the time Celestine made it until the time it reached Mrs. Reynolds' hands. No she hadn't noticed anything peculiar about it.

When he came to his question as to whether she knew of any reason that someone might want to kill Mrs. Fitzhugh, she threw back her head and laughed out loud.

"I should say I do. I can tell you ten, fifteen people not a bit sad that lady dead."

"Well, I gather from my talks with some of the others that Mrs. Fitzhugh was not the most popular woman about. Can you be more specific?"

"Oh, sure. Me, for one. I hate that woman very much, I tell you.

She yell at me, she call me a slovenly hussy--she had no call. No call to do that. I not too sad to see her dead."

"Well, I must say--"

"I not kill her," Aurore shrugged, "but I got no reason to be sad, either. You take Lady Heloise, now. That lady, poor thing. Miz Alida say mean things to her, oh, yes, she say the meanest things about how Lady Heloise a poor relation, not worth nothing, all that. I bet Lady Heloise not too sad herself."

"Interesting."

"And Mr. Dominick--he hate her so much he hurry up, marry Miz Jess so he wouldn't have to marry up with Miz Alida."

Rhodes blinked. "What do you mean?"

"I mean, he hear that Miz Alida coming down here, had her head set to marry up with him. He say, huh, he married to her witch sister, he not gonna marry her. So he quick marry Miz Jess. She just s'posed to be the secretary."

"How do you know these things?"

She shrugged. "I hear things. You know."

"Um. Go on."

"Bet Miz Jess happiest of anybody to see her dead. She give Miz Jess one bad time."

"How was that?"

"She say she above Miz Jess, you know? Miz Jess not from the society like she was. She say Miz Jess beneath her. She told Miz Jess she gonna take Mr. Dominick, that she don't care if she married to him or not, she gonna have him. In fact, I know for certain-sure that she in Mr. Dominick's room one night. I saw her come out."

"Do you think Mrs. Reynolds knew about that?"

"Don't know how she could help it if she got ears to hear. Miz Alida got real loud when she had one, two drinks. Which was about always. If I been Miz Jess, I be real mad."

"Um, yes, I can see how you would." His mind was racing over the possibilities. Jessalyn was the last person to see Alida Fitzhugh alive. The opportunity. She might suspect her of having an affair with her husband. The motive. And the weapon--poison was typically a woman's weapon. Men tended to do violent murders--guns, knives, strangulation, that sort of thing. Might he be able to prove any of this?

Would it be possible to tie her to Alida Fitzhugh's death? Right now he merely looked up and said, "Than you. I suppose that will be all, then." And Aurore left the room.

When he wandered out of the office in search of Dominick Reynolds, he was alternately cheered and frustrated. As a constable, as the representative of the law on Tobago, he must, of course, find the murderer. Or murderess. He would be gratified to find that person so quickly. Still, he would much prefer that it not be young Mrs. Reynolds. She was not at all the sort he'd wish to find guilty of a crime. What a pity that wicked Mrs. Fitzhugh had to be the victim instead of the perpetrator. From what he knew of her, he'd not regret having to send *her* to the gallows.

He found Dominick Reynolds in the drawing room. "Ah, Mr. Reynolds. Could I speak to you for a moment?"

"Certainly."

"I want to ask where you keep your rat poison."

The constable had not asked whether the planter kept the poison; the rodent population was a constant problem on Tobago. All planters kept a supply of poison and of cats to deal with rats and mice.

"Back of the kitchen in a pantry."

"Could you show me, please?"

"Of course."

He led the constable through the kitchen to the back pantry and reached up to a shelf to remove a container. He opened it, displaying the poison to Rhodes. "This what you're looking for?"

"Um. Indeed." He looked about the room. Small, windowless pantry. Typical. Containers sealed, metal mostly, to keep insects and rodents out. A rodent would be in for it if he found that container, he thought. He looked on all the shelves, not certain what, if anything, he was looking for. He poked among the boxes and finally ran his hand along the shelf on which the container of poison had set. Nothing, He did the same with all of the other shelves. Finally, he sat back on his haunches and ran a hand under the edge of the shelves along the floor. "Hello. What's this?"

Just under the edge of the bottom shelf, a trace of something pink. He picked it up. "A feather. Flamingo feather, from the looks of it. Your cook in the habit of keeping flamingos for pets, Reynolds?"

"I couldn't say. She keeps almost everything else."

"Where might this have come from, do you think?"

Dominick Reynolds opened his mouth to say I don't know, when suddenly, he realized he *did* know. He could remember quite clearly a day in the jungle garden, Jessalyn, a book--and two flamingo feathers she had used as bookmarks.

"It could have come from almost anywhere," he said finally.

"Odd, though, finding a flamingo feather in the pantry. I say," he stepped into the kitchen and spoke to Marguerite. "I found this in the pantry just now." Marguerite looked up at him and squinted across the room. "Do you have any idea what it is? Or where it came from?"

Marguerite came over slowly, wiping her hands on her apron.

"Uh. I know *what* it is," she said, taking it from him. "Flamingo feather. What I don't know is, how that thing get in my pantry."

"Mr. Reynolds and I were wondering the same thing. Anyone around here have a flamingo for a pet?"

"Huh." Marguerite looked at him as if she'd hardly heard such a stupid idea. "Nobody have a *flamingo* for a pet." She went back to the bread she was kneading. "In fact, only time I ever saw one of those feathers was when Miz Jess had one."

"Mrs. Reynolds?"

"Uh-huh. She probably dropped that one in there."

"What makes you say that?"

"She in and out of that pantry a lot, for one thing. That where she kept Marmles till he got big enough to take upstairs."

"Marmles?"

"Her cat. I had an old cat, had kittens a while back. Kept 'em in that pantry. Miz Jess in and out a lot."

"I see."

"She probably dropped it in there."

Walter Rhodes looked at Dominick Reynolds and saw that the man's jaw was clenched and the scar across his face stood out with white clarity against his tanned skin. Interesting. I'd bet almost anything that he thought of his wife's bookmark, too. Aloud he said, "Reynolds, let's go back into the office, shall we?"

In the office, Rhodes sat behind the desk again, and Dominick sat across from him.

"Just a couple of questions I wanted to ask you here," he said. "Did you remember your wife having that feather?"

"When Marguerite pointed it out, I did recall, yes."

"Why do you suppose you didn't remember sooner?"

Reynolds shrugged. "I suppose it just didn't make much of an impression on me. Bookmarks are not a major part of my life, you know."

"Um. One other thing. Were you having an affair with Mrs. Fitzhugh?"

"Good god, no! I couldn't stand the woman."

"I can appreciate that, but do you think your wife had any reason to believe you were?"

"If I understand correctly what you're getting at, constable, let me assure you that jealousy is in no way a factor in this situation."

"Can you be absolutely certain of that?"

"I believe so."

"Um. Would you fetch Mrs. Reynolds and bring her to the office, please? I'd like to talk to both of you."

When Reynolds ushered his wife into the library, Rhodes glanced up at the pair and frowned. There was something, he thought, odd about the two of them together. Something--not quite right, It wasn't as if they were unkind to each other. Perhaps just the opposite. They seemed somehow--uncomfortable with each other. Not at all like a married couple, he thought. Not even like a newly married couple. They were almost afraid to touch each other. More like a recently introduced couple, who, while attracted to each other, are not yet friendly enough or well enough acquainted to feel at ease together. Strange, he thought. Most couples seem more relaxed than they, even during their courtships.

"Mrs. Reynolds." She looked up at him, her gaze direct, unintimidated. If she's the one, he thought, she's extraordinarily cool about it. "There are a few aspects of this case that are confusing to me, and I called you back to see if you could help clarify a few things."

"Certainly, if I can."

"You were, by your account and everyone else's, the last person to see Alida Fitzhugh alive."

"I believe so."

"Further, you admit administering the drink that probably contained the poison, am I correct?"

"What do you mean, 'admit'?" Dominick interrupted. "You make it sound as if she's trying to hide something."

"Sorry. Just a phrase. You did pour the drink, am I right?"

"I suppose so. I poured the last drink she had."

"Mrs. Reynolds, did you have any reason to believe that Mrs. Fitzhugh was having an illicit affair with your husband?"

She opened her eyes wide, her mouth opened as if she were going to say no, but nothing came out. She hesitated. Then she said, "I'm not quite sure I know what you mean."

"Quite simple. Did you believe your husband was having an illicit affair with Mrs. Fitzhugh? What is it that you don't understand about that question?"

"Now see here, Rhodes--"

"Quiet please, Mr. Reynolds. I've asked your wife."

"I--I--I don't know," she finally whispered.

"I've told you before, Rhodes, I couldn't bear the woman. I was not having any sort of affair with her. I didn't even like her."

"That's not the question, Reynolds. The question is whether your wife believed that you were. I think she did."

"That's nonsense, at any rate, Rhodes. It wouldn't matter whether she thought I was having an affair or not. Frankly, our marriage was an arranged marriage, a marriage of convenience. Purely a business arrangement. She wouldn't care whether I had a dozen affairs."

Rhodes glanced at Jessalyn Reynolds. For the briefest moment, she looked so incredibly stricken that he thought she might cry, but the expression passed, and she merely looked at her hands. How could anyone have a "marriage of convenience" with a woman like that! How could he keep his hands off her--well, he thought, none of my business at any rate. He said only, "Is that true, Mrs. Reynolds?"

"Yes," she murmured. "It was a business arrangement." Her voice was so low he could barely hear her and she said the words as if by rote.

"Um. Well." He leaned back in the chair and tossed his pencil on the desk. "Quite frankly, I don't have enough evidence of any sort to justify an arrest, but I must be honest with both of you. If I were to make an arrest at this moment, you would be my prisoner, Mrs. Reynolds."

She looked up, startled. "I? But I didn't kill her! I had no reason!"

"That remains to be seen. You had the opportunity, which you've freely admitted. You had the means--we've found this quite near the poison." He held out the flamingo feather.

"My bookmark!" she said.

"And it may well be that you had the motive. However, given the nature of the victim, I freely admit that there may have been others with motives, too. Still--and this is quite unscientific, you know-- poisoning is the sort of thing women do. Men don't use poison often. Violent murders are more their style."

She seemed to slump a bit. "I didn't do it," she said, and he thought there were tears in her eyes. "I didn't kill her. I never even considered such a thing."

He rose from behind the desk and came around to hand her his handkerchief, his expression not unsympathetic. "I do hope not, Mrs. Reynolds. I certainly hope not."

"What are you going to do now?"

"Wait. I have more inquiries to make. Meanwhile, don't leave the island, will you? I'd like to be able to reach you if I need to."

# *Chapter Eighteen*

WHEN WALTER RHODES LEFT, Jessalyn started up the stairs to her room, climbing slowly, weighted down with the burden of her feelings.

"Jessalyn."

"Yes?" She stopped, but she didn't look back at Dominick Reynolds.

"Please come back. I want to talk to you."

"I don't want to talk to *you.*"

He bounded up the stairs after her. "I *need* to talk to you. I need to explain."

"You don't have to explain to me. Ours is a business arrangement. Nothing in the contract says that you have to explain your actions to me."

"Damn you!" His face was dark with anger, the muscle in his jaw throbbing with controlled fury. "Don't you understand?"

"Apparently not." She started up the stairs again, but he grabbed her arm and pulled her up the steps behind him.

"I refuse to talk to you on the stairs where all the servants can hear. Come with me."

He almost dragged her into his room, then he slammed the door behind her and spun her around to face him. "Listen to me. I was not having an affair with Alida Fitzhugh. I despised Alida Fitzhugh. I despised her sister, and I was married to her. I'd have sooner crawled into bed with a snake. Do you understand that?"

"But she said--"

" 'She said, she said.' Alida Fitzhugh was incapable of telling the truth; don't you realize that? Didn't you learn anything about her in the time she was here?"

"It wasn't just that." She was frightened now. He was holding both her wrists so tightly that she couldn't move, and she couldn't think with him this close to her. "I heard you. I heard you in here one night."

"What did you hear?"

"I--I--heard voices, and I heard her laugh, and I thought--"

"That I'd invited her, is that it?"

"Or at least that you'd accepted her."

He looked down at her, silent for a moment. Then he said, in a different sort of voice, "Were you jealous?"

"I--it was just that--after you'd said to me--"

"Said what?"

"You *know* what you said. You said that perhaps--"

"Perhaps we could have a real marriage."

"Yes."

"Answer my question. Were you jealous?"

"Yes! Yes, I was jealous!" She looked up at him, her face furious, her eyes flashing. "Yes! I hated her!"

"Ahh." He smiled at her. She lowered her head. He loosed her wrists and lifted her chin to look into her face.

She turned her head. "But you were right. I had no cause. We had a business arrangement, just as you told the constable."

"Jessalyn, didn't you understand why I said that?"

"Because it was--Oh!" She stopped, suddenly, seeing the whole thing differently. "Because if it were only a business arrangement, then I'd have no motive. I wouldn't care about what you did. You wanted him to think I had no motive."

"Exactly."

"But suppose I did?" she whispered.

"No more than did I," he said.

"Because of Bellefleur, you mean."

"Of course."

"I--had--considered that."

"And do you think I did it?"

"No."

"Why not?"

"I don't think you're capable of it."

"Oh, I may be. I may indeed be. Certainly, I considered murdering my wife."

"But you didn't, you see, and if you'd been going to, you'd have done it then. At least, I thought that. Besides it seems to me if you'd been going to kill Alida, you'd have simply done it. You'd not have used poison. That's sort of, well, uncertain. Suppose it only made her sick."

"Rhodes said poison was a woman's sort of thing."

"Or the sort of thing used by someone who thinks like a woman, perhaps."

"Anyway," he said, "I'm not the guilty party, you are incapable of murdering anyone, and who does that leave?"

"I don't know. I don't know," she said, closing her eyes and shaking her head. "I don't even care at this point. I'm quite tired of Alida and her death and all the trouble she's caused. I wish we could just leave her buried and forget her."

"So do I. I also wish I could take you with me to Trinidad next week. You could use a holiday."

"You're leaving next week?" She turned troubled eyes on him.

"Yes. But not for long. I'm becoming less fond of time away from you. I'll be gone a week. Meanwhile, I'm delegating Simon to take you on some trips around the island. Rhodes said you couldn't leave the island, but he didn't say you couldn't leave the house. And, if you don't get some time away now, you'll be shut up for a long time during the rainy season. It becomes more difficult to get around when the rains start."

She smiled at him, and it was a smile that made him want to stay with her, that made him regret the decision to make the trip to Trinidad. It was a smile that made him want to make up to her for all the things she'd suffered at the hands of men, of Alida, even the things she'd suffered because of him.

He pulled her to him, and he felt her body stiffen, resisting, and her face became wary. "Jessalyn," he said, touching her hair, "I know you don't have any reason to trust any man, even me. Perhaps especially me. But try to, anyway. Please try."

She lowered her head. "It--perhaps it isn't you," she said. "Perhaps it's me. I've trusted Simon, and nothing bad has come of that. He saved me, in a way. And I've trusted you, in so far as I've been able. But--" Her eyes were cloudy, uneasy. "It's as if my loving them gave them--I don't know--power to hurt me, somehow. It isn't you. It isn't *just* you. It's--maybe I'm bad luck."

"Nonsense. There's no such thing as bad luck or a jinx or what have you. You've not had a smooth life, and that's an understatement. But I promise it will be better. I promise." He lifted her face to his so that she looked into his eyes. "Do you believe me?"

"I'll try."

"Promise me?"

"I promise that I'll try."

"Good." And he kissed her forehead, her eyes, and her mouth, very gently. She shuddered the length of her body.

*  *  *  *  *

An odd sort of metamorphosis had overtaken Lady Heloise since Alida's death. She'd not liked her niece. She hadn't liked either of the twins, actually. She'd thought them badly raised, spoiled little girls, and when they were grown, they were spoiled women. She had not bothered, most of the time to conceal her dislike for them. Recently, it had become politic to pretend, at least, some devotion to Alida. When she was assigned the task of chaperoning her on the trip out to marry Dominick Reynolds, she had thought that the one saving grace of the journey would be that she'd have a place to stay for a time where she would have some use, where she wouldn't be reminded of the superfluity of her very existence. But that had fallen apart when they had arrived and Dominick was already married. How furious Alida had been! She hated being thwarted. Even as a child, she exacted revenge for every real or imagined injury. And when she'd arrived to find Dominick married to that "dreadful little nobody," as she had so unoriginally put it, she'd been in a fierce temper. Indeed, Lady Heloise wouldn't have put it past Alida to have administered the poison herself. Of course, she'd have meant it for Jessalyn, not for herself. She'd have planned to kill the girl, and then she'd have been too drunk to tell the difference. But that was farfetched, of course. Alida wasn't smart enough to have thought of anything as subtle as poison. She'd have done something more vicious, like pushing her down the stairs. Or the sort of thing the two of them did to poor Caroline. They'd arranged it to look an accident, but she'd been sure then that it was not, and she was sure now. Wretched girls, the two of them. She knew that when they were alive, and then when only Alida was alive, but now that she was dead, it became easier to pretend that what others seemed to think was the truth--that perhaps her death was a tragedy. She had been murdered in the most dreadful fashion, and perhaps someone should suffer for that crime.

People had come around to pay condolence calls, and Lady Heloise was the one who received them. Dominick had no reason to mourn the sister of a dead wife. Jessalyn had no reason at all to regret her death. So the task--or at least the duty of receiving the expressions of sympathy fell to Lady Heloise. And as they came in, no matter that she knew they were insincere formalities, she began to decide that perhaps poor Alida had not been such an awful person. She'd lived a sad life, in face. A loveless first marriage to a man thirty years older than she was, a brutal villain who misled her from the start. Of course, he was Irish, by ancestry, with the failing for liquor so common to that lot. The death of her beloved twin at such a young age. The loss of the man she'd planned to marry. Oh, dear, no wonder she drank. No wonder her life was a bitter one. Poor thing. Poor thing.

And as she convinced herself that Alida was a dear, misunderstood, sad, lonely woman, she set about to place the blame for her death on someone. Who could it be? Jessalyn, of course. The dear woman had tried so hard to befriend that silly girl, and even tried to teach her how to handle herself among her betters, and she'd been repaid for her kindness by absolute treachery. It made a wonderful, dramatic scenario. Lady Heloise was quite pleased with herself for having thought of it. How beautifully it told. And it did reflect well on the Trentons, too. It simply wouldn't do to have the local people misunderstand and think that Alida was drinking and mean and all of that. There had to be some justification, the blame had to be placed somewhere. By the time she'd constructed her story, she was quite satisfied with it and quite convinced that it was true. She had nothing against Jessalyn, actually. In fact, she'd rather liked the girl early on. She was quick witted, and had come to be rather attractive, and Lady Heloise had been secretly amused to find her installed as Dominick's wife, so thoroughly defeating Alida.

But in the end, her loyalties were with Alida. With no one around to correct her version of the story, she became quite taken with her little tale, with being the center of attention for the first time in her life, and with the sense of power she gained from being able to manipulate her audience.

It had begun almost innocently. Bethany Basil had asked her if the constable had any idea who had done such a thing, and Lady Heloise had said, "No. But I've every reason to believe he has his *suspicions.*"

"Do you, indeed, Lady Heloise? Do tell me what you think."

And after that it had been easy. "Well, of course, I'm not at liberty to say. After all, no one has been arrested, and of course, I wouldn't want to say anything that might be misunderstood, you know."

"Oh, I certainly agree. I surely do. But you can tell me. I shan't repeat a word."

"Well, in all confidence, you know that Dominick's marriage was--well, a bit of a hasty thing, don't you?"

Of course Bethany knew. The whole island had talked of nothing else for days.

"Well, just between us, I'm quite sure he regretted it, but that's neither here nor there. Alida told me before she died, poor dear, that there was every chance that Dominick planned to have the marriage annulled. Alida had every reason to believe it had never even been--you know--" her voice dropped to a whisper--"consummated."

"Really!" Bethany's eyes grew large.

"That's what Alida said. At any rate, she had reason to think--at least she said she did--that Dominick was thinking of putting aside his marriage to that girl and marrying Alida."

"Was he! How fascinating!"

"Now, you mustn't breathe a word of this, of course, because all I know is what Alida hinted at before--" a long sigh. "You know. Poor thing."

"Does the constable know about this?"

"Well, I really can't say, but I do know this much. Jessalyn--isn't that an awful name?--was the only person he talked to more than once.

And I feel quite certain that he has her under suspicion. At least, I heard that he had told her not to leave the island."

"No!"

"But you must promise not to breathe a word."

"Oh, of course."

But naturally, she couldn't avoid stopping off on her way home to tell her best friend, and Kitty Anderson hadn't promised not to tell, and within days the story was all over the island.

It fell on the receptive ears of Lacey Delaney, who laughed when she heard it, and promptly did everything she could to help it along. Poor Dominick. He had no luck with women. His first wife died--of her own doing, Lacey understood--and now the second was quite likely to be hanged, it seemed. This time he'd need consolation. She was quite ready to give it.

For a time after Dominick left, Jessalyn was rather sequestered at Dragonsong. She'd made no calls; she'd received no one. She simply didn't feel up to it, and so she was unaware of the gossip, the rumors swirling about her. She was even unaware of how her withdrawal fueled them. She wasn't withdrawing on purpose; but to the outside, it appeared as if she were trying to hide.

She saw few people even inside the house, and none from outside it, and Marguerite and Simms and Celestine and Aurore and George were unlikely to repeat what they were hearing. She had to find out eventually, and she learned it by accident.

She had gone down for breakfast a bit earlier than usual, and Marguerite had given her a special treat to take to her cat. Ordinarily she wrapped it and put it in her lap so she'd remember, but this morning, she had left it beside her plate, and she'd been halfway up the stairs before she remembered it.

"Marmles would never forgive me if I forgot his breakfast treat," she murmured to herself, turning back toward the kitchen. Her hand was almost on the swinging door before she was stopped by the sound of her own name.

"...what they say about Miz Jess, Celestine." It was Marguerite's voice. "I don't believe nothing like that. Miz Jess just not that kind."

"Well, I'm just telling you what that skinny maid over at Delaneys' say. She say Miz Jess gonna be arrested any minute now for killing

Miz Fitzhugh. She say they gonna find out Mr. Dominick planning to marry with Miz Fitzhugh, and that why she killed her."

"Trash. That skinny Delaney maid trash. Telling gossip about Miz Jess. Stupid gossip, too. Mr. Dominick hate that woman. He didn't even like her sister much, and she his wife. He never marry up with that Fitzhugh woman. That Delaney maid got no good sense."

"Don't matter if she got good sense or not, Mama, she just say what everybody been saying, that's all."

Jessalyn pushed the door open and they turned, startled, guilty. Her face was pale, her voice harsh as she asked, "Is it true? Is that what they're saying about me?"

"Now, Miz Jess, you ought not pay no mind to stupid gossip. That Delaney maid, she got one big mouth and one pea brain. No reason for you to--"

"But they are saying it, aren't they, Celestine? They are saying I killed Alida Fitzhugh?"

Celestine looked at the floor, then at Jessalyn, then nodded.

"Thank you," Jessalyn whispered, and left, closing the door softly behind her

She walked through the house, out the front door, down the steps, across the lawn. She didn't know where she was going, nor did she care. She simply had a compelling need to get away, to hide. She reached the gravel drive and followed it down through the trees until she finally came to the beach. There she stopped, breathless, and began to walk along the expanse of golden sand, watching the waves rush in and break, pushing flecks of foam ahead of them onto the sand.

She walked for a distance, looking out over the water, contemplating her future. Suppose Constable Rhodes decides I did murder Alida, she thought. Then, of course, the future is quite simple. They will hang me. I shall die, as my brother died. The thought of Jamie hanging in that awful courtyard flashed through her mind, and she tried to push it out. The image was not one she wanted to dwell on.

But suppose that they can't prove who did it, that they haven't enough evidence to arrest me. Suppose I have to live with this slow sort of death by dissection. This death of being talked about, of being the subject of such gossip that people hush when I enter the room. I couldn't bear that, she thought. How could Dominick stand having a wife about whom people talked so viciously?

What shall I do? What can I do? Suppose I could find the murderer--and suppose it should be Dominick? No, I won't think that. I can't think that. He didn't do it. He couldn't do it.

So engrossed was she with her concerns that she didn't hear Simon Alderly when he first hailed her from the grove of palms back down the beach. In fact, he had called her three times before she heard and turned back toward him, her hand shielding her eyes from the sun.

"You seemed to be miles and miles away," he said as he approached her. "I called you several times."

She did not return his smile. She raised troubled eyes to his and said without preamble, "Simon, do you know what they're saying about me?"

He frowned down at her and took her arm. "The island gossips? Yes, I've heard."

"Do you believe it? That I poisoned Alida Fitzhugh?"

"Good heavens, my dear, of course not. I can't think of anyone less likely to have done it."

"When we talked the first time about my coming to the island, you said you wanted to be able to assure your employer that you were not bringing an axe murderess into the house. Are you certain you've not brought in a dealer of poisons? I did dress as Lucrezia Borgia for the ball, you know. Perhaps I was trying to tell you something."

He laughed. "Not likely. If you'd been that sort, You'd never have dressed the part. You'd have been done up as a Botticelli angel or some such innocent thing."

"The constable doesn't agree, you know. He thinks there isn't anyone *more* likely to have done it. He says I had the motive, the opportunity, and the means. Evidently those are the three touchstones of criminal detection, and now it's all over the island, evidently, that I'm the one most suspected. They all seem to think I'm guilty."

"If by 'they' you mean such celebrated purveyors of rumor as Margaret Harrington and Lacey Delaney, let me assure you that you can put your concerns behind you. Most of them, including Margaret and Bethany Basil and Kitty Anderson, haven't the wit to recognize the truth if they had maps to it, and as for Lacey--well, let's just say that

Lacey never passes up a chance to repeat a good story, even if she has to make it up. As for Walter, well, he spends way too much time reading theories of detection, with the lingering hope that he may someday get to use some of them. Besides, I have every reason to suspect that the source of this gossip is much closer than any of the women I've mentioned."

"What do you mean?"

"How much have you seen of Lady Heloise lately?"

"Lady Heloise? Hardly anything, actually. I don't have tea with her; she seldom dines with anyone. She has a tray in her room. She's been receiving all the callers. After all, it was her niece, not a relative of mine who died, and--Oh. That's what you mean, isn't it? You think she started the gossip."

"I have some reason to think so." Actually, he was quite certain of it. He had made some effort to trace the stories back to their source, and they all came out of the Reynolds residence.

"But why? I've never done anything to her. I rather thought she liked me, even. We've never had a quarrel."

He sighed. "Jessalyn, don't forget this, ever. Dominick did, and it was to his detriment, eventually. The members of the so-called aristocracy always--*always*--stick together. Even if they hate each other. Even if they have better reason to stand up for someone else. They may babble on about honor and the gentlemanly thing to do and all of that, but when it comes down to it, they'd slice a throat to save one of their own without a thought or a backward glance. Alida Fitzhugh was a witch, a vicious and evil woman, a wicked, despicable vixen. Furthermore, Lady Heloise knows it. She knows it so well that she's had to spend some time trying to clean up that bit of dirty linen, and if she needed a victim to help her do it, well, I'm afraid you were the nearest at hand. Do you understand me?"

"Yes, I think so."

"Good. Then I came here to talk of more pleasant things. Dominick said that I must get you out of the house before the rainy season started in earnest, and I'm here to do just that. Dominick will deal with the other when he returns, I've no doubt, and meanwhile, I'm to lighten your spirits. This is a small island, but we do have some fine sights that you've not seen, and I'm going to take you to see a few of them. What would you say to a picnic tomorrow?"

"Ahh, I'd love it." She glanced at the sky overhead. "It's getting cloudy already, though. Do you think it will be clear tomorrow?"

"I doubt it very much, but we'll take rain gear. The showers won't last long, and we'll do a bit of exploring."

"I'd love that. Will we ride?"

"Yes, I thought we would."

"Good. I'd love a ride. I hope the horses aren't too frisky after being penned so long."

"They may be, but we'll work that out of them right away."

As they neared the house, a light rain began to fall, and they had to run the last bit to the porch to escape being soaked.

Jessalyn was breathless by the time she reached the veranda. "I'm glad I had a chance to talk to you. I'm feeling better. You've improved my state of mind."

"Mrs. Reynolds, you always improve mine. Shall we say seven in the morning?"

"Yes, that's fine. Where will we go?"

They stood in the foyer and he made his way toward the office. "I've been thinking of Ma Rose Point. It's a good long ride, and it will give you a chance to see a great deal of the island."

"Good. I'll have Marguerite pack a picnic for us."

They heard a gasp and turned toward the stairs to see Lady Heloise draw herself up, a horrified expression on her face. "A *picnic?*" she said, her lips curling around the word as if it were something obscene. "Have both of you forgotten that this is a house of mourning?"

"It will be a house of insanity if I don't get out of it for a time, Lady Heloise," Jessalyn said.

"Actually, Lady Heloise," Simon surveyed her with no loss of composure, "you're quite wrong. This is a house of some thanksgiving, now that Mrs. Fitzhugh has gone to what I'm certain is a just reward." Lady Heloise choked. "Not only is no one here mourning her-- including you, I might add, no matter what your pretense to the contrary--but wherever she is, our behavior could hardly make any difference to her."

"Of all the thoughtless, unfeeling--"

"Oh, do pack it in, Lady Heloise." Simon rolled his eyes skyward. "No one on earth was more thoughtless and unfeeling than the late unlamented. If you want to carry on in this fashion, do so elsewhere."

Her ladyship turned and stalked up the stairs, muttering and looking back over her shoulder. Jessalyn began to laugh, stuffing her fist in her mouth to conceal her giggles until Lady Heloise had slammed her door.

"I'd never have had the nerve to say that," she said, wiping her eyes.

"Nothing lost by it. She is a thoroughgoing old hypocrite, isn't she?"

"I should say. The way she talked to Alida when she was alive was--quite different."

"Then I shall see you tomorrow?"

"Indeed."

Jessalyn reentered the kitchen in quite a different frame of mind from that in which she had left it, prompting Marguerite to say, "Why, Miz Jess, seems like something sure cheered you up."

"In fact, something did, Marguerite. Mr. Alderly is taking me on a picnic tomorrow. I came back to see if you would make a lunch for us to take."

"Oh, sure! Glad to see you go, get out of this gloomy house for a while. Anything you want special?"

"No. I'll leave it up to you. But I would like some of those little tarts, if they're not too much trouble."

"No. Not any too much trouble."

Aurore, sitting at the end of the table peeling a mango, looked up at her through thick lashes. "Where you gonna go?" she asked.

Jessalyn frowned, trying to remember. "Someplace, he said, like Mama Rose Point. Is that right?"

"Ma Rose Point," Celestine corrected. "Not get me up there."

"Nonsense, Celestine," her mother said. "Miz Jess like that place. It has one fine view of the sea."

"Besides," Aurore scoffed, "you don't believe all that ghost stuff, do you? You the one say they no such things as ghosts."

"Didn't say they was, didn't say they wasn't, neither," Celestine said. "Way I see it, no point in finding out, one way or the other."

"What are you talking about?" Jessalyn looked from one to the other. "What about ghosts?"

"Ma Rose Point s'posed to be haunted," Celestine said.

"Why?" Jessalyn asked. "Who haunts it?"

"Ma Rose," Marguerite said. "At least, she s'posed to. It's an old story. Back long years ago, all the black people on this island was slaves. White people bring them here to work the cane. Same like now, only no pay. Anyway, they have these overseers, some of them pretty bad men. Some of them beat those people with whips. They this one plantation up by Charlottesville, have this bad overseer. He *mean*. He so mean, he always look for reasons to hit the slaves. One day, this old woman, they call her Ma Rose, she carrying a bundle of cane, and she old, you know, slow. He told her to move faster, and he snap that whip at her. He always carry a whip.

"She try to hurry, but then she fall down on her knees, and he hit her again. She try to get up, he hit her again. She real angry now, real mad. So she throw down that bunch of cane, and jump up and run over, grab him. She like a tiger. 'Fore they can pull her off, she bite his throat right clean through it. Kill that overseer dead.

"Well, 'course this make the owner upset, you know. He gonna take that old woman out the next day, he gonna have her tied to a tree, he gonna have her whipped to death. Show all the others. Only, next day when they bring her out, she get loose from the guards. She run fast, faster than her guards, faster than old woman's s'posed to run, and she jump off the cliff. She rather die her own way.

"Now they say, she still hang around there, her spirit stay at that place. Sailors go by there when the sea is rough, they say Ma Rose is thirsty. They pour a little rum in the water, keep her happy."

"Has anyone ever seen her?" Jessalyn asked.

" 'Course not," Aurore said scornfully, standing up. "How can anybody see her? She not real. Ghosts just stories, that's all."

Tell that to Alida Fitzhugh, Jessalyn thought, but she said, "Oh, I don't know. Some of the old houses in England are supposed to have ghosts that show up now and then."

"Huh." Aurore's lip curled in contempt. "That so much nonsense. Nobody but old women and little children believe in ghosts."

"You sure silly, Aurore," her sister said. "You scared of cats, but you not scared of ghosts."

"Cats real, ghosts not." And she went out the back door.

"You never mind her, Miz Jess," Celestine said. "She don't believe half of what she *can* see, never mind what she can't."

"That the truth," Marguerite said. "Anyway, you leave it to me. I make you one fine picnic. Give me something to do. Hardly get no chance to cook any more, Mr. Dominick gone, nobody here eat much." She paused, thinking. "I can make you some *pastelles*, they good for picnics. Maybe a little bit roast chicken. You don't worry. I fix you up fine."

"Good. Then I'll go out to the stable and tell the men to have the horses ready."

When Jessalyn picked up the picnic hamper the next day, she decided that Marguerite had made a mistake and thought that the picnic was to include at least ten people, rather than the two of them. Simon Alderly agreed when he lifted the hamper.

"Are you sure you told her there were only two of us?" he asked. "I'd swear she has enough food here for half a dozen people."

"More likely for a full dozen. Marguerite lives in fear that I might possibly lose an ounce or two."

The hamper was a wicker affair made in two sections to fit over the horse's rump. Simon swung the baskets over his own mount behind the saddle and helped Jessalyn onto her mare.

"I've decided to save Ma Rose Point for another day and take you instead to Buccoo Reef. You haven't seen the reef, have you?"

"No," she said, "although I shall be sorry to miss the haunted point."

"Haunted--oh, Ma Rose Point. You must have been listening to Marguerite."

"And Celestine. And Aurore. I think they believe Ma Rose still lurks about the place."

"Not likely. I'm sure she went to her reward years ago."

"Aurore says the same. She says only children and old women believe in ghosts."

"For once the contentious Aurore and I agree. But don't tell her so," he said. "If she found out, she'd change her mind."

Jessalyn laughed. That did sound like Aurore, she thought.

The day was lovely, the sky blue and clear, the breeze from the ocean pleasant. The ride to the place where they'd take the boat to the reef was invigorating, just what she needed, Jessalyn thought, to take her mind off her troubles.

Simon had hired a boat to take them out toward the reef. It was a small fishing boat, aboard which, he said, they would have their picnic. They left their horses tied to a small house back from the ocean with a young boy who was hired to watch them.

At first Jessalyn was afraid that she would have a reoccurrence of her seasickness, but the queasy feeling passed. They sailed out to the reef and around it, Jessalyn hanging over the edge of the boat to see the colors of the coral reef. The water was clear and the day was perfect. They sailed along the coast for a way and had their picnic. The crew was spirited and happy, singing calypso tunes that Simon translated (and censored) for Jessalyn. She laughed and enjoyed herself, trouble seemed far way, and she was sorry to see the day end.

When they left the boat, Simon put the hamper back on his horse and they rode down the beach a way. There had been enough food for them and for the crew, who had licked their fingers and exclaimed over Marguerite's delicacies. Jessalyn gave the frisky Josephine her head for a short stretch of beach, then turned and called to Simon, "Toss that hamper away for a bit, and I'll race you down the beach."

"Done," he said, reaching back to free the hamper, "but come back here first. You don't get a head start."

She walked Josephine back to the place where Simon was waiting, turned, and at his shout, urged her mare into a gallop. Josephine needed little urging; she was eager to be off. Simon passed them, and Jessalyn, intent on making at least a decent showing, leaned forward and touched her mount with her quirt.

Suddenly the mare screamed in pain and reared, spinning half around and throwing her startled rider into the sand. Then she raced away down the beach.

Jessalyn sat up, stunned, holding the shoulder on which she had landed. It felt curiously numb. Simon, who had been a few feet ahead of her when she fell, had spun his horse around and returned to her. He jumped off and ran across the sand, kneeling beside her.

"Jessalyn! Are you all right? What happened?"

She shook her head. She was a bit dazed and she looked up at him with eyes faintly out of focus. "I--I'm not sure I know. One minute we were racing along, and the next she reared and threw me. She's never done anything like that before."

"How do you feel? Are you in any pain?"

"No--yes, actually, my shoulder hurts a bit. I think I landed on it."

He touched her shoulder and moved her arm, examining her injury as best he could.

"Nothing seems broken or dislocated," he said finally. "It will probably be badly bruised, though. We'll call the doctor to take a look at it when we get home. Can you stand?"

"Oh, yes, I'm really all right. I just can't understand what made her do that. She's never given me even the faintest worry."

"I've never seen her do any such thing, either. Lucky for one thing, though. If you had to fall, at least it was on the sand. If we'd been riding along the cliffs at Ma Rose Point--" He stopped and she shuddered.

"You're right. I'm lucky. What made her do it, do you think?"

"Hard to tell. I want to check her before you remount. Something may have worked its way under the saddle. Can you hold these reins?"

She took them, and he started down the beach for Josephine, who came to him now, quietly dragging her reins in the sand. He approached the mare, taking the reins and walking up beside the saddle. He ran his hand under the edge of one side of the saddle, feeling for something, anything that might have hurt her. Nothing. He moved around to the other side, running his hand along, looking for something that might have chaffed or stabbed her. He felt nothing at first, then as he started to withdraw his hand, he gave a sudden grunt of pain and jerked his hand away. Blood oozed from a long scratch across three of his fingers.

"Did you find something?" Jessalyn was standing on the other side of the animal.

"Hmm." He lifted the edge of the saddle, raising the fender on his side. Protruding from the leather was a sharp object that proved to be the point of a tack driven through the flap. It was placed at such an angle as to be unnoticeable as long as the rider was sitting upright, barely penetrating the felt saddle blanket. But if the rider leaned forward, as one would do in a race, or in looking over a cliff-- He withdrew the tack and tossed it away, angry. Someone had placed the tack in the saddle, someone who wanted the rider to fall from a swiftly moving horse or to lean forward at the edge of a cliff, startling the horse into a sudden jump. The scratch on his fingers stung so that he suspected the tack or the blanket or the horse's hide had been doctored with something to make the wound sting.

To Jessalyn, he said merely, "Looks like a splinter or something like that. Must have stabbed her and she reared. Probably came off the stable railing."

No point in alarming her. Why tell her someone just tried to see that she was injured--or killed? Poor girl has enough on her mind. But damn! I should have saved that tack. I ought to get to Walter Rhodes and give him this little bit of information.

Back at home, Jessalyn was mothered and pampered by Simms and Marguerite, who insisted that she be tucked into bed immediately and plied with all the dishes appropriate to the proper healing of such wounds.

Celestine, delegated by her mother to take care of Jessalyn, helped her out of her riding habit and into bed.

"Celestine, I hardly think this is necessary. It's just a bruise, you know. I'll be fine."

"Miz Jess, you got to humor my mama. She say you go to bed, you go to bed. Doctor be here pretty quick, and she already send up some salve she say I got to rub on that shoulder, make it not so sore in the morning."

The doctor arrived, pronounced Marguerite's treatment acceptable, and left.

Jessalyn submitted to the treatment, and she had to admit that the shoulder did feel better. Marmles climbed up the covers and curled at her feet. Outside, she could hear the drip of water from the roof. What was happening to her paradise, she wondered as she lay in bed, on the verge of drifting off. Why did it suddenly feel so ominous? The silence had seemed calming, peaceful at first; the sounds of the insects and the night birds calling had been pleasant. Now the sound of the rain drip-drip-dripping from the eaves seemed somehow threatening.

What's going on in this place? She brooded drowsily. Marmles stirred beside her. Why is there such--what? Fear? Unhappiness? Foreboding? She drifted off, her mind uneasy, but her body tired and demanding sleep.

*     *     *     *     *

Simon Alderly sipped his brandy and set it on the table beside him, gesturing impatiently as he did so. "I think you've been mistaken in the tack you've taken on this, Walter. I think you're seeing it in the wrong way."

Across from him, Walter Rhodes shrugged. "I don't know, Simon. I'm not certain you're right. Still, it does raise interesting possibilities. Jessalyn Reynolds seems the perfect choice except for one thing--I simply cannot, no matter how hard I try, see that young woman as a killer. My reason says one thing, but my--what? Intuition? Feeling? --says another. Interesting. Alida Fitzhugh would seem the perfect killer too, except for one thing: she's quite dead--the victim."

"I know better than anyone how deceiving appearances can be. I remember very well how Adelaide Reynolds seemed to me until the first time I ever saw her shed that lovely façade in a flaming rage. Even I had been fooled by her, and I thought myself something of an expert on human character."

"What you are suggesting, if I understand you, Alderly, is that Alida Fitzhugh was not the intended victim at all; Jessalyn Reynolds was."

"That's precisely what I'm suggesting."

"That would put all of this in a much different light, of course, but it brings me back to the first question. Who would want to kill Jessalyn Reynolds?"

"Who indeed? You're right. Alida Fitzhugh would be my first choice, but the fact that she's dead must prove that she had no such plot in mind."

"And you're certain that this accident with the horse today was no accident?"

"Positive. I've cursed myself for throwing that tack away in a fit of anger, but there it is, and I'd never have found it on that beach. I do have the wound on my fingers to show, but that proves little. I could show you the hole where the saddle was punctured, but that wouldn't do much to prove my point either."

Walter Rhodes waved his hand. "I've no reason to doubt your word, personally. A jury is something else, of course, but I feel quite sure you're telling the truth. Did you tell the girl what you suspected?"

"No. I thought there was no point in frightening her."

"Hmm." Rhodes stared off into space for a moment. "If only we'd been able to check that glass or that flask. Either of those would have been proof. Of course, the flask would have been more valuable, but even the limeade would have told us something."

"But if you'd had only the limeade, it might have had poison in it, in any event, had she poured the poisoned rum into it."

"True, but the solution would have been weaker. The poison in the rum itself would have been stronger. The rum would have been diluted by the poison-free limeade."

"I see. Did you ever ask Miriam where she got the rum?"

"Yes, of course. She got it from Dominick Reynolds."

"Did that give you reason to suspect Dominick?"

"No. You see, she said that when he gave it to her, he poured it from a cask into a decanter. Both of them were untainted, although the decanter was cleaned before I examined it. Miriam said that no one handled the decanter between the time she took it upstairs and the time Mrs. Fitzhugh died except herself, the victim, and Mrs. Reynolds. No, I never suspected Dominick. I'm certain the poison was either in the limeade or introduced into the flask."

"Did you learn why Dominick locked the liquor cabinet and then continued to supply rum to Mrs. Fitzhugh?"

"He said he'd hoped to limit her drinking by locking up the spirits, but he soon saw it was doing no good. I can see his point. On a plantation where rum is distilled, there's hardly any difficulty in obtaining it. As I see it, he just gave it up as a bad job, and hoped to keep her quiet until she left."

"Then, just for the sake of argument, let's eliminate Jessalyn and Dominick Reynolds from our list of suspects. Who else might have done it?"

"No one has a motive as strong, as I see it. Dominick had the motive, but not the opportunity. He told me himself about his estate,

Bellefleur, is it? But I cannot place him at the scene. Jessalyn had, possibly, all three essentials, but if we make her a potential victim, not a killer, we have to look elsewhere. How about the servants?"

"Always a possibility, but I wouldn't know where to begin to look."

"How about that strange Simms?"

"Odd one, that," Simon agreed, "but I can't tie her in to a murder. Though I know for a fact that she had no love for the Trenton women. Still, she likes Jessalyn, or seems to, and had nothing to gain from her death."

"How about the Douglases?"

"Umm. No. They all seem to adore Jessalyn."

"How about an outsider?"

"Possible. Almost anyone could have come into the house."

"Come now, Alderly. Without being seen?"

"I think so, if they were careful. You've been at Dragonsong, Walter. You know how big the place is. And with as few residents as there are, Dominick keeps a small staff for a man of his means. I've wandered about the place for five minutes without running into a soul, and I was *searching* for someone. Yes," he said, "someone could have come in from the outside unobserved."

Rhodes sighed. "Well, if you're right--and I'm not saying you are, mind--that gives us two problems. It means I have to start over and consider everyone on the island suspect. No small task. And it means that Jessalyn Reynolds is in grave danger, you know." He looked at Simon over the rim of his glass for a long moment. "Have you any idea why anyone would want to kill her, any idea at all?"

"No. You realize, of course, that I don't know much about her, but I have no idea at all."

"Well, if she is the target, whoever it is has now failed to kill her twice. The next time he--or she--may not fail."

"I've thought of that. I think we'd better get Dominick Reynolds back here as soon as we can."

# Chapter Nineteen

DOMINICK REYNOLDS WAS LIVID. There had been no shortage of people to tell him about Lady Heloise and her sudden change of face in his absence; the servants were all too eager to fill him in. That, and Jessalyn's "accident" were the main topics of conversation on his arrival. He had no need for information about either. Simon Alderly had briefed him thoroughly about both of the situations. His first act was to go up to see Jessalyn.

She was reading when he entered, and the pleasure she felt when she saw him, the jump her heart gave, surprised her.

"Simon told me you'd taken a fall. Are you all right?" She was stretched out on a chaise, holding her book, when he came in, and she'd not risen.

"Oh, yes. I'm quite well. Simon frets too much."

"He said you hurt your shoulder."

"Yes, but it's only bruised, the doctor said. That and my dignity, I suppose." She smiled at him. He reached over and took her hand.

"I'm sorry about it. I shouldn't have gone and left you here."

"Why not, for heaven's sake?" She was certain that her heart could not beat faster, but when he took her hand, it did. It very definitely did. "It was a minor accident, not at all serious. You surely couldn't have prevented it, even if you'd been here."

"No...no, I suppose not. But if anything serious had happened to you, I'd not have forgiven myself." His face was dark, almost angry. She had an irrational urge to touch his cheek, to smooth out the lines from his face with her hand, assuring him that everything was fine, but she did not. There was silence between them for a moment, and she thought that surely he would hear her heart pounding. Then he stood, still holding her hand, and turned it palm up and planted a kiss in the center of it. Her fingers curled about his cheek almost involuntarily, and he raised his head and looked at her for a long moment. "I have some things to take care of," he said softly, and he turned and left the room. She stared at the door for a full five minutes after he'd gone, holding the hand he'd kissed to her mouth.

He sent Simms to bring Lady Heloise to his office, and he was sitting behind his desk when she entered.

"Sit down, Lady Heloise," he said.

"Dear Dominick, that was certainly a quick trip. We really didn't expect you home so soon."

"I found it necessary to return. There were one or two problems that arose during my absence that I found necessary to deal with."

"Problems? Oh, nothing serious, I hope."

"You should hope, Lady Heloise. One of them concerns you."

"Me? I certainly don't understand why."

"I've heard--from several sources, by the way--that you are responsible for certain rumors that are circulating about the island concerning my wife."

There was a long pause. Lady Heloise raised her chin sharply and looked down her nose at him, but he returned the stare, and she dropped her eyes. Finally she said, "I can't begin to think what you mean."

He leaned forward on his elbows, glaring at her. "I mean, Lady Heloise, that you have managed to spread about the island the story that my wife murdered your niece. Have you any shred of proof of that?"

"I'm sure I did no such thing, Dominick. Besides, if I did happen to mention your wife in passing, it was only because the constable seems to think she had something to do with it. After all, he did order her to stay on the island. And, anyway, who else could have done it?"

"I suppose I could have, for one. You could have, for another."

"*I!* How dare you! She was my niece, and I loved her like a daughter. Like the child I never had. She and Adelaide were as dear to me as--"

"Stop it. You know better, and I have witnesses to the fact that you had roaring fights, frequent and bitter. Shall I send those witnesses to discuss the matter with Walter Rhodes?"

She looked, at first, outraged, then as she considered what he had said, she blinked, her eyes shifted, and she twisted her hands a bit in her lap. "Well, certainly we had our disagreements, I mean, after all, even parents and children disagree sometimes, but that certainly doesn't mean that I ever considered--*ever*--doing anything to harm her. I mean it would be most misleading to say--"

"It is most misleading to allow others to believe such things of my wife, Lady Heloise."

"But if not her, then who?"

"I don't know. Nor do you. Nor does Walter Rhodes."

"Well, under the circumstances, I hardly think I've done anything to be censured for, and besides, I've not said anything, really. Not much, anyway."

"Then, of course, you won't mind in the slightest retracting it."

"I certainly would mind! To tell people that I've *lied*--outrageous. I certainly will not do any such thing."

"Then let me see whether there is anything I can do that might change your mind. Simms!" he called. "Will you come in, please?"

Simms had evidently been waiting outside the door, because she came in almost at once.

"Simms, do have a chair. There's something we have to discuss with Lady Heloise."

Simms sat down across from the angry woman. Neither of them spoke.

"Lady Heloise, I've asked Simms to relate to you a story of which I have no doubt as to the authenticity. Simms has never told this to anyone but me, and she wouldn't have done that had I not had reason to need to know it. It concerns both the sisters and a cousin. Do your remember a cousin named Caroline?"

"Oh, dear, yes. A tragic thing, Caroline's death. Poor child. She was only fourteen."

"The same age as the twins, yes."

"But what on earth can that have to do with anything now? Her death was a terrible accident, but it happened years ago."

"That's what we're about to tell you, Lady Heloise. Simms, why don't you begin?"

Simms wasn't accustomed to telling stories; she fidgeted for a moment before she finally said, "Where should I start then, sir?"

"Perhaps with the way the twins felt about Caroline, Simms. Just as you told me."

"They were always jealous of Miss Caroline, sir, her being an only child and all, they thought--"

"Nonsense!" Lady Heloise spat. "They were prettier, smarter, better at everything. Why should they have been jealous?"

"Please don't interrupt. Do go on, Simms."

"Well, Lady Heloise may be right, perhaps sir, but the fact was Miss Caroline was an only child. And as her father didn't gamble the way the earl did, the young lady always had more money, you know, the best of everything for that girl. Probably she was quite spoiled, you know, but she was a pretty little thing, and always polite and all."

"A milksop of a child," Lady Heloise muttered.

"Perhaps, ma'am, but you know, servants always know who's kind and who's not. It's easy to be nice to your betters, but it's not so easy to be nice to them that's beneath you. Anyway, Miss Caroline was sort of a darling among the servants, you know. The young misses didn't like her for that. Or for her pretty clothes. Or for her getting to do just about anything she liked. The only thing they had over Miss Caroline was that they were good riders, and she wasn't a rider at all."

"No nerve, no nerve at all."

"I don't know about that, ma'am. She'd fallen off a horse when she was a little thing, and she was scared to death of them, you know. The young misses was always twitting her about it, saying she was scared, and a coward, and all that. And she was, I suppose, when it came to horses. She was terrified of them, that was true. Miss Adelaide, she used to scare her about being afraid of horses by riding her own horse up so close to Miss Caroline that the poor thing would go white as a ghost.

"When they were about fourteen, as you say, ma'am, she was visiting over at the Trentons' and Miss Alida had a terrible row with her. Over some dress. Miss Alida was used to just taking whatever she wanted to wear, and when she took one of Miss Caroline's new dresses and wore it and spilled something on it, before Miss Caroline even wore it herself, you know, Miss Caroline got real angry, like, and told on her, and Miss Alida was in such trouble.

"Well, I don't know when they planned what they did. I never asked them. Sometime that night, I suppose, but they set it up so that the next day, they sent a message back up to the house that Miss Caroline was to come down to the stables. They didn't sign their own names on the message; they knew she wouldn't come for them. They signed their mother's name. I guess Miss Caroline didn't think anything of it. She went down and they grabbed her. There was a horse stabled there--the earl had won him in a card game, I guess--and he was mean. No one could ride him, not even the earl, but he was handsome, and so the earl kept him. They shoved her into that stall with him, you know, and that horse trampled her. Killed her, and her screaming and screaming. They murdered that child, ma'am."

Lady Heloise had gone white. "But that's not true! They admitted teasing her about the riding until she got so angry she went in the stall, but they didn't--they wouldn't have--"

"I saw them do it, ma'am. I had gone in Miss Caroline's room, you know, after she left, and I saw the note, and I knew right away it wasn't their mother's writing. I took off after her, but I wasn't quick enough. They'd opened that stall and shoved her in and were holding the gate closed when I got there. Miss Caroline was screaming and the horse was kicking and tramping at her, and I pulled open the gate and tried to get her, but I couldn't get past him either, and he kicked her head. That's what killed her."

"It's a lie!" Lady Heloise hissed. "I vicious lie!"

"I'm afraid not, Lady Heloise," Dominick Reynolds said. "Apparently it was the only thing that Adelaide ever had a guilty conscience over, because when she was dying, she babbled about it. That's when Simms told me the story. She swore me to secrecy, just as she and the girls had sworn years before. But of course, now with both of them dead, the vows are broken, you see."

"But why didn't you tell? Why did you keep it secret?" she asked Simms.

Simms paused. "I don't really know, ma'am. I should have told, I guess, but I knew two things would happen. The girls would get off, because they were the earl's daughters, and I'd lose my place and be made to look a liar." There was a short silence. "Miss Adelaide never rode again after that. I don't know why.

"Besides," she went on, "having something to hold over them gave me some power, like, and I couldn't resist that. They'd give me such a terrible lot of trouble, you know. I liked the thought of having them step to my tune for a while."

"Blackmail," Lady Heloise said contemptuously.

"Is that worse than murder?" Dominick asked.

"Besides, it would have been your word against theirs."

"No, ma'am. You see, I had the note. I still have it, in fact."

There was silence for a moment. Then Lady Heloise said, "I don't see what all of this has to do with anything. You couldn't tell this story without blackening the name of your late wife, Dominick, as well as Alida's name, and to do that to the woman who died while carrying your child--"

"That's another part of the story, Lady Heloise. You see, we've always allowed people to think that Adelaide died as the result of a miscarriage, but that's only partly true."

"What do you mean?"

"Adelaide induced the miscarriage. She tried to lose the child, and she succeeded, but she killed herself in the process." Had she been watching him, had she been at all sensitive to anyone except herself, Lady Heloise would have seen the pain it caused him to have to admit this, the agony that the memory still held for him. But she did not. She was blind with her fury.

"So," she said icily, "what are you telling me?

"That unless you mange to find a way to retract, gracefully, all that you've said about Jessalyn, I will arrange for everyone on the island to know the truth about your nieces--that they were murderesses, and that there was nothing of which they were not capable. In fact, I'll see to it that the stories reach England and are told in the most public places I can arrange."

She went pale. "But I don't know how--I don't know what to say--I don't see how I can--"

"You'll think of something, Lady Heloise. You're quite creative, I've learned."

She spread her hands, defeated. "I--I'll do what I can. Whatever I can." She paused. "Are you going to send me back to England?"

"Not if you do what I've asked."

"I--rather like it here you know. And I've no place else, really."

In spite of his anger, Dominick felt rather sorry for her. She was a useless old woman with little besides a title and some remnants of pride. "Lady Heloise, this is a large house, and you're welcome to stay here as long as you like. I don't want anything--*anything*--to hurt my wife. Is that clear?"

She nodded.

"Aside from that, you've the run of the place as far as I'm concerned. When Jessalyn and I have children, you might take a hand in supervising their educations."

She stared at him. "Children?"

"Yes. People do have them, you know."

"But I thought that you--"

"Thought what?"

"That you hadn't--"

"Hadn't what?"

She shook her head, bewildered. "Nothing, nothing," she said. "It was a mistake, that's all. Thank you. I appreciate your offer. I'll try to undo--my--mistake."

She did, of course, and she managed to handle it in such a gracious manner that her confidants came away feeling positively flattered. "My dear," she would begin, "I do hope you can forgive me. I've made the most dreadful mistake. It's what comes of listening to servants, you know. They only have half the story most times, but dear me, I'm so gullible. It's about dear Jessalyn…"

As she left the room, Simms turned to her employer. "Do you plan to tell Mrs. Reynolds about this, sir?"

"Probably. Some day, anyway. Now I've got to leave, Simms. Thank you for your help. I know it was difficult for you. Now I've got to go sharpen my blackmailing skills on Lacey Delaney."

At the Delaney mansion, he reined in his panting horse and handed him over to the boy who raced out to take it. He took the steps two at a time, knocked, and waited impatiently as the butler went in search of Woodrow Delaney. He stood in the entryway, alternately tapping his foot on the polished floor, and striking the top of his boot with his riding quirt.

"Why, Dominick." The musical voice that had been no small part of her success on the stage floated down from the steps ahead of Lacey Delaney, and he looked up to see her gliding down the stairs. "How good to see you. Won't you come into the drawing room? I'll ring for some tea. Or brandy, if you prefer."

He looked at her, his face immobile. "Sorry, Lacey. I haven't time for the social amenities. I came to see Woodrow."

"Woodrow?" She frowned, then smoothed her features into what she hoped was a fetching expression. "And I had hoped you were here to visit me. Are you sure you can't stay a moment?"

He didn't answer; Woodrow Delaney had just entered the foyer. "For heaven's sake, Lacey," he said, "don't keep Dominick standing here. Take him into the drawing room and give him a drink of something."

"My thought exactly," she drawled, "but he's evidently in a frightful hurry. He insists that he can't spare a minute. You must convince him, my dear."

" 'Course you can stay, Nick. A minute, anyway. Come in, come in."

Dominick shook his head. "I'm not here on a call, Woodrow. I have a bit of business to see you about."

"Um, I see. Then come into the library. You can sit down a minute, anyway."

Dominick looked at him, then at his wife, and said, "On second thought, this concerns your wife as much as it does you. Maybe she should join us."

"Lacey? Concerns her? What on earth?"

"Woodrow, are you aware that since Alida Fitzhugh died, there has been a great deal of gossip about my wife's part in it?"

"Gossip? What sort of gossip?"

Lacey colored.

"The stories being spread about indicate that my wife murdered Alida."

"Murd--What nonsense! What complete nonsense! Fine woman, your young wife. Not capable of anything so foul."

"I know that. Evidently some others don't."

"How'd this get started, Nick?"

"As nearly as I can tell, her aunt Heloise began the stories. I've dealt with her about it, but I've come to ask Lacey's help in stopping the rumors."

" 'Course she will. No need to ask. 'Course she will."

"Well, certainly, Dominick," Lacey murmured, picking at the lace on her sleeve, "although I have no control over what people say, now, do I? I mean, after all, people will talk, and there's very little--"

"There's a great deal, Lacey." His voice was cold, and Woodrow Delaney looked up at him, surprised. "There's a great deal you can do, and I intend that you shall do it."

"Nick what is this? Are you accusing Lacey of something?"

Dominick paused. "I have every reason to believe that while Lady Heloise started the stories about Jessalyn, Lacey has been doing all she can to spread them and even to add to them."

Delaney's mouth dropped open, and he looked from Dominick to his wife and back again.

"Dominick," Lacey said coolly, "you're quite overwrought. I don't believe you know what you're saying."

"I believe I do."

Lacey's face flushed with anger and she bit her lip. "There isn't a word of truth in what he says, not a word." She had turned, appealing to her husband. "I've not had anything to do with that gossip, not that I haven't heard it, of course; everyone has. But I certainly can't be responsible for what people are saying."

"Let me tell you something, Lacey." Dominick was fairly biting off his words now. "When you came to this island, you were accepted by the women here for two reasons: Susan Newell liked you, and I forced Adelaide to call on you. After that, the others followed suit" Lacey's chin went up, her teeth clenched. "If you have any doubt about the truth of what I say, you can ask any woman you know.

Her husband nodded. "*I* know," he said. "Known all along. Should have thanked you for that, Nick. Never did." His wife turned toward him and gave him a withering glance.

"At any rate," Dominick went on, "you can disclaim responsibility all you like, but unless you make every effort to stop the talk, your social acceptance on this island may suddenly become quite limited."

"Nonsense," Lacey snapped. "You may think you're the wonderful, the powerful Dominick Reynolds, but you can't manage *that* little bit of magic. I've become the most popular hostess on the island. Maybe your help was needed to get me started, but people come now because they enjoy my parties. You can't stop them."

"Don't bet on it, Lacey. I stopped by to see Susan Newell on the way over here. She quite likes Jessalyn, you know. One word from me, and she'd be very willing to withdraw her sponsorship of you."

"Let her. I don't need her, either."

"My dear," her husband said softly, pulling at his pipe, not looking at either of them, "I don't think you fully appreciate the situation here. Dominick Reynolds controls the shipping from this island. If he refuses to handle a planter's sugar, the planter can't move a teaspoon of the stuff. One word from him, and there's not a husband on this island who would allow his wife to cross your threshold."

Her eyes widened, and she looked from her husband to Dominick. "You wouldn't do such a thing."

"I didn't say that I would."

"You didn't have to," Woodrow Delaney said. "Situation is obvious. I know what you did for Lacey when she came here. Owe you a favor, I say. *I'm* grateful, whether she is or not. I know how important those parties and such are to her. You have my word," he said with a meaningful look at his wife, "that we will do everything in our power to help. Everything."

"Thank you, Woodrow," Dominick said, extending his hand. "Sorry I was rude. I've been upset over this."

"Understandable. Completely understandable."

Lacey had risen and was standing stiffly, listening to the exchange between the two men. Dominick turned to leave, and she watched him go. Her husband, without looking at her, went back into his office. Suddenly she scooped her skirts into her hands and followed Dominick out the door, down the steps, to where he stood in the drive, waiting for his horse to be brought around to the front.

"Dominick!"

He turned and looked down at her, his gray eyes cool.

"I meant no harm to your wife--please believe me."

"I believe you, Lacey. I'm quite sure it was just amusing gossip to you. After all, what would you have to gain?"

"What, indeed? In any event, your friendship is of more value to me than such nonsense."

"I'm glad to hear it."

"Dominick." She moved close to him and looked up, her eyes wide. She put her hand on his arm. "Dominick, you know that you mean--a great deal to me. I've always--admired you." She moved her hand up his arm, stroking it gently. "I wouldn't like something of this sort to come between us."

He lifted her hand from his arm. "It needn't."

"Dominick, surely you know--I mean, surely you realize--is there any way I can make myself more clear? I'm offering you more than friendship, if you're willing to take it."

His expression didn't change. "I'm glad of your friendship, *Mrs. Delaney*, but may I remind you that I am married and so are you. In fact, your husband is less than fifty feet from this spot, and he is my friend. Surely a little discretion is advised."

"Is it?" She moved back, stung, but she looked amused. "Were you terribly discreet with Mrs. Fitzhugh? Surely given your frozen little wife, the late Mrs. Fitzhugh must have been quite a change of--temperature?"

"I had nothing to do with Alida Fitzhugh. You of all people ought to know that. Do you think I'd walk back into another alliance like my last marriage? Do you have any idea what that was like?"

"I can imagine. I can also imagine that if the opportunity offered itself, there might be some appeal in--shall we say, a short fling?"

"Shall we say you have a vivid imagination, Mrs. Delaney?"

"Perhaps. I have other desirable qualities, too. If you should change your mind--"

"I won't." He swung into the saddle and was gone without a backward glance.

\*       \*       \*       \*       \*

Simon Alderly was convinced that Dominick had made a mistake by going to the Delaneys to protest the gossip over Jessalyn. His opinion was that gossip is a bit like smoke--impossible to fight, but given enough time, it dissipates. Had he been consulted, he'd have recommended a more moderate course of action, but Dominick had acted impulsively, and, he thought, might have stirred up more rumors as a result.

The year moved slowly, inevitably, into the rainy season, and the residents of Dragonsong were largely confined to the house. Jessalyn, at her husband's urging, made some social calls and was warmly received. Susan Newell went with her on some of them, determined to back down any resistance to Jessalyn, but in fact, they encountered none. They were received with welcomes and without suspicion. Still, Jessalyn found going out unpleasant. The rain poured, hour after hour, and eventually the road was nearly impassable. Floods had washed out parts of it, an annual occurrence, she learned. She gave up the calls and stayed at home, taking care of Dominick's correspondence and reading. Simms was teaching her how to knit--"Come in handy, once you have little ones, ma'am." Jessalyn blushed at that.

"Simms, it's too warm here for knitted things. What do you do with the things you've knitted?"

"I send them to my sister's children in England, ma'am. They can use them in England."

The confinement and the constant rain began to take their toll on the dispositions of the residents of Dragonsong. Marguerite snapped at her when Jessalyn went down to the kitchen one day, and was instantly contrite.

"Think nothing of it, Marguerite. This weather is enough to make us all crazy. How much longer do we have?"

"Oh, my gracious, Miz Jess. We only into the rainy season two months. We got at least four more."

"Four more? Of this? We'll be berserk."

"Naah. Rainy season start a little early this year, but it raining too much to keep it up forever. Anyway, another month, month and a half, usually July or August, maybe we get a *petit careme*."

"A what?"

"A *petit careme*."

"A 'little lent'?"

Marguerite laughed. "That what we call it. It be a week, two weeks, three weeks, rain stops. Sun comes out. Wind blows. It is a wonderful time. Everybody goes on picnics, gets out to visit--like a holiday. Gives everybody time to breathe before the rain starts again."

"That sounds wonderful."

"You wait. We get one. Every time the rainy season starts early, we get *petit careme*."

The only saving grace of the enforced stay at home was the time she spent with Dominick. They had dinner every night, tea most afternoons, and even worked together in the office in the mornings. It was wonderful being with him, she thought. She was becoming more comfortable in his presence, more trusting, more relaxed with him than she had ever been with any man. They talked, they shared jokes and stories, they argued amiably; it was a pleasant time for her in that sense. Still, it was, she thought, an uneasy time. The rain and the humidity didn't entirely account for it, though those things didn't improve the situation any. Tempers were frayed, generally, and the residents were tense. Servants had taken to bickering among themselves, quarreling over insignificant trifles. The most equable of them seemed to have turned moody and snappish. Marguerite had circles under her eyes; she told Jessalyn she wasn't sleeping well. Aurore and Celestine argued and fought with each other like two caged cats. Even Simms, never talkative, seemed more silent than ever.

Simon Alderly had heard of Marguerite's dreams; he knew she had, or claimed to have, the "sight." He had his sources of information regarding what went on in the main house, and he knew that Marguerite was suffering under the burden of what she had "seen." He knew, too, that Lady Heloise, confined to the plantation by the rain, was irritable and unpleasant; she wasn't quite over her humiliation at Dominick's hands. This was not a good time, he thought, especially for Jessalyn. She never mentioned anything to him, but he knew that the situation preyed on her mind. She was almost through half of her year as Dominick's wife; would she stay, he wondered? He'd have bet that Dominick would have her stay, if the choice were his. Interesting how that had worked out. Rather a surprise, too. I wish that I had Marguerite's famous "sight," he thought. I'd use it to see what is to become of Mrs. Reynolds. If it should be that Dominick doesn't manage to keep her here at the end of the year, perhaps...He pushed the thought from his mind. Jessalyn Reynolds was a lovely and unusual woman but she was married to his employer and friend. No point to think of anything beyond that.

It was midsummer when Jessalyn awakened to what she thought, at first, was a strange sound. She lay still in her bed for a few moments, listening. Then she realized that it wasn't a strange sound at all; it was the absence of sound, a kind of silence. There was no rain dripping from the eaves, from the banana trees. The sun was out, in fact, its early rays lighting a corner of her room. She sat up. This must be it, she thought. The *petit careme*. It's come! The rain has stopped for a time. She rose and padded to the window to look out. For the first time in weeks, the early morning sky was clear, and there was a faint breeze rustling the leaves outside her window. She felt suddenly exhilarated and excited, and she dressed quickly, washed, brushed her hair, and let it hang loose to her waist. She slipped out the door and down the stairs. She wanted to get out, to be outdoors for a time, to run, to work out the dragging malaise that had settled upon her during these last few weeks.

She threaded her way through the palms at the edge of the sand, and slipping off her shoes, walked a way down the beach, ran a bit, skipped over the sand, felt the cool dampness beneath her feet. Glorious! The sun had not yet risen enough to warm the sand, and it felt soothing. She walked close to the water's edge, just past the foam-laced place where the waves had smoothed the beach, and then skipped back, turning to watch the footprints she had left, seeing the water come in and reduce them to hollows, cups with a bit of water in each.

She lifted her skirts in her arms and walked a bit further out into the water, letting it wash over her feet, feeling it surge almost to her knees. The sensation was delightful, invigorating, and she felt that she was washing her mind and her spirit as well as her feet. The burden of suspicion that Walter Rhodes had placed on her seemed lighter this morning. He had been back to the house several times, asking questions, poking about; he had not arrested her, although she had been tempted to beg him either to put her in jail or to let her loose from this half-bondage. But nothing had happened. He had said little to her, other than the occasional question. She pretended his visits were social calls. It was a silly sort of charade, she thought.

She hiked up her skirts and raced down the beach, dancing in and out of the waves, and when she turned to race back, she almost ran headlong into Dominick Reynolds.

"OH!" she yelped, startled. "I didn't know you were here. I thought I was alone on the beach."

"I know," he said, falling into step beside her. "I saw you leaving the house, and I thought I'd bring you breakfast."

"Breakfast?"

"Breakfast," he said, holding out two fresh coconuts and extending one of them to her. "Hold this a moment." He pulled out a machete--the cane workers' "cutlass"--from his belt. He chopped off the top of the coconut he held and handed it to her so that she could drink the milk. He followed suit with the other, then he cut out a small wedge from each nut and showed her how to use that to scoop out the soft jelly inside. They strolled along the beach, eating the coconuts, and when they had finished, he tossed the husks far out into the surf.

She spread her arms and whirled about on the sand. "I'm soooo glad the rain has stopped. Will it stay clear for a long time?"

"A *petit careme* lasts up to three weeks," he said. "We can hope."

"That would be lovely. Then I could stand the rest of the rainy season."

He watched her as she skipped across the sand, this lovely child-woman, the light in her hair, the sun on her face, and he thought her the most beautiful creature he had ever seen.

"We can go riding," she was saying, "because I'd bet that Josephine is frantic, being shut up with so little exercise, and Spaniard will be kicking his stall down, and I can understand why they feel that way because I feel just like that myself--" She looked up at him and thought that he wore the oddest expression she had ever seen. "What's wrong? Do I look odd? Why are you looking at me like that?"

He inhaled sharply. "Because, Jessalyn Kirke Reynolds, I think you are the most beautiful woman I've ever seen, and because I'm very much in love with you, and because I think it's time to begin our marriage."

She stopped quite still, her face alight, but her body a bit tense and wary. "I--I--don't know--" she began.

"It's all right. I know. There's still something between us, something you have difficulty getting past. But I assure you, nothing matters. There's no one else for me, there never has been, really, and having found you, I know that there never will be again. I will never have another woman in my life, Jessalyn. You are my life's love."

Not Aurore, she wanted to ask, not Adelaide, not Alida. But she didn't speak. She wanted to believe him, wanted very much to think that his words were true.

"It's time, Jess."

She gasped for breath, she touched her hand to her chest as if to put more air in her lungs.

"I think it's time, Jess," he repeated.

She struggled for air. He stood there, tall and dark and beautiful in her eyes. Everything in her heart screamed Say Yes! Say Yes! But some dark, frightened corner of her mind hung back.

"That might be a mistake," she finally whispered. "How would it look to the constable if we should suddenly become a loving couple after having assured him that our marriage was only a business arrangement?"

"I say let Walter Rhodes go to the devil. I'm at the point of telling him to let you go unless he has something to base this stupid house arrest thing on. I want to take you to Trinidad with me next month, and I would like to be free to take you anywhere we want to go. He can't prolong this forever."

She nodded. But she said nothing.

"Jessalyn." He moved close to her and she was torn between the urge to step away from him and the urge to move into his arms. She didn't move.

"Jessalyn," he repeated, "tell me what you think of me."

"I--I--I'm a bit--that is--I think--I think I'm afraid of you."

"Of me? There's no one less likely to harm you. Are you sure you aren't afraid of yourself?"

"I don't know." She breathed, not looking at him. "I'm--just--afraid."

"Because all the other men in your life have betrayed you? Treated you wretchedly? I'm not all the others, Jessalyn."

"I know, but--"

"But it's hard, anyway, isn't it?"

"Yes." Very softly.

"I know. I didn't want to be in love with you, you know. After Adelaide, I didn't ever want to be in love again."

"No?"

"Never. But I love you, Jess. I want you. I want you to be my wife, to have my children, to live with me for all of our lives. Can I be any clearer than that?"

She shook her head, feeling her throat constrict, feeling tears come to her eyes.

"Do you love me, Jess?"

She couldn't speak. She rubbed the back of her hand across her eyes, but she nodded quickly.

He pulled her to him, and raised one hand to tip her head back to kiss her, a long slow kiss, the sort of kiss that belongs to love that has plenty of time. She clung to him, her arms around his neck, feeling her tears on her face, tasting them on her lips, on his lips. At last he released her, smoothing her hair, and said, "Then it's all right, love. Everything will be all right. Trust me, my own."

He held her hand, and they made their way slowly back up the gravel drive.

At the veranda, they were met by a foreman from the sugar mill who told Dominick he was urgently needed there. Dominick turned, kissed her quickly, and started off toward the stables. About ten steps away, he stopped and called to her, "Jessalyn."

"Yes?"

"Give this thing to Douglas, will you?" He handed her the cutlass, extending the handle to her. "He'll take care of it. I don't want to take it on the horse."

She took it and went up the steps, waving goodbye to him.

Douglas was not inside the door, and so occupied was she with her thoughts that she was in her room before she looked down and noticed that she still had the machete in her hand.

"Oh, good," she murmured to herself. "Just what I need, a cutlass in the room. Maybe I can use it to trim the lamps."

She stood it against the doorframe where she would remember to take it back down to Douglas later. Marmles was sleeping in a patch of sunlight on the floor of the gallery, and she picked him up and took him downstairs to have his breakfast, leaving the machete in the room.

Dominick wasn't back for tea. She went word up to Lady Heloise asking her to come down and join her for tea, but the lady said she was suffering from a vicious headache and asked to be excused. When Simms came in, Jessalyn asked her to sit down and share a cup of tea. Simms hesitated.

"I'm not sure how that would look, ma'am."

"I'm not either, Simms, but my husband isn't back from the mill, Lady Heloise has a headache, Simon is goodness knows where, and I'm lonely. Do sit down for a moment. If it will sooth your feelings, we can pretend to discuss the affairs of the household."

"Since you put it that way, ma'am, I'm sure I don't mind." Simms took the cup of tea and sipped it, then she said to Jessalyn, "What this place needs, ma'am, if you don't mind my saying so, is a houseful of children." She blinked at her own temerity, then added, "Begging your pardon, Mrs. Reynolds."

Jessalyn blushed, and Simms added quickly, "Of course, that's none of my business, ma'am, I'm sure, and you may not even want children for all I know."

"Oh, no, it isn't that, Simms. I do, of course, but you know that Mr. Reynolds may not care for them."

"Oh, dear, Mrs. Reynolds, I'm sure no man ever wanted children any more than Mr. Reynolds. I know he grieved more for that child than he ever did for his dead wife."

Jessalyn spent the rest of the afternoon and early evening in the library reading with her ear turned to the door to listen for Dominick's step. But at twilight, he sent word that he would be late and not to wait dinner for him. She sighed, put the book away, and ate dinner alone.

After dinner, she went out to the back and called Marmles, who came bounding across the grass of the back yard and sprang up to land in her outstretched arms. She laughed.

"Spoiled cat," she murmured, nuzzling her chin against his head. He purred and stretched his neck to rub his ear against her shoulder. She carried him, scratching him under the chin and behind his ears. It was getting dark in the house. She stopped to light a candle and with the cat under one arm and the candle in the other hand, she started up to her room.

As she approached her room, the cat suddenly began to twist under her arm and growl in his throat, the hair on his body standing on end.

"Marmles, what's the matter?" Jessalyn paused in front of her door. "Settle down, now."

He continued to growl and turned, trying to climb her shoulder.

"Ow!" She jumped as his claws dug into her flesh. He yowled and writhed under her arm, finally freeing himself. He jumped down and landed a few feet away, backing away from the door and hissing.

"What on earth is the matter with you, you beastly cat? That hurt! You behave as if I'd taken a dog in there. Come on, now."

But the animal backed away from her, still hissing, his fur standing up, his back arched, his teeth bared.

"Honestly, silly, nothing is wrong here. Come *on*."

But Marmles turned and ran down the hall, yowling. Jessalyn shook her head as she watched him go. Well, I suppose you'll come back when you have a mind to, she thought. I'm too tired to chase you. She opened the door and entered the room

The bedroom seemed stuffy, and she frowned as she glanced across to the blinds, lowered over the closed French doors. "No wonder it's warm in here," she murmured. "I thought surely I'd left these windows open. Who in heaven's name would have closed them?"

She set the candle on the dressing table and crossed the room to raise the blinds and fling open the doors. The breeze that came through felt good, and she stood for a moment on the gallery. Then she turned back to the dressing table, standing in front of the mirror to brush her hair. As she raised her arms to remove the pins from her hair, she thought she caught sight of some movement behind her reflected in the mirror.

She turned toward it.

She saw nothing.

Then as she turned back to the mirror, she saw a shadow move across the floor.

When she faced the shadow, she froze.

She was looking into the eyes of a huge snake, which was moving steadily toward her.

The creature must have been eight feet long, banded with alternating sections of black and vivid salmon pink. Its snout was blunt, and the small eyes focused squarely on hers. The tongue flicked in and out, and the reptile continued to move relentlessly toward her.

Forcing herself from her paralysis, she began to back away from the serpent, and she screamed at the top of her lungs.

The snake edged forward, the back half of its body coiled into a great loop, the front half-poised, swaying slightly, moving inexorably toward her. She backed up and screamed again, shaving a chair into the path of the creature. The snake withdrew for a small space, then moved forward again, pouring itself like oil among the rungs of the chair.

She looked about quickly, choking back her panic. She had backed herself into a corner, cut off in both directions form the doors. She screamed again, calling for help. She reached out behind her with her left hand and felt the drawer pull of a desk. She grasped it, and yanking hard, flung it at the snake. It backed again, briefly, then moved into the open drawer and across it, the rasp-like skin reflecting the candlelight as if it were made of wax.

Jessalyn moved along the edge of the room, feeling behind her for something, anything. She flung a book at the creature, missed, and hurled a candlestick. The candlestick hit it in the middle part of its raised body, and the snake coiled into a tighter circle and slowed a bit, but as Jessalyn searched for another weapon, the serpent moved back into the larger circle and began creeping forward again.

She grasped the desk itself and shoved it at the snake, attempting as she did so to move around behind the desk and use it as a shield. The serpent pulled back, then began to move beneath the desk. She shoved the desk from her, tipping it over on the body of the snake, temporarily pinning it to the floor.

She jumped out of the way, leaping out of the corner. At that moment, the door sprang open, and Dominick Reynolds burst in. "Jessalyn, what is going on in--"

She screamed again and pointed to the snake oozing its way from beneath the desk.

"My god! A bushmaster!" Dominick snatched a cover from the bed and flung it over the snake, then looked frantically about for something with which to kill it.

"The cutlass!" Jessalyn screamed. "Behind you, beside the door!"

He spun around and grabbed the machete. He chopped viciously at the roiling coverlet, striking through the fabric to kill the snake. Blood spread over the peach cover, then it was still. He pulled back the spread and looked down at the dead serpent. He dropped the machete, breathing heavily.

Then he turned to his wife, who was leaning against the door. She was pale, her eyes were wide, her body was pressed against the door, and her palms were spread beside her, seeking escape.

"Jessalyn--love--are you all right?" He stepped across the coverlet to her. "He didn't strike you, did he?"

"No," she breathed, moving her head from side to side. And then her hands were still, and silently, she slid down the wall in a dead faint.

# Chapter Twenty

S HE CAME TO, BROUGHT out of the faint by the acrid scent of the smelling salts Simms was waving under her nose.

"It's all right," Simms murmured, recapping the container when she saw Jessalyn's eyes open. "You were right. She wasn't bitten; she just fainted."

Jessalyn was lying on a bed, but it was not her own. Dominick was holding her hands in a vice grip. "Jessalyn, what happened?" he asked. "Where did that snake come from?"

Se struggled to sit up. She was in Dominick's room, lying on his bed. The door between the rooms was open; evidently they had brought her in that way. She breathed deeply and shook her head to clear it, then she said, "From under my bed, as nearly as I could tell. If you mean how did it get there, I've no idea."

"Hmm." He frowned. "I suppose it could have come in from the veranda; there's the possibility it could have climbed the vines, I guess, although I've never known one to do that. Wonder how it got on the island? They aren't native."

"No. That couldn't have been. The French doors were closed."

"Closed?" His frown deepened. "The doors to the gallery were shut?"

"Yes. I had opened them when I came in. They'd been closed for some time, I believe, because the room was stuffy, and the first thing I did was open them."

The room was quite still. Dominick Reynolds looked at her, then at Simms, then back to Jessalyn. "Do you understand the implications of that?"

She closed her eyes and clutched his hands tightly as the situation became clear to her. Then she said, "It means someone put it there. Someone put it in my room deliberately."

"Yes."

"Someone is--someone wanted--to--kill *me*."

"Apparently."

"Then--" her voice was tight and high pitched as other things suddenly became clear to her. "Then it wasn't Alida who was supposed to die at all. It was *me*. Someone has been trying to kill *me*. But why? I haven't hurt anyone. Why would it be me? Why me?"

"I don't know," he said. "If I did--well, it doesn't matter. Simms, have someone clean up that mess in Mrs. Reynolds's room, will you? And tell them to be careful of that snake, even if it is dead."

"Yes, sir. Before I leave, could I show you something, Mr. Reynolds?"

"Certainly. What is it?"

"Perhaps if you'd come with me, sir..." He looked up at her. Whatever it was, she didn't want Jessalyn seeing it.

"Just a moment, Jess." He followed Simms into the hall. She took something out of her pocket and extended it to him. He took the bit of paper she had given him and frowned at it. In the dim light of the hallway, he could just make out burned scrap of paper with fragments of words written on it: --lyn Reyn--.

He looked up at Simms. "Someone put the light on her. Where did you get this?"

"One of the servants brought it to me this morning. I should have given it to you earlier, perhaps, but I haven't seen you, and I didn't think--"

"It's no matter." They had both lived on the island long enough to know the *obeah* ways, the *obeah* tricks. "This is a native thing."

"Or a native hired by someone else."

"Simms, don't mention this to her, will you? She's frightened enough already. No point in getting this voodoo nonsense planted in her mind."

"As you say, sir. Shall I let you know when her room is ready?"

He paused, looked at her and said, "No. No, that won't be necessary. I'm not letting her out of my sight until we find out who's doing this. She'll stay in my room."

"Very well, sir."

When he went back into the room, Jessalyn was sitting at the head of the bed, her knees drawn up almost to her chin, her hands clasped in front of her tightly. Her eyes were wide and dark with fear, and she was shaking.

"It's over, love." He sat down on the bed beside her and took her hands. "It's over. Nothing is going to hurt you." He could feel her trembling.

"The horse," she said, not looking at him. "That wasn't an accident either, was it? That was someone trying to kill me, too."

"We think so."

"That's why you came home so soon. Simon sent for you, didn't he?"

"Yes."

"But Dominick," her voice was a whisper. "Why? Why me? I haven't done anything. I'm not important enough--"

"Hush, love. Hush. It's all right." He pulled her to him, gathered her into his arms, stroked her hair. And for the first time, she clung to him, wrapping her arms about him, burying her head in the curve of his throat, still shaking, but warmed by his touch and his love. "I'm not letting you out of my sight. You're going to be fine, I promise. Don't be afraid. It's all right."

"I'd better go back to my room," she murmured, but she didn't move from his arms. "I'd best--"

"No."

"No?"

"You'll stay here tonight. I'm not sending you back in there. You can stay here. You're never going back in there. You'll be here tonight. Every night."

"But Dominick," she whispered.

"Shhh. We've delayed our wedding night too long already," he said, and he felt her body relax against him.

He kissed her, and he loosed her hair, burying his hands in that heavy golden curtain, murmuring her name against her skin, against her mouth. He stretched out on the bed beside her, pulling her body close against him, moving his hands over her, unbuttoning her dress, slowly undressing her. She gasped when he moved his hand gently across her bare breast, but she didn't move away, she merely held him tighter, her fingers digging into the flesh of his arms.

And then she was naked, and he smoothed his hands across her creamy flesh, and after she'd have sworn he had kissed every square inch of her body, he whispered, "This may hurt you, love."

She clung to him, and he was right--and wrong. She felt the pain, was aware of it, but lost it somehow in the rest of their love, in the joining, the coming together, and she felt the sudden perfection of the moment. She called his name, and he whispered, "Yes, my own love," and she felt as if she'd been separated from half herself until that moment, that she had never known or given love until now, that she had not been quite complete. The two of them were worth everything, all the pain, all the loss, all the agony--everything. To have him, to belong to him, to have him belong to her--tears filled her eyes and he saw them and kissed them away, and everything that it had cost her to get to this moment she have done twice over.

He held her until she slept. When she woke in the night, dreaming of the snake, gasping and shaking, he wrapped her in his arms and stroked her hair and whispered to her until she slept again.

She woke in the morning to find him already awake, propped on one elbow, regarding her. His eyes were dark in the pale dawn light, and he was winding a lock of her hair about his finger.

She watched him without moving; then she said softly," I love you, Dominick Reynolds."

He smiled, leaned over, and planted a row of kisses along her collarbone. "That's fortunate," he murmured. "It will make your life easier."

She giggled, and stroked his hair. "If my life were any easier, I'd have servants employed for the sole purpose of peeling grapes for me."

"Umm. I can arrange it."

"I'll bet you can. They you'd end up with a fat dumpling of a wife."

"Like Margaret Harrington?"

"Dominick, you're wicked. But yes, like her, poor dear."

"Poor dear, indeed. The woman's a horror, and not just because she's fat, either."

"Well, it must be difficult for her, knowing that her husband prefers his mistress." She sat up in bed, pulled the sheet up under her arms, and glanced sidelong at her husband. "Do you have any mistresses?"

"What! Woman, what a question. No, I have no mistresses. I have one extremely difficult wife, who, although she's been shirking her marital duties lo these many months, seems to be showing a wonderful tendency toward reforming."

She blushed. He rose and walked toward his dressing table and opened a drawer from which he took a flat, square box.

He brought it to her and placed it on the sheet in front of her. "Mrs. Reynolds--and you are, finally, Mrs. Reynolds--these are for you."

She looked at the box, she looked at him, then she picked it up and opened it.

Lying on the pale gray velvet lining was a sapphire and diamond necklace and matching earrings. The necklace had seven large, deep blue stones, each surrounded by diamonds. The earrings had a single sapphire surrounded by diamonds, pendant from large diamond stones.

"How beautiful," she breathed, "how very beautiful."

"They were my mother's," he said. "They were handed down to the oldest daughter in the family, but since I was an only child, they were to go to my wife. They were all that we had left from--before." He paused. "I never gave them to Adelaide. I don't know why. I simply never felt--I don't know. I haven't felt as if I had a wife. Until now."

Her eyes filled with tears, and she dashed them away with the back of her hand.

"Don't," he said. "It's all right if you cry." And she did, leaning her head against his chest, sobbing.

At last he said, "Now. Get into your riding habit. We'll take the horses out for a run before breakfast." She started for the door between their suites, but he called after her, "Let me go first."

He pulled on a dressing gown, opened the door, and preceded her into the room. He poked under the bed, checked the wardrobe and drawers, searched the dressing room. Finally he said, "I think it's all right now."

"The next thing I know, you'll be tasting my food for me."

"Not a bad idea. Either that or cooking it myself."

"Marguerite would never let you into her kitchen."

"Nonsense. This is my plantation."

"It may be your plantation, but it's Marguerite's kitchen, and if you want to keep your cook, you'd best remember it."

"A mere bride, and giving me orders already. I've a terrible life to look forward to." He kissed her before he went back to his room. "Hurry up. I'm not waiting a second longer than five minutes."

She was longer than five minutes, but he didn't seem to mind. They were out of the house and on their horses quickly.

He saddled both mounts himself, checking her gear very thoroughly.

"Where are we going?" she asked.

"Around the coast to the boat house," he said. "I have a little sailboat I want to show you. We can sail around the island to Robinson Crusoe's cave."

"Can we really?" her eyes widened.

"Well, we can really sail, but it isn't really Crusoe's cave."

"Do people say that it is?"

"That's the story, and a good story, too. But hardly true. Crusoe was fiction."

"Well, yes, but sometimes there's a true story at the bottom of a made-up one."

"Perhaps. You've never been to Italy, have you?"

"I've never been anywhere except England and here."

"Well, I'll have to remedy that. In Verona, the required stops are at the houses of Romeo and Juliet. Great fun to see, but so much rubbish, of course."

"The play was beautiful, though."

"Yes, I suppose. Although I can't enjoy it as much as I should, because I've very little patience with people who kill themselves to escape their problems. As long as you're alive, there's always another way."

"Perhaps they were too young to know that."

"That's the only excuse I'll allow them. Up with you now." He helped her mount, and she raced off a little way, spun her mount about and raced back.

"My, she is frisky this morning."

"So is this old devil. Spaniard, mind your manners, sir. This way, love. We're off along the coast road."

They galloped along the coast road for a way, then slowed the horses to a walk, still arguing about Shakespeare's tragedies. She defended the stories, he attacked the logic. Finally she threw up her hand in mock dismay. "Dominick, you have no romance in your soul!"

In answer, he pulled Spaniard close beside her mount, leaned across, pulled her to him, and kissed her thoroughly. "Nonsense," he said, releasing her, "I am entirely romantic, though rather more in practice than in theory. Come along, the boathouse is just here."

There was a long narrow pier out over the water to the boathouse, and he held her arm to lead her up the steps. The boathouse itself was unlocked, merely bolted from the outside, and he opened the door and let her enter. Moored in the dim recesses of the house was a sailboat that looked as if it needed repair. Dominick jumped down into the boat and began checking it over.

"I'm going to have to do some work on it," he said. "It's been longer than I remembered since I sailed it." He checked the boat, tapping on this, knocking on that. "Have you done any sailing?" he asked.

"No, not if you mean on a small boat like this one."

He stood up, his hands on his hips, and looked at her a long moment. "Do you realize how little I know about you?"

"No less than I know about you. You could have a scandalous past, for all I know."

"I'll never tell." He jumped out of the boat. "Come on. I'll get some men down here to work on this and take you out while the *petit careme* holds. Meanwhile, let's get on with our ride. Where would you like to go?"

"Let's stop by the Newells'. I haven't seen Susan in a long while."

"Gladly."

As they left the boathouse, Jessalyn glanced around with a puzzled look. "Dominick, isn't this rather far from the house? I'd think a boathouse here would be inconvenient."

"No, not really. We came the long way. Look." He pointed toward the growth at the edge of the beach, and following his arm, she could see a small path emerge from the jungle. "This path comes out just back of the jungle garden, and is quite short, actually. You come across instead of going around. Much shorter than the way we came."

"Yes. Yes, I can see it would be."

"This cove is much more sheltered than the one where the ships dock. That's deeper; that's why I put the docks there. But this is more out of the wind. A bit of protection in case of storms."

"Are there storms here? Bad ones, I mean, not just the rain."

"Not usually. Oh, the occasional one, but we don't have hurricanes like most of the West Indian islands. Too far south. Still, once in a while, there's a fierce one. In '36, a hurricane destroyed most of the crops, and many of the planters went under."

"Is that another reason you don't keep everything tied up in the sugar crop?"

"Precisely, my bright and beautiful wife. Any number of things can happen to a one-crop plantation. I diversify on this plantation, and I have the other holdings that you know about."

"More of the others should do that."

He shrugged. "Some just don't want the bother. But let's get back on the road. I'm taking you in to talk to Walter Rhodes, and if we're going to the Newells' first, we'd better get riding."

Early as it was, Susan Newell was in her flowerbeds, weeding. She greeted the Reynolds with great enthusiasm.

"Do come in for a bit of breakfast," she said. "Jessalyn, my dear, you're looking quite ravishing. Lovely riding habit."

"What's this, Susan? You didn't say how ravishing *I'm* looking."

She laughed. "Dominick, actually, I've never seen you looking quite so well. Marriage must be just the thing for both of you. But, Jessalyn, I didn't want to tell him that. Turn his head, you know."

She ushered them into the breakfast room, and handing her hat and gloves to a servant, ordered breakfast for them all. "I did want to get at those flower beds, you know. Have to take advantage of the weather. You never know how long this nice spell will last. So, where are you both off to this morning?"

"A ride around the island, Susan," Dominick said, not mentioning the proposed trip to the constable. "Jessalyn wanted to get out and give the horses a run for the same reason you were so eager to get into those flower beds."

"We do have our hobbies, Dominick What do you do when the weather is foul, Jessalyn?"

"I've been doing correspondence for Dominick and reading, of course. Always reading."

"Oh, good. Dominick always has all the latest books. Do you have the most recent by Mr. Dickens?"

"No. I looked through the latest batch. No Dickens."

"I do have it, so let's trade something. I'll bring it over tomorrow, and we'll make a swap. By the way, Dominick, have you seen Lacey since your little set-to?"

"What set-to?" Jessalyn asked.

"Umm. You wouldn't have told her, now would you? Let's just put it this way, my dear. Dominick confronted Lacey over some rumors she was spreading about you regarding Alida's death, and he told her to stop it or else. She stopped it, of course."

"You did that?" Jessalyn looked at her husband, amused.

"I did. The woman's vicious."

"More than you know, Dominick," Susan said, frowning over her tea. "I'd be careful of that one, if I were you."

"I'm not afraid of Lacey Delaney, Susan."

"Oh, dear, I know you're not. But watch out for her, all the same. I do adore Lacey; always have. She has a wicked tongue and a devastating wit. She's the cleverest hostess on the island. Nonetheless, when she gets a grudge going, she can be very unpleasant. You be careful, both of you. She can attack in the most vulnerable places."

*    *    *    *    *

Walter Rhodes gazed at the pair across from him. Something had happened to them, and while he wasn't sure what it was, he knew that the relationship was different. A business arrangement, indeed. Of course, it was obvious why Reynolds had said it. If they had only an arranged marriage, there would be no need for the young woman to be jealous of Alida Fitzhugh. But the man quite clearly dotes on her. Any fool can see that.

"Now, let me get this straight," he said. "You say someone put the snake in Mrs. Reynolds's room?"

Dominick stirred impatiently. "Of course, Rhodes. You know as well as I do that bushmasters aren't indigenous to this island. It would have to have been brought across from Venezuela. Besides, I've told you. The doors were shut. The place was closed up. I've had the servants save the snake's body if you want to see it."

"You have witnesses, of course."

"Certainly. I'm tired of the suspicion that's been centered on my wife, Rhodes. I want you to tell her that she's cleared and get on with finding the person who is trying to kill *her*."

"Well, under these circumstances, I do suppose that confinement to the island seems--if not silly, certainly dangerous."

"I suppose, under the circumstances," Dominick said, "you'd be advised to consider releasing her from that confinement. According to my lawyer, you have no reason to restrict her movements indefinitely without charging her."

"Umm. You're right, of course. But the bushmaster thing gives me a new source on which to operate. It might be a point worth investigating. If someone brought one of those things over here, there's more than one person who knows about it. I'll give that some thought."

Jessalyn, quiet until now, leaned forward in her chair. "Constable, do you still have any doubts about my innocence?"

He paused, looking first at her, then at her husband, then at her again. "Quite frankly, Mrs. Reynolds, I'm not sure my doubts or lack of them have any bearing. It is possible--though not likely--that these, um, events that have occurred could have been arranged carefully by the two of you to throw suspicion elsewhere."

"Rhodes, that's nonsense, and you know it." Dominick was furious.

"Very probably, Reynolds, very probably. But look at this from my position. I must consider all possibilities. You know that."

"I suppose," Dominick muttered.

"Would you like an honest opinion, both of you?"

"It would be a pleasant change, Rhodes."

"Quite frankly, I've had a difficult time casting Mrs. Reynolds, here, in the role of murderess ever since I met her. She just doesn't fit the part. Of course, that means nothing. Most innocent-looking lad I ever saw had slit the throats of three women. Still, I've had to hold her up for scrutiny, because she had the three essential elements of a murderer: motive, opportunity, means. But suppose I accept your story as quite true. I'll verify it, of course, but you both must understand, Reynolds, Mrs. Reynolds, that if it is as you say, Mrs. Reynolds is in great danger."

The couple glanced at each other.

"We know that," Dominick said. "That's why we're here."

"Very well. Let me work at it from the snake angle for a time. Heaven knows, I've made very little progress until now."

Jessalyn breathed a small sigh. "I do feel better about this, you know."

"You shouldn't." Rhodes stood up. "If you are not the perpetrator, you were obviously the intended victim. You should be terrified."

"She has no reason to be," Dominick said. "I'm not letting her out of my sight from now on. No one can touch her."

As they left the office, Walter Rhodes moved around to the window and watched them out of sight. Interesting problem, he thought. If the lovely Mrs. Reynolds is not the guilty party, she might make the most effective bait for the one who is.

He stood by the window a long time after they had gone.

*     *     *     *     *

When they arrived at the house, Marguerite had a late breakfast ready, and no protestations that they had eaten would stem her fuss over Jessalyn.

"You poor chile," she said. "You come in here and sit down and let me fix you breakfast. Poor thing! What an awful night for you! Sit down. You too, Mr. Reynolds. I fix you something." Amid bustling and clucking over Jessalyn, Marguerite served up strong hot tea, muffins and marmalade, and eggs, insisting all the while that the two of them eat, eat!

"What a bad shock," she muttered. "Poor thing, you eat. That make you feel butter."

"Marguerite thinks," Dominick said when she'd left the room, "that anything not curable by a hearty meal is probably terminal." But Jessalyn did feel better after her second breakfast.

"Marguerite," she said, "can you cure anything with strong tea and hot food?"

Marguerite smiled, her eyes crinkling in her round face. "I think I can't cure *everything*, Miz Jess, but if I can't cure it, I make you feel better to put up with it."

"By the way, Marguerite, have you seen Marmles? He ran off last night when I tried to take him into my room, and I haven't seen him since."

"Oh, yes. I have seen him. No getting rid of that hungry cat. I fed him a while ago and put him outside. He be out back somewhere. You call him. He come."

Jessalyn went out through the kitchen and called for the cat, but he did not immediately appear. She followed the gravel path around the house, calling him, and as she came toward the front, she spotted him getting ready to pounce on a small bird.

"Marmles!" He turned and started toward her, gliding across the grass and curling himself around her ankles as if birds were the furthest things from his mind.

"You are a total fraud, cat," she said, scooping him up into her arms. "What a wicked thing you are, and what a hypocrite. I don't know why I tolerate you."

With the cat in her arms, she strolled back to the kitchen the way she had come. Dominick had gone back to his office, and as she entered, she heard the sounds of voices raised in anger. She walked through the door to see Celestine and Aurore squared off in the midst of a furious fight.

"I am tired," Celestine was saying loudly, "of doing everything around here while you sit around doing nothing! I wish Mr. Dominick get rid of you! You one worthless girl!"

"Celestine," Marguerite snapped. "Don't you talk to your sister that way!"

Celestine spun to face her mother. "But it is true! You have said so, you yourself! You know how lazy she is! You know it. You always spoil her, you do!"

"Ha!" Aurore's lovely face was red with anger. "Spoil me, indeed! All she ever tell me is how good you are. Celestine so-o-o good. Celestine work so-o-o hard. Celestine this, Celestine that. When does anybody around here pay any mind to me?"

"You just lazy no good!" Celestine shouted. "You worthless girl!"

"You just jealous," Aurore sneered. "You just jealous because you getting old, past marrying age, and nobody want to marry with you. You jealous because *I* marry anybody I choose. You jealous because I so pretty, you so not."

She turned then and swept past Jessalyn, giving Celestine a look of contempt as she left the room. Celestine stood in the center of the room, reduced by her rage to a helpless fury. Finally she screamed, "Someday I kill her, Mama! She made me so mad!"

Marguerite shook her head, frowning. "You do no such thing, Celestine. You right about her. She lazy, she good for nothing. But," she shrugged, "someday she get married, she have babies, she settle down. You see."

"Maybe somebody not let her live that long," Celestine said darkly, and stormed out of the room without a backward glance.

"What on earth was that about?" Jessalyn asked. "I've never seen them so angry."

"Ahh," Marguerite sighed, "bad blood between them. I don't know if Celestine ever get over it. Aurore have a mean streak. She take away one of Celestine's gentlemen, just to show she able to do it. She don't want him. She just want to have him because he Celestine's. They always fight, but after this, it get worse."

She stopped, sighed, shook her head. "Maybe it the weather."

"But it's a lovely day, Marguerite."

"Umm. But it been a long rainy season, it gonna be longer. They get on each other's nerves. It strange, Miz Jess. I think we in for one big storm. One big, big storm."

"A tropical storm? A hurricane?"

"Maybe."

"But Dominick says we don't have them on Tobago."

"We have had. We will again."

"Oh, Marguerite, not for years, maybe. Maybe--"

"Soon. I have seen it."

"Seen it?"

"I keep seeing one, Miz Jess."

"What do you mean, 'seeing one', Marguerite?"

Marguerite sighed and glanced at her sidelong. "I mean, Miz Jess, sometimes I just *see* things. I just know them, sometimes from dreams, like I been having lately. Sometimes just--they just come to me." She shrugged. "I don't know why. Just do. Always have."

"What sort of things do you see?"

"Different things." She looked at the floor, at Jessalyn, then away, at her hands. "I know you gonna be a beauty, first thing you came here. Never mind you looked like a scrawny chicken. I know."

"Maybe you just guessed that I couldn't look so bad as all that."

"No. I know more. I knew about Miz Alida."

"You knew--" Despite the head, Jessalyn felt the touch of something cold. "You knew she was going to--die?"

"I know, Miz Jess." Her voice was almost a whisper. "I didn't tell anybody. Nobody believe me anyway. But you--you have to believe me, Miz Jess. You have to. You in awful danger."

"But Marguerite, the constable has told me I'm not under suspicion any more. There have been some--things, but Dominick says--"

"That don't matter. You still in danger. That storm comes, you hide, hear me? The storm comes, your brother not save you."

"My brother---" her heart gave a strange lurch. "Marguerite, I never told you I had a brother."

"I know. He dead. But he not, you know? He stay around, stay around you. He save you from Miz Alida that time she throw that thing at you."

Jessalyn put her hand to her mouth. How did Marguerite know? How did she *know*? Servants' gossip, it must be. But they didn't know, either, they couldn't have guessed. There was nothing, nothing...

"I'll take care, Marguerite."

"I wish you leave this island."

"I can't, Marguerite. I wish I could, too, but I can't."

"Then you be careful, like you say. Don't go nowhere you don't know about. Stay close to this house. You safer here."

"I wonder. That thing with the snake--and besides, this house seems to be--I don't know--empty, I guess. Spooky, sort of. It's so big and lonely."

"This house not really spooky, Miz Jess. It just empty and lonely, like you say. This house be fine if it had five, six children in it."

"I suppose. I guess children can chase the ghosts out of any house."

"Huh. They do that."

*     *     *     *     *

The *petit careme* went, and the rains started again. Dominick and Jessalyn had one sail in the refurbished boat before the rains resumed, but he put the boat away after that, telling her they'd have to wait until the dry season started.

The weeks dragged on, warm and wet, seeming to Jessalyn to pile one damp day on another. Everything not carefully dried mildewed rapidly; keeping the linens and clothes fresh was difficult. The beds felt damp when sleepers crawled into them at night. And the predominant sound coming into the Reynolds's bedroom was the drip-drip-drip of the rain from the broad leaves of the banana trees.

Tempers flared and subsided; the residents of Dragonsong began avoiding each other. August slipped away and wasn't missed. Calling, among the island women, renewed during the *petit careme,* dwindled again.

Lady Heloise, bored with nothing to occupy her, kept up her calling as long as she was able, but it was the rare and brave lady who would risk the torrents of water that cut through the roadways or poured down the centers of roads.

For this reason, Jessalyn was surprised one drizzly afternoon when George Douglas came into the office where she was working to tell her that Lacey Delaney was calling.

Jessalyn hurried out to the foyer. Lacey, dressed in spotless lilac, was folding a deep purple umbrella, and appeared to have made the trip through the mud and damp without picking up a droplet of water or a spot of dirt.

"Lacey," Jessalyn said, "how good to see you." The response was genuine. If Lacey Delaney was not her favorite person--and she was not--Jessalyn was eager enough to have someone to talk to that she could greet her with unfeigned enthusiasm.

"Jessalyn, I simply had to get out of that house. I'm going mad in there with no one to talk to but Woodrow. And even he isn't really available. He has his head in one of those endless, boring histories he's always reading."

"Do come into the drawing room. I'll send Aurore for some tea."

Aurore came in, and when Jessalyn sent her for tea, Lacey watched her out the door, a faint, amused smile flickering about her mouth.

"My, she is lovely, isn't she? I'd never allow her to work in *my* house."

"Aurore? She's George and Marguerite's daughter. They're the Douglases. The whole family works here."

"Well, my dear, I suppose you know what you're doing. You certainly know whether you can trust Dominick or not."

"Oh," Jessalyn said lightly, "I'm sure I can."

"Well, perhaps he's reformed. I do know that poor Adelaide couldn't have an even halfway attractive housemaid in here. That's one reason the staff was always so small."

Jessalyn stiffened in her chair. Lacey noticed her discomfort with some satisfaction. "She'd be certain to get rid of *that* young lady."

"Perhaps," murmured Jessalyn, "*she'd* have had cause."

When Aurore returned with the tea, Jessalyn poured for the two of them.

"By the way," Lacey said, "has the constable fastened on anyone else to use as a suspect in Alida's death? It must be ghastly for you. I'd be frightened to death to stay in the house."

Jessalyn rattled her teacup in its saucer, but she said only, "I'm not really afraid. But I don't know about the constable. He doesn't confide in me, you know."

"Speaking of confiding, I really do need to see Dominick about a rather touchy little matter. Where is he, by the way?"

"He's up at the sugar mill, I believe. They're having a terrible time drying the sugar this year."

"You 'believe?' Well, I suppose one excuse is as good as another. I did need to talk to him, though. When will he be back?"

"Shortly, I suppose. I really have no idea."

Lacey laughed, a mirthless, nasty sound. "I see," she said. "Goodness, you *are* a trusting soul. With Dominick's reputation--but of course, that was all before he met you. I'm sure it's quite different now."

Jessalyn gritted her teeth. She wanted nothing so much as to pour the pot of tea in Lacey's immaculate lap. "I've no idea what you're talking about," she said. "Further, I'm not sure I want to. I have no intention of following my husband about the plantation simply because there are women on it."

Lacey raised one eyebrow. "Ah, well, your concern, I suppose. I'll be leaving then. Just tell him I wanted to talk about Marianne."

"Marianne?"

"My personal maid. Rather pretty young thing. I've just discovered she's expecting a child."

"Why should that concern Dominick?"

The other woman gave her a long look and rose. "Why should it not?" she said. "I do need to know whether Dominick might give me some idea as to the most--expedient way of dealing with the problem."

She swept from the room, leaving Jessalyn sitting behind the teapot, stunned.

# Chapter Twenty-one

WRINGING THE TRUTH FROM her took some time, but Dominick, concerned about her obvious agitation, eventually compelled her to relate the story to him. When he heard it, he laughed, amusement tinged with anger.

"Damn that Lacey!" he said.

The laugh had been so unexpected that Jessalyn was startled. She regarded her husband with bewilderment and surprise.

"Jessalyn, I know that the maid--Marian? Marianne?--is expecting. I also know that her husband is quite delighted about it."

"Her husband?"

"Indeed. I'm sure Lacey neglected to mention him. They've been married for three years now. The husband is Marguerite's cousin, and all I've heard in that time is how awful that there were no children. Now there is one. They're both quite happy about that fact."

"But Lacey said--I mean, she implied--"

"That I was the father, right?"

"Yes."

"That witch. I'm going to go over there and--"

"No, Dominick. Please don't."

"Don't? I can't have her doing things like this to you. Good grief, every day she'll start a new rumor."

"No. I think this was revenge for your making her retract the story about me."

"But Jess--"

"She's very clever, Dominick. If you go over there, I know what she'll say. Since she never actually *said* you were the father, she'll just say something like, 'I've no idea what you're talking about. All I wanted to know is whether you'd help me find a new maid since Marianne is to be confined now.' "

He regarded her a long moment. "You're rather clever yourself, Mrs. Reynolds. That's just what she'd say, as a matter of fact."

"Let it go then. If she does anything else, you can go to Woodrow about it. But until then--I think she's done her worst."

He pulled her to him in a long, hard embrace. "It didn't work either, did it?"

"No," she sighed, leaning her head against his shoulder. "But I don't mind telling you she frightened me."

"Don't be frightened. Not of that. You're coming to trust me, you know, almost in spite of yourself."

"No, love. Because of *yourself.*"

*    *    *    *    *

September disappeared. The days passed, rainy, humid, uneventful. Jessalyn worked and read and pottered about the house. Dominick dined with her, keeping her close at hand for most of the time, leaving her only to do his rounds at the sugar mill.

The rains continued.

Nothing happened.

And then, something did.

The weather turned inexplicably clear and unusually hot. The ocean breezes, which usually kept the island pleasant and which were the highlight of the *petit careme*, died, and heat seemed to sit on the plantation like a smothering blanket, oppressive and unrelieved. The house was empty and still, unpleasantly hot and humid. Even Jessalyn became irritable. She sat at the desk and tried to write, but her hand perspired and stuck to the pages, leaving a mark. Perspiration dripped from her forehead, blurring the ink and her eyesight. After the last letter she was working on was marred, she tore it to shreds and flung it away.

She went out into the jungle garden where the leaves of the banana trees hung limply, unstirred by a single breath of air. She had the sensation that the world was holding its breath, waiting for something, but she had no idea what that something was.

At night, she and Dominick moved their bed out onto the gallery in the hope of catching any breeze that came up, but virtually none appeared. The night was so still that she lay on the bed beneath the mosquito netting, watching the hot stars gleam through the dense night air, listening to mosquitoes buzz around them.

Marguerite Douglas was sleeping badly, restlessly. Once when she cried out in the night, her husband awakened her, but she refused to talk about her dream except to mutter, "It was very bad, George, very bad."

Celestine and Aurore screamed at each other when they were talking at all. Celestine became increasingly irritated at Aurore's irresponsibility; Aurore became increasingly arrogant and pettish. The climate was very bad for tempers.

Simon Alderly watched the residents of the big house and the residents of his own house and wondered how close some of them were to snapping. Strange, he thought to himself, the feeling of impending disaster is so strong that I wonder whether I'm getting superstitious or if the weather is affecting me, too.

Lacey Delaney wandered through the rooms of her house, seeing nothing in her path, her thoughts turned inward, numbering the days, staring from the windows, moving through her activities with unusual preoccupation.

*       *       *       *       *

On the fifth of October, Jessalyn slipped from her bed early, trying to avoid waking her husband. It was just light, but already the heat was great enough that her pillow was damp from her perspiration. She dressed quickly and left the house, off to the beach where she could slip off her shoes and wade in the waves. The water was cool, the only coolness she'd felt for the last few days. She strolled the length of the beach and watched the sea gulls wheeling overhead, their raucous cries mingling with the sounds of the waves splashing on the shore.

The sun rose, red and hot, coloring the high streaks of clouds to match the flamingos, Jessalyn thought. She stared up at the sunrise and thought that she had never seen a sunrise so bright. Rather more like a sunset, she thought. There should be a rainstorm before the day ends, if the old saying holds true.

She looked out over the ocean, slate blue in the sunrise, and thought how quickly she had become accustomed to the sights and smells of the island. She had never lived so close to the water, but she had come to love that proximity as if she had been born to it.

She walked barefoot back up the beach, stopping to slip on her shoes when she reached the driveway, and picking idly at a blossom that drooped over her path.

Dominick was standing in the middle of the drive, staring up at the sky and frowning. He handed her an orange as she approached him, saying, "I think there's going to be a storm."

She began to peel the orange, putting the peel in her pocket, and turned to follow his line of vision.

"Marguerite thinks there will be a hurricane," she said.

"I have great respect for Marguerite's intuitions--she's been right too often to be discounted--still, we don't usually have hurricanes on Tobago."

"You didn't say *never*, though."

"Well, as I've told you, they're not unheard of. Some of the old ones remember the last. But most of the planters haven't been here that long."

"Have you ever been in a hurricane?"

He glanced down at her. "Once. On Haiti. I'd as soon no go through that again."

"What was it like?"

"Like nothing you've ever seen before. Think of the worst storm you've ever seen in England and multiply it by ten--no, fifty--and you wouldn't be close to what a hurricane is like. The wind sounds like screaming banshees and it rips trees out of the ground as if they were so many dandelions, and the rain comes down like, well, like no rain you can imagine. Let's hope it isn't a hurricane. For one thing, it would wipe out the sugar crop."

She bent down to pick up Marmles, who had rounded the corner and was curling about her ankles. "Would that hurt you badly? Financially, I mean."

"Hurt *us*," he said. "I'm not in this alone any more. And no, that is not to say that we wouldn't be damaged. We would. But it would ruin some of the planters."

"Could they recover?"

"Some could. That would depend on how heavily they had borrowed against the crops."

"How about the Delaneys?"

He smiled. "Why? Would you like to see Lacey brought down a peg or two?"

"I can't say I'd shed any tears for her, but no, that wasn't why I asked. I know Woodrow is a good friend of yours."

"Yes, he is. And I think he's safe. He shares my philosophy about investments. But he is one of the few."

He watched the sky for a moment longer, then shook his head. "I need to see Simon, get his advice. But frankly, I think we'd better prepare for the worst. Go in and tell Simms, will you, love? Tell her we may be in for quite a blow and to start closing up the house and getting the place sealed off."

She left to do as he'd asked, and he strode off down the path toward Simon's house.

Simon was standing outside surveying the clouds. In the last hour, they'd gone from high streaks to lower, gathering clouds, and he was watching them stream overhead. The horizon had taken on an ominous light. He turned when Dominick appeared, lines of concern on his face.

"I think we're in for a storm." Simon turned back toward the sea.

"I'm sure of it," Dominick said. "How bad, do you think?"

Simon shook his head. "It's hard to say. I hate to think of a hurricane, but--" He shrugged. "I think we'd best consider it."

"Our resident prognosticator says we're in for one."

"Is Marguerite seeing things again?

"Yes."

"Well, that's hardly scientific, but we could do worse. All my indicators support her. I think we'd better prepare."

"I was afraid you'd say that. Well," he sighed, "better to prepare and look foolish than not to prepare and have the place ruined."

"How will the house stand the storm?"

"Dragonsong? Probably quite well. It's built for it, at any rate. I want you to come up there for the duration. I'll send people to seal your place, but I'd feel better if you'd come up to the main house."

Alderly nodded. "Where are you going to put the cane workers? Those places of theirs will fold like card houses in a big wind."

"I think most of them can go into the warehouses, and some of them can stay in the main house. Can we seal up those warehouses, do you think?"

"I'm sure we can. We'll have to put in a good supply of water and food, but the warehouses are strongly built. I'll see to getting that done."

"Tell them to bring whatever they can--household goods, clothing, whatever they can bring. We'll make room."

"They'll be frightened, you know."

"I know. So am I, if it comes to a hurricane. I'll do my best, and you can, to reassure them, but better frightened than dead. I don't want to take any chances."

Back at the house, Jessalyn thought that the deadly calm that had settled on the island was more threatening than a storm could be. Not a breeze stirred, not a curtain lifted. The heat was stifling, and as the men arrived to put up the shutters, the closed windows in the big house added to the sense of muffled, smothered, sullen quiet. The tension of waiting had the nerves of the house's inhabitants at the breaking point

Simms had been through tropical storms before, though not a hurricane. She knew what had to be done, and she organized the servants thoroughly.

In the main house, Jessalyn was supervising the lowering of the great chandelier in the dining room. Two men had come to help take it down, letting it into a crate packed with pillows and bed linen. Marguerite, watching, paced back and forth like an anxious mother.

"They best watch that, Miz Jess. They best be careful. Look out there, you! You gonna break that! Mr. Dominick sent for that all the way across the ocean, you best be careful!"

Finally, when they had successfully completed the maneuver, she wiped her head as if she had done the whole thing herself and said, "I am glad that one is done. Now, I can't be in this house any more for now. Miz Jess, you get Celestine and Aurore to help you go through those cupboards and pack up that china and crystal. If this house start to shake in that storm that I hope don't even come, I don't want none of that stuff falling out of the cupboards and breaking."

"It's all right, Marguerite. You go take care of your own things. The men are bringing in crates and barrels to pack up all the dishes. We'll take care of it."

"You need cloths to wrap them in. I got plenty in the pantry. Celestine, you know where they are. I go to my house, gather up things to bring here. Anything you want special, Celestine?"

"I got my clothes up here already, Mama. Just bring that little box I keep my earrings in."

"Huh," Aurore said, "those ugly earrings better blown away. See about my things, too, Mama."

"You gonna need some help mama?" Celestine asked, ignoring her sister.

"There she go, being goody-goody. 'You need some help, Mama?' " Aurore mocked. "Try to make me look like I never help nobody."

"You don't. You don't do nothing somebody *need* doing. You do what good for Aurore."

"You stop that fighting!" Marguerite almost screamed at the two girls. "Bad things happening here! Stop your silly fights!"

"It's all right, Marguerite," Jessalyn said, giving a warning look at the girls. "You go do what you have to do. We'll do this."

Marguerite followed the path that led toward her house, but turned off to the sheds before she got there. She spotted Dominick among the workers at the sheds, and she stopped and told him she thought Miz Jess was going to need more crates. He nodded and sent a man to take care of getting them. She left him there, returned to the pathway, and set out for her house. As she mounted the steps, she lifted her head and stared at the sky. Over her head, the tops of the trees were beginning to move in the breeze.

Outside, Dominick felt the breeze spring up, and he urged his workers to hurry. They were moving everything not nailed down into the storage sheds and tying down those things that could not easily be moved. Inside the sheds, workers were stacking barrels to make room for the people who were beginning to move in small groups toward the warehouses.

Simon Alderly and his helpers moved from house to house in the compound where the workers lived, urging them to hurry and gather their belongings and their families and move up to the big house or to one of the warehouses. His helpers responded to the varying degrees of fear and apprehension by reassuring the workers as best they could, finding help for those who were to old to gather their things, helping the mothers with their children, but always moving quickly, their sense of urgency increased by the growing breeze.

*       *       *       *       *

George Douglas, helping to seal the shutters on the French doors at Dragonsong, felt the wind pick up and looked toward the sea and frowned. If Marguerite is right, he thought, it is beginning now. I wonder, he pondered to himself, a thread of worry pulling at the back of his mind, if there is something she hasn't told me. Surely it isn't just a storm. What is it about *this* storm? He shook his head and returned to his work. I suppose a storm could be bad enough, he thought, but is there something more? She didn't tell me everything, he thought, suddenly certain. She has seen something else.

*       *       *       *       *

Lady Heloise admitted the workers to her quarters to seal up her windows. The possibility of a storm frightened her, and she was visibly shaking. "Are you sure those shutters will hold?" she asked. "Shouldn't we put up more latches, more--" she didn't know what. She paced her floor as they sealed the windows. "What do you think will happen?" she asked the workers. They shook their heads for the most part, muttering. "Don't know, ma'am." Or some such noncommittal response. I shouldn't have come here, she thought. This is my punishment for coming here, for keeping silent. If I survive this, it will be different. I swear it will be different.

*       *       *       *       *

From the windows of her mansion, Lacey Delaney could see her husband ordering the servants in their preparations for the coming storm. She turned from the window and crawled back into her bed, allowing her maid to replace the damp cloth on her forehead. Why this? She thought. And why now? She gritted her teeth and moved uneasily on the bed, feeling the now-familiar sensations spring to life. Perhaps if I just lie here, very still, she thought…An image of Dominick Reynolds flashed across her mind and seemed to recede, like a memory of something long past. Ah, well, she thought, farewell to *that* forever. Nothing like a dose of reality to put an end to fantasies. She turned toward the window, through which she could just catch a glimpse of the tops of trees, tossing in the growing breeze. The sensation of waves rising and falling caused a momentary queasiness, and she closed her eyes to shut out the sight. Nothing to do now but get through this, she thought, and she gripped the sheet tightly. It could be for the best, after all. She clenched her teeth. It *will* be for the best. I shall see to it. She sighed and drifted off into an uneasy sleep.

*     *     *     *     *

Jessalyn standing on a chair to reach the goblets in the top of the china closet, handed one down to Celestine. "Give me some more cloths, Celestine," she said. "I'm out."

Celestine looked into the rag box. "No more here. I'll go get some out of the kitchen. How many more do we need?"

"Um, we have two, four, six, oh about a dozen glasses left."

Celestine rose from her place beside the packing crate and started out. As she was leaving, Aurore came into the kitchen. "You still working with Miz Jess in there?"

"Yeah, I'm still working with Miz Jess in there. You think I run off somewhere--like you?"

"Course not, Miss goody. You tell Miz Jess Mr. Dominick want to see her."

"Huh. I tell her. Where he at?"

"Down to the boathouse path down back of the jungle garden. I take her to him."

Celestine shrugged and went back into the dining room.

"Miz Jess," she said, "Mr. Dominick said he need to see you. Aurore's s'posed to take you down to the boathouse path."

"The boathouse? What on earth for?"

"Can't say I know. I just deliver the message."

"Oh, all right. I guess you can finish these few things."
She removed her apron and went to look for Aurore.

*     *     *     *     *

Along the coast road, Walter Rhodes felt the carriage shake as a sudden gust of wind hit it, and he urged his horse into a faster pace. His passenger glanced sideways at him and looked out at the trees beginning to bend in the wind. Rhodes was almost sorry he'd started the trip today. He'd thought he'd have time, but it looked as if the storm would catch him. They might have to wait it out at Dragonsong. He had to do this today; he was running out of time.

*     *     *     *     *

At her cabin, Marguerite finished gathering all of the belongings that she could carry, and she was packing the things that she'd send George for. She turned to the last of the chests, Aurore's things. She had packed most of the clothing, and now she reached into the little chest where Aurore kept her jewelry and personal belongings. She took out the jewelry, the squares of bright cloth that the girl wrapped about her head, some ribbons, and odds and ends of girlish items.

She glanced into the box to see if she had everything. In the corner of the chest, wrapped in a napkin that had been taken from the big house, was one last object, and Marguerite reached for it. The napkin was soiled, and the object appeared to have been hastily shoved under the other things. Marguerite unwrapped the wadded cloth, uncovering the smooth, flat shape of a silver flask.

She turned the object over in her hands. Even in the gloom of the cabin, it caught the light, gleaming as she examined it: a silver flask. She frowned. What would Aurore be doing with such a thing? Her first thought was that it had been stolen, that Aurore with her longing for pretty things had taken it from the house. But that made no sense, she thought. Why a flask? Why not jewelry? Why not something that she could dispose of or use, if she had to steal. Why a flask like this one?

What was it about a flask? she asked herself. Where had she heard something about--When Miz Alida had died, that was it. That constable, going around asking everybody had they seen a flask. Why?

What did that have to do with this flask? A sense of foreboding and then of déjà vu swept over her, and she felt for a moment as if she would not be able to rise, as if her knees would not support her. She had been here before, had held this flask before. She had seen this moment. But why? What had it to do with her? Or with Aurore? She closed her eyes and rocked back and forth a moment. Damn the fate that had given her the cursed sight, anyway. It wasn't ever enough to see all, to know all the things about what she saw. It just gave her enough to make her sorry that she knew anything.

Still shaking, she rose and gathered the bundle of her belongings, and tucking the flask in on top of them, started down the steps, leaning into the growing wind.

*     *     *     *     *

From his position on the upper gallery where he was finishing the last of the shutters, George Douglas saw the two young women leave the house, Jessalyn following Aurore down the path. Why would they be leaving now, he wondered. They shouldn't be leaving the house; it's too dangerous now, with the wind picking up. He called to them, but the wind was too strong. He couldn't shout over it. Ah, well, he reasoned. They probably know what they're doing. Probably on some errand for Marguerite. He turned back to completing his work.

*     *     *     *     *

Dominick Reynolds and Simon Alderly dashed to the front of the house at almost the same moment from opposite directions. Dominick struggled with the front door, holding it open against the wind and leaning against it to close it.

"Are they all in?"

"Yes. I put most of them in the warehouse and some in the other wing of the big house," Simon told him. "We put in enough food and water to last through a storm and to use afterward if the water supply should be contaminated. No way to know how long this will last, but they'll be fine for some time."

"Good. Can you think of anything that we've missed?"

"No. I think we've covered everything. Now all we have to do is wait it out."

"Umm." Dominick smiled. "All, indeed. Well, come into the library, and we'll have a brandy before the worst of it hits and we have to start worrying about whether this place will hold."

The wind had risen enough to howl around the corners and rattle the shutters. Dominick lit a lamp on the desk to ward off the darkness of the office. The room was warm, and with the shutters closed, quite dim. He poured the drinks and handed one to Simon; it was a moment before his eyes adjusted, and he realized that Marguerite was standing inside the door, her face tight, something clutched behind her back.

"Oh, Marguerite," he said, "come in. Mr. Alderly and I were having a drink before we--Marguerite, is something wrong?"

For an answer, she jerked her head up and down and approached the desk. Still silent, she stood a few feet away from him, looked at him, opened her mouth, closed it, licked her lips, and finally, extending her hand to him, said, "I have found this."

She held out the silver flask.

He looked at her, puzzled, and took the flask. Simon Alderly leaned toward his chair. "Is it--"

"It's Alida's flask. It has the earl's crest on it. But Marguerite, where did you get it?"

"I found it," she said softly, "at my house. With--with Aurore's things."

"Aurore's?" He looked at her, his eyes narrowed. "With Aurore's things?"

She nodded.

He twisted the cap from the flask and smelled its contents. Frowning, he tipped the nearly empty container to drain a few drops into his palm. He touched his tongue to the liquid.

"Rum." He handed the flask to Simon and extended the palm for him to smell. Simon ran a finger around the neck of the flask and tasted the liquid.

"I don't taste or smell any poison in this," Alderly said. "Tastes like pure rum to me. That means that--"

"The poison was in the limeade. We were right. It *was* meant for Jessalyn."

"And if you found this with Aurore's things, that must mean that Aurore--But why?" Simon looked at Marguerite. "Why would Aurore--"

The sound of someone pounding at the front door interrupted him. George Douglas was not back inside yet, so Dominick ran to open it and admit Walter Rhodes and a tall, slim black man.

"Constable, what on earth--"

"New twist on this murder thing, Reynolds." They shoved the door shut. "This is Adam Crane, ships on the *Edmund Roy*. He has an interesting story. But I think the part you'd be most interested in is that he recently delivered a bushmaster in a sealed box to a person on this island."

"That wouldn't be Aurore Douglas, would it?"

"No. That would be Celestine Douglas."

"Celestine? But Aurore's mother found this among her things when she was packing to come here." He extended the flask to the constable. "Pure rum, as nearly as we can tell. You'll want to have the doctor check it, of course."

"That would substantiate the story about the poison being directed at Mrs. Reynolds, then."

"It would."

"But--where are the Douglas girls now?"

George Douglas had entered the room. "Celestine is in the kitchen. I just saw her."

"Marguerite, would you have her come in here, please?" Dominick asked. "Where is Aurore?"

"Dominick, where is Jessalyn?" Simon looked around. "Shouldn't she be in here by now?"

"I don't know. Perhaps she's with Simms."

"I'll go look for them." Simon left in search of Jessalyn and Simms, and Marguerite returned with Celestine.

"Miss Douglas, we have a few questions to ask you about--" Rhodes began, but Adam Crane put his hand on his arm and was shaking his head.

"That not her, sir."

"No? Aren't you Celestine Douglas?"

"Yes," Celestine said. "Why?"

"That not the woman I gave the snake to, sir."

"What do you mean?"

"Well, she say her name Celestine Douglas, but this not her. That other one, she smaller, she lighter, she real pretty."

"Then who was she?" No one answered.

Finally Celestine shrugged. "Sounds more like Aurore to me."

Simon Alderly entered the room with Simms. "Dominick, we can't find Jessalyn."

Lady Heloise descended the stairs behind them. "Can't find her? What do you mean you can't find her?"

"Mr. Dominick, I saw her going toward the jungle garden with Aurore, maybe half hour ago," George Douglas said.

"That the truth," Celestine said. "Aurore said you wanted Miz Jess. She took her down to the boathouse. She said you down there."

*     *     *     *     *

By the time they left the house, the wind was tossing the trees about, and Jessalyn's skirts whipped about her. "Where are we going, Aurore?"

"This way," she said, raising her voice over the wind. "Down by the boathouse."

"The boathouse? What on earth is he doing down there?"

But Aurore didn't answer. She turned and started down the path.

The branches around the flailed the air, and Jessalyn had to put an arm in front of her to prevent them slashing her face. The path was longer than she'd thought. She'd never been to the boathouse this way, only on the horseback route. They seemed to be some distance from the house, and the path twisted through the jungle growth, away from the cane fields and toward the ocean. At least, she thought it did. She had no way of locating herself, and with the sky darkening and the jungle pressing in around her, she found it difficult to get her bearings.

Then the path sloped gently downward, and she could see the end of it ahead of them. She could see a patch of gray ocean, and it wasn't the calm, soothing sea she was accustomed to. This ocean was raging, its vast waves smashing at the shore, seemingly eager to grasp the little island and take it down to the depths.

There at the end of the green tunnel was the boathouse. Already the waves were washing around the steps, creeping up on the pier. Usually, the steps stood on dry land, even at high tide, but no longer. Within a short time the pier and the steps would be covered with water. Jessalyn balked at the edge of the waves.

"Aurore, are you sure he's here? Why would he be here now?"

Aurore shrugged. "I can't say, Miz Jess. I just do what he say."

"Well," Jessalyn said, "I suppose it must be important." She hitched up her skirts and kicked off her shoes and waded to the steps. Aurore followed her. Jessalyn could feel the pier shake beneath her feet as she padded down its length to the boathouse. The bolt had been removed and lay on the planks. She flung open the door and shouted, "Dominick, where are--"

Then she was shoved forward so violently that she fell on her face, and the door was slammed shut behind her. She heard Aurore drop the bolt into place.

"Aurore!" she screamed. "What are you doing? Where is Dominick? What's going on?"

"I'm sorry, Miz Jess." The voice from the other side of the door was almost lost in the sound of the wind and the waves. "I'm sorry for you," she said, "but I have to do this. He never notice me long as you here. You one lucky woman. Now you die."

"Aurore, don't! Please! Let me out! Don't do this! Why are you doing this to me?"

"I want him. *I want him!*"

"Aurore!" Jessalyn was fighting a mounting hysteria. "The water is rising! The boathouse won't hold! Please let me out, Aurore! Let me out! Let me out!" She paused to listen, and she realized she was shouting to the wind. There was no one on the other side of the door.

*     *     *     *     *

Aurore hurried back up the path and let herself into the kitchen. She began to smooth her hair into place, to straighten her disarray. Deliberately she slowed her breathing, struggling to bring herself into her usual state of calm control. By the time she left the kitchen, moving slowly down the hall, her appearance was as ordered as if she had never been out in the raging wind.

"Aurore?" She turned toward the voice and saw Dominick Reynolds striding down the hall toward her. "Where have you been? Where is Jessalyn?"

Her brow puckered in a small frown. "Miz Jess?" She shook her head. "I do not know. Last I saw of her, she was leaving to go down to the boathouse. I haven't seen her in twenty, thirty minutes."

Dominick grabbed her by the arm and half-dragged her toward the front of the house. "We'll see," he said. "Come with me."

In the foyer, Adam Crane stepped forward. "That be her," he said. "That the one say she Celestine Douglas."

"Don't be stupid. I'm Aurore Douglas. Not Celestine. I don't know you."

"Sure you do. I brought the snake. You sent to Venezuela for a bushmaster. I bring him. You remember."

There was a moment of silence. They all looked at her. Tiny beads of perspiration appeared on her upper lip, but her composure remained flawless. "I don't know what he talking about," she said. "I never see him before, ever."

"Where is Jessalyn?" Dominick Reynolds spun her around by the shoulders and shook her. "Where is my wife? What have you done with her?"

"I do not know," she said. "I have not seen her. I don't see her, I guess, since--" Behind Dominick's shoulder something moved, and as her gaze shifted, her face went rigid. Her eyes opened wide, and her hands went to her cheeks, and she began to shake her head back and forth, gasping, "NO! NO!"

Dominick glanced over his shoulder. Nothing was there. Aurore wrenched free from his grasp and began to back toward the door. "No!" she was whispering, then her whispers became screams. "NO! Get away! Get away from me!"

"What is the matter with you? Where is Jessalyn?" Dominick was confused and angry. "Where is she?"

Aurore flung herself at him, clutching at him, her face a mask of terror, her eyes huge. "NO-NO-that man! Can't you see? He--look! Stop him! He coming to get me! Don't let him get me!"

"What man?"

The watchers moved uneasily, and Dominick held the terrified Aurore at arm's length and shook her again. "There's nothing there," he said. "Stop this nonsense and tell me where Jessalyn is!"

"He's there! He is! I can see him! He have a rope around his neck and I can see *through* him! I can see right *through* him!"

"Stop this right now, Aurore. Tell me where Jessalyn is."

She turned her face toward him, her eyes horrified, almost uncomprehending.

"The boathouse," she said, looking back and forth from him to the apparently empty space. "The boathouse. She there."

Dominick flung her from him and rushed out through the front door.

Before anyone could stop her, Aurore ran after him, screaming, "Let me be! Let me be!"

Simon Alderly ran out after his employer. He saw Aurore disappear into the jungle garden, but he ignored her, following Dominick down the path to the boathouse.

*     *     *     *     *

Jessalyn had pounded on the boathouse door until she realized the futility of that effort. The water was rising inside the house, and the waves breaking against it shook the place. Water from the waves was seeping in the cracks as high as her head. She looked about for a way out. There wasn't one that she could see. There were no windows. The end of the boathouse was open and she could see only raging water through it. She was not a good swimmer, but she'd have been frightened of those waves if she had been. As nearly as she could see, that was certain death. The pier entrance offered the only hope she saw.

The boat beside her was rising. The water was coming over the ledge where she was standing, and the hems of her skirts were wet to her knees. Think, I have to think, she said to herself.

Perhaps there's something on the sailboat that could help me. She knew little of sailboats or of boating, beyond the bit she'd seen when she'd gone out. But she climbed over the rail into the boat and began searching for something, anything. After what seemed hours, during which the water level had risen another few inches, she came across a toolbox that contained a most useful item--a small hatchet. She snatched it and climbed back out of the boat onto the ledge. The water was up to her shins now, and her skirts were weighing her down. She stripped them off and flung them aside. Rage had replaced her hysteria. Fear had given way to fury, and she struck the door with all the strength she could muster. She would not die like this, she thought. Not in this futile, silly way. She'd survived so much that she had no intention of succumbing to this--this plot, this selfish little plot. She was not going to be killed like some silly sheep so that Aurore could take her husband.

She hit at the door again and again. It was a strong door, made to withstand the corrosive effects of the sea, but it wasn't made to take this attack, and eventually, it started to splinter. Over and over, she struck at it, wearing herself out, stopping now and again to take a breath. The water was up to her knees now, and the house was swaying, battered by the waves. Finally, one last blow, and she had opened a large enough hole to put her hand through.

She lifted the bolt and dropped it into the waves and pushed on the door. The water held it back, but she finally opened a slot large enough to get through. As she stepped outside, the wind caught her and almost ripped her off into the water. The pier and the steps were covered, and the water was racing up almost to the edge of the jungle garden. She hung on tightly to the door, considering what to do next.

As she held on to the door, being soaked by the salt spray, Dominick Reynolds plunged out of the jungle, onto the beach, fighting to stay upright in the wind and the water.

"Jessalyn!" he shouted. She saw him, saw Simon Alderly close behind him, then raised an arm to show she'd seen them.

She couldn't hear them, but she saw them pointing to her, gesturing, leaning close to each other to hear.

Finally Dominick turned to her, shouting something over and over. She couldn't hear him, She strained to hear, tried, but the wind blew the words away. Frantic, he gestured and shouted again. A rope! They needed a rope. She made her way back into the boathouse. There would be plenty of rope on the boat. She climbed back into the boat, which had risen so that it was difficult for her to get over the rail.

Still she got the rope. Now to get it to him. She couldn't throw it that distance. But perhaps--where had she put that axe?

There. She had left it on a rail beside the door. She grabbed the axe and tied it to the rope. Careful. Can't risk losing it. She shoved against the door, holding on to it, forcing her way through. She raised the rope to show them that she had it. Dominick nodded and made frantic motions about his waist. They wanted her to tie one end of the rope around her waist. She wedged herself into the door opening, reached inside and put the hatchet on a rail, and scrambled to find the other end of the rope. There. She had it. Her hands were wet and the rope was wet, and she dropped it twice before she got a good knot solidly about her waist. Back on the pier, she held to the door and tried to toss the hatchet carrying the end of the rope to the men. It wasn't going to work. She'd have to let go of the door long enough to swing it about. She watched the waves, judged her moment, then, as the waves made their backward sweep, she began to whirl the axe over her head, making larger and larger circles, finally releasing it and grabbing the door just in time to same herself from being swept loose. The axe hurtled toward the beach, landing in the water, and Dominick plunged in after it. He came out of the water with the hatchet in his hand and gave it to Simon, who pulled the rope taut.

"Jump!" She saw, rather than heard, the word, and as Simon pulled on the rope, tugging her from her place into the waves, her husband plunged into the surf, holding the rope, making his way toward her.

She struggled against the water, barely able to make out Simon's figure moving toward her, pulling her to the shore. It seemed to take forever until she felt Dominick's arms grab her, lifting her out of the water and dragging her onto the beach.

# Chapter Twenty-two

WHEN SHE RECALLED IT later, Jessalyn felt as if the struggle to reach the house had taken an eternity, but it could not have been more than a few minutes. By the time they had reached the edge of the jungle, the boathouse had begun to sway; it would not last much longer. The wind was so strong that it fairly pushed them along, and limbs torn from the trees twice crashed in front of them

They were admitted to the house by the frightened residents who then leaned against the door to close it. Two men moved a chest against the door to hold it shut.

"Where's Aurore?" Dominick asked.

Walter Rhodes shook his head. "I don't know. She ran after you, screaming, and frankly, I wasn't about to go after her."

"No point. If she survives this storm, there will be time enough to search for her."

Marguerite, weeping in a corner, was being comforted by her husband.

In another part of the room, Adam Crane was sitting beside Celestine, talking softly to her.

Simms took control of her domain, ordering servants about to prepare a bed for Jessalyn, sending for tea, escorting her to her room to remove the soaked garments and to get her into bed.

Jessalyn, exhausted, was only too glad to place her well being into Simms' capable hands.

If the residents of the house had thought that the storm was nearing its peak, they were wrong. The screams of the wind grew louder and the force of it increased until it seemed certain that the house would be torn from its foundations. Rain roared against the shutters.

At one point in the storm, Dominick cracked open a shutter on the lee side of the house to assess the situation, and would have sworn they were in a green blizzard. Leaves were being stripped from the trees so that they swirled about the house like so much green snow.

A limb was thrown against an upstairs window, ripping off a shutter. The men rushed up to try to cover it, finally shoving a wardrobe over the hole.

Several hours into the storm, the winds died, and a curious golden light broke over the landscape. The clouds seemed to lift, and the sun broke through in a hazy warm light.

"Ah, good," breathed Lady Heloise. "It's over. I have to admit, I was quite frightened, but it didn't last as long as I thought it would."

"Not yet, Lady Heloise," Simon Alderly muttered. "This is only the eye, the calm center. We are only halfway through the storm."

He was right. The calm lasted about twenty minutes; then the full fury of the storm was on them again. Throughout the rest of the day and part of the night, the frenzied winds tore at the shutters and battered at the doors. But by dawn, Jessalyn woke to the sound of the drizzling rain pattering on the gallery outside. She rose and opened the French doors, then the shutters, and stepped out into the cool gray dawn. Around her the landscape looked as if angry giants had ripped and torn at it. Trees were uprooted, limbs were scattered about. Some trees like thin skeletons, stripped of their leaves, stood nearly bare against the dim sky. Leaves not torn from the banana trees hung in limp shreds. Branches and twigs were scattered about the gallery.

Dominick and Simon were out as soon as they were able, riding across the plantation to survey the damage. Walter Rhodes and Adam Crane were still up in the house and would be for a time; the roads were impassable for carriages and only barely manageable for horseback riders.

Jessalyn and Simms set about putting the house to order and getting the plantation organized to help the cane workers restore their dwellings. The homes in the compound were destroyed, flattened, and the materials of which they'd been constructed scattered over acres of land. The women arranged to distribute food to the families, and

Marguerite and Celestine began boiling vats of water for drinking. Dominick feared that the water supply might be contaminated, and he was taking no chances.

The men returned to the house about noon.

Dominick found his wife in the dining room, putting away the last of the crystal.

"Jess?"

She turned to him. "Is it quite awful?" she asked.

"Yes. Very. Come out onto the veranda with me, will you?"

He stared out over the cluttered expanse of lawn, silent for a moment, then he said, "We found her."

"She was--dead, then."

"Yes. Crushed beneath a tree."

"I see." She stood beside him, not touching him, not looking at him. "Dominick, was she mad?"

"I don't know. I had known for years that she had a kind of --crush on me. But I thought she was a child, that she'd outgrow it. I wish I'd--"

"What, love? What could you have done?"

"I don't know. Sent her away, perhaps."

"Do you think she'd have gone?"

He shook his head. "I don't know. I don't know."

"I saw her one night with you. I saw her touch your face, and I thought perhaps you were--"

"Having an affair? No, never. I'd played with her when she was a child. I don't suppose I noticed when she stopped being one."

They were silent for a time.

"Is the sugar crop quite ruined?"

"Oh, yes," he said. "Absolutely flattened. I'd be surprised if there's a stalk left standing on the island."

"It will be bad for the planters, won't it?"

"Yes, very. I don't know what they'll do. Some of us who are able will be lending some of them money, I suspect, but--" he shrugged, "it won't be possible to help them all."

"So where do we go from here?"

He looked down at her, then drew her to him, resting his chin on her hair. "We clean the place up and go on. We do what we have to do, just as we always have. The sugar will come back. We'll have to repair the warehouses and the docks, all of that. But it isn't important. The important thing--the only important thing--seems absolutely undamaged."

"Good. What is that?"

He smiled. "You, love. You."

# *Epilogue*

J ESSALYN SHIFTED HER WEIGHT in the hammock, trying to find a
comfortable position. It wasn't easy in the eighth month of pregnancy,
she had learned, to be comfortable in any position. She glanced up to
see her husband striding across the lawn toward her, and she lifted her
hand languidly in greeting.

"You're certainly getting lazy," he said with mock severity. "Are all
prospective mothers as indolent as you?"

She smiled. "They are if they have you for a husband and Marguerite
and Simms for watchdogs. I think the lot of you would keep me in bed
the whole term if I'd stay."

"We just want you to be careful, that's all."

"Careful! Marguerite would spoon feed me if I'd allow it. Well,
were there any letters?"

"Yes. One from Trenton offering to sell Bellefleur to me."

"Well, well, well. I'm impressed. And are you going to buy it?"

He dropped down on the grass beside her hammock. "Probably. It
doesn't seem vital any more, but I do think it might have its uses. What
would you say to sending Lady Heloise to England to run Bellefleur?
That way, when the children go back there to school, they'd have a
place to spend holidays."

"My, you are in a hurry. We don't even have a child yet, and you
already have a crowd of them in school. But, yes, looking ahead, I think
it sounds as if it would be a good idea. Do you think Lady Heloise
would do it? She seems to like it here."

"I don't think she'd pass up a chance to run her own house in England. I think she'd love the idea."

"And any other letters?"

"Also interesting. A letter from one of my agents regarding your Captain Scarsdale."

"Not *my* Captain Scarsdale. That villainous man."

"Not anybody's Captain Scarsdale, any more. Seems that when he stole the money from you, there were some rings, some personal items in with the money. Do you remember?"

"Um. Yes, I never got rid of them. I just left those things in with the money."

"Well, the good captain tried to sell them and was caught. Your old favorite, the Duke of Bennington, identified the rings, and Scarsdale was arrested and hanged for being an accomplice in the robbery."

"But--he wasn't guilty. Not of that, I mean."

"He was guilty of enough things he hadn't even been accused of. I can't work up much sympathy for him."

"Didn't he tell them where he got those things?"

Dominick shrugged. "I don't know. The letter didn't say. He stole them, in any event. But you've already seen how much effect any story has against the word of the Duke of Bennington."

"Yes. It's almost too bad, in a way."

"Well, anyway, enough about depressing subjects. Let me help you out of that hammock. The Delaneys will be over shortly, so I'll walk you back to the house."

"Is Lacey bringing the baby?" she asked as he helped her to her feet.

"Does she ever go anywhere without him?" he responded, and they both laughed.

"Motherhood has certainly made a different person of Lacey," she said.

"Nonsense, Jess. She's simply going at motherhood the way she goes at anything else--full tilt."

"I'd never have believed it of her, any more that I'd have believed that she and I could--after a fashion, at least--be friends." She leaned on his arm as they strolled across the lawn. "Do you think Marguerite is right?"

"About what?"

"About ours being a girl."

"Probably. Have you ever known Marguerite to be wrong about anything she 'sees'?"

"Never. Will you be disappointed if it isn't a boy?"

"Not for a minute. Not for a single minute. Not if we have ten girls. I'm just jealous enough to enjoy being the only man in your life."

She laughed, feeling the child move beneath her heart. Overhead, a scarlet ibis flashed against the sun, a splash of red against the blue sky. A good omen, she thought. A very good omen.

## THE END

LaVergne, TN USA
27 October 2009
162094LV00003B/1/P